KEYS of LIFE

KEYS of LIFE

Book Two
SWORD of FIRE

Carolyn Schield
Tom Vorbeck

ISBN (print): 978-0-9916670-5-5
ISBN (e-book) 978-0-9916670-4-8

Book design by Maureen Cutajar
www.gopublished.com

Acknowledgements

Special thanks to our outstanding copy editor Alexandria Arnold, for her incredible patience and great talent. Her tremendous courage was inspirational for this huge project. Pat yourself on the back, Tom and Andrew Aker for this incredible cover. Our families get big thanks for all their support and love. Our parents deserve credit for encouraging us to follow our dreams.

We couldn't have done it without our test readers so thanks Kevin, Stephanie, Sandra White, Brad, Julie, and Kay Gambill. We give a great big hug and thanks to Jennifer, Tom's wife for giving her time and helping us find such talented people.

Kay Gambill took on the extra job of proofreader and helped edit our book and thank you so much Kay for an excellent job.

Marty Johnson gets a round of applause for his illustrations in the book. His artwork is phenomenal and so creative. Tom and I have been blessed with wonderful families and friends. Thanks to all of you, we did it, again.

CONTENTS

PROLOGUE

The distinguished scholar enjoyed looking at his latest rare find. De Villiers stroked Isis, his precious cat, between her furry ears as he gazed up at a painting depicting a moment that changed the course of history, Caravaggio's *The Taking of Christ*.

In 1990, Caravaggio's lost painting *The Taking of Christ* was discovered hanging in a Jesuit dining room in Dublin, Ireland. Art experts had declared the magnificent artwork a copy but after a good cleaning, Sergio Benedetti revealed the truth. Caravaggio's work came out of hiding and into the light. Two graduate students in Rome discovered evidence of the painting's existence in an ancient book that detailed Caravaggio's commissions. He painted the amazing work for Ciriaco Mattei at Pallazo Mattei. He came in contact with a well-known artist, Pietro da Cortona, who held the esteemed position of Director of the Guild of Saint Luke. Cortona believed a painting could illustrate many subplots connected to a central concept and create richness and depth. Carravagio demonstrated this technique in this artwork. The original painting hangs in the Dublin Museum today.

Twelve known copies of the painting exist today and one copy belonged to de Villiers. The devious man watched the frozen scene in the painting thaw before him. In the painting, Judas, who betrayed Christ for a bag of thirty silver coins, kisses Jesus as greed, injustice, and betrayal lurk in the shadows. De Villiers' eyes landed on the hands of Christ. The hands of one of the most famous Pure of Heart in history are folded in a mysterious crisscross pattern, revealing his knowledge of the coming events and his submission to sacrifice his life for the good of mankind. The symbolism of the intertwined hands, seen in other art such as statues of Magdalene, were thought to be signs for the Pure of Heart, reminding the viewer how everything in life is connected with each other.

A light shines in the arm of the soldier taking Christ, like an ancient Egyptian perfume bottle on its side for holy spikenard oil. Love, loyalty, and devotion shine through the dark oppressive shadows. The tilted white perfume jar used by Mary Magdalene to anoint Jesus before his death illuminates the oppressive armor of the Dark Watcher grabbing Jesus. Her sacrifice of precious perfume and her premonition of Christ's death set into motion Judas' betrayal. The once-devoted follower was angered at the wastefulness and loss of money as Mary anointed her king with precious oil. De Villiers' eyes darted from figure to figure on the canvas. The events that followed led Judas to deliver his friend Jesus to his enemies.

The Dark Watchers grabbed the Pure of Heart on orders of the Children of the Nephilim, who held prominent positions in the Jewish Sanhedrin. The Light Watchers tried to protect the Pure of Heart, but Jesus' death set in motion a movement that changed the world. The destruction of a corrupt Rome followed, leaving the world in chaos.

The prisoner in the painting knows what the future brings and is ready to make the sacrifice. De Villiers smiled. *Sacrificing one's life for mankind is a typical, foolish trait of a Pure of Heart,* he thought.

Dark Watchers would not be taking any more orders from the weak and crumbling Children of the Nephilim. De Villiers planned to change the power structure that had existed for thousands of years. *It's time for the Dark Watchers to claim what is theirs*, he thought.

One painting technique used by Caravaggio called chiaroscuro dealt with illumination and light and dark colors which produced a three dimensional feel. At age eleven, Carravagio was a talented painter but also a controversial one. He murdered a man and fled for protection under the Knights of Malta, who ultimately imprisoned him. He later escaped, but the artist was always on the run for his life and hunted by his enemies. Who could he trust? Some investigators believe Carravagio died from his enemies' poison, others, a fever. De Villiers sat in deep thought, listening to the soft purring of his loyal friend and stared at his copy of Carravagio's painting in the boardroom of the Dark Watchers. *Let all Dark Watchers be warned by the mesmerizing Carravagio artwork of the price of disloyalty and treachery.* The painting reminded the puppet master to never trust anyone. *All present will be reminded that betrayal is the greatest of all sins.*

CHAPTER 1

Revenge Is Sweet

Machine guns roared as Cordy jumped from the helicopter, barely dodging the bullets that speckled the night sky. Gravity instantly pulled her down into the dark, freezing waters. The force of the water knifed through her and nearly knocked her unconscious, but her karate-toned physique allowed her to kick to the surface and fill her lungs with much needed air. Once she caught her breath, Cordy feverishly scanned the water around her in search of her great-grandfather, Chief Saunhac, and Ash.

A light flickered in the water. Cordy caught a glimpse of Ash's blonde hair and followed the shimmering rays into the unknown depths of the frigid ocean. As she reached the light, she saw Ash holding onto the wounded chief's hand. Blood flowed around the elderly man's body, gushing from a bullet wound to the chest. Ash's sad eyes turned to her – the chief had sacrificed his life to save him. Cordy gazed into the old man's eyes and knew he didn't have much time. His ancestors called to him and he fought to stay with them as long as he could.

In this instant, time slowed to a crawl. Cordy heard his soft, calm voice in her head, murmuring, "Let me go, Star Child, for I go to join my ancestors and loved ones. You are the protector of the ring now." Chief Saunhac pulled from his neck a silver chain with a gold ring on it and handed it to her for safekeeping.

He turned to Ash and handed him a crystal ball from under his blood-soaked shirt. The eyes of the Mi'kmaq chief became fixed for his old heart had ceased to beat. Hypothermia, blood loss, and asphyxiation sent the wise warrior on his journey home.

Ash and Cordy touched the crystal ball together and a glowing light started to radiate from the orb. The energy pulsating from the ball pushed Cordy and Ash rapidly to the surface of the water. The strong force field around the sphere caused Cordy to drift in and out of consciousness.

The next minute, she was wearing a shimmering, silver gown and a jeweled crown. The silky dress hugged her curvaceous body; her long, golden brown hair draped over her back. She walked on clouds and felt weightless. Cordy thought for a second that she was in Heaven, but Antar, the leader of the fallen angels and the Children of the Nephilim, stood close to her. The handsome angel both attracted her and repulsed her like no man she had ever met. Cordy first encountered Antar in a cemetery next to her parents' grave at the Miraculous Medal Shrine. It was at this same hometown shrine she found the interlocking crossed hands of the Pure of Heart revealed by the woman in the shrine painting of the *Passion*. How appropriate it was to meet the revenge-seeking father of the Children of the Nephilim in a sacred place of death. The burial place of her assassinated parents seemed the best place for warrior to meet warrior.

The interlocking crossing of hands in prayer symbolizes how evil and good are linked together, fighting throughout history. The Jerusalem Cross, known as the Crusader's Cross, formed a square of interlocking crosses. Chief Saunhac's ancestor, the Templar Grandmaster Guilliame Saunhac, was killed in the Crusades. The Saunhac families were warriors who fought gallantly for humanity and produced generations of Pure of Heart.

Antar whispered in her ear, "Another Pure of Heart dies a gruesome death. What a pity. I'm hoping for a better fight from you." His eyes, filled with desire, scanned the woman before him. "I feel your anger and understand your wanting to get revenge for their deaths. I will regret your death, lovely Cordelia. Don't you feel the thirst for revenge, that fire burning through your veins? In this place of death, let the anger consume your heart. Don't give up, Cordelia. Who will avenge the chief and make them pay?"

Suddenly, a bright light radiated around Cordy like a halo. Sadness engulfed her at the thought of being left alone again. "Why do they leave me?" Cordy whimpered. "The chief and my parents are gone, and now I'm all alone." Loneliness penetrated her soul and chilled her heart.

Cordy thought about how her parents and great grandfather were killed fighting an ancient war that raged through the millennia – the Pure of Heart versus the Children of the Nephilim.

Cordelia felt the fire of revenge stirring within her heart. Antar sensed the rush of her life force. He placed his lips upon hers, sending a light pressure and strange vibration tingling through her body. He took a deep, intoxicated breath and moved away, looking into her alluring eyes.

"Revenge, Cordelia," he breathed, "That is what this is about. The lesson to be learned is about sweet revenge and even sweeter betrayal."

A grinning Antar disappeared, replaced by her grandfather Chief Saunhac dressed as a Crusader knight. He wore his Mi'kmaq Indian war bonnet of feathers and the Red Cross on his white tunic. Saunhac's eyes gazed at her intensely.

"Star Child, you are never alone. Your family is always near you. The crystal ball and ring are your inheritance. They have come from the past. The treasures given to you must be protected. They were brought to Earth from our great heavenly family. Revenge brings only grief and sorrow. The Children of the Nephilim want the Keys of Life and will hunt you down. Star Child, love will guide you, for if you do not succeed then all life on Earth may die. A wise man said the best revenge is not to be like your enemy."

He disappeared into the clouds of her dream.

Cordy struggled to stay on the surface, but her arms grew heavy. A hand grabbed hers. A muscular man pulled her onto a burning ship. She had aspirated water and went limp. The man with a bullet hole in his captain's cap yelled at her, but all Cordy wanted to do was sleep.

She found herself pulled through a tunnel with great force. At the end sitting on a rock, a smiling Uriel, the leader of the Pure of Heart, gazed upon her.

"You have much more to do, Cordy. The battle to save Earth begins. We hear her cries. You carry the ring of Solomon, so use it wisely."

The tunnel again came whirling around her. Cordy awoke to cold and pain. She was aware of lying on a ship. A dark-haired man with a black mustache appeared distressed and very mad.

What the hell is he mad about? Cordy thought. *I'm the one lying on the deck. Is he still mad that I shot him?* All she wanted to do was to go to sleep and for him to leave her alone.

"C 'mon, cherie! Breathe, dammit, breathe!" he shouted.

He put his lips on hers and she felt a fire shoot through her veins and into her heart. She rolled on her side and coughed up seawater. Bullets zipped through the air around them, riddling the boat with holes. Her rescuer pulled her into his arms. Jon Lafitte gave her a devilish grin and placed the harness on her. As she was pulled up on the helicopter, Ash hugged her firmly. Cordy snuggled close to Ash's warm body and enjoyed his strong, protective arms around her. A heat rushed into her body, and she realized that with Ash by her side, she would never be alone.

The boat descended lower into the icy waters and a furious fire raged on deck, but Jon smiled at her. Cordy could only grin as he held up his cap and waved at her. The gray smoke pluming in the sky reflected a war in which friends became enemies and enemies became friends.

Ding! A bell went off in the airplane. Cordy relived that horrific day over and over again in her dream. A stewardess nudged her elbow.

"Have you decided what you would like for dinner?"

Cordy lifted her head off Ash's shoulder, which smelled of musk from his aftershave, and smiled.

CHAPTER 2

Trouble Ahead

The seawater engulfed Ash as he swam in a desperate attempt to grab the wounded, dying chief. The old man's eyes grew dimmer, but he had that amazing grin on his face; his floating arms waved a final farewell to them in the water. In his mind, Ash heard the chief laughing at him.

"Lil' Rabbit, it is time to hunt for the Swords of Air, Water, Earth, and Fire. You can use the crystal ball and the ring to find them. The lovely girl with the blonde hair likes you, Lil' Rabbit. You made an impression." The chief smiled, "You must take the ball and ring to the Great Temple. Place the ball in the right spot and someone will be revealed to you. Do not let the Children of the Nephilim possess the ball and ring, and beware of the Dark Watchers."

The chief gave him the crystal ball before he took his last breath. The minute Ash grabbed Cordy's hand, the ball lit up with a brilliant light and a force propelled them both to the surface. In a flash, a vision rushed into Ash's mind.

9

He was transported into space, surrounded by galaxies. Ash spotted the sun and then he gazed at the wonderful blue planet. Earth was home to billions of people and animals. The world shone like a priceless gem, and he gazed at the beautiful Earth from the moon on which he stood.

Uriel the Archangel, dressed in a black leather biker jacket and holding a whiskey bottle, patted Ash on the back.

"What a view!"

Uriel smiled. "Amazing, isn't she? Mother Earth, she's home to so many and yet mankind, in its greed for power, would destroy her. The planet is a sentient being. Don't mess with her, or you'll regret it. We hear her cries for her children."

Uriel took a gulp of whiskey and handed the bottle to a surprised Ash.

"A war is in progress, and Earth is in great peril. The Pure of Heart have to stop the Nephilim and Dark Watchers. The ancient technology given to mankind by Noah must not fall into their hands or Earth and its inhabitants will experience another extinction-level event. This isn't the first time Earth has been placed in danger. Your ancient ancestors left the Pure of Heart the tools to save her from devastating destruction. The weapons and sacred knowledge given to them long ago from the time of Noah and the Egyptians protected them. Do you understand the severity of the situation, Ash? Every living thing on Earth is in danger and the Pure of Heart must rise."

Ash took a gulp from the bottle and felt its delightful warmth slide down his throat. The smoky, woody taste of the whiskey tantalized his taste buds with fruits and molasses. If Mother Earth had a taste, whiskey would be one. Ash felt the buzz. He passed the bottle back to his familiar friend, remembering how the angel saved his life at Abu Simbel and aided him in his discovery of the Keys of Life. His life had changed from that moment and led him to Montreal where he met Cordy. He felt her smooth skin brush against his shoulder and her hair smelled of roses. If Mother Earth had an aroma, her perfume would be like Cordy's. His solitary life had changed in that instant and he wanted to be with this woman more than anything. He fell in love with her at first sight. Ash answered with confidence, "Big deal, Uriel. The Pure of Heart can handle them. We got this."

Uriel took another gulp from the whiskey bottle and a slow grin spread across face. "That's what I like about you, Ash. You're an optimist."

Cordy touched Ash's elbow gently and Ash woke from his dream. The cute stewardess started to flirt with him and asked what he would like for dinner, finishing with a wink. Cordy gave her a hands-off look. Ash noticed it and smiled.

CHAPTER 3

Edinburgh Castle

Ash and his father, Han, promised not to call one another in case the Dark Watchers were listening. Han knew double agents in both the Light and Dark Watchers' organizations who could aid him if Ash wasn't on the run. The thing is, though, Ash was on the run and time was of the essence.

Han dialed his son's cell phone, knowing he might be putting him in harm's way. But he had no choice. He had to reach his son and needed help. The phone rang again and again, triggering a voicemail. Ash's dad made one last desperate attempt, and this time a male voice answered at the other end.

The ex-Navy SEAL and vice president of Cordy's company felt Ash's phone ring in the pocket of his gray business suit. Cordy had needed an experienced money manager to keep her fortune safe from the shark-infested waters of Wall Street. She hired him on the spot at Bingo's restaurant, where he had worked as a waiter. His life completely turned around. Now, he had just gotten done with a television interview on how Cordy's company was changing the lives of the poor by donating equipment to help produce clean drinking water.

Bob knew it had to be important. Bob carefully picked up Ash's old cell phone and answered it with a simple hello. A man's voice yelled back, "Hello? How did you get this number? Who are you?"

There was a long pause.

"How did you get this phone and who are you?" Han demanded in a now-worried voice.

Cordy's friend wondered who the old man was and how he'd gotten this number. He'd known Ash since he saved his life in Nova Scotia. The crazy archeologist gave him the phone to keep in case of emergencies so he needed to be very careful here.

Bob laughed, "No, that's not how it works. You see, I have the phone and you called me. I'm holding all the cards here, or in your case, the phone." There was a long silence at the other end of the phone. Bob waited for a response.

"How do I know if I can trust you?"

Bob playfully answered back, "Well, now, you don't, so I will have to be going. I will tell you this: time is *good* money lost and I have a lot of *good* things to do." Bob knew he was tipping his hand by emphasizing the word good.

Ash's father picked up on it and knowing that the person on the line was not Ash, he replied with, "Asho" and nothing else. Two can play this game.

Bob's ears caught the name Ash hated all his childhood. "Well now, we are getting somewhere. I know that little asshole. Well, he's not so little; you could call him a big asshole!"

Han angrily answered back, "Hey! That's not funny. I gave him that name and this is his father."

Bob's instincts had told him it was Ash's father on the line. It had to be Ash's dad because only a few people knew Asho was Ash's childhood nickname. He felt a little bit of sympathy for Ash knowing how the kids must have taunted him. Bob quickly apologized, "I'm sorry, sir. I didn't mean any disrespect."

For the first time, Han understood what Ash had tried to tell him about the trouble his name caused him through childhood. "You did mean it, and you aren't funny. That was just downright disrespectful. It's people like you who made him change his name to Ash. Damn, what bad luck that I get you instead of my son."

"No, sir, quite the opposite. If you didn't name him Asho, he would be dead by now. He's a survivor and knows how to fight. I've seen him in action. Sometimes, our past battles prepare us for the future ones. What kind of cellphone are you calling from anyway?"

"I bought a disposable, prepaid cellphone," Han explained. "I won't call on it again. I understand what it's like to be on the run. The phone can't be traced."

"Running and being chased must run in the family," Bob chortled. "Well, I shouldn't be telling you this on the phone, but I work for a Pure of Heart. We discovered Asho was a Pure of Heart and everything we had to do came into focus. My boss and Ash are together as we speak, headed for Ireland. She's researching her family history and Ash is helping her find something very important. They are in grave danger. Everyone is looking for them now. I am not a man who easily gives up hope, but I'm a pessimist when it comes to their chances."

"Ash's mother said it was going to be bad," Han sighed. "Do you have a way of getting in touch with them?"

"Yes, I do. They have encrypted phones. These phones can't be tracked as long as they don't let them out of their hands. The problem is, I can't give you the number over the phone because we can't be 100 percent sure that no one else is listening."

Han spoke quietly, his voice cracking at the end. "What I have to tell him is of grave importance. It's a matter of life and death."

Bob realized it was serious. "Just give me the information, and I will make sure it gets to him."

"I can't do that. I have to make sure he gets it directly from me," Han explained.

There was a long pause on the other end until Bob finally said, "All I can tell you is that if you look for *who* your son is, you will find him. *Who* is your son? *Who* is Ash? I have to go now.

Don't forget to tell the asshole I said hello." Bob then abruptly hung up.

Ash's father stood there in shock with the phone still cradled between his shoulder and ear. He was pissed. "The man on the other end of the phone is not a nice guy. He didn't even tell me how to reach Ash! He only said to look for who Asho is and that we would find him. Who is Asho? He's my son! How does that even help?" Han threw his hands in the air.

Ash's mom thought for a second. "*Who* is Asho?" she pondered. "Asho is our son. He's tall. He is an archaeologist. He's a man. He's a Pure of... that's it!" Aziza exclaimed.

"Give me your phone and a piece of paper and pen." She opened the phone's keypad and started to write on the paper: P=7, U=8, R=7, E=3, O=6, F=3, H=4, A=2, R=7, and T=8. Let's see, old man, his phone number should be 787-363-4278. There, call your son."

"No way," Han protested. "It can't be that easy. You gotta be joking!"

"Well, honey, sometimes it takes a woman to figure out these puzzling and mysterious secrets. That goes for the bedroom and in the real world." She smiled and patted his back.

Ash's father dialed the deciphered number as he shook his head and looked at his wife with skepticism. "No way," he muttered. He heard the phone ring and ring and expected a wrong number.

Ash and Cordy were still on the plane, taxiing to the private gate Bob had arranged for them in Dublin, Ireland. Both of their phones started to ring at the same time. Bob had configured the phones that way so that when he needed to talk to someone, he had a better chance if both of them would get the same call. They wouldn't have to put anything on speaker for both of them to hear.

Cordy picked up first. "Hello?"

The man on the other end stammered, "I am sorry, miss. I must have the wrong number."

Cordy could hear the man talking to someone in the background. Ash's father admonished his wife. "I knew it was going to be a wrong number." At that instant, Ash hit the talk button on his phone.

"Father?" he asked. There was a long pause.

"Is that you, my little Asho?"

Cordy chuckled loudly and quickly covered her cell phone with her hand. She grinned ear-to-ear. She knew how much Ash hated that name. School bullies teased him throughout his childhood because of it. Ash's father, who had been thought to have been dead, was proud of the name. Ash rejoiced at the news his father lived, but his patience grew short every time his father used the name he'd grown to hate. Cordy, who he knew would never want to hurt him, was the only one who could get away with teasing him about it.

"Yes, Father, it's me. And I thought you weren't going to call me that anymore." Ash looked over at Cordy and mouthed the words *hang up*, with a very serious look on his face. Cordy giggled and shook her head no.

Ash threw his hands in the air and thought, *This is going to be just great.*

"Asho, we are on the run," his dad explained. "Your mother and I are in big trouble."

Ash sat up from his chair with his ears perked. He asked, "Grave trouble?"

"I am afraid so. Who was that laughing? It sounded like a woman."

"That was Cordy McDermott. But what kind of trouble are you..."

Han cut him off before he finished and asked in surprise, "Is she good looking?"

Ash's mother got excited and pulled the phone from her husband's hand. "Is she single and still of child-bearing years?" Ash's father took back the phone and gave his wife a scolding look.

Ash rolled his eyes and thought to himself, *Enough of that, or I will hang up!*

Still listening on the line, Cordy shook her head and threw up both of her hands in exasperation at Ash's crazy parents.

Ash tried to get his parents back on topic. "What is so important that you would risk a phone call? What do you mean big trouble?"

Ash's father started to explain. "Do you remember Brother Michael? Your mother and I were in hiding with him when he got a call from a desperate Pure of Heart that had defected to the Dark Watchers. He told Brother Michael that he was looking for sanctuary because the Children of the Nephilim were trying to kill him. The Dark Watcher, and Brother Michael had been close friends at the monastery at Mount Carmel. This man dealt in antiquities and was an expert translator in Aramaic. He had a tip that one of the original copies of the ancient scrolls of the Book of Enoch was stolen. He had a chance to see the book and remembered some of the pages he translated a few years ago in the archives. Some of the pages were quite controversial and contained diagrams.

"They were going to be destroyed but he found something extremely important to the Pure of Heart. He said that once the book was destroyed, the chances of a Pure of Heart "golden age" would come to an end. He had a vision of an angel who came to him in a bright light. The angel told him these pages were needed. They were contained in the Book of Dreams. The book came from Noah's great-grandfather and was purposely left out of the Bible because there are secrets within its pages. It's one of the scrolls and an unknown chapter in the Book of Enoch. The book was hidden away by the Dark Watchers but he knows where they put it.

"Only two religions talk about the book of Enoch, and few Christians even know it ever existed. But, I am getting off track again. Asho, my son, an angel told him that a man and a woman needed the book. The Dark Watcher was moved by the angel's prodding to call someone he trusted ¬—Brother Michael — and go to his hometown as soon as possible. Brother Michael lives in Edinburgh, Scotland, where the historic Edinburgh Castle was built on an extinct volcano."

"Slow down, Father. I am taking notes, and you are going too fast," Ash said.

Cordy looked at Ash with disbelief at what she was hearing. "We're on the run and now you guys. Where are you now?" she asked.

"Oh, Ash, she has a soothing voice, just like your mother! She sounds pretty," smiled Han.

"Dad, cut it out," Ash admonished. "Keep your eyes on the task at hand. Focus! Cordy and I are in Ireland investigating and re-searching some of the artifacts we possess. We think some of the answers we're looking for can be found here. And now you believe an ancient scroll from the Book of Enoch contains important in-formation that can help us."

As if he didn't hear a word his son had said, Han clamored on, "I used to say that all the time when I was on my dig sites! Keep fo-cused! And I am focused believe me. Listen to me! We are at Edinburgh Castle on the North Hill looking for the Book of Dreams one of the chapters in the Book of Enoch. We were to meet Michael's friend on the north side of the Edinburgh Castle hill. He told us that in this spot in 1754, some workmen discovered a subterranean cham-ber and found an image of the Virgin Mary wearing a crown made of white stone. The books have to be placed on sacred ground or be in possession of a Pure of Heart. It was then, when I recognized it was you and Maggie that the book belongs to. You both belong to the Pure of Heart as well as to us. We need to work together."

"No, Dad. Maggie is a little girl," Ash corrected. "Cordy is the Pure of Heart and she is who I am with. And yes, Dad, I think you're right. You wouldn't believe what we have been through these past few days. Do you have the book?"

"I was just getting to that. When we arrived at the North Hill of the castle, we saw a man dressed in a monk's robe and four men just a little ways behind him. Then all of a sudden, they disap-peared into the hillside. We followed them and found a hidden entrance to some passageways, but it has been a long time since I was underground, if you know what I mean. I have no experience with castles. Only pyramids. Well, I guess I hate to admit it, but I am very scared for your mother. I want you to talk some sense into her. She listens to you."

Ash reassured him. "No, you did the right thing by calling. Whatever you do, don't let Mom go in. It's too dangerous. Tell her I said no way she goes in. OK, we learned in school that in most cases, castles had to have a hidden exit so if the king wanted to escape, he could. They usually had to have a hidden water source, like a well, in case they were under siege for a long time. I hope this Book of Dreams is worth all this trouble." Ash looked at Cordy, "Any suggestions?"

Cordy shrugged her shoulders. "You're the guy who has played in the dirt all his life. What do I know of rabbit holes, Little Rabbit? I'm not Alice in Wonderland." She smiled back at him.

Ash closed his eyes and racked his brain, letting his memory guide him through all the facts he catalogued in his head. "OK, Dad. I remember a story about Edinburgh Castle that had a piper play his bagpipes in the hidden tunnels below so those above could keep track of him from the sound of the bagpipes. All of a sudden, a great quiet came from below, and the piper disappeared in the labyrinth of the passageways."

Han anxiously replied, "Son, I was hoping for more than a ghost story."

"Hear me out. I think it may have the answer to your problem. If you're hunting for the Book of Dreams, it's probably in that secret chamber where the piper stopped playing. In the maze of the underground passageways at Edinburgh Castle, there are many hidden tunnels. I bet the monk knew which one went to the chapel with the Virgin Mary. He probably knew which one led to where the piper's music died. You know how archeologists follow the passageway that has the breeze coming down the tunnels? I think if you follow the one that doesn't have any air movement, you will probably find the hidden well. That might explain why the men didn't come back out. The other possible explanation is more fatal. If I remember correctly, the castle was built on volcanic rock and there are caves down in the tunnels that expel poisonous radon gas. Either way, it will be very dangerous. Whatever you do, don't let Mom go in."

Han sighed, "Either way it looks like we could be out of luck."

"Sorry to say, but, yes, that is pretty much it, Dad. Tell Mom I am in Dublin. Cordy's aunt, Sister Agnes told us we needed to come here. I think it has something to do with the Keys of Life. Mom is welcome to come join me, though I don't know how safe it is here either."

"If you don't hear from me in a week, your mother will be on the way to meet you. Goodbye, my little Ash. You are a good son and I'm very proud of what a great man you have become. The Pure of Heart will win this war. The Book of Dreams reminds us our dreams are important and to learn from them. It is written, 'Let every evil work be destroyed.' I love you very much." The phone went dead. It was the first time Han had called his son Ash and a small tear rolled down his cheek.

Ash put down the phone and wiped his face. He never thought his dad would call him Ash. "You know, if he doesn't get the book, it will be up to us."

Cordy put down her phone. She rubbed the tense muscles in his shoulders and tried to reassure him. "They'll be okay. He will make it, and they'll find what they're looking for."

Ash wasn't as optimistic. "I hate to say it, but I'm one of the best when it comes to underground exploration, and I don't think even I would make it out alive from something like that." The plane finally reached the gate and Ash and Cordy prepared to disembark. All they could do now was wish his parents good luck.

*　　*　　*

Ash's father used Brother Michael's cell phone as a flashlight. Brother Michael couldn't go in because of early cataracts in his eyes and Aziza knew not to ask. "Well, I will be back in a minute," Han announced. He moved back the vines that hid the entranceway and went in search of the well. He walked for only 10 minutes before he came to a split path. Contemplating his son's advice, he took out some matches from his pocket and lit one; it flickered from the breeze coming down the tunnel. Ash's father did the same to the other tunnel, but this time there was no movement of the flame. Suddenly, a cold sweat broke out over his forehead and his hand began to shake as the match burned to his fingertips.

He took a deep breath. "OK, here we go," he said aloud to himself. Han made it about fifteen yards before he felt himself starting to free-fall. He stopped and regained his balance just in time, thanks to a hand that grabbed the back of his shirt. It was Ash's mother. Aziza had followed him, even when he had told her to stay put.

"Hang on, honey," she grunted. "I won't be able to hold you for long. You are much heavier than when I first met you."

Han's feet started to slip. Any sudden movement would send him, and maybe even his wife, careening into the abyss below. "Reach back and grab my arm slowly," she instructed. "I will try to pull you back on the ledge."

Han was surprised by his wife's strength as she hauled his body back onto solid ground. He turned to her and they squeezed each other until it hurt. After taking a few moments to catch their breath, they realized they were standing on the edge of the well. They both peered down.

Glancing at the bottomless well, Ash's father said, "I bet I know what happened to the piper. Come on, my love, let's keep going to the other passageway."

Ash's mom scoffed. "You get the idea of me going back out of your head right now!"

"Why? You're doing better than I am." They proceeded up the other tunnel. In an instant, it turned downward and broke off into a fork.

Suddenly, Han's instinct took over and he said, "Stop. There is a hidden passageway here." He pushed on the rock wall and felt for a latch. Han had seen this mechanism in some of the temples in Egypt. He lifted it and the wall rotated, leaving a small opening. They walked into a fourteen by fourteen-foot room. In the corner, a man dressed in a monk's robe laid on the floor.

Ash's mom ran over to him without hesitation and asked, "Are you OK?" It was then that she saw blood dripping onto the earth and pools of red surrounding him.

The wounded monk whispered, "They have killed me, but I sent a few of them ahead of me." He was bleeding so much Aziza couldn't tell if he was shot, stabbed, or both. "Here is the book, but I must tell you, something isn't right here. I can see you're a Pure of Heart from the compassion in your eyes. The keeper of the Book of Dreams was entrusted to keep it out of the hands of the chairman of the Nephilim. I give it to you to protect now." He gasped for air and his eyes started to close.

"Dear sir, don't leave us yet," Aziza pleaded as she shook the dying monk's shoulder. The wounded man held the ancient scrolls next to his heart.

"I think," he gasped, "I think they are using the book as bait to lure us. What is in this book could bring light to the world; it is priceless and unique." With that, the monk took his last breath.

"Maybe this time, we should just leave this book behind," Han said. "I wonder if it is cursed."

Ash's mom shook her head. "No, we need to get this back to Ash as fast as we can. The chairman of the Nephilim wants it for some reason. Nothing good, I am sure of that."

"Let's get back to Brother Michael," Han said. He picked up the ancient scrolls and helped his wife to her feet. He started toward the doorway to the tunnel.

Aziza looked defiantly at her husband. "Ah, honey, no way are you getting me back down that hole." She walked passed him and out of the main doorway. "Not gonna happen, you hear me?"

Han yelled out in frustration, "It's easier living like a monk than being married to a woman."

Ash's mom winked at him. "Yes, but the late-night perks are better. Oh and did I forget to mention your late-night escapades have made you a father again? It is a good thing you married a younger woman to keep up with you."

Ash's father ran to catch up with his wife. He grabbed her by the shoulders and looked into her eyes. "I didn't think it was possible, but if it is to be, I am the happiest man alive. A miracle, you've given me such joy." Tears started to cloud his eyes as he smiled at her with love. At that moment, his heart felt like it would burst with happiness.

Aziza tenderly looked up at her husband. "I, too, thought the well had dried, but you managed to fill it up again. You must have gotten my hormones flowing. Anyway," she spoke as they continued to exit the tunnel, "a woman can tell when she is pregnant. It's bad enough having young perky breasts start to swell, but try having large, saggy breasts that are swelling. It is not a pretty thought, aside from the fact that we are on the run as well."

They climbed down the hill as fast as they could. Han spotted Brother Michael in the distance, waiting next to a different car. He asked, "Michael, what's with the car?"

"Well, I saw you pop out at the top of the hill and there weren't any of the four men behind you. They left the keys in their car, and it was so much better than ours." The silver haired monk smiled at both of them.

"We got the book, but everyone else is dead. The protector of the Book of Dreams managed to kill them but died in Aziza's arms. And I am going to be a father," Han said.

Brother Michael seemed shocked. "When did you decide to join the priesthood? You are happily married."

"No, no, not a father in the priesthood! Everything is religion with you. A father as in my wife is pregnant!" shouted Han.

Aziza scolded him, "Oh, dear me. Both of you get in the car. Han couldn't wait five minutes to tell someone. Drive, Brother Michael, and close your mouth. You do know that is what husbands and wives do don't you? Make babies?"

Brother Michael gave Ash's father a high five and yelled, "You the man!"

Ash's mom sat in the back of the car. "Does anyone have any clue on how we're going to get out of this mess?"

Brother Michael drove down the hill. "Well, I called my friend in Ireland and he has a connection with a smuggler who will take you to any destination you wish. To get there, we will drive to Cairnyan, Scotland. It should take us about two and half hours by ferry. We should be in Ireland in about 6 hours." He smiled and looked in the rearview mirror at Aziza.

"My, Brother Michael, how you've become the travel agent."

Ash's mom tapped her husband on the shoulder. "Call your son and tell him to meet us down by the marina in Belfast. And don't tell him he is going to be a brother yet. It is our secret."

CHAPTER 4

Words of a Dead Man

Ash and Cordy got the call about his father and mother escaping to Ireland from Scotland. They headed to meet them in Belfast.

The pair arrived and passed through Irish customs with no problems. The crystal ball, with its made in China sticker on it, and the ring of crystal quartz, with its precision detail engraving, appeared to be New Age jewelry. The ancient alchemical symbol etched on the ring would someday fit precisely but where remained a mystery. All they knew was it possessed great power; Chief Saunhac had given the ring to Cordy before he died.

No one at the airport noticed anything out of the norm. The Keys of Life still had on its handle the price tag from a cruise ship gift shop from when Ash brought it through Greek customs. Security never suspected they were real antiquities. He had one large golden ankh filled with miraculous seeds and a smaller golden ankh, that of Osiris, which opened up the hiding place of the stone boxes carrying the golden triangle and a small rock quartz jar with honey from the Tree of Knowledge. Ash wanted to take the crystal ball to Newgrange. He had a hunch the golden ankhs could unlock more hidden treasures of the Pure of Heart. The temple dated back before the pyramids. The Celtic cross resembled the Egyptian ankh and his intuition felt these ancient civilizations were connected. His first priority though, was to help his parents get somewhere safe.

Ash emailed his former intern, Linda, asking for her help in locating a safe place for his family to stay. As a diplomat's daughter, she had access to many places.

Linda emailed back that she had their accommodations ready. Because hotels require passports and identification, Linda made arrangements for them to stay in a safe house belonging to the Diplomat Brats, a global organization of diplomats' children working together to aid each other.

Linda was so glad to be able to assist Ash and his parents. She owed him so much for healing her of a debilitating stutter. She thought the world of Ash but her former teacher made it perfectly clear that he was too old for her. One thing about Ash was that his moral compass directed him on the right path. Linda respected him for that.

Bill McDermott, Cordy's grandfather, head of the Light Watchers, arranged for one of his men to meet the two at the airport. He told Cordy that he wanted the Light Watchers to help her.

Mark McDonough waited for Cordy and Ash as they exited the airport. McDonough came from an old Irish family who were loyal Light Watchers. Bill explained to Cordy that one of the men who signed Ireland's Declaration of Independence was Seán Mac Diarmada, Gaelic for John MacDermott, one of the leaders of the Irish Rebellion in 1916. Sean died by firing squad, sacrificing, his life so Ireland could be independent. Cordy's family history was tied to Ireland and her ancestors' courage documented. They came from a dynasty of warriors just as the chief had told her. Sister Agnes wanted her to come back to her roots and Ireland was her family's long lost home.

Bill believed that Seán was a Light Watcher or a Pure of Heart. He wanted Cordy to walk on the street named after Seán MacDermott in Dublin and visit the Lough Key where the ancient McDermott Castle stood. The Lough Key is a legendary Forest where the ancient McDermott castle called the Rock dated back to 1184. The mystical lake is in the Irish Annals of the Four Masters, which talks about Irish history all the way from the Great Deluge. Bill wanted his granddaughter to see her ancestral home. Cordy promised she would.

Ash shook hands with a smiling Mark McDonough, who was obviously smitten with Cordy. He hadn't taken his eyes off her since the minute she walked off the plane. Ash watched the stocky Irishman try to impress the girl, bothered that Cordy seemed to fall for his charming little jokes. He couldn't wait to get rid of Mark at the earliest convenience. Ash realized that for the first time in a while he was getting jealous over a woman, but brushed it away. Ash decided to go along with the program until Mark showed them their mode of transportation. He pointed to two motorcycles parked over by the driveway.

Ash stopped in his tracks. Cordy looked over her shoulder at his pale face, "What's the matter, Ash?"

"I've never driven a motorcycle before," he admitted.

Cordy and McDonough glanced at each other and shook their heads. The archeologist had led a boring life until now and was in for a treat.

McDonough chuckled and whipped out his cell phone. "Let's use a video to show you how."

Cordy laughed, "Get on the damn bike, Ash, and just go in circles. You'll love it. You need some practice but we'll never make it to Belfast in time without them."

Ash looked doubtful, but figured what the hell. He couldn't let Cordy think he was a wimp. He hopped on the seat and started the engine. Cordy jumped on her bike and put on her helmet, motioning for Ash to do the same.

"You need to learn how to shift gears," she shouted over the roar of the engines. Cordy demonstrated how to use the clutch and pedal.

Ash slowly got the hang of it and started to ride in a circle. He did great, getting faster and faster. It was just like riding a bicycle. He felt exhilarated and realized riding a motorcycle wasn't so hard after all. Until he started to turn too fast.

"Uh oh! Where the hell is the brake on this damn thing?" Ash cried.

Cordy yelled, "On the handle! The brake is on the right handle."

Ash put on the brake and flew head first over the bike and onto the grass. McDonough and Cordy closed their eyes and prayed he hadn't broken anything. Ash got up cussing and disheveled, yet nothing was broken but his pride.

"You are really doing great, Ash. I think you are ready," Cordy encouraged. If looks could kill, Cordy would have been dead. The one thing she loved about Ash was how he picked himself up after adversity. Nothing kept Ash down for long.

McDonough waved goodbye and told them to keep in touch. "If you guys ever need anything, give me a call. Especially you, Cordy," he winked. Ash rolled his eyes.

Ash and Cordy rode down the highway, heading for Belfast. The day could not have been more gorgeous. Ireland's grassland was a beautiful green — it wasn't called the Emerald Isle for nothing.

Suddenly, a tour bus drove straight at them, honking wildly. The bus driver drank his pint while he motored along the road. He laughed with his chums not paying attention and weaving all over the road. Everyone on the bus was singing and partying.

Ash yelled at Cordy, "What the hell do we do? Is the bus driver drunk?"

Cordy screamed, "Get out of its way!"

Ash veered to the right and rode the shoulder of the road. Cordy veered to the left. The bus screeched past them and when it passed, Cordy was nowhere to be found. Ash started to panic. Where the hell did she go? He shouted her name and noticed a gravel road leading to a small pond. Cordy had skidded and flown over the handlebars, landing in the water. She emerged soaked and furious. Ash sat back, smiling at how her wet shirt clung to her shapely body. She saw him grinning and that only made her angrier.

"Don't say a word, Ash, if you want to live," she threatened through clenched teeth. Without saying anything else, she hopped on the bike behind Ash. They got back on the road and hurried toward Belfast.

CHAPTER 5

Second Honeymoon

Brother Michael was on the phone with his best friend. They were eight years old when they first met and had remained close ever since.

"OK, Jimmy, we will meet you in about three hours down by the ferry docks."

He ended the call and looked over at Ash's father. "Jimmy O'Sullivan will be meeting us when we get off this thing. He's arranged for us to go to a boat marina near where the ferry docks. Tell Asho that we..." Han put up his hand to stop Brother Michael from talking.

"Let's get in the habit of calling Asho, Ash from now on," he interrupted. "I know it will take some time for us to change since I've always called him my little Asho, but he is a man now and he can call his own shots. He wants to be called Ash." Brother Michael nodded his head. Aziza was listening in and reached over and squeezed her husband's arm.

"Okay, tell *Ash*," Brother Michael emphasized, "that we will be at the Maritime Marina where the ferry docks. It is by Legg Park just off of A2 to Maritime Drive, near the town of Carrickfergus. Tell him to come quick if he is planning on sailing tonight. Jimmy will take us to safety."

"I'll be right back," he said. Han went into the main cabin to get out of the cold air and make the call to Ash.

Atop the deck, Ash's mom questioned, "Brother Michael, how well do you know this Jimmy?"

"Well," he answered, "he is a longtime friend. I would trust him with my life. My last name is Murphy and we Murphys are fighters. Every time I got in a fight, Jimmy backed me up, so I have no doubt he will be there for me this time, too."

Aziza gave him a warm smile. "Well then, Brother Michael Murphy, if Jimmy is our best shot, I'm in."

Ash's father came back on deck. "Ash and his girlfriend Cordy will be about one hour behind us. They said they will meet us at the Marina and can't wait to see the Book of Dreams."

"I am going to get some sleep for the next two hours, and I recommend you two do the same," Brother Michael yawned.

A loud horn announced the final warning signal for the ferry's departure. Men started to tug back the untied ropes and the ship pulled away, heading out to sea. Ash's parents felt like it would have been impossible for the Dark Watchers to follow them onto the ferry, but what they didn't consider was that someone was going to find the car that Brother Michael had taken and left at the pier.

Trying to make the most of the moment, Aziza cuddled up to Han. "This is like our second honeymoon. Oh, I forgot. You are required a first honeymoon before the second one. And I don't think a dig site in northern Egypt for two months counts. Now we are finally on our first romantic cruise and I'm already pregnant," she quipped. They both broke into laughter, holding each other as if they would never let anything ever separate them again.

Time slipped by and what seemed like only fifteen minutes was actually two hours and twenty minutes. The horn blared as the ferry moved in for docking. Yet, it was the best two hours and twenty minutes Aziza had ever had. Not once did her husband stop holding her, and now she began to cry.

Han hugged her. "What is wrong my darling?" he asked with alarm.

"I am worried we will not make it," she confessed. "I can't see the future of my new child. All I am getting is a bunch of broken feelings, and the future scares me. With Ash, I could see him as a teenager just weeks into my pregnancy. Something is wrong and I just can't put my finger on it."

Han didn't say a word as he felt her tears roll down his shoulder. It was the first time he had ever seen his brave wife cry like this and his heart broke as she sobbed. All he could do was keep her close and reassure her. Brother Michael came through the door just as Aziza wiped the last tear way from her face.

"We are almost there," he said. "I can see Jimmy O'Sullivan over to the left where all the pedestrian foot traffic is coming off the ferry." Brother Michael started to wave. Jimmy spotted him and signaled back.

The trio gathered their things and as they got close to the exit, Jimmy started to chuckle. "Oh my, Michael! Look how fat you have gotten. I thought you monks were supposed to pray all day, not eat," he teased. They both laughed and hugged each other. The real joke though was that Jimmy was twice the size of Brother Michael.

Brother Michael smiled at his friend. "And here all these years I thought you were with the starving Irish. Now I know the reason they were starving was because you already ate everything," he retorted. The two started to laugh again. "Jimmy, let me introduce my friends Donna and Tim Smith." Brother Michael decided to give them fake names just to keep everyone safe. They shook hands with one another and then Brother Michael decided, "We better get off the streets. Someone could be watching."

Jimmy nodded. "Aye, that's a good suggestion. My van is just around the corner." Brother Michael's friend whispered in his friend's ear the owner of the boat's name who would be taking them. He led them over to a new van. As they got in they could smell that new car smell.

"How do you like my new van, Michael? I just picked it up today."

"It's great, Jimmy. How can you afford this? You never had any money," Brother Michael asked.

"I just got a promotion and it came with a hefty pay raise," Jimmy bragged.

"Congratulations, Jimmy! Now, how long will it take us to get to the marina? I need to wait out front for the other two I was telling you about."

Jimmy gave him a surprised look. "You mean they weren't on the boat with you?" He turned looking at the crowd leaving the ferry. "I thought they were just trailing behind."

Brother Michael shook his head. "No, they are driving up from Dublin and should be an hour behind us."

Jimmy scanned the area nervously. "Well, let's get going before we're spotted."

They drove for only about fifteen minutes and pulled up to a large, luxurious marina that had everything from small sailboats to large yachts. Aziza's eyes lit up. "Wow, how much do they cost?" she asked.

Jimmy pointed toward the biggest one. "See the one over to your left? She has three stories. The owner named the boat after his divorce – 'She Didn't Get This.' You're looking at about 3 million dollars."

Ash's mom spotted the magnificent yacht. "I always wondered what a million dollars looked like. That's impressive. Is your friend's boat that big?"

"No, but my friend's boat cost more. Sometimes bigger isn't necessarily better, at least not in his line of work. Let me show you the way to his ship."

Brother Michael nodded. "You go ahead. I will wait for the others. I could use the fresh air."

Jimmy disagreed with his plan. "Well, I wanted to introduce you all to the captain at the same time. He won't want to be interrupted twice. Back to back, and..."

"Relax, Jimmy," Brother Michael cut him off. "I won't need to be shown around. Ash will be looking for me and if he doesn't see me he will leave in an instant. Take my friends and get them settled."

"OK, but don't be long." Jimmy headed down the ramp to the marina and Ash's parents followed. Jimmy yelled back at Brother Michael, "They will send someone to get you."

Brother Michael stood breathing the cool sea air for a few minutes when he recognized Ash on a motorcycle accompanied by a lovely woman. It didn't fit Ash's profile. He had always considered Ash a studious, quiet archeologist not an adventurous bad boy who attracted beautiful women. The surprised Brother Michael walked over and waited for the two of them to dismount. He smiled at Ash, "How was your trip up and are you going to introduce me to your enchanting friend?"

Ash gave Brother Michael a big hug. In the short time they had known each other, Ash felt like the older man was a long-lost uncle. He could tell Brother Michael loved it.

"Brother Michael, I learned how to ride a motorcycle today. Luckily for me, it's easier than riding a camel. We made great time. But I can't believe how dangerous the roads are in this country!"

Cordy's face showed her impatience. Ash had not introduced her yet, so she reached out and grabbed Brother Michael's hand. She pulled him closer and leaned in for a small friendly hug.

"Hi, I'm Cordy. If we wait for him to introduce us, it may take a while. You see, we went on a helicopter ride and a plane ride but we skipped the pony ride." All three of them laughed. Ash gave Cordy the *OK, I get it* look.

"Oh my, Ash, your adventures have loosened up the serious archeologist," Brother Michael grinned. "Your parents are aboard the yacht already with my friend Jimmy. His friend will take us somewhere safe after you receive the Book of Dreams. They discovered the ancient scrolls under the castle in Edinburgh and escaped. Your father believes this rare copy is one of the oldest and contains some interesting surprises." As he started to turn, he recognized Jimmy walking up the other ramp out of the marina and into his new van.

He drove off in a hurry, his tires smoking and screeching. The monk's face showed surprise as his friend sped away into the darkness.

"Oh no, Ash, this doesn't look good. Jimmy's run off without saying goodbye and your mother and father weren't with him. I suspect something is terribly wrong. I hate to say this, but he may have led us into a trap and they already have your parents on the boat."

Ash realized they had to act fast. "Brother Michael, where is the yacht and what does it look like?"

"I don't know, Ash. I never got down to see it," Brother Michael said with confusion. "I was waiting for you." Cordy and Ash could tell how scared he was by his quivering voice.

Ash asked him, "Do you have the name of the yacht or the name of the owner?"

"I don't know the name of the boat, but Jimmy did say the ship belonged to John O'Leary."

Ash thought for a second. "Cordy, you and Brother Michael stay here and keep an eye on the boats in case they take my parents somewhere else. I will try to find the yacht. I know someone who can help us."

Ash reached into his pocket and pulled out his wallet. He opened his black address book and a business card fell to the ground. Ash picked it up and handed it to Cordy. "Call Dottie," he instructed, "she may be able to find out the name of the yacht. Dottie's new husband is a harbor master and can get the name or home port of almost any large yacht or ship."

Dottie had given Ash a card with her cell phone number and a short note, "For a good time, call Dirty Dottie." Ash started down the ramp to the marina and yelled back at Cordy, "Call Dottie! She may be our only hope." Ash knew his dad and mom could soon be dead if he didn't find them soon.

Cordy shouted back, "Ash, wait! Don't go! We are stronger if we stick together!" But it was too late. Ash had already disappeared down the ramp.

Brother Michael urged, "Cordy, call that number and get the name of that yacht and hurry. Ash is going to need your help. He's worried to death about his parents and not thinking straight. He may make mistakes because he can't see past his parents being in danger."

Cordy immediately dialed the number on the card.

CHAPTER 6

Ellen's Replacement

The chairman gazed at the magnificent skyline view from his office in the high-rise tower he created. New York, the financial capital of the world, glistened as the sun shone on the windows of her skyscrapers. All the golden light reflected from the sun hurt his eyes. The Tower of Babel, built again with his help, was invincible. His empire would not fall.

Where the hell did she go? he pondered. Ellen, his programmed slave since childhood, went off the Nephilim's radar. He never saw Ellen miss a report or fail a mission; besides, she always called in. Her obedience was never questioned and for good reason. He controlled her with fear. Any insubordination brought pain and cruelty. The chairman had stripped the kidnapped little girl of her identity and created Ellen, a vicious and deadly assassin. The little girl, Julia, died long ago with her parents.

Ellen might have been killed on assignment but it didn't really matter to him if she lived or died. He did admit he would miss his morning cocktail. Ellen made the best damn Bloody Mary. He drank the crappy one in his hand that Ken had made. Ellen could have at least shown someone how to make a decent drink before she left. He was disappointed in her.

A knock at the door came and the chairman yelled, "Come in."

Ken, his new head of operations walked in, looking like a younger version of the chairman. He smiled and said, "I want to introduce you to Mindy. She's your new assistant since Ellen hasn't reported in." A very young and beautiful blonde gave the chairman a seductive smile. Mindy's figure would turn any man's head. Ken watched the chairman nod his approval as he stared at the young woman. Ellen's dark hair and fiery nature made a stark contrast to his new blonde and submissive assistant. He wanted a change, and Mindy suit him just fine.

"She will do anything you want," Ken explained. "I mean anything. Mindy has been well trained."

Mindy nodded. "Whatever the chairman wants, I can do it," she agreed.

The chairman laughed. "Can you make a decent Bloody Mary for me, Mindy?" he challenged. "After that, I'll check out what other talents you have."

Mindy giggled, "Yes, sir." She grabbed his drink and sauntered over to the bar to make another one.

"I felt you needed a change, someone younger and different. Ellen started to bore you. I could tell."

The chairman nodded. "Ellen, as she got older, expected way too much. I think she wanted my job. Women are only really good for one thing, don't you agree, Ken?" His eyes met Mindy's, which promised an afternoon of fun.

"Absolutely, sir. I do need to report a serious problem though. The profits of our corporations are down lately. A new power player in the stock market has been buying the companies we have bankrupted and sold. He's rebuilt them and is now our competitor. Our mission is to take down and destroy this new player, but we first need to discover who he is."

The chairman nodded and then asked about his top-secret project. "How is the biogenetic program doing?"

"Excellent. The Neanderthal DNA obtained at Vindija Cave is working. The latest specimen is stronger, taller, and more obedient. The test results coming in are amazing. We have created a super soldier. Neanderthals interbred with Homo sapiens and many Asians and Europeans carry Neanderthal genes," Ken reported excitedly. "Maybe they didn't go extinct but merged with their cousins. We possess the pure bloods. I'll email you the file."

"I'm very pleased, Ken," nodded the chairman.

Mindy brought the Bloody Mary over to the chairman. He took a sip and grimaced. Mindy's cocktail tasted like crap. Ellen still made the perfect Bloody Mary. He began to hope she wasn't dead yet. The dark-haired minx had her uses.

As he gazed at Mindy's voluptuous figure and perfect skin, he thought to himself that surely she must have other talents. It was time to get rid of Ken so he could enjoy playtime with his new assistant. Mindy needed to be broken in.

"Ken, I want you to investigate who the troublemaker is and take care of it. We need to make an example of him so other upstarts don't dare defy us. Now, if you don't mind, Mindy and I have important business to conduct." Mindy giggled because she knew what kind of business he referred to. Ken had told her that the chairman had a hankering for the exotic and erotic. Mindy knew she could please him.

CHAPTER 7

Dirty Dottie Comes to the Rescue

R*ing, ring, ring.* No one answered and the call went to voicemail. Cordy mumbled under her breath, "Shit, shit, double shit."

The phone's automated message began, "This is your hot momma Dirty Dottie. I am so excited that you have reached out to touch me. Leave me a dirty little message at the beep, and I will try to fit you into me as soon as possible." A woman's voice chuckled innocently, "Oops, I mean, I'll try to get back to you as soon as possible, but only if you leave me a dirty message." A shocked Cordy watched as a frantic Ash ran all over looking for the ship.

Cordy hung up in disgust. "Ash is such a jerk. He shouldn't be playing around, not at a time like this. Who the hell is Dirty Dottie? Is she some kind of pervert?"

Cordy sprinted down the ramp to the shipyard to help Ash when her phone started ringing. She looked and it was the same number she had just called. Cordy let out a big sigh of frustration, "Oh great, now a hooker agency has my number."

Cordy answered, "Hello, this is Doctor Cordelia McDermott."

"Oh my, you're a woman?" a surprised voice on the other end replied. "Honey, sorry, I don't play with girls. I only like the one-eyed trouser snake, if you know what I mean."

Cordy rolled her eyes. "Yes, I do understand what you mean. I think there has been a mistake."

The woman's puzzled voice on the other end of the phone continued, "How unusual! Are you a secretary?"

Cordy snapped back, "No, I'm a doctor."

"Well, Doc, I hate to disappoint you, but I'm not sick."

Cordy couldn't believe she was even having this conversation with a hooker and was getting very annoyed. "I am a veterinarian," she said tersely.

"How weird. My dog, Precious, isn't sick either."

"Listen lady, I think my friend Ash gave me the wrong number to call. He's in trouble so I have to go."

"Hold on, honey," the woman countered. Then, a loving sigh came from the other end of the phone. "Sorry, I'm reminiscing about Ash. What a fine specimen of a man! Are we talking about that gorgeous Ash from Egypt?"

Cordy laughed, "Yes, the one and only."

"Well, honey, you can call me Dirty Dottie. I must say just hearing his name was enough to make an old lady tingle all over. Of all the hundreds of men I have encountered in my life, Egypt's Ash is number one by far. I just melted when he put his hard chiseled body against me. I grabbed those firm, drive-it-home butt cheeks and I could feel his large rigid..."

Cordy cut her off before she reached the climax of her story. "Dottie, Dirty Dottie! Stop for a second! Ash is in big trouble!"

"Well, I'm not surprised," she answered back quickly. "About how far along are you, Doc?"

Cordy couldn't believe this woman and just wanted to scream. She took a deep breath and broke the news gently. "I'm not pregnant. Dottie, Ash is in real trouble. He said you would be able to get the name and description of a yacht if we gave you the owner's name. Can you please help? Time is of the essence."

"Does a virgin want to have sex?" Dottie bantered. "You betcha, I can help. What's the name of the owner?"

Cordy quickly answered, "John O'Leary."

"Doc, I am going to place you on hold. Give me a minute."

Dottie called her husband's office and a man picked up the phone. She recognized the familiar voice of her husband's best friend. "Hard-on Harry, is that you?"

The man chuckled at the other end. "Yes, Dottie. You know your husband is going to fire me someday if he hears you call me that again."

Dirty Dottie laughed, "Well, Harry, you are the only man I know that gets hard just by talking dirty to him. Hard-on Harry, men have told me I have a special touch and someday Harry, you must give it a try." Dirty Dottie let out a wicked laugh.

"Not as long as I work for your husband!" Harry replied seriously.

"Careful, Harry, I may have to have you fired just to get a feel." She let out another wicked laugh.

Harry answered back, "Seriously Dottie, what do you need?"

"I am looking for the name of a ship. All I have is the owner's name. It's John O'Leary."

Harry went to his computer and cautioned, "Dottie, you know, I'm not supposed to do this."

Dirty Dottie laughed. "Well, Harry, you're talking to a woman who does everything she isn't supposed to do. A girl has to have some fun."

Harry sighed in submission. He never did have it in him to say no to this woman and she knew damn well he couldn't either. "Hold on, Dottie, it's starting to pop up," he said as he searched the yacht records.

"Oh, I just love when it pops up," Dottie gushed.

Not thinking while looking at his computer screen, he replied, "Here it comes."

Dirty Dottie seductively answered, "Oh give it to me, Harry."

"Dottie, here you go. I found your ship. It's a private yacht. Wow, you don't see this one every day!"

"Oh, Harry, don't I know it. You're a one of a kind." Harry tried to ignore her and concentrated on the computer screen.

"The name of the yacht is 'Unpunished.' She is a gaff-rigged topsail schooner. Construction is a teak on oak with a teak deck. The builder is Will Mire and Sons of USA. The designer, Will Mire, built her in 1931. It was last refitted in 2007. She now flies under a British flag. This yacht cost a lot of money and is used in smuggling. Here it says she has many secret compartments and a large one under the aft main quarters. Many times they use this kind of ship in illegal human trafficking. My advice, Dottie: stay away from this guy. He's bad news."

"Thanks for the info, honey. Now you can go and take care of that hard-on, Harry."

"Always a pleasure and glad to be of service. You can call me anytime, Dottie."

Dirty Dottie just laughed and clicked the phone back over to Cordy.

"Doc, are you still there?"

"Yep, what do you have for me?" To Cordy, it seemed as if Dottie had taken an eternity on the other line.

"It's not good Doc," the woman replied. "The name of the yacht is 'Unpunished.' You will recognize her easily. She is worth a lot of money. She is a top of the line schooner with sails. Now the bad part. Doc, they use her to smuggle sex slaves into the country. My guy told me there is a hidden area in the aft under the main cabin."

"Thank you so much for your help, Dottie! I have to run," explained Cordy.

Dirty Dottie thought she would give Cordy a farewell she wouldn't forget. "If you see Ash, pat him on the ass for me. Tell him I'll never forget our time together." All Cordy could hear when she hung up was Dottie laughing.

Cordy ran halfway down the shipyard wondering why she gave a damn who Ash had slept with. This was a side of him she never knew, but she cared for his parents and didn't want him to lose them. Thinking about the ship being used for hiding sex slaves really pissed her off. It brought back bad memories of poor, beaten Minah, a girl she saved in St. Louis from being killed by the Children of Nephilim.

Cordy came around the corner and saw the name 'Unpunished' painted on the back of a yacht. Dottie was right; it did look like big money. Ash wasn't around anywhere but she thought this must be where Ash's parents were being held. Two men stood by the side of the ship on the deck where passengers boarded. She needed a plan to get aboard.

She fed the seagulls some sunflower seeds she'd been munching on at the end of the pier earlier. She had half a bag left in her coat pocket. Cordy started to walk down the pier throwing the sunflower seeds in the air and a huge flock of sea gulls started to gather around her. As she moved closer to the ship, the two men became nervous and their feet fidgeted as she approached. Cordy could see they carried guns underneath their coats. They started to turn toward her and at that exact moment, Cordy threw the rest of the bag of sunflower seeds in the air. In her mind she chanted a Mi'kmaq song her grandfather taught her to summon God's creatures to do her bidding. The seagulls heard her call and attacked the two men standing guard.

It looked like a scene out of the Alfred Hitchcock movie, *The Birds*. The two men started to freak out, waving their arms and hands to protect themselves from the swarming seagulls. They never saw Cordy's karate kicks coming. She had both of them on their knees and out of breath in seconds. With lightning speed, she grabbed one of the guns from its holster. She hit one of the guards with such force that it knocked him out instantly. Cordy put the gun up to the second man's head.

"Get up and take me to your captives if you want to live. Otherwise, I'll feed you to the birds." A grisly scene took place before their eyes as the birds pecked at the unconscious man's face, splattering blood everywhere.

He nodded and stumbled up the deck; Cordy pressed the gun to the back of his head. When they got to the main cabin, she whacked him in the head with the handle of the gun, dropping him to the ground. Cordy kicked the cabin door wide open and there in the center of the room was Ash, tied and gagged in a chair. Ash had never been so glad to see a woman in his life. An angry Cordy stomped over to the chair and as he lifted his hand up to be untied, she slapped him across the face. Ash's face registered pain and surprise at her attack.

"That's for humiliating me by making me talk to your hooker friend. Dottie knew more about your body than any woman should know. She knew about sex slaves and smuggling, and just when I thought I met a man who was different" she seethed through her teeth.

"Oh! Oh! You womanizer!" And she slapped him again.

Still gagged, Ash was trying to explain when, without warning, Cordy yanked off the duct tape that sealed his mouth. Now Ash started to get mad. "Cordy, I can explain, but not now. John O'Leary is down in the radio room reporting to the Dark Watchers. He captured me and tied me up."

Cordy untied Ash and he stood up. "My parents are here somewhere. John O'Leary possesses the book. I searched the ship before they caught me but I couldn't find them. I noticed the boat had the symbol of the Dark Watchers, the dark seeing eye." Ash pointed to the door she had just kicked in which bore the symbol.

"It's OK. Your prostitute friend Dirty Dottie told me where to find them. Dirty is an understatement, by the way."

"Hey, cut that out. Dottie saved my life," answered Ash.

Cordy shot back, "Yeah, sure, I bet. With what, five dollar blowjobs?" Turning back to the task at hand, Cordy whispered, "Help me move this rug. According to Dottie, there should be a secret hiding place under the main cabin."

Ash pulled the rug away and there it was, the trap door. When he pulled open the door, he could see his mom and dad were still alive. They were bound and gagged but otherwise appeared to be OK. Ash jumped down to help them out. Ash cut his mother's ropes from her hands and the moment her hands were free, she slapped him on his head. Ash defensively covered his head, "Mom, what are you doing?"

Aziza whispered angrily, "You didn't say anything about knowing a prostitute, and what does a five dollar blowjob have to do with saving your life?"

"Mom, did you hear everything?" Ash groaned.

"Yes, everything. And don't forget I see more than most."

Ash's dad got between them. "We don't have time for this. Son, go to the desk and get the book," he pointed. "I saw John O'Leary put it in the bottom right drawer. The Dark Watchers want the book because it contains secrets. And Cordy, give me that gun!" As soon as she did, the cabin door opened. Han surprised the armed Dark Watcher and fired right between the eyes. As a trained East German officer, he was a perfect shot.

Everyone stood dumbfounded until Ash yelled out, "Let's get the hell out of here!"

CHAPTER 8

Ash, Mom, and Dad on the Run

Ash's dad fired four shots in the air so the guards on the yacht would take cover. The four of them ran for their lives to the gang plank. The mercenaries on the yacht panicked when they caught a view of the pairs emerging from the captain's cabin. They sounded the alarm. The fact that Ash's father carried a gun in his hand helped the guards scatter. They got to the gangplank and Ash stepped on one of the bloodied men still knocked out on the ground by Cordy. Ash thought, *I bet those guys regret tangling with her*, and he rubbed his jaw where she slapped him. Bullets started flying around them. "Stay low and keep running," yelled Ash.

As they ran down the dock of the marina, Ash started to feel a little regret. Cordy put her life on the line to save him and his parents. He knew he would never be able to repay her for what she had done. Even trying to save the dying Chief didn't come close. If anything happened to Cordy, he didn't know how he could live without her. He made sure he covered her with his arms as the bullets rang around them.

Cordy's anger melted away when Ash placed himself as a shield around her. She felt sorry for yelling at him because she knew Ash's heart was always in the right place.

As they got to the parking lot, Ash noticed someone who had unloaded his car and was walking to a small sailboat at the end of the dock. Ash had an idea. "Everyone this way!" he shouted. Brother Michael, who kept a lookout at the other end, heard the commotion and started towards them.

Ash cried, "Get a move on, Brother Michael! We leave in one minute."

The four of them arrived at the open car. Ash prayed that the keys were somewhere nearby. The angels must have been looking out for them because lo and behold, the keys were left in the ignition. The owner watched stunned as everyone got in his car. He started to run back to his car, yelling, "Stop, stop!" But it was too late. Brother Michael was already closing the back door. The hatchback of the car was still popped open and everything spilled out as they made their first turn. What a sight to behold, as groceries and luggage fell out onto the road!

"Cordy, call Bob and see if the jet is still in Dublin."

"Yes, Ash. That's a great idea." She called Bob's cell phone. It buzzed but got no answer. Just as the phone was going to voicemail, Bob was calling her back. "Bob, where have you been?"

Bob's calm voice answered, "Out havin' fun with your money and doing a phenomenal job I might add. You'll see some headlines in the news that will make you proud. Now, what can I do for you?"

"We are on the run and need transportation."

"What the hell happened to the Harleys?" he demanded.

Cordy broke the bad news to him. "I wrecked mine and Ash had to leave his behind."

Bob teased, "I was hoping that it would be just the opposite – Ash wrecked and *you* left *him* behind. What are you looking for, Cordy?"

"We're in Belfast and hoping the jet was still in Dublin."

"Cupcake, I know where you are, silly. You're still wearing the bracelet I gave you. I could tell you where to turn to get to the next hotel or restaurant. But I could also tell you that I already have a jet in Belfast fueled and ready to go. And I do, so will you and Ash be there in a few minutes or do you want me to tell you how to get to a great pub? Oh and tell Ash, if he is going to the airport, he needs to make a left at the next light."

Cordy smiled at the silver friendship band, "I love your bracelet, Bob. It's like we're engaged, but not," she remarked. "Oh, Ash, Bob said you need to make a left at the next light if you're going to Belfast Airport. He has the jet ready to go. Are you having people track us, Bob?"

Bob laughed. "I have many people doing many things; the hard part is finding good people that I can trust. By the time they get out of college, they've been pretty much corrupted or are completely fallen. But enough of my whining. Yes, I'm tracking you. Is anybody following you? Where are you and Ash headed?"

"Nope, we ditched O'Leary's men. It's not for Ash and me. The jet is for his parents and a monk named Brother Michael. It's a long story; they need a safe house."

"What did you have in mind, boss? Do they need a ride somewhere or are we talking someplace to live for a long time? Are we talking similar to the FBI witness protection, with new passports and everything?"

Cordy thought for a second. "I'm pretty sure we are talking witness protection with new everything." Cordy told Bob she would call him back. She looked over at Ash's mom and asked, "Do you have a preference on where you want to live?"

Aziza smiled. "The safest place you can find for me and my baby," she said rubbing her belly. Cordy's eyes widened and a smile spread on her face.

Ash, behind the wheel, looked at his mom from the rearview mirror and said, "I'm going with Cordy, Mom. Not with you and Dad."

Cordy grinned. "I don't think she's talking about you, baby. I think she is talking about the new baby."

Ash's confused eyes searched Cordy's face. "The new baby? What do you mean new baby?" The car started to swerve and Ash abruptly pulled over to the side of the road. A big cloud of dust and gravel flew everywhere. He turned to his mother and looked at her smiling face. "Is it true, is it really true?" he asked. She took his hand off the back seat and placed it on her stomach.

Ash's mom grinned. "Yes, Ash, it's true. You're going to be a big brother and yes, I am sure. I'm as surprised as you are but after four pregnancy tests and the fact that I had to buy a new bra already, I am sure. Miracles do happen."

Han, who had married the beautiful young Aziza late in his career, chimed in, "I'm still in happy shock, if that is a condition. We wanted to tell you before we parted because we don't know when or if we'll ever see or talk to you again. Your mother's visions into the future have ceased since she found out she's pregnant. All she's picking up are mixed, jumbled visions. This has never happened to her before. I know you're in shock, son, but we're in the middle of being chased so do you think we can get moving again?"

Ash beamed with the news. He leaned over and hugged Cordy. He yelled with pride at Brother Michael, "I'm going to be a big brother! Cordy, did you hear that? I am going to be a big brother."

Cordy patted Ash's shoulder and smiled at him, but pointed to the steering wheel. "Uh, can we get moving, Ash? Before the baby comes?"

Ash was very excited, but he slowly pulled back on the road. He drove for only a few seconds when he noticed a car following them. Ash asked everyone to hold on as he turned off the highway and onto a small rural street. It was a typical Irish roadway — very dark and narrow with a rock wall on both sides. Ash showed expert precision as he navigated through the tight space with their car. As he started to pick up speed, he could see an eighteen-wheeler heading right for them and he yelled out, "Uh oh, what should I do?"

Cordy thought about the games of chicken she played in her small hometown in Missouri. "Don't back down; just keep on your side of the road," she advised. Ash moved over closer to the rock wall, nearly scraping the side of the car. Then they heard a smashing sound. The passenger side mirror pulverized to nothing. The truck flew by them and there was another sound of crash and smash. Everyone screamed as they saw sparks and heard metal grinding. The driver's side mirror and the passenger side of the car were damaged the whole length of the car.

Cordy started to laugh to relieve the tension in the car since everyone sat stunned.

"You know, Ash, car repair is the second leading industry in Ireland. The first is Irish whiskey. You put the two together and it isn't pretty. How are you going to pay back the man you stole the car from?" asked Han.

Cordy knew honest Ash needed reassurance. She held up some anonymous gift cards that she picked up at the airport security deposit box placed by Bob's minions. She and he long agreed the gift cards would be used to help the needy. If there was ever an example of being needy this was one of them. Ash smiled back at her and left them in the glove box with a note and a check worth triple the amount of the car. "Thanks, Cordy. I don't think I could have done this without you."

She took her hand and tenderly touched his. "Nope, but together we make a great team."

After the near collision, Ash got back on the highway and followed a sign that said two kilometers to the airport. He checked the rearview mirror and didn't see the car behind them anymore. "We must have lost them."

Han's hands gripped his seat. "I've been very patient and have tried not to comment on your driving, son, but you just scared the hell out of me. I hope you don't do that again. You are supposed to run from bad guys, not die running from them." He let out a big sigh and then smacked Ash's head.

Suddenly, Cordy turned around to talk to Ash's parents. "I think I know where the safest place is. Ash, what do you think about the chief's house?"

"I can't think of a better place, and we know they can be protected there," he said. "Grey Smoke would make a great watchdog and playmate for my future brother or sister." Ash let out a little happy chuckle at the picture forming in his mind of the great, gray wolf dog playing with a child.

Cordy called Bob back. When he picked up, they both simultaneously said, "The chief's house."

"You see, Bob, great minds think alike. Ash thinks it's a great idea too," said Cordy.

Bob grumbled, "So much for great minds. How did he become a doctor anyway?"

"Now, Bob, that's not nice. Give the little asshole some slack."

Ash and his father turned around and yelled in unison, "Hey, cut that out you two."

Cordy felt instant remorse and apologized. "Sorry guys, I'm trying to tell Bob to back off."

"What about the paperwork and passports?" Cordy asked Bob.

"I see everyone is a bit touchy over there huh? Don't worry about that government stuff — I got connections. I will have them ready when they land. My people will follow my instructions and get them safely there. Cordy, you do know what this means. I will have to get your grandfather Bill involved. Do you think we can trust him?"

Cordy paused and thought about it. "He told me he would do whatever he could. We are all that's left of the family." She remembered the day when she met her estranged grandfather and in Montreal. He wanted to patch up things between his family. They agreed to let the past go and try to unite the family again. Bill headed the organization of the Light Watchers who tried to protect the Pure of Heart and mankind. "I trust him," she decided. "Let's get this done."

"You got it, boss. I'll make it happen."

Bob called her grandfather. Bill picked up his cell phone and saw that it was Bob, Cordy's right hand man. "Howdy Billy, this is Bob. Did I almost say Billy Bob? Never mind, seems apropos since last time we met we were holding machine guns shooting bad guys out of a helicopter. We make a helluva great team." Bob got down to business. "Before we get started, Cordy is OK but on the run as usual. She's made quite a few friends over the last few days. Unfortunately, they're on the run as well."

"Oh, thank God. Is she hurt? My early reports said they were captured early this morning and there are casualties. I've been worried sick thinking about my granddaughter being tortured or worse," Bill anxiously answered. "It's made me rethink everything. She is all the family I have. I'll do anything, Bob, to help Cordy. What can I do?"

Bob reassured him, "Don't worry. That little girl can take care of herself. And once again, she is alright. Cordy asked me to call you for a favor. I warned her it might not be possible for you to help, but she assured me you told her to ask for anything and you would try your best. So here we go. Your reports were right. Some of her party was captured but they escaped and now they need a safe place to hide for a long time. It will be two men and one woman. Here is the hard part - I need to get them into Halifax, Nova Scotia without any of the Dark Watchers seeing them. I think this is impossible, but Cordy thought you would be able to find a way to keep them off the grid."

The relief in Bill's voice was audible. "You were right to call, Bob. I know you don't trust me yet, but I do keep my promises to that little girl. It means taking the risk of losing it all, but it doesn't matter anymore. If my reports from Ireland are correct, I already came close to losing everything that means anything to me and that is Cordy."

"Bill, I left something out. The woman is pregnant and at some point will need medical assistance. I won't tell you the final destination over the phone until we meet in Halifax," Bob said. "Oh, by the way, we will be arriving in the next five to six hours."

"Nothing is out of the realm of possibility when it comes to my granddaughter. I'll be at the airport waiting and will have your back. No one will have a clue where they go. I'm on it."

The way Bill spoke cast doubt on Bob. Bob's father always said that if something sounds too good to be true, it probably is. Right now, they didn't have many choices. "OK, Bill, I'll call you when the jet is about an hour out. I'll have all their documents ready when they arrive. Don't worry about them."

"Sounds good. Tell Cordy I love her and that I wish I would have understood what was really valuable in my life. It's not money or power. Tell her I want to be part of her life always and I wish my dead son knew I'd changed. I have lots of regrets." Bob could hear Bill getting choked up on the other end of the phone.

Bob knew Bill loved his only granddaughter. "He knows Bill, and so does Cordy. I've got to go, Bill. I have a lot to do in the next five hours. Goodbye."

Bill dropped to his knees, put his palms over his eyes, and began to cry. He couldn't catch his breath. He knew his life didn't mean as much as his granddaughter's. For the second time in his life, it wasn't about him, but about her. Bill remembered how scared he felt when Cordy dived into the freezing ocean after the dying chief. How life would be so empty now without the old chief if it weren't for his lovely granddaughter. Everything changed in that moment, when he knew her life was in danger. He would do anything he could to save her.

Bob called Cordy back and told her everything was a go. He let her know what her grandfather said but deep down he remained skeptical. *Could a man change after all these years?* he wondered to himself.

After Cordy got off the phone, she turned and gave them a thumbs up. "Ash, it's a go. My grandfather will meet your parents and Brother Michael at Halifax. He assured us that no one will know where they are going."

Ash pulled up the car at the office outside where the corporate jet was. "Well, Mom and Dad, this is it. Time to say goodbye. Call us when you know if it is a boy or a girl. Dad, congratulations. Not bad for an old man. I didn't know you had it in you." They laughed out loud as he hugged his mom and slapped his dad on the shoulder.

Ash went to shake Brother Michael's hand. The elderly man pulled him in for a hug instead. They didn't exchange any words, just looked into each other's eyes; they both knew how close they had become over these hard times. Finally, the three boarded the private jet. Ash and Cordy couldn't wait for the plane to take off so his parents could start their life anew. As the plane pulled away, Ash put the car in drive and accelerated. In the back of his mind, he wondered if he would ever see them again or get to meet his future brother or sister. Time would only tell.

Six hours later, the jet was taxiing to its private terminal. Bob, dressed in jeans and a dark windbreaker, and the elder Bill, wearing a baseball cap and sweater, sat waiting on the side of the building. Their green van had the name of a fuel company, Blue Fuel, on the side. The two men didn't wait for the jet to come to a stop before they headed out to meet it. They pulled up to the aircraft and down came three people with coats on and hoods covering their faces; they drove off together in a hurry.

Bob and Han did a quick introduction. On the walkie-talkie, Bob could hear an emergency call go out from the main terminal. Bill's distraction worked and true to his word everyone focused on the emergency down farther on the other runway. His men had pulled it off.

No one noticed Bill pulling the van up along four trailers in the shape of a square. He told everybody to get out and follow him. He went into the center of the four trailers and to Bob's astonishment, there stood a small, four-passenger helicopter. Bob was impressed. No one could see who was getting in because the trailers blocked everyone's view.

Bill ordered them to board. "OK, everyone, get in the helicopter. Bob I know you can fly this bird. I read your military dossier and if you fly low enough no one will be able to track you. It's better for me not to know where you're going."

Bob, carrying a black bag, smiled, "Son of a bitch, Bill, you stayed true to your word! I thought we'd be in a fire fight by now."

"You better get moving or you may still get in one. Just leave the helicopter in a store parking lot. Someone will complain and we will get it back to its owner." Bill smiled and shook Bob's hand and patted him on the back. Aziza, Han, and Brother Michael expressed their thanks.

As the helicopter took off, Bob reached into a small duffle bag in the helicopter and passed out new identities to everyone. "Here are your new names. Study them because you will need to know them when we land."

Ash's father took the opportunity to reprimand Bob. "You're the one who likes to make fun of my son's name. I want you to stop. Do I make myself clear?"

Bob hoped his bad joke on the phone wouldn't come up, but Ash's dad wanted to make a point. He smiled at Han and said, "Well sir, I admit I have a sick sense of humor. I didn't think Ash would make it being a studious professor type; he has no military training like me. You see, my main job is to keep my boss, Cordy, alive and he was a big question mark in my book. He's a terrible shot, but he is one lucky brave guy. Ash told us his real name Asho meant Pure of Heart. He is the real deal and I trust him but his marksman skills make me nervous. I have to say I never thought his dad would be sitting here next to me with a gun. I'm going on record as saying I'm sorry for teasing him."

Bob started to laugh and so did Ash's dad. They reached across and shook each other's hands.

Han smiled and instantly took a liking to Cordy's right hand man, "Thank you for all you have done, Bob. We owe you our lives."

Aziza pointed to the ground below. "Look, Brother Michael, is that snow on the ground?" She had a big smile on her face. "I've never seen snow before. It's so beautiful! Look how it sparkles when the light shines on it. I'm sure it's a good sign for a new beginning for all of us." Han hugged his wife and hoped Ash would find more clues about the Keys of Life.

CHAPTER 9

So Close

De Villiers strolled around the meeting room of the Dark Watchers headquarters drinking his brandy. He couldn't resist gazing at Carravagio's painting on the wall. Betrayal is the worst crime. Judas betrays his best friend for money and power. A true Dark Watcher in every way, the traitor should be admired rather than vilified. If only he had a few more capable traitors working for him now, his job would be easier. His agents infiltrated and placed themselves in positions of power and like Judas, discovered all their enemies' secrets. He finished the job by setting them up for slaughter. De Villiers chuckled at the chaos within the painting. A good puppet master stands behind the curtain and watches while he pulls the string. He grimaced at the stupid puppet who escaped his grasp.

Ellen had such potential to be groomed as the next Judas but she just couldn't pull it off. A disappointment in every way, Ellen did serve her use for setting into motion Chief Saunhac's death but she didn't kill Lafitte nor did she bring back the Pure of Heart's treasures. The woman didn't even have the decency to die. His minions reported she still worked for the Nephilim but was demoted to menial jobs at headquarters. She was no good to him anymore. He would have killed her himself but rumors had it the chairman would take care of her soon. The Dark Watcher leader held her dossier in his hands, fully aware of how the chairman programmed little Julia Villars into femme fatale Ellen Villars, the top enforcer of the Nephilim organization.

She didn't know who he really was but De Villiers didn't want the Nephilim suspecting the Dark Watchers involvement with her. The seductive Ellen believed he loved her and he would betray the Dark Watchers. The master of intrigue used her ambition to try to impress her superiors to go rogue and bring back the treasures of the Pure of Heart. He suggested she contact Lafitte and use his services. All along she thought he was the fool when she was his puppet on the string. De Villiers' men were going to take out Ellen and her team, Lafitte, and the Pure of Heart. Their treasure should be in his hands but alas Ellen wasn't as efficient as Judas. At least he had the decency to die by his own hand.

He gazed up at the painting and saluted Judas with his glass.

"If one wants something done right then he must do it himself. A good puppet master doesn't leave any loose strings in which he can get tangled."

He smiled at Isis and then gazed up at Carravagio's painting.

"Like you Isis, if I had a mouth, I would bite. If I had my liberty, I would do what I liked. In the meantime, let me be that I am and seek not to alter me. Shakespeare's Don John inspires me. It must be not denied, but I am a plain dealing villain. A damn good one to boot." The cat hissed and De Villiers chuckled.

CHAPTER 10

Ireland's Giants and Dream

A handsome tour guide on a sightseeing bus in Ireland held his microphone and looked out at his audience. They're young couples, retired couples, and an elderly nun visiting the Emerald Isle. The day's setting was perfect for his mysterious tale as a misty fog fell over the land.

He ran his fingers through his thick red hair and began, "Long ago legends tell us, a race of giants called the Formorians lived on the island of Ireland. Survivors of the great flood, the giants ruled the country until a misty day, such as the one we are having now. A foggy cloud swept in a new race of people called the Tuatha De Danann. They came and landed on the great mountaintop. The natives called the Tuatha De Danann the Forevers. Keepers of great magic, they defeated the Formorians with great weapons.

"The rulers and great warriors eventually made peace and in time, the races intermingled," the tour guide continued. "Later on, the Milesians landed on Ireland and defeated the Tuatha De Danann. They disappeared into myth and the mist of time. Legends say these supernatural beings' magic still existed, even to this day, and they became the sidhe or fairy folk of long ago stories. Magical beings or Tuathe De, meaning tribe of the gods, invisible to the eyes, fought their foes with shields of white and lances of blue. Their weapons of incredible power were used to destroy the giants and save Earth's children.

"Legends say the Tuathe De came from the heavens to teach mankind how to live in peace and teach them about mathematics and give them knowledge of the stars. Dagda, meaning the "good god," brought his magic cauldron, filled with magical seeds and food. When the people saw famine and starvation, they were fed from his cauldron of plenty. Like a cornucopia, no one would starve eating from it," he spoke into the microphone as he rubbed his belly. "Another myth told of those who drank from it being healed of their injuries like the Holy Grail of Galahad. Dagda also owned a magical harp," he said as he pretended to pluck the air, "that rallied the troops in battle. It could make anyone laugh, cry, or fall asleep. The idea of using different frequencies is explored today in the study of psychoacoustics.

"The monks of old wrote about the legends and called them "people of God" or another name for Israelites. Some have connected them with the ancient tribe of Dan. They explain it is from Jerusalem where they brought their secret super-powered weapons and knowledge given to them from the Heavens.

"The Sword of Nuada was a flaming sword that no one could defeat," the tour guide continued, slashing the air with his finger like a blade. "The possession of the Spear of Lugh meant being undefeated in war. You can compare the Spear of Lugh with the spear of Michael the Archangel defeating the forces of evil. The Stone of Lia Fail would cry out who the King of Ireland was if he stood beneath it. A comparison can be made to the Scottish Stone of Scone which when a ruler sits upon it makes them king or queen. Five magical treasures of the Tuatha De Danann were brought to Ireland from their ancient home," said the young man. "Who knows, on this trip, we may just find one of them." Everyone gave a cheer on the bus.

As the sightseeing bus drove down the road, the tour guide pointed to a huge green mound surrounded by a circle of white quartz rock. "That mysterious mound covers over one acre of land. Built in 3200 B.C., it's older than Stonehenge and the pyramids of Egypt," he explained. "Archeologists believe it was built either in reverence to the dead or to the stars. On winter solstice at Newgrange, the sun's rays enter the doorway and for 17 minutes the chamber floor is illuminated. Legend wrote that Newgrange was the home of Dagda and his son Oengus who brought his friend Diarmaid to see it. He decorated his home with magical symbols and beautiful artwork. Newgrange's megalithic artwork carved on its ancient stones still remains today. Some archeologists believe Ireland is host to a network of these mounds, which are interconnected and use the stars as their compass. The ancient people seem to have far more knowledge of the stars than we thought. Scientists have concluded other mounds at Knowth, Dowth and the Lough Crew Cairns could be monuments with astronomical importance," he said.

The redheaded tour guide's nametag read Uriel. His eyes stared deeply into the wise eyes of the quiet nun on the bus; a great calm and peace fell over her. Uriel smiled at the frail elderly woman, dressed in her blue habit with a veil over her head, and whispered into her ear so no one else could, "You need to come home, Sister Agnes. Your journey is coming to an end. He knows you broke the contract and now he wants revenge. Oh, Pure of Heart, a sacrifice must be made and we await you. You've fought an honorable battle against the Nephilim and their partners. I salute you."

Sister Agnes touched the Miraculous Medal close to her heart. Two hearts engraved on the medal surrounded by stars held the symbol for the Pure of Heart for her. She smiled at the charming Uriel and showed no fear. "I'm ready to go home my friend, and see my family. What better place for my next journey to begin than in the land of my forefathers. You'll protect Cordy."

Uriel nodded and his eyes filled with great determination of a warrior.

Sister Agnes understood Uriel's message. Her bargain made with De Villiers long ago to protect Cordelia after her parents died had ended. The devious man figured out they had hidden the child's birthdate from the Nephilim by delivering her at home and falsifying the records. He promised to leave her alone as long as she never interfered with the Dark Watchers' agenda. Agnes broke the contract when she gave Cordy her trust money and revealed the battle of the Pure of Heart and Nephilim and Watchers. She had no choice after Cordy exposed herself saving Minah, a young woman kidnapped by a sex slave trader. De Villiers' temper would want revenge and retaliation. He himself had tested Cordy, discovering another Pure of Heart and her true name, Cordy Mcdermott. The Dark Watcher leader used her as bait to kill Chief Saunhac, and she led him to the treasures long hidden from the Children of the Nephilim. De Villiers hoped to kill his opposition Jon Lafitte and take Chief Saunhac's Pure of Heart treasures plus get his revenge by killing Sister Agnes's niece for her betrayal. Cordy possessed the Pure of Heart treasures and Lafitte survived.

Chief Saunhac and Sister Agnes had protected the ancient treasures for years. The Swords of Fire, Earth, Air, and Water, hidden away treasures of the ancient races like the Tuatha De Danaan, were in trusted hands of the Pure of Heart or their allies. De Villiers thirst for revenge after she deceived him could only be quenched by Agnes' death. He also wanted information about the Pure of Heart. Sister Agnes didn't have much time left. Uriel gave her the message loud and clear. Newgrange flashed by her window on the bus in her mind. She smiled as all the ancient temples held their secrets close.

Sister Agnes awoke from her vivid dream. The sun shined on her small convent bedroom at Marrilac. She picked up the phone and booked a ticket to Ireland, hoping to see Cordy one last time. She told Cordy she needed to trace back her ancient family history. Sister Agnes made one more phone call to say goodbye to an old loyal friend, Master Wong. He taught Cordy karate and trained and protected her through the years, although her niece never knew her guardian and protector's connection with her aunt. The next day, the frail tiny nun hugged her fellow sisters' goodbye and left for Ireland. One nun watched Sister Agnes leave and headed for the phone to let De Villiers know she left for Ireland. The Dark Watcher hung up the phone, knowing no one can hide from him.

CHAPTER 11

Good Vibrations

Cordy's low spirits made her very emotional. It had been a long time since she'd been around a real family. Even as dysfunctional as Ash's family was, she could see the closeness and love that was there. She wondered if she would ever be so lucky or live long enough to have a family of her own. Her eyes glanced over at Ash as she struggled with her emotions. Ash had risked his life for her family and she knew in her heart he was one of a kind.

It was the calls from his girlfriend Linda and his second girl-friend, possible hooker that troubled her. Dirty Dottie and the black book in his wallet all pointed to what her girlfriends in St. Louis called, a *real player*. Cordy made a point to stay clear of them in the past, but this guy pulled her in early with those piercing eyes and chiseled body. This one was different. As she looked at Ash as they drove away from the airport, she admitted that yes, dammit, she was jealous of that Dirty Dottie.

She knew she shouldn't feel that way but she envied the woman. Ash was always a perfect gentleman to her but Ellen's first request of the archeologist was for him to pull down his pants. Cordy started to smile at Ash, and he smiled back at her not knowing she was reminiscing about that moment. Cordy thought, *What are you thinking? Is he an animal or a predator? He just wants to get you in bed and then you will be just like all the other Dirty Dotties out there. And why in the hell did you just smile at him? Are you leading him on? Do you want to go to bed with him?*

Cordy straightened up in her seat next to Ash. Now she had worked herself up into frenzy. She reached into the side door, pulled out a map, and started to fan herself. She started to perspire; her hands began to sweat as well. Cordy thought, *Oh my, it's like I'm eighteen all over again. Get ahold of yourself, woman!*

Ash slammed on the brakes and pulled over to the side of the road, tossing everything in the car around. His irresistible voice yelled, "That's what I was looking for!"

Caught off guard, Cordy seductively breathed, "Take me, Ash!"

Ash's eyes looked deep into her lust filled eyes. He grabbed Cordy's shoulder and then pointed out the window. "How would you like that between your legs? That's what we are taking to Dublin!" Confused, Cordy placed her hand on her chest and took a huge deep breath. She blushed with embarrassment as she realized what Ash really wanted. He was looking at a 2006 Harley-Davidson Softtail Fat Boy, not her, parked in a hotel parking lot and had stopped next to it.

"Well, Mr. Ash, you have been on only one motorcycle and now you have an addiction for them. We call that bitten by the bug. It's something you will have for the rest of your life!"

"I don't know what it is but it looks cool, doesn't it?" Ash asked.

"You're not thinking of taking it, are you? There is a saying, 'Big bike, big biker.'" But Ash was already getting out of the car. He walked up next to the bike and searched for a hidden key, but there wasn't one. He glanced back at Cordy who remained seated, shaking her head. Ash threw his hands up in the air. Cordy threw her hands up too, as if to say, "Come on, let's get going!"

Ash shook his head no and pointed back at the Harley.

"I'm begging you help me. If I'm going to die, let it be on this bike."

Cordy opened the glove box, dug out some papers at the bottom, and found a screwdriver. She grabbed it up and swung open the car door. She shook her head again, "Don't think just because I've been around motorcycles that I know how to steal one. I did, once upon a time, date a biker boyfriend who did, and I saw him do it. I was pretty young and that was the last date I had with him. So, it doesn't make me an expert just to let you know." As she passed Ash, she handed him a gift card Bob had given her so its owners might find a nice surprise.

"Cordy, are these cards worth 50 G's? I saw you give my mom four of them."

"They gave up everything for you and they were going to need some seed money," she replied.

"What is seed money?"

Cordy forgot that Ash wasn't from the U.S. "It's an expression farmers used where I come from. Someone they knew would give them money so they could buy seeds and when their crops came in, the farmers would pay them back."

"If you gave my parents $200,000, they will have a hard time paying you back," Ash cautioned.

Cordy sighed. "Shut up and get your bag from the car. When we start this baby up, everyone on the street will know it, and like I said, big bike, big biker."

Cordy jammed the screwdriver into the lock on the bike. She took her foot, gave the bike a karate kick, and then pulled out all the wires. Before Ash could return from the car, Cordy started the bike. The roar of the engine scared him to death but exhilarated him at the same time. The loud thump, thump, thump was something he had never heard before. Ash ran back with the bag of artifacts, hooked it on the back bar, and jumped on behind Cordy, putting his hands around her waist. He snuggled close and Cordy admitted she liked where his hands rested. For the first time, Cordy didn't say anything but smiled on the inside. She just slammed the

Harley Fat Boy in gear and off they went. Luckily for them, its owner slept like a log in the hotel.

They had only gone about two miles before Cordy pulled over. She told Ash, "You'll have to drive the rest of the way to Dublin. I'm exhausted."

Ash was excited to take the driver's seat. They changed places and Cordy pulled herself unusually close to him. Ash looked back at her and smiled, then put the bike into gear and raced off. He had never felt a power like this in anything he had driven before. Pressing herself even closer to Ash, Cordy knew what she was doing. They only drove on the road for a few minutes.

Cordy put her hand inside Ash's shirt and rubbed his chest tenderly, as if to say thank you. In the next second, Ash unexpectedly took his hand off the throttle and placed it on top of Cordy's hand. He squeezed it as if to say, I've got you. Cordy wiped off her tears on Ash's shirt and held him tightly.

Thirty minutes outside of Dublin, Ash pulled over to call Linda. Cordy rolled her eyes; she had forgotten about Ash's other girlfriend in Ireland. She imagined her to be about twenty-five and great looking. Cordy was upset that Ash would still call an old girlfriend. Reality hit her. Cordy was thinking about him getting rid of his old girlfriend and for the first time she wanted to be Ash's new girlfriend. *I mean, after all,* she thought, *We've been through so much together. It would only be natural for Ash to like me. I'll be keeping my eye on Linda.*

Then she heard Ash say, "OK, Linda, we'll see you there in thirty minutes. I've missed you too." Cordy reached out to Ash and asked, "Do we have to get Linda involved? Can't we just find some place on our own? What if it's a set up?"

"Cordy, calm down, it will be OK. Linda can be trusted."

Ash started the Harley up and headed down the road to the Crown Plaza Hotel. Linda told Ash that there was too much security at the embassy, so she made reservations for Ash and his friend for three nights under her parents' names, Robert and Beatrix. Linda had the keys so they had no reason to go to the front desk and could remain undetected.

Ash pulled up on the backside of the hotel. A black BMW flashed its lights at them. Ash knew Linda's signal. Cordy already hated the girl before the car door even opened, but to her surprise, out popped a cute petite teenage girl. Cordy was convinced that the girl's mother would come out of the other door, but the car door didn't open. Cordy thought the little girl couldn't be more than a freshman or sophomore in high school. She punched Ash in the shoulder. He threw his hands in the air with frustration. "I told you it wasn't that way, she's just a friend," he said as he chuckled at Cordy's surprise.

As they started to walk toward Linda, she ran to Ash. He put his hand out to shake hers, but she pulled him in for a big hug instead. Ash patted her back as if to say, that's enough. Cordy was all smiles. The young girl was just that, too young for Ash. He was right. Linda wasn't what she had thought. Cordy watched the bubbly teenager squeeze Ash. So what, Linda had a crush on him, and so did she. What was there not to like about Ash?

Linda turned around to greet Cordy. "Hi! My name is Linda, and Ash cured me of stuttering. I'll always remember that day, and I'm forever in his debt. We worked together at Abu Simbel on a photo shoot. He's such an amazing archeologist. I want to be just like him." Now everything made sense. Linda explained that after Ash cured her, she had felt exhilarated, scared, exhausted and intoxicated with amazing energy. Linda idolized Ash, and he was her hero. Cordy started to feel like a fool.

Linda told them, "The embassy is on high alert, and I couldn't get any military protection for you two. Besides, the wall around the hotel is so high, I don't even think Ash could get on top of it." Cordy remembered the past phone calls to Linda which caused some jealous feelings when she heard them discussing something about how Ash didn't like using protection and who was going to get on top. She had meant the wall around the hotel. Ash smiled from ear to ear. It was like he was reading Cordy's mind and loving it. Cordy punched him in the arm and then with true relief and excitement, pulled Linda in for a hug. The girl sported a typical schoolgirl's crush on Ash. Linda gushed at the sight of him. Cordy went from disgust to relief in three minutes, but she didn't forget about Dirty Dottie.

Ash gave them their instructions. "OK, you two, you look like you're long-lost sisters and you're saying goodbye."

"Here are the keys to the room," Linda said. "You have them for three days. It was all the money I saved." With that, Cordy handed her a gift card out of her pocket and smiled. She knew Linda would be surprised the first time she used it and got the balance. Linda hugged them both and started to drive off, but she stopped next to Ash for a second. "I'll be back in three days to check you out of the hotel." She reached out of the car window and squeezed his hand. "You know, I still have a crush on you but if I lose to this one," Linda said, jerking her head toward Cordy. "I would understand."

Ash grinned, "Get out of here you nut." As Linda drove into the night back home, her parents slept, unaware of her nocturnal escapade.

CHAPTER 12

A Special Vision

The late hour arrived. Ash and Cordy staggered into a luxurious, king-size room, carrying only the clothes on their backs and a bag of artifacts. Although exhausted, both of them still felt a nervous energy and tension. Ash admitted to himself that he had never been alone in bed with a hot woman in his life. With his head spinning, the responsible Ash thought, *Stay on your life-and-death game. Focus, man, focus. Don't let your guard down, and don't get distracted.* He couldn't help but be nervous because surely Cordy's boyfriends in the past knew what they were doing when it came to romance. The shy archeologist felt awkward and fumbled around like a schoolboy.

"Alright, now let's get you out of those clothes and into the shower. If we're going to have something clean to wear tomorrow, we have to do our laundry tonight."

Ash's brain still hung on the words *let's get you out of those clothes.*

Cordy pushed him into the bathroom and said, "Take off your clothes and put them in the sink. Then give me a call and I'll wash them when you're in the shower."

"You got it. Just give me a minute."

When Cordy heard the shower start with steam filling the air, she came in and took off her clothes. She put their dirty clothes in the water-filled sink and started to rinse them out, washing them with a bar of lavender soap. Cordy wrapped a towel around her, but couldn't help looking at the steamy shower door. His muscular shadow filled the misty window, which she knew hid a prize.

Ash yelled out, "I'm done. Can you get me a towel?" Cordy handed him a washcloth and started to laugh. "You mean this one?" He didn't grab it and waited. "Oh you mean this one?" After a second, she handed him a large towel.

Ash laughed, "Very funny. I'm coming out now." He stepped out of the shower, his thick blonde hair dripping and muscles glistening. A towel was wrapped around his waist. Cordy's eyes feasted on every bit of him, and her chest felt a slight flutter.

Cordy had all the clothes washed and hanging all over the room. It was her turn for the shower, and she jumped in. She tossed out her towel and began to sing; she always sang in the shower.

Ash went to the bedroom and pulled out an extra blanket from the closet. He took two pillows from the four sitting on the bed, folded the blanket in half on the floor, and threw his pillows down, opting to play the role of the perfect gentleman. What he didn't know but decided in this magical moment was that Cordy was the one and if he waited this long, he knew she'd only respect his efforts not to take anything for granted. Ash could hear the water stop and his heartbeat like a racehorse just out of the gate. He had his back to the bed and window so she could come and get in bed without feeling uncomfortable.

Cordy started to get nervous knowing she was going to be alone with Ash in such close proximity. Linda had already made it to Cordy's good side because she gave her a small care package, which had a brush and some lotion in it. She brushed her long, thick hair as she stood naked in front of the mirror. Cordy let out a Mi'kmaq war howl and headed for the bedroom in all of her bare glory. She walked out of the bathroom door and looked to her left, only to see

Ash, the gentleman, turned with his back to her, sound asleep on the floor.

She stood for a moment at the bathroom doorway, gazing out of the bedroom window into the starry night. Tonight, a full moon's light shone over Ash's firm and muscular body. She thought to herself, "So, great grandpa Saunhac, so much for my war whoop call." Ash didn't move. She stood there for a second thinking about how much she'd fallen for him. She realized that for the first time, she couldn't be the aggressive one. If Ash felt anything for her, he'd have to show her to win her over. Cordy always wanted to be in control but not this time.

What she didn't know was that Ash could see her reflection the whole time in the mirror above the dresser. Time stopped for a moment and he stared at a masterpiece of art. He could hardly control his emotions and silence. Ash whispered to himself, "I do believe in angels, for this must be one." Cordy closed the blinds and crawled into the king-size bed. She gave Ash one more look and then closed her eyes.

CHAPTER 13

Newgrange

Early in the morning, Ash and Cordy set out on their motorcycle in search of more answers. They first headed to Newgrange to see the tomb mound that dated before Stonehenge. They both suspected the Keys of Life dated to the time of the Great Flood so Newgrange could hold some clues for them. Ash and Cordy saw the large circular mound surrounded by white quartz stones in the distance. The tours came and went throughout the area but for twenty minutes Ash and Cordy got to explore the inside alone.

Ash explained, "Newgrange is older than the Egyptian pyramids. It's aligned with the sun and on winter solstice the sun floods the chamber with light." They entered deeper inside and the crystal ball that Saunhac gave them lit up. The light could be seen peeking through the sides of Ash's backpack. Both Ash and Cordy tried to cover it over with one of their jackets.

Cordy yelled out in frustration, "I wonder what's activating the crystal. Where is the on and off switch on this thing?"

"I think it's on a ley line and the quartz around the circular structure picked up some kind of energy," Ash answered. "We should check at the other older site called Knowth. Maybe, we can drive there later tonight. It won't be so crowded there. The chief knew its power, and everything in his book he left you pointed us in this direction. Plus, add your aunt's suggestion to come to Ireland. Something's going on with the ball. The ancient Irish called quartz the 'stone of the sun.'"

Cordy nodded in agreement. "Let's do it. What are all these designs carved on the stones? I've seen these symbols in some Native American paintings and rock carvings."

Fascinating and magnificent, the ancient stones outside Newgrange were carved with spirals, which appeared as the galaxies of the universe. She pointed to a tilted chessboard pattern of interconnected squares, or more like lozenges or diamonds. Cordy was reminded of the interconnected crosses forming a square in Magdalene statue's hands at home.

"Geometric patterns and spirals are found everywhere in Central America, China, Malta, and Columbia. They occur in nature, too, like in seashells, flowers, and DNA. The lozenge is a rhombus. I've seen some of these patterns in Nova Scotia too. The Mi'kmaq Indians used some of the same patterns for their sacred symbols like the cross and crescent moon."

Ash smiled "Good catch, Cordy. The stone engravings carved here are examples of Neolithic art. Some archeologists believe they make reference to the stars and galaxies. Primitive man knew more about the stars than we give him credit. We're still learning about the Egyptians, Mayans, and Sumerians observations of the stars. Their precise calculations demonstrate their advanced astronomical education, and, remember, they didn't have our computers. The heavens were considered sacred to their priests. We may be looking at a sophisticated ancient culture not a primitive one like history tells us. I've always suspected our history books are missing a few things."

Cordy's face showed surprise. "The Book of Enoch talked about Uriel and other angels instructing Enoch on the stars and moon.

He passed the knowledge down through his family to Noah. You think Ash, Newgrange is connected to the story in Genesis of the Nephilim? The children of the Giants — did they live around here?"

Ash nodded. "The Irish have myths and legends about giants. The Giant's Causeway is where the giant Finn McCool fought, and the Fomorians, who were an ancient race, were referred to as giants. It's all legends and stories from the past. The geometric symbols could be a universal language. I know the Egyptians considered their symbols sacred, and the Pyramids' structure is mathematical. Newgrange is built in a geometric circle symbolizing infinity and the number pi. They needed geometry to be the great builders, and in the Book of Enoch that information was handed down generation to generation.

Templars used the lozenge symbol on their castles. The mounds share a connection with a mother goddess cult. I think ancients knew more about the Earth's energies and the power of water than modern man. They understood the concept of how everything is connected to one another. The brilliant Da Vinci realized how everything connects to everything else. Modern man can't seem to grasp this concept. A big lesson needed to be learnt because mankind's survival might depend on it. I think our dreams and visions guided us here for that purpose. "

Cordy looked at the crystal ball still lit in his backpack. "I'm beginning to think there is some truth in these legends. Newgrange's awakened the ball. Maybe we're near an activation point? I read in the brochure about how the tomb complexes connect with one another. Newgrange aligns astronomically with the winter solstice where others align such as Loughcrew, with the spring and autumn equinoxes. I'm looking at the engravings on the rocks and one sign appears to be the astrological symbol Aquarius. Water plays a big role as one of the Keys of Life. The water-carrier symbol brings a new Aquarian age. We're entering in that age right now, and one symbol seems to be a boat. Noah's ark was built to save the world from the great flood. I think we're on to something here. Let's go see Knowth's tomb tonight. I've got a funny feeling you're right. We've got a few more hours so let's visit a sacred place with healing waters, Our Lady of Knock."

CHAPTER 14

Our Lady of Knock

Ash and Cordy continued on their way to see the shrine of Our Lady of Knock. The plan had always been to follow Cordy's Irish family history to see if any other clues or treasures showed up. Chief Saunhac gave her a family diary, which explained the history of those ancestors who had dedicated their lives to protect the treasures of the Pure of Heart. Cordy's story began with a statue of Mary Magdalene with her hands folded in a mysterious symbolic way. It led her to the Miraculous Medal Shrine where she found the same mysterious hands on a painting of the passion in the shrine of Our Lady.

The statue kicked off her whole journey and led her to Ash. The hands were interconnected crosses in a form of a square. Ash said it resembled the symbol for the five-fold Jerusalem cross of the Crusaders, which he had seen in Jerusalem at the Church of the Holy Sepulchre. On one of the church walls, crosses were carved by the knights who made quests to the Holy Land. The crosses on the wall numbered in the thousands, touching one another, and offering proof of the Crusaders' dedication and faith. Legend said the Templars discovered ancient treasure from the time of Moses. The McDermotts had served in the Crusades. The Jerusalem Cross symbol could be seen on their heraldry crest.

A stop at the local pub for lunch bought Ash and Cordy time to talk while eating some delicious shepherd's pie and drinking Irish beer.

"My great-grandfather witnessed the lights of Our Lady of Knock," Cordy explained. "A Fenian hedge schoolmaster, he taught not in school but on the hillsides and farms to the poor because they were forbidden an Irish education by the English. The hedge master taught Gaelic, Ovid, Virgil, Irish folklore, and music. Their school, forbidden by the British, could be found in the hiding spots of the hedges and woods.

"One night, coming home to his family, he discovered the bright lights at Knock. He later heard of the close-up visions from his neighbors. I promised Sister Agnes that I'd stop here on my journey. She's guided and protected me all through my childhood. I appreciate you coming along with me, Ash. I know it sounds crazy, but my family believed in the power of Knock's vision. They survived some desperate times in Ireland, and the visions gave them hope. They escaped to America to find a new life just like Noah searching for a new home. Magdalene, Acadians, and Irish refugees flying from oppression share a similar story of escaping death in boats and finding freedom. They brought their priceless treasures with them and I believe the crystal ball was one of them."

Ash answered before he could think, letting his heart talk, "I think the chief wanted us to do this together. I couldn't think of a better person to be with than you." A moment of silence passed and Cordy's eyes locked with Ash's for just a moment. After what seemed like an eternity, their eyes parted.

Ash stood up and asked some men at the bar for directions to the shrine.

"Ahhhh, laddie, you be goin' down the road and turn by Michael's pub!"

Ash and Cordy shook their heads. God invented GPS because of an Irishman's directions. They had to stop almost every ten miles, looking for the next pub, to get directions and grab a pint just to be friendly and blend in so as not to raise any suspicions. After visiting every Irish pub on the way to Knock, they finally found it.

They discovered a narrow street lined with cars and parked their bike. Cordy explained more about the shrine to Ash.

"The vision of Knock came at desperate times for the people of Ireland, during the Great Famine. It wasn't that there was no food, but that the poor were being starved to death by their British landlords. The food they produced was sold to Britain and meanwhile, their children starved. Genocide of a certain standard, it had all the signs of the Children of the Nephilim's handiwork. They hunted down the Pure of Heart and killed them. If they didn't die of starvation, they died of sicknesses on the boats. Placing the sick in close quarters, with no physicians, meant death sentences for most of them. Families were driven apart, but Ireland fought and gained her independence.

"On August 21, 1879, witnesses discovered a woman dressed in white, her head crowned with golden crosses called Our Lady. One of the witnesses said they went to kiss the vision but encountered only a wall. Cures followed the vision and the water of Knock gave drinkers and bathers healing properties.

"The visions of Knock were similar to the Fatima visions of the Miracle of the Sun in Portugal witnessed by thousands. Angels appeared in both visions. The third secret prophecy of Fatima, revealed later to the public, talked about an angel with a flaming sword pointing it toward Earth while a woman in white held his hand and sword from destruction. The angel's words announced a warning, *Penance, Penance, Penance.* A warning to the Children of the Nephilim about their impending destruction."

Cordy filled an ancient alabaster stone jar engraved with the symbol of the Keys of Life ankh with water from Knock to keep as a souvenir for her grandfather Bill. The water was considered powerful and pure with special gifts.

Ash got her message. "I know all about the angel with the flaming sword. He isn't to be taken lightly. Water contains the essential ingredient of life, produces electricity, and, incredibly, is a byproduct of star formation. Scientists talk about how unique water is — it can present as a liquid, ice, or steam. Researchers have found water carries memory, and certain emotions change the molecular structure of water. Our bodies consist mostly of water. We're connected to water. It's the sacred ingredient in religious rituals in many cultures. I do believe there is such a thing as holy water. The Egyptian desert taught me a hard lesson on how precious a gift pure water is. Knock is a sacred place for the Pure of Heart. I understand why."

"You know, Ash, I've noticed that the Celtic crosses look very much like the Egyptian Key of Life, the ankh. Did you see it too?"

"You're right, Cordy, they're similar. An Irish legend of an Egyptian princess named Scota popped up in twelfth century Irish books. Some historians say Scotland's name comes from the legend of Scota. The Celtic cross and ankh are connected through time."

Cordy immediately noticed the Vincentians and Daughters of Charity house located next to the shrine.

She whispered to herself, "I wonder if Sister Agnes lived here in her younger days? I think the McDermott's ancestral castle lies near the Lough Key. It's a mystical magical place, a lake created in legend by a great Druid named Ce who fought an ancient evil. The ancient druid was a follower of the legendary Nuada, leader of the magical Tuatha Da Naan and when they dug Ce's grave, water rose up from the ground creating the Lough Key. "

Ash's head shot up, "A druid, of course. They were Pythagoreans. Legends say they could heal others and communicate with animals. It fits."

All of a sudden, Ash and Cordy stopped in their tracks. They observed the large sculpture of the Crucifixion with Mother Mary and John. Below them, kneeling and looking straight at Cordy and Ash, was a statue of Mary Magdalene, her hands folded the same way as the Magdalene in St. Louis. You could still see the symbolic hands of the Jerusalem Cross, though age had chipped away some of the stone. "I can't believe it. No wonder my aunt wanted me to come here." A murder of crows sat on the statues. One black bird began loudly cawing at Cordy, followed by the whole group. "OK, I'm getting a creepy feeling."

Ash and Cordy knew the birds were a sign. A calm silence surrounded them. Cordy blinked at Ash with tears in her eyes. A tingle spiraled down her spine. "I think my aunt is in grave danger or maybe dead. Something awful has happened to her. The crows are giving us a warning. My mother said they warned of a loved one's death."

Ash put his hand around her shoulder and tried to reassure her. "Why don't you call Bob and maybe he can check up on her. We need to start heading back to Knowth so we get there by nightfall."

Cordy called Bob and left the message on his voice mail. "Bob, do me a favor and check on my aunt, Sister Agnes. I think she's in grave danger. My aunt isn't answering her phone."

CHAPTER 15

Knowth

Ash and Cordy decided to hide their motorcycle behind some bushes near the road and hike in the dark to the mound at Knowth. The full moon helped light the way. A mysterious place located in the valley of the River Boyne, the Great Mound at Knowth was 5000 years old and surrounded by a group of smaller mounds. They proceeded through a cow pasture and found the cement path surrounding the huge mound. The path led to the front stone opening of the mound's door. Ash and Cordy saw the spiral and lozenge engraved on the outside rocks, like at Newgrange.

Cordy whispered to Ash, "Do you feel the vibration? Something is strange."

"I feel it too. It reminds me of a feeling I had in Egypt before I found the Keys of Life," Ash whispered.

"Wasn't Knowth a tomb? Oh look, the ball is lit. The light shines brighter here than at Newgrange."

Ash shook his head. "People make the same mistake about the pyramids in Egypt. They think all of them are tombs but some are temples."

Ash pulled out the crystal ball and the light illuminated their way. The crystal brightened with greater intensity as they got closer to the doorway. They scanned the area for people, but no one was around.

Ash whispered, "Yes, Knowth mound is reportedly a tomb. I've spent my life investigating ancient temples. This one is in a similar shape to the Keys of Life. It's a circular mound, and the inside passageways are built like a cross, sort of like an Egyptian ankh. The symbol for life, the ankh is the key to opening the door to another life. So, you can see why the symbol could be used both for a temple and a tomb. Let's go to the eastern chamber."

They walked farther into the long, stone tunnel until they came to a blocked wall. A stone basin stood in the corner. Carved into the basin was a handprint, or what some might say looked like an angel with wings.

Ash was surprised. "Oh, wow, this is amazing! I think the handprint wants to hold the crystal ball."

Ash placed the crystal ball into the basin and set it on the open hand. A beaming, bright light filled the chamber and the tomb began to shake. Ash and Cordy started to run, but a woman in white stood in front of them and blocked their escape. Cordy and Ash fell on the ground looking up at her.

"Welcome, Pure of Heart," she greeted them. "I have been waiting for both of you. Please recite the password, Star Child, and place the golden triangles over the hand with the crystal ball in the center to prove that you are a Pure of Heart."

Ash took out the golden triangles - one discovered by him in Egypt and the other given to Cordy in St. Louis by a cat named Isis. He never noticed how the triangles fit together, one on top of the other, forming the Seal of Solomon, the six-sided star. The crystal ball sat on top of the star. He looked at Cordy with a confused expression. "What's the password, Star Child?" he asked her.

The chief called her Star Child. She thought for a second and remembered long ago Chief Saunhac singing to her as a little girl. Cordy sang the lullaby her great-grandfather sang to her over and over again.

"Twinkle, twinkle, little star..." The musical notes resonated through the stones of quartz. The crystal ball illuminated the whole room with an even brighter light.

"I am the Guardian. How can I help you?" the woman in the white dress announced.

Ash and Cordy's mouths fell open in astonishment. Ash asked her, "Guardian of what?"

"I am the Guardian of Terra and her children, left here to protect Terra by the Forevers."

Cordy asked, "What is Terra?"

"Terra is what you call Earth," the Guardian answered. "I've been sleeping for a long time and will try to adapt my language to yours."

Ash said, "Who are the Forevers?"

"They lived here on Terra long ago and instructed me to protect her and the Pure of Heart. You possess the crystal ball, which is the energy source of the Forevers. You activated me. I scanned the bag you carry, and you possess some of the Keys of Life."

"Where are the other Keys of Life?" Cordy asked.

The Guardian showed surprise at her question. "You possess the Ring of Power over the Forevers. Be careful, for this power can be very dangerous. You must place the quartz laser disc on the hand of the Forevers on the basin, over the golden star. Then place the crystal ball on top of it. The disc contains the answer to your questions."

Ash set the quartz disk Cordy found at the Miraculous Medal Shrine on top of the golden star in the basin. He placed the crystal ball atop it.

"Look at the stone wall behind you." The Guardian pointed to the stone. Pictures and massive amounts of data projected in holographic forms appeared on the wall.

"The laser disc contains all the information from the Forevers' library. The sacred places are interconnected around the world and lie on Terra's energy lines. The artwork at this site shows the ball of energy and the Keys of Life," the Guardian explained. A holographic picture of a stone carving flashed on the wall, with the ankh cross inserted into the crystal ball. "The crystal sphere can be oriented in many ways for power. The cross above the ball is for activation of sacred places; the crystal ball above the cross is for energy and realignment of Terra. I've disclosed the two functions of the ball of power. The openings for the golden Keys of Life will open the door when touched by the crystal ball. Terra's position in the cosmos is of great importance for the balance of the solar system. She is filled with life. We honor her children. All things in the universe are connected, for we are made from the same star dust, brothers and sisters united.

"A long time ago," she continued, "the Keys of Life activated the gateways, one to leave Terra and another to return to Terra. The Keys of Life were placed in the protection of the Pure of Heart and me. All of the Keys of Life are hidden in case of another impending catastrophe. We've detected an imbalance in Terra and an extinction-level event is a possibility. Terra and all her children may die. In Terra's history, ancient civilizations recorded a similar event called the Great Flood. It is why the Pure of Heart have been called to serve. You will be able to activate the library of the Forevers at any time with the crystal ball. The library contains knowledge of an advanced civilization from long ago."

Cordy asked, "What do we need to prevent this extinction, Guardian?"

"Swords," she answered. "The Sword of Air, once known as Nuada's sword, controls the winds. The flaming Sword of Fire guards the Tree of Life. The Sword of Sacred Waters, birthed from two places where waters cure the sick, is held within a sacred vessel engraved with the symbol of the Key of Life. Oceans, springs, and rivers obey this sword. The Sword of Earth, the Destroyer, produces powerful lightning and controls weather and earthquakes. One more called the Sword of Heaven can unite them and all evil falls when it is wielded. The Dragons have awakened and the swords can control them."

Ash's eyes met Cordy's. "What dragons?"

"Dragons' spirit energy consists of geomagnetic power which flows throughout Earth's core. These creatures influence the magnetosphere of Terra, which guards the planet from solar radiation. Without it, all life would die.

"You both possess special gifts. Ash's healing powers. Cordelia's gift of communicating with animals. Great devastation came when the Great Flood occurred. The Keys of Life contain seeds to help replenish Terra's gardens in case they perish, seeds touched by cosmic rays in outer space. Use these gifts well or all will die. You must repair the imbalance and take these treasures the Forevers left to the Pure of Heart in order to save Earth's children. I will contact you again and give you further instructions. I'm with you as long as you have the crystal ball, but for now, I must go."

The crystal ball's light dimmed, leaving Ash and Cordy sitting in darkness, stunned by what the Guardian had told them. They decided it was time to go before they were discovered. Both of them gathered the precious treasures, stumbling through the dark tunnel of the Neolithic passage where souls were believed to pass to the other world of eternity. A cell phone provided light to get them to the doorway. The stars shone bright in the stillness of the night. Spooked, they ran down the hill as fast as they could. Cordy glanced at Ash as she jumped on the back of the motorcycle.

"I need a drink, real bad," she gasped. The pale-faced woman held tight to Ash's waist.

"I know where every pub is in Ireland, so hang on tight."

CHAPTER 16

Message from Jon Lafitte

A sh and Cordy settled into a booth at the far end of the pub with their beer. Both of them were overwhelmed by the responsibility placed on their shoulders. Meanwhile, everyone at the bar cheered on their favorite soccer team, not even noticing the quiet couple. Cordy pulled the crystal ball out of her coat pocket and set it on the table. With the light from the ball gone, it looked harmless.

"What the hell is going on? We talked to the Guardian," Cordy gestured with her index and middle finger, "who broke the news that Earth is headed for an extinction level event. Did I hear that right? You saw her too?"

Ash started to answer her, but the crystal ball's light flickered. Surprised, they scrunched up farther back in their booth. They watched the ball with care and the Guardian's face showed up in the orb, staring right at them.

Her voice answered, "Your hearing is correct, Pure of Heart. I am demonstrating how you will be able to communicate with the

Guardian through the crystal ball. Jon Lafitte's family knows the whereabouts of the other Keys of Life. Contact has been made. I will monitor your progress." The Guardian's face disappeared and so did the light.

Ash and Cordy took big gulps of their beer. They simultaneously said in disbelief, "Contact? What the hell? This is so crazy!"

"I'm going to need a few shots of whiskey. I'll be right back." Ash walked over to the bar and bought a bottle and two glasses. He poured and they downed their drinks. The shaking in their hands calmed and they felt the familiar warm feeling of sanity returning.

Cordy took the Guardian's tip and checked her emails. Someone had indeed contacted her via her video on the internet called "Looking for Magdalene." The video had helped connect her with Ash. The statue of Magdalene in the film had the same

interweaving hands as the statue of Magdalene at Our Lady of Knock. Cordy remembered the Guardian's words, *everything is connected in the universe.* They were connected now again that Lafitte had found her through the video.

"Well, I'll be. He did make contact. Lafitte wrote, 'The man with the hole in his hat would like to meet with the lovely lady who put it there. I possess something of great importance to you.'" Cordy knew exactly who wrote it. He had saved her life after she almost drowned trying to rescue Chief Saunhac. Her grandfather, Bill, recognized him as the Dark Watcher named Jon Lafitte. In the message, the man gave her his email. The email seemed so anonymous, but she had a good feeling about it. Plus, the Guardian foretold it. Cordy emailed him back. Next, she checked in with Bob, but there were no messages or emails from him about Sister Agnes.

Cordy grew sad as she looked at Ash with concern. "Bob hasn't gotten back to me about my aunt. That isn't like him. I'm really worried."

Ash nodded, "You're right, not like Bob at all. But you know, he has been a bit distracted with Julia. He's head over heels in love with her. She's keeping him busy and he loves it. Anyone else email you?"

Cordy showed him the text. Ash was a little surprised to remember their rescuers, especially the blonde who pulled him out of the water. He also remembered her kiss after he saved her life.

Ash answered, "Lafitte wants us to meet him at the Dublin Museum tomorrow afternoon. He has something important to show us." He paused and then said, "Well, I guess we're going to the museum. We better hope it's not a trap."

Cordy gazed at the crystal ball to see if there was an answer but got nothing. "Ash, what do you think about all of this?"

"After all the crazy stuff we've been through, you're asking me? I've seen the incredible buildings constructed by what some historians depict as primitive cultures. I don't see how stones weighing tons could be created with the primitive tools on hand, and the Guardian confirms the idea of an ancient civilization possessing incredible knowledge and technology. The Book of Enoch you found talked about Enoch receiving the knowledge of the stars and moon from the angels. I'm wondering if these angels could be the Forevers.

"Plato talked about Atlantis being destroyed by its wars or technologies. We might be doing the same thing and endangering Earth with nuclear weapons. History might be repeating itself. The Newgrange, Knowth and Loughcrew sites are connected. Many have said the ancient people understood Earth's energy field better than we do now. I'm not surprised the Guardian picked Knowth as a rendezvous point. It sounds like the Keys of Life are an ancient technology left by the Forevers. I can tell you, if we're looking for them, then the Nephilim and the Dark Watchers are too. We better be very careful tomorrow."

Ash and Cordy left on their bike and headed back to the hotel, stopping only to buy some essentials.

CHAPTER 17

A Storm is Coming

The Pure of Heart network had expanded into an international powerhouse. Thousands of talented recruits sent in their resumes. The word leaked out that his company treated their employees to tremendous benefits. Bob needed to know what companies the Children of the Nephilim targeted and owned. Julia volunteered to go back in to get him those names. A spy infiltrating the Children of the Nephilim's headquarters couldn't be any more dangerous, but any information brought back was incredibly valuable.

Bob and Julia decided to financially destroy them. The Children of the Nephilim were nothing without their money, seeing as how money meant power. The Nephilim enjoyed destroying good companies, draining their assets, and then discarding them, leaving employees' lives in shambles. The organization hid its money in overseas accounts where it paid no taxes. While its structure was immense in size, only a few knew all of the secret projects.

Bob realized early on that he loved Julia. Why was he attracted to wild women? He remembered his little classmate Peggy Sue who wanted to give him a kiss on the playground in front of all their friends when he was just six. She was the one who made his heart sing, rather than the little goody two-shoes Sara, who told the teacher on them. He admitted to himself that he was an adrenaline junkie. Something about Julia made Bob feel more alive than anybody or anything.

Julia, once known by the Nephilim as Ellen, made passionate love to him on an elevator after he got sacked by the chairman, and her advice to get out of town saved his life. Bob ended up paying her back for that favor when he rescued her from being poisoned by the Wishing Cup, which had been filled with the honey made by the bee hive in the Tree of Knowledge. The poisoned honey sent Ellen on a journey that helped her to break free from the Nephilim's mind control. Chief Saunhac explained she was the daughter of the Villiers, who were killed by the treacherous chairman. Julia may be a bit messed up but her programming guaranteed total obedience. What a passionate and talented woman! He knew she wanted revenge, but he tried to talk her out of going back. Deep down though, Bob knew she was right. The Nephilim needed to be destroyed, or else nobody would be safe.

Julia wouldn't listen to him so he had resigned himself to helping her. She wanted closure, but Bob knew that mind control and post-traumatic stress could have dangerous side effects. He worried that she would suffer a split personality. Who would win, Ellen the trained killer or Julia the Pure of Heart, rescued by the chief who sacrificed his life for her? Bob had recognized her on the helicopter after she drank the snake venom in the honey. She almost died, but Julia was resurrected and given a new start. He loved her and knew she had to be one of the bravest women he'd ever met. Bob saw many of his comrades go undercover but this was different. He was nervous, and it showed as he paced around the office.

His cellphone buzzed and he could see Julia's number. He answered it.

"Hi honey, tell me you changed your mind and we're going on a cruise."

"I'm getting ready to go in. I just wanted to hear your voice one more time. I want to tell you Bob, just in case I..." Bob stopped her before she could finish.

"You and I are going to take that cruise, lock ourselves in our cabin, and have wild sex the whole trip. I love you. Don't you ever forget it."

"Sounds good to me. Bob, never forget I love you so much, too! I'll stay in touch. Ellen is returning for one final show."

"Julia better return, or I'm going in to get you."

The phone clicked off and Bob looked out the window at the New York night sky. "I wouldn't want to be the chairman," he muttered. "A storm is coming. Ellen is back."

CHAPTER 18

Forgiveness

Sister Agnes had dedicated her life to helping the poor and nursing the sick. As a young woman, she took the vows of a Daughter of Charity. The Pure of Heart recruited her early on and she served them well.

She hid Cordy from the Nephilim but made a pact with the devil. DeVilliers promised to aid her but only if Cordy never knew of her family's role in the Pure of Heart organization. Agnes had broken the promise to him and knew her time was running out.

Sister Agnes and Chief Saunhac had agreed Cordy's birth needed to be hidden from the Children of the Nephilim. Her star charts predicted great things in her future. The Children of the Nephilim produced star charts on millions of possible Pure of Heart candidates and then snuffed them out. Cordy's birthday chart showed great promise amid a very dangerous path. The elderly nun sent Cordy on a mission to find more of the missing Keys of Life. She knew prophecies made long ago by the Pure of Heart revealed that Earth and mankind were heading for another extinction level event. Her niece couldn't fail.

Cordy had gone to Ireland in search of the treasures of the Pure of Heart but she was now in danger. Sister Agnes decided she might be able to protect her. The elderly nun had contacted her friends in Ireland and they were excited to see her after so many years. Long ago, she served at the Vincentian community at Knock.

Bill McDermott, Cordy's grandfather, had visited the nun at the convent a couple of weeks before and told her about Saunhac's death. Bill warned her to be very careful because she was being watched. He gave her a necklace as a gift, telling her to keep it with her for protection. It was a Miraculous Medal with hearts on the back. Her family's connection with the medal couldn't be denied. She grieved for the chief; his loyalty to the cause of the Pure of Heart was unquestionable. She knew he died a happy man, seeing his great granddaughter one more time before he died. She hoped for a death like his, not one lying in a hospital bed.

The nun arrived at Dublin Airport and planned on giving Cordy a call when she arrived at the hotel. Sister Agnes had her luggage loaded in a cab, but as soon as she got in, a man dressed in a black sweater entered from the other side of the car and pointed a gun at her head.

Sister Agnes was calm. "You're a Dark Watcher, aren't you?"

The man, still in his early thirties, looked at her coldly. "How did you know?"

She answered, "The tattoo on your arm with the dark all-seeing eye gives you away. What do you want from me?"

"Mr. de Villiers wants you to answer some questions and then hopes to kill your niece. Any other questions?" He hit the elderly woman's head with his gun and Sister Agnes lost consciousness.

Darkness surrounded her when she came to. The brave, tiny nun sat in a chair, tied up by two Dark Watchers. "I'm honored, you came yourself to kill me, de Villiers."

De Villiers, dressed in black, wore gloves over his hands. She had double-crossed him and now it was time to pay her back. Cordy turned out to be formidable like her aunt.

He looked coldly at her and sneered, "The head of the Pure of Heart deserves the best. Did you notice where I brought you? It's

94

the McDermott Castle on the Lough Key. You think she'll get the message?"

The formidable nun remained silent. "I want the ring," he continued. "Does she have it? Did Saunhac give it to her before he died?" Sister Agnes didn't even bat an eye.

"You trained her well," said de Villiers. "Did you know I tested her and she passed? She is a true Pure of Heart. I don't care about any other sacred items, but I want the ring." He paused for a minute, contemplating the swan-like curve of her neck. "Where is it? Let's make this easy."

Sister Agnes looked at him defiantly and spat, "I will die before I tell you anything."

De Villiers stared intensely at her. "You leave me no other choice," he sighed. "So be it, but know that your precious Cordy will also die. In fact, the enchanting young lady should be dead in just a few hours. A shame really, she's quite charming. Perhaps I'll order my men to give her some *special* attention before she dies." His men bunched their fists up, waiting for his orders to begin. "Time runs short, Sister Agnes. I believe at the end, you'll tell me everything I want to know."

The elderly nun gazed up into the night sky as the full moon shone with such brilliance. "I forgive you, my brother, for what you do but know this, you'll suffer for what you have done. I'm giving you one more chance to get on your knees and beg forgiveness." De Villiers smirked, "Alright, I see you've decided."

He raised his hand and his men approached the defiant sister. She spoke so all could hear her. "Shakespeare said, 'We must not hate people who have done wrong to us. For as soon as we begin to hate them, we become just like them, pathetic, bitter, and untrue.'" The nun's face glowed. "I do not hate you, all. The Pure of Heart are here to break the cycle of hate with forgiveness and respect for all life. Our day will come and so will yours. A sacrifice must be made." She folded her hands then just as Christ did in the Carravagio painting.

De Villiers lashed out. "Finish her, she's boring me." His men nodded and surrounded her.

A loud scream could be heard in the darkness of the forest but then cold silence. De Villiers showed his disappointment at her quick death. Her heart had failed before she could talk. A dark mist fell on Lough Key, and a chill filled the air of the resting place for one more McDermott.

CHAPTER 19

Tender Embrace

After quite a few drinks at the pub, Cordy and Ash still couldn't believe what they saw at Knowth. After the long and confusing day, Cordy walked into the hotel room and threw herself on the bed. She grabbed her head and rolled from side to side and moaned.

"Too much information, too much crazy unbelievable information!"

Ash sat down in a chair. "You're telling me, but I do understand the possibility of ancient civilizations with advance technology far surpassing ours existed. Crystal balls are in legends throughout history. I've seen the crystal ball in a painting." Ash pulled up da Vinci's *Salvator Mundi* painting on his cell phone. "Look, Christ holds a crystal ball in his hand."

Cordy gazed at the photo in shock.

"It's the Pure of Heart's crystal ball. Merovingian kings were buried with crystal balls. Historians called them the "sorcerer kings". I've seen pictures of a crystal ball found in King Childeric's grave from the 480s and it looks just like ours and da Vinci's. They may have encountered the Guardian. My father's family bloodline descends from them." Ash pondered for a few minutes. "What I don't understand is why us, why now? The Guardian must believe a cataclysm is coming." He shook his head and rubbed his forehead, then as he dug his fingers through his hair. He cried out, "Too much, it's too much!"

Cordy sat up and looked around. "Is there an echo in here? That's what I just said, Ash, the whole thing is just too much!"

Ash pulled out a fresh white T-shirt from a backpack they bought earlier that morning; he also pulled out a pair of fresh white boxer shorts. Cordy laughed to herself thinking that this guy could pass for Mr. Clean when he came out of the bathroom. A woman sure could bring some color into this guy's life.

"I'm going to grab a shower and I don't want to meet any angels or guardians in there, understood? If you see any out here tell them it is not, OK, to come in. I just need some time, alone."

"I'll watch your back if you'll watch mine," Cordy answered.

"I don't need any one to wash my back but if you're volunteering, I won't stop you," Ash teased. "I would surely wash yours if you let me." He stopped at the doorway to the bathroom, turned, and smiled.

Cordy picked up a pillow and threw it at him. "I said watch your back, you heard me W-A-T-C-H." She giggled playfully with hope in her heart that he would never change and always remain easy going. He was one of the only men Cordy felt relaxed and comfortable around.

It was a good thirty minutes before Ash opened the door to the bathroom. A small amount of steam slipped out and by no means did he look like Mr. Clean. Underwear manufacturers would die to get this hunk in their TV ads. Cordy jumped up with a white cotton nightie, and a pair of white high-cut cotton bikini underwear in her hand. She'd purchased the clothes when she was shopping earlier that day. She was thinking, conservative, hot, and casual. As she passed Ash, she leaned in for a deep breath of a hot, clean man and he didn't disappoint. She didn't shut the bathroom door all the way, almost offering an invitation.

Cordy stood by the shower. "You know, Ash, I'm glad it's you on this journey with me. I'm not sure I could have held it together by myself. I pride myself in thinking that I've got everything under control, but I realize, I don't want to be alone. I think you make me stronger. We're a great team."

"I feel the same way, but do you think it could be controlled terror?" They both started to laugh.

Cordy turned the shower on and Ash could see her taking off her top and bra from the small crack in the door. She let her pants slide down to the floor ever so slowly. Ash moved onto the edge of the bed to get a better look, just to make sure he wasn't dreaming last night. The image of Cordy standing naked in the moonlight was burned into his heart forever. He wasn't disappointed. Cordy shut the door. Ash rolled over on the bed and let out a quiet sigh. "She's killing me," he grumbled.

Cordy dried off and left just a bit of water on her skin to let her nightgown cling to her body. She couldn't wait to go to the bedroom, so she wrapped her wet hair in a towel and headed out for the main event. When she opened the door this time, she saw Ash sitting in bed. He had piled up the pillows behind him and sprawled every artifact out across the bed. He was in archaeologist heaven.

With all of his books face open, he read with a passion for learning; she could see it in his face. Ash looked up at her and said, "Wow." In the next instant, he beckoned, "Come here, I have so much to show you." His face beamed like a little kid. He threw back the covers and motioned for Cordy to get in. She did so, but there was only one thing she wanted to see.

She leaned into his shoulder and Ash instinctively put his arm around her, wrapping around her tiny waist and under her left breast. It made her breathe with excitement. Ash read the ancient text aloud to Cordy. She put her head on his shoulder and snuggled in. She couldn't ever remember feeling loved this much before in her life, not a physical love but a heart-to-heart kind of love. In five minutes, she was asleep. Ash read and looked at everything for another hour and then got up and put a pillow under Cordy's head. He gathered his mess and thought for a second about putting down a folded blanket on the floor next to the bed. He pulled the covers back on his side of the bed only to catch a glimpse of Cordy in her nightgown and panties. He slid in next to a sleeping Cordy, turned out the light, and in a soft voice said, "Goodnight, my love."

In the morning, Cordy woke up first, aware of Ash's soft, sleepy breathing, and rubbed up against his back. She knew he was a perfect gentleman. Ash sleepily rolled over. His arm stretched under her pillow and came out next to her shoulder. His other arm was draped over her hip and his hand caressed her stomach. She put her hand in his outstretched palm and rubbed it gently and then shook his hand, whispering, "Ash, wake up. We're late."

He started to pull her in closer and she told herself, just five more minutes," but knew they needed to get moving. Cordy broke loose of his love hold and sat up. She let out a forceful Mi'kmaq war whoop and yelled, "Ash, wake up!"

He sat straight up. "I'm up, I'm up."

Cordy jumped out of bed and saw her tousled hair in the mirror. Rule number one: never go to bed with wet hair. She shot off to the bathroom, grabbed some washcloths, and headed in for damage control.

Ash could hear the water running in the bathroom and shouted, "I can explain." But did he want to? Ash knew he'd held Cordy in his arms half the night before he fell asleep. It was the best night of his life and for a few seconds, he just rolled over, hugged the pillow, and smiled really big.

CHAPTER 20

Dublin Museum

Ash and Cordy decided it was time to say goodbye to the motorcycle, parking it in the forest. Ash would miss it and Cordy agreed that they had some very good memories on the Harley. They switched to a double-decker tour bus to fulfill a promise she had given to her grandfather Bill. He wanted her to see Sean McDermott Street, named after one of her relatives who signed the Proclamation of the Irish Republic in his Gaelic name Sean Mac Diarmada. He died at 33 by firing squad. Cordy's family history was filled with Pure of Heart who changed the world.

Along the street, Cordy spotted the Church of Our Lady of Lourdes and the Vincentians' office. She thought about her aunt and hoped she was wrong about her gut feeling. She regretted leaving her, but the elderly nun had insisted she go.

They headed for downtown Dublin. They wanted to do more research. Trinity College in Dublin housed the most famous ancient manuscript, the Book of Kells. Ash wanted to show Cordy the illuminated pages because he believed the Guardian's past might be linked.

Cordy was amazed at how intricate and complicated the designs were. Ash told her the book was made by monks in the 800s A.D. It was a miracle that the book survived all these centuries. The monks at the Abbey of Kells had protected the masterpiece from the Viking raids. Golden page after golden page showed four angels: the bull angel, the eagle angel, the lion angel, and the man angel. In modern interpretation, they represented the four Gospel writers.

Cordy told Ash that some believed they represent the constellations Leo, Taurus, Scorpio, and Aquarius. Cordy pointed. "Look at this page, four are in a square, surrounding a center. The four elements are water, air, earth and fire. They may represent the four swords the Guardian talked about. I think we need to remember this. My gut is telling me this page is important."

Ash whispered, "They represent the four archangels, Michael, Gabriel, Raphael, and Uriel. You can see the crosses each one carries like swords. The Celtic knots intertwine and the center seems to be the key area between them all. Interesting!"

Cordy smiled. "They are seen in the Book of Ezekiel where he meets angelic beings from Heaven. All of these books tell similar stories.

The Guardian said, "'Forevers have been around a long time.'"

Ash checked his watch. "The connection is angelic beings with wings. The Book of Enoch is all about the war between the angels. The Egyptian hieroglyphs contain their winged gods like the Sumerians. The Celts had their angels and so did the Egyptians. They're all over different cultures. It makes me wonder if the monks knew about the Nephilim and the war. We better get over to meet Lafitte."

They both headed for the National Gallery of Ireland looking for Lafitte. They decided to split up so they could cover more territory. Cordy couldn't help looking at the different masterpieces such as Poussin's *Lamentation of Christ*. She thought, *another Pure of Heart put to death but whose sacrifice changed the world.* She looked closely at the one cherub kneeling in prayer and a child crying at the death of Christ. Cordy wondered how many Pure of Heart were killed by the Children of the Nephilim. They were hunted down and killed as soon as possible. Dossiers filled with names and birthdates were scrutinized by astrologists to determine their potential to be a Pure of Heart. Hit lists were created. Hired assassins were then ordered to kill them. All their deaths were hidden from the public and made to look like accidents, just like her parents'. She was only alive because her aunt and parents hid her birthdate from the state. She moved along the hall.

What stopped her in her tracks was Carravagio's painting *The Taking of Christ*. It sent chills up her spine. The hands of Christ folded in the same way as the Magdalene statue she found in St. Louis, the same folded hands she had found on the painting at the Miraculous Medal Shrine and at the Knock. It couldn't be a coincidence. Perhaps the hands indicated that a Pure of Heart secret lies here in Ireland. The painting represented betrayal by a friend. *Lots of that going around*, she thought. Lafitte betrayed the Dark Watchers to save Ash and her and the Nephilim betrayed Julia. A great secret did lie here in Ireland. The Guardian discovered and activated by the Pure of Heart was in fact a secret. Cordy wondered if Jon was trustworthy or like Judas in Carravagio's painting, looking for his thirty pieces of gold?

Cordy walked closer and closer to the painting when she heard a man softly whisper in her ear with a seductive voice. He smelled of sandalwood and musk.

"Magnificent, isn't it? I'm sure you notice the hands of Christ are similar to Mary Magdalene's in your video. The loyal woman named Apostle to the Apostles is in the painting." He pointed to the dark knight's arm glistening in the light, where an ancient Egyptian perfume jar could be seen on its side. "It's quite a coincidence but is it?" She stared right at the symbol for Magdalene's jar, which carried the spikenard used to anoint Jesus.

"Mary knew before any of the Apostles what was coming. They knew sometimes we need to make a sacrifice for the greater good. They possessed the power to see the future. Who would guess Magdalene Islands held the precious secrets of the Pure of Heart? Could Ireland be another spot for their hidden treasures? I believe

I've found one of them standing before me. You, my dear lady, are quite the prize. Let me introduce myself. I am Jon Lafitte, and I believe you are the enchanting Cordelia McDermott."

Cordy turned and gazed deeply into his mischievous, dark eyes. "I am and the last time I remember, you saved my life. I wanted to say thank you and ask why you saved us. You betrayed the Dark Watchers to whom your family owes allegiance. Are you like Judas? I hope not. He didn't live very long," she said, pointing to the painting with her head.

"Shall we say, at the time, I thought it was a good idea. We Lafittes honor our debts and we do not follow madmen. My family owed a debt long ago to your family and it was time for us to repay it. You are very lucky that I spotted the McDermott pin or you would be dead. I'm not Judas, but perhaps your savior. Remember, I brought you back from the dead.

"Judas betrayed Jesus for a bag of thirty silver coins. De Villiers doesn't care about the Dark Watchers. He's using them to gain power over the world, and he's betrayed the Dark Watchers to the Children of the Nephilim. We betrayed de Villiers to save you, but betrayal depends on a certain point of view. Judas played his part. I know we must stop de Villiers or everyone in the world will die. I think he wants total control of the Pure of Heart, Light Watchers, Dark Watchers and the Children of Nephilim. He's the puppet master, pulling everyone's strings while he gets what he wants. He must be stopped."

"Why did you want to meet?" she asked.

"You and your friend are in great danger. I can offer you my protection. You won't leave Dublin alive unless you come with me. I'll take your friend, too, but we must go now. Trust me, if you want to live, come with me," Jon said.

Ash found them standing in front of the Caravaggio. Cordy's attention was completely focused on Jon. Ash didn't like how Jon looked at Cordy. Everything about Lafitte screamed ladies' man. He rushed over.

"Cordy, there you are. I see you found Lafitte."

Jon smiled at Ash. "Hello, Monsieur Ash, I presume. One of my blonde-haired commanders told me to say hello. How could she forget that charming moment? I thank you for saving her life, and I am in your debt. Both of you, follow me and we'll leave by my car in the back. The sightseeing trip is over for right now. The Dark Watchers have you on their most wanted list. You both are in grave danger. We must hurry." Lafitte walked a few steps away from them and talked on his cell phone.

Ash's troubled look spoke volumes. "I don't know if that's a very good idea, Cordy."

Cordy nodded. "I know, Ash. But the Guardian said Lafitte knows where the rest of the Keys of Life are, so we have to go. I know it's crazy, but I trust him."

Ash reluctantly gave in. "Well, as long as I'm with you, then we'll go with him. You still need to check in with Bob."

Cordy agreed as they followed Jon downstairs. His black limo and chauffeur waited at the back of the museum. Jon Lafitte told his driver to take them to the airport for they were flying to Paris.

Cordy smiled at Jon. "I've always wanted to visit Paris."

CHAPTER 21

One Last Stop

In the car, Ash told Jon, "We need to go by the hotel. Cordy and I need to meet up with a friend and say goodbye."

Jon glanced at Ash with a raised eyebrow. "You two better make it a fast good-bye because the Dark Watchers and Nephilim are close."

"We'll be quick, Jon. He just needs to pick up some packages," Cordy said.

Jon got back to business. "Is the friend important, chérie, or rather the artifacts he possesses?"

"Statements like that don't give me confidence in our alliance," warned Cordy. Lafitte ordered the driver to take them to the hotel.

The car pulled up outside the front door of the hotel. Ash told an impatient Jon to wait for them. Ash and Cordy jumped out and made their way to the door. As they passed the doorman, Jon saw him take out his hand radio and talk to someone. It wasn't a good sign. The Frenchman ordered his driver to pull the car around to the side entrance, and ran inside. Jon prayed he was being overly cautious.

Ash and Cordy passed the front desk and headed toward the elevators. The lobby was filled with visitors checking in and an ice cream and dessert cart stood by the elevator for their guests. Once again, one of the front desk clerks pulled out her hand radio and began to talk on it as soon as Ash and Cordy passed by. The two of them rounded the corner and continued to walk to the elevators. Ash pushed the up button. The door opened and there was happy-go-lucky Linda.

Linda smiled, "I went to the room and saw you hadn't packed yet, so I did it for you. The hotel called me on my cell and said they needed the room. I got worried because check out time was noon." She threw two backpacks at Ash and Cordy.

Ash put his hand out to thank Linda. With no hesitation, she grabbed it and pulled him in for a hug. Ash looked back at Cordy and smiled. He put both hands in the air in surrender to Linda's hug. Cordy grinned and threw up her hands. Ash winked back at her.

As Linda came out of the elevator, she stepped right in front of Cordy and came to a stop. Ash and Cordy turned to look at what she saw and spotted two suspicious men in black suits walking toward them with a threatening look. The men realized they had been seen. Their hands went into each side of their suit coats, pulling out small pistols. They opened fire on all three of them. The first three shots ripped through Linda's body. The first one into her lower left stomach, the second into her lung, and the third bullet was a shot to the head. Her body was lifted off the ground from the impact and velocity of the bullets as they tore open her young body. As the bullets exited, blood sprayed Cordy and Ash.

Ash reached in his bag and pulled out his Glock and started to return fire. His adrenaline pumped and he shot everything except the two men. Vases shattered and people ran for cover. Cordy's inner calm kicked in. She cradled Linda in her arms as bullets flew all around her. Her only concern was for the young girl as she kept pressure on her wounds. With her last breath, Linda whispered to Cordy, "Use the network." Time slowed down for Cordy in that moment.

A hand reached for Cordy's shoulder. She blocked it and standing there was Uriel the archangel. Cordy looked up at him with tears in her eyes and asked, "Why is evil raining down on us? Why?" Uriel wasn't alone; a tall angel stood next to him.

Uriel yelled at Ash, "Get behind the steel cart! The steel will shield you from the bullets." Ash dashed behind the ice cream cart and a jar of candy exploded from a bullet. Uriel looked down at Cordy, "You're going to have to let young Linda go. You can't help her anymore. Gabriel will take her now."

"She's in the best of hands. Now run, Star Child, run!" Cordy gazed at the limp body in her arms. Linda was gone and she heard the chief's voice in her head calling her by name.

The two men sprayed bullets at the steel cart but all of the bullets ricocheted; none were able to penetrate the metal. Shots rang out behind Ash and Cordy and the two men fell to the ground, both shot in the head. Jon Lafitte cried out, "Let's get the hell out of here, mademoiselle!" Jon grabbed Cordy's arm and she gently set the girl down and started to follow Jon.

Ash stayed a few seconds longer to make sure no one was going to shoot at Cordy again. The room was demolished, with people whimpering in fear. Ash took another look at Linda in a pool of blood. He hated to leave her but Cordy needed him. He followed down the back hall covering their retreat. They jumped into the limo and the sound of screeching wheels filled their ears. The driver swerved to avoid police cars, sirens blaring, racing to the hotel. Ash saw Linda's blood splattered all over Cordy, yet she still maintained tremendous inner calm and had only silent tears for the young girl running down her cheeks.

"Cordy, are you hit?" he asked.

"Why Linda and not me?" she whispered.

Ash felt a tear run down his cheek. "I know. I wish it would've been me and not her. No, it's not right, but the fact remains innocent people die during war. All we can do is keep fighting. I know that's what Linda would want."

Jon winced. "Well, hey you two, if it's any concern of yours, I've been hit in the shoulder. I warned you that going back to the hotel would be dangerous." Cordy looked over and blood flowed from his shirt. She attempted to stop the bleeding by putting pressure on the oozing wound but he was starting to lose consciousness.

Jon yelled out to his concerned driver, "Get us to the airport, fast!"

CHAPTER 22

Sad News

McDonough reported the bad news to Bill as soon as they found her. Sister Agnes' body was discovered in the woods near the McDermott castle. McDonough had seen another man get into her taxi but lost the car in traffic. The tracking device on Sister Agnes worked well enough to let them know the kidnappers entered the forest of the Lough Key. The trouble for McDonough was that he was hours away. He needed to call the Light Watchers for help.

McDermott Castle stood surrounded by water and deep dark woods. McDonough and his men launched a search, and found the boat used to take Sister Agnes to the island. The nun lay bruised and beaten on the ground. Her rosary with the GPS was found in the brush about a mile away. A note pinned on her body said, "I'm giving a warning to the rebellious and honorable McDermott family: defy me and die!" De Villiers demanded their treasure as soon as possible or more of the family would die. McDonough called Bill, his commander, to tell him the bad news.

Bill called Bob with the sad news of Sister Agnes' death. Neither knew how to tell Cordy. Earlier, Bob had received a phone message from her asking how her aunt was. Cordy mentioned her feeling that Sister Agnes was in grave danger. Bill took care of the funeral arrangements but he was worried about Cordy's life.

McDonough had more bad news. A young girl who was aiding Ash and Cordy had been shot and killed at their hotel. The newspapers said she was accidentally hit in the crossfire of a drug deal gone wrong. Bob and Bill agreed the cover story placed by the Dark Watchers hid what had really happened.

"What are we going to do, Bob? Cordy's all I have left now. McDermotts don't negotiate with killers. De Villiers is going after my granddaughter." Bill's voice broke with emotion.

Bob reassured him, "Now Bill, you know Cordy can take care of herself, but I do worry about that idiot she's with. Ash couldn't hit the side of the barn but he's got tremendous courage. She's not alone. I'll get on her private jet and search for them myself. But first, I've got more bad news. Jon Lafitte's involved. I wouldn't trust him with my dog, that's for sure. And trust me. Freddie, my Chihuahua, can hold his own."

"Lafitte owes us a debt and believe it or not, he will aid and protect her," said Bill.

"Thanks, Bob," he continued. "I'll have my men work on finding them, too. Ash is quite resourceful when he has to be. They make a good team. As far as Lafitte, he saved Cordy at Magdalene Island so if he wanted to kill her, that would've been his best chance. No, he's helping them for a reason. "

Bob hesitated for a second and said, "I'll tell Cordy about Sister Agnes when I see her. I think she would want me to tell her in person not on the phone. What did they want from the poor old lady? It's pretty obvious they were trying to get her to talk."

"A warning to the McDermott family," Bill said. "De Villiers is also looking for Saunhac's treasures. He'll kill anybody to get his hands on them. I'm used to threats to the McDermott family, but I'm worried about Cordy. She isn't safe if she's on de Villiers' radar screen. He's a big-wig in the Dark Watcher elite, and he's not going to be happy with Lafitte helping Cordy."

"These treasures, what are they? The Hope diamond and a chest of gold?" Bob asked.

"Nope, Bob, they are much more valuable. They are very powerful and give the Pure of Heart command over the universe."

Bob choked while drinking his coffee. "Did you say over the universe?"

"Yep, that's what I said," Bill answered. "I'm going to call the Lafitte family. I know Jon's grandfather, Poppa Jon. You've met his grandson Jon. Do you remember what he looks like, Bob?"

"How could I forget him? Handsome and cocky as hell, and the Frenchman knows how to fight, too. He showed up just in time. Lafitte's got guts. Can you trust him?"

"I can trust him. His family follows a code and they will aid my family. They proved it. The Dark Watchers seem to be going through a power struggle. The Lafittes are in danger. I'm going to give Poppa Jon a call and warn him about de Villiers. We've shared information over the years. In intelligence work, as you well know, Bob, things are never just black and white. The Lafitte family can't be pinned down which makes them very powerful and dangerous."

"I guess I better get going. I'll call you when I find them, Bill."

Bob hung up the phone and texted Julia. "Honey, gotta go find Cordy and save the universe. Don't wait up for me."

CHAPTER 23

Bloody Mary

Ellen entered the all-familiar corporate headquarters of the Children of Nephilim, but strangely, things also looked foreign to her. She wasn't the same Ellen after she drank from the Wishing Cup. Julia Villiers had returned from the dead. The chairman killed her parents and kidnapped the child later becoming her legal guardian. The child tested positive as a Pure of Heart but entered into mind-control programming conceived by the organization. The child, Julia, was abused by the chairman and her identity stripped away. As her replacement, the cold-hearted Ellen followed orders without question and became a loyal member. The awakened Ellen was on a new mission, centered on the absolute destruction of the Children of Nephilim. She strolled into the headquarters with ease. Everybody looked surprised to see her as she headed to the chairman's office. . She felt something had changed from the way everybody stared at her.

As her hand twisted the knob on the chairman's door, she could hear a woman giggling. Ellen opened the door to see the chairman fondling the breasts of a girl who looked barely 25. She was sitting on his lap. *It didn't take long to replace me,* thought Ellen. *I knew he always thought I was dispensable. Coldhearted bastard, he's in for a surprise. I've been trained by the best to be poisonous viper. I'll wait patiently before I strike with no warning.*

The chairman stared at her and the fury on his face was priceless. He'd been caught and he didn't like it.

"Where the hell have you been?" he snapped.

"I killed Saunhac, Chief of the Pure of Heart, and brought back the Dark Watchers' prized Wishing Cup. That is where I have been. I see you've been busy." Ellen held out the Wishing Cup, a beautiful white cup with Egyptian hieroglyphs on it. She thrust it at him so he could examine the precious cup for himself. The chairman didn't pick it up and in fact flinched and pushed away from the poisonous cup like a scared rabbit.

"Set it down, Ellen." She could hear the nervousness in his voice.

Ellen smiled. "Oh, don't you want to drink from it or hold it? Some say all the knowledge of the Universe will be at your fingertips if you drink from it." She pushed the cup closer to him and he moved away. The chairman showed fear in his face. Ellen enjoyed his reaction. He knew only a Pure of Heart could handle the power of the cup.

"Who's the new toy on your lap?"

The chairman wickedly smiled, "Your replacement. Isn't she beautiful and so youthful? I've decided to try something younger and newer. You're to work in Operations under Ken. During your absence, I promoted him. I want a full report of where you've been and no excuses."

Ellen realized everything the chief had told her was true. "I'll leave this here and let you have your fun." On one hand, Ellen knew he had found a new play toy, but on the other hand, he'd put an expiration date on her. Ellen could see it in his eyes. She didn't have much time. He'd play with his new toy. He appeared to be enjoying the girl's special talents very much.

"Oh, Ellen, I want you to teach Mindy how to make Bloody Marys. You make the best ones, and since you'll be out on assignment, Mindy can make them for me."

Ellen turned her back on him and smiled. "I'll be glad to teach her. " She shut the door.

A smiling Ken handed her a pile of dossiers and busy work. "We'll want a full report on what happened. How did the other operatives die?" he asked.

"Shot, both of them by the Light Watchers. I killed Saunhac and grabbed the Wishing Cup. I got lucky and escaped," she explained. "Oh and congratulations, boss, on your promotion."

Ken grinned. "What can I say? The best man won the job, and don't you ever forget it. Get back to work."

Ellen gave him a look of resignation and sighed, "Yes, sir."

He walked away and headed for the chairman's office and knocked on the door. "Enter," commanded the man within. The chairman motioned for him to come in and shut the door.

"I gave Ellen a bunch of busy work and told her to give me a report. She took it better than I thought," Ken described. "Aren't you worried she'll want revenge? I can take care of her if you want. In fact, it would be my pleasure."

"We don't have to worry about Ellen taking revenge on me because her programming will not allow her hands to kill me. If she tries, her coded response is to commit suicide. Trust me on this, Ken. I want her to train Mindy and give us all the details in her report. You don't have anything to worry about with Ellen. She's well trained and served her purpose by killing the leader of the Pure of Heart. We've tried to kill that old man for years and I admit, he made a formidable adversary."

Ken smiled, "Good, the programming has worked perfectly so far. I've had confirmation from our intelligence group Saunhac died of gunshot wounds, hypothermia, and drowning. Newspapers reported his death as an attack by fishing pirates protecting their territories and blamed the thieves for killing him. Ellen's in the clear.

"I admit the Wishing Cup is mesmerizing." He pointed to the white alabaster cup with hieroglyphs standing on the shelf on the wall where Ellen set it. Ken couldn't help touching the exquisite priceless cup then set it back on the shelf. The Chairman watched calmly as he did it.

The chairman explained, "Saunhac had a triple death like Merlin the Druid, playing the role of the ultimate sacrifice. A very dramatic exit for a great sorcerer. He died in the ancient traditional way. He's been a pain in our sides for a long time but, thanks to Ellen, no more." He sat in his chair twirling his thumbs.

"Now, we have one more to take care of and you know who that is," he continued. "Put the hit out on her. The Pure of Heart will be completely decimated without their leaders. The Children of the Nephilim will finally win the war and gain complete power over the world."

Ken nodded and bowed. "I live to serve," he said, walking out of the office. The chairman knew Ken had signed his death warrant by picking up the Wishing Cup. Legend claimed that only a Pure of Heart could possess it, so anyone else who touched the Wishing Cup would die a horrible death. Ken didn't hold to superstition but the chairman did. His arrogant assistant would regret it.

Mindy smiled seductively at Ken and their eyes met as they passed each other. She proceeded to walk into the chairman's office and get back to her job. Ken laughed to himself. Mindy would report everything the chairman said to her. "Who really runs the Children of the Nephilim now?" Ken smugly smiled to himself.

CHAPTER 24

Hidden Secrets

In the old days, Ellen despised the Operations Department. It was the most demeaning, lowest-level office job of the Children of the Nephilim. Ellen knew Operations was boring, but the job would place her at the heart of the organization. It meant access to records, passwords, and files in every department. Bob would be in heaven with the information she gathered here. Instead of a punishment, Ken had given her a gift.

All the money, corporations, money laundering, cartels, and secret information came through the databases and computers of Operations. Ellen smiled and thought Operations to be the perfect place for her to destroy the organization.

She never saw or had contact with the chairman after she was sent to her new department. Ellen went upstairs to his office only to teach Mindy how to make his damn Bloody Mary just right. She sighed and glanced at her watch, "It's time to see Mindy for her lesson."

Mindy gave Ellen her private security code to access the headquarter's main office. The beautiful girl had her hands full meeting the demands of the chairman and Ken. Her bartending skills were pitiful.

The secretary had ordered Ellen to come up and mix a couple of drinks for the chairman and place them in the fridge. Ellen rode up the elevator and accessed the office door with Mindy's code after no response at her knock. The chairman's door closed and Ellen glanced around, seeing no one in sight. Her eyes turned to the files laying on Mindy's desk.

Mindy felt Ellen was her minion. She enjoyed the subterfuge of the job. Ellen knew Mindy played both sides. She told Ken everything the chairman did, and she told the chairman everything Ken did. Ellen had to give her credit for being an excellent scheming, ambitious, and vicious replacement. Mindy probably hoped for a big promotion such as Ken's job. They all deserved each other.

In the empty boardroom, Mindy waited for her at the bar. Ellen surveyed the room and thought, "Hard to believe how things changed and yet changed." She remembered when it was her sitting at the table. She had enjoyed playing the game but now she hated it.

Ellen used to play a major role in boardroom decisions, but now she sat in a cubicle downstairs. Guilt flooded her for the lives taken in those meetings. She knew her time was running out. Mindy smiled at Ellen. She acted the part of Ellen's friend in the hope of prying all of Ellen's secrets out of her.

"I've got all the ingredients, Ellen, just like you told me. I can't believe how angry he gets when I don't make it right. Yesterday, he slapped me for making it too salty."

Ellen remembered how the chairman had slapped her and knew Mindy would be regretting her job more and more.

Ellen patted the girl on the shoulder to comfort her and pulled out a tiny metal jar with red seasoning. "I've brought you my secret ingredient, cayenne pepper from French Guiana. It's a male aphrodisiac. I used it to control him. He never knew. I wouldn't tell him if I were you because you can control him with it, too. A secret among sisters, shall we say? He's addicted to it." Ellen handed the small container of red spice to Mindy.

Mindy's eyes gleamed with excitement, "Oh, thank you so much, Ellen! How much do I put in?"

"Two dashes of cayenne, four dashes of salt, two dashes of pepper, a dash of lemon juice, and a layer of Worcestershire sauce. Add some cracked ice and make the tomato juice thick and you'll make him so happy. Good luck. And tell me how it goes. If you need any help, let me know."

Mindy started mixing the drink. "Bye, Ellen," she ordered. "You don't want to be here when the chairman gets here. He really doesn't like you anymore."

Ellen walked out of the boardroom thinking to herself, *He has to be stopped at all costs.* Deep inside her mind, a picture arose of a scared, little child, Julia, crying and unable to hit him. Her stomach twisted and her breathing became erratic. It was the failsafe put in her programming. Anytime she thought of killing him, she felt terribly ill. She'd seen the chairman test the programming by beating an unrestrained agent. The mind control didn't allow the agent to fight back. The chairman himself lit the man on fire. Ellen knew what awaited her. She understood how impossible it would be for her to kill him. Best thing she could do was kill the massive corporations he built.

She placed large sunglasses over her eyes and set a wide-brim hat on her head. The elevator came. No one except her stepped on, and she pushed the button to the basement. Pea Brain, her deceased former subordinate, had, under her orders, placed surveillance cameras in Ken and the chairman's office. At the time, her ambition drove her to out-maneuver everyone for a promotion, but now she realized that deep down she knew this day would come.

Steam filled the basement. Ellen used a janitor's closet as her secret surveillance room, for which only she knew the code. Pea Brain's death was convenient in the fact that no one knew about the other cameras. She studied the surveillance cameras in the chairman's office and obtained all his passwords. She listened to each report coming in on the Nephilim's agenda. The cleaning closet became Ellen's secret command post and hideout.

Ellen discovered where they kept the antiquities they'd stolen. And the best part was finding the names of companies that worked for the Nephilim and the government officials all over the world on their payroll. She sent the passwords, codes, and dossiers on the Pure of Heart who were being hunted down to Bob through encrypted messages on a tablet he had given her. Ellen smiled and wrote, "Bob, make me proud."

A text message popped up. "I love it when you talk dirty. They're so screwed."

Ellen grinned. *Bob will show them no mercy,* she thought. She put her sunglasses and hat back on and took the elevator up for lunch. Her mission was almost complete.

CHAPTER 25

Dragons Arise

Master Wong sat meditating on a cushion with incense burning in the simple white room. He looked through space and time with his mind. His old friends, Chief Saunhac and Sister Agnes, smiled down at him. The three of them had fought against the Children of the Nephilim for years. His friends spent all their lives protecting the Pure of Heart. Each of them brought unique skills and gifts, working as one. Unlike their enemy's use of chaos and death, Master Wong and his friends formed an intricate web of cooperation and loyalty. He knew then, as his comrades stood before him, both friends had passed onto the other side.

The chief's grave face stared at his trusted friend. The Mi'kmaq warrior wore his headdress and war clothes. "The war takes a turn for the worse. We need the dragons to rise to Cordy and Ash's aid."

Tears fell from Sister Agnes' eyes and a light illuminated the frail nun. "We come to warn you that Cordy and Earth's children are in peril. The Guardian awakens, my dear friend. Time is running out. De Villiers possesses the cursed thirty pieces of silver of Judas. He's been using this great evil to unite the Nephilim and the Dark Watchers. Help us, old friend, before it's too late." Both of his friends disappeared when he opened his eyes as he awoke from his deep trance. A long time ago, Wong trained at monasteries on meditation and martial arts of various forms. He'd dedicated his life to training others to fight in the war. He remembered when Sister Agnes asked him to take Cordy under his wing. The young girl surpassed his expectations, but even she couldn't fight this evil alone.

He called out to Peter Woo in the next room. The door opened and the younger man, dressed in white with a black belt around his tunic, knelt before the wise old man. "You called, Master?"

The man nodded. "The time has come for the dragons to rise. We will come to the aid of the Pure of Heart. No longer can we stay in the shadows." Master Wong stood up and walked into a large training room where fifty men knelt, placing their swords on the floor as a sign of loyalty and reverence.

Peter yelled out, "Your command shall be carried out, Master! Dragons, arise!"

Master Wong raised his hands for his men to stand. "My brothers, long have the dragons stayed in the shadows. Our power has relied on our great stealth and invisibility. But the war is intensifying and protection of the Pure of Heart is critical. Mother Earth and her children need our help. Long live the dragons! Like smoke we will rise and smother evil."

All of the dragons raised their swords in salute.

Peter stood next to Master Wong. "You don't need to worry about Cordy. You trained her well."

Master Wong nodded in agreement. "I'm not worried about Cordy but I feel an imbalance in Earth's energy. Judas' thirty pieces of silver possess great evil and endanger mankind. They poison anyone who touches it. If de Villiers touched the silver, evil infected him like a virus, slowly creeping into his heart. He'll turn into a monster. The Guardian has awakened and that means danger exists for planet Earth. Scholars have reported strange readings, and I've seen the signs. An extinction level event may be coming."

"Are you talking about a Great Flood as is written in the ancient texts?"

"Yes, but even worse."

Peter Woo started to worry. Master Wong was always right. He would send the call out throughout the world. Master Wong patted Peter on the shoulder.

"Pack our things because we will meet up with Cordy. She will need us. I know where she is heading and who is protecting her. I don't know if she can trust him or if he is leading her into a trap. Let us prepare."

CHAPTER 26

Stones of Truth

Bob's office consisted of a group of highly dedicated and loyal men and women. All the Pure of Heart in Ellen's confiscated dossiers were warned and notified that they were on the list for termination by the Nephilim. Safe houses were created to protect them but some of them wanted to help. Many of them came to work for Bob's agency.

He proceeded to sabotage the Nephilim's agenda of buying, robbing, and destroying good companies. They believed in monopolies and the idea that any competition must be destroyed. The Nephilim's favorite strategy was selling the stock of a stable company, driving them into bankruptcy and confiscating the assets sold, as well as the retirement funds of the employees. Paid, corrupt government officials sat back and watched the well-run companies be destroyed. Thousands of families were destroyed because of the jobs lost. Economic warfare, the weapon of choice of the Children of Nephilim, caused so much damage, while giving the Nephilim more power. No one stood in their way.

Bob used Cordy's money to buy the bankrupt companies' stock on the cheap and turned the companies around before selling them for a huge profit. The employees shared in the profits and could buy shares in their company. Bob's companies protected the environment with honest policies and peaceful objectives. The Nephilim's corporations lost billions in weeks. They placed short options on the companies they destroyed but Bob's rescue of them drove up their prices, blowing up the Nephilim's strategy in their faces. Meanwhile, the reputation of Bob and Cordy's money fund benefitted and increased in popularity. Their monopoly shattered the Nephilim's economic power, making them weaker than ever.

Bob worried about Ellen every day. She had told him about the programming she was subjected to as a child. He decided it would be up to him to save her. The chairman's ruthless tactics were well known by everyone on Wall Street, but Bob could be pretty ruthless too, especially against a child abuser. He texted Ellen that everything was working according to plan and that she needed to get the hell out of there before they suspected her.

He had loved the crazy, beautiful woman ever since he made love to her on the elevator. It was love at first sight on the tenth floor. Ellen emailed him. She wanted a picture of him in the Bingos waiters' hat he wore when he worked at the small hamburger joint in St. Louis.

Cordy and Bob had met at Bingos, where she had a panic attack over how she'd handle the millions of dollars she inherited from her billionaire grandfather. Grandpa Bill decided she was old enough to manage her own trust. Bob had just left New York for the quiet life, but when Cordy asked for his help, he couldn't say no. Bob's financial genius brought volunteers in droves as word got out that his corporation was a great place to work. Cordy and Bob's plan worked like a charm. They were devoted to developing companies that helped mankind, nature, and animals.

Organizations over the world wrote to Cordy's company with ideas for solar power, food production, and helping animals survive endangerment. Gift cards would show up to help people afford shelter, food, and healthcare. Bob bought foreclosed homes and let homeless families live in them in exchange for helping fix them up. Neighborhoods started to thrive. They also supported the schools with the latest equipment.

Everyone in New York wondered how Bob got so lucky, recruiting such fantastic people with loyalty and incredible talent. The chairman tried to infiltrate Bob's organization but none of his men could ever get hired. The Nephilim wondered how Bob knew who to hire?

Bob had a little help from two sacred amulets Ash had brought back from Egypt. The Nephilim originally stole the amulets from a museum during the Egyptian riots, but a young friend of Ash's named Mahd saved them from falling into their hands. Ash left the priceless amulets with Bob for safekeeping.

Ellen used the search engine in the Nephilim's database and found how precious the amulets were. She sent all the information to Bob. He started reading about how the Egyptians believed the magical amulets possessed special powers. Both would reveal a speaker of Truth, according to the Egyptian Book of the Dead. Bob stared at them on his desk a little confused. He felt the hair on the back of his neck start to tingle.

"Ah, I see you possess the Stones of Truth. Aren't they magnificent? I believe they're from Egypt," said a strange voice. "Hello, Bob, remember me? Uriel? We met at Chief Saunhac's funeral. You offered me a job."

Bob's eyes shot up quickly and saw the smiling, redheaded Uriel in a gray suit, sitting in the chair opposite him.

"How the hell did you get in here?" Bob asked. "Wait a minute, I remember you. We met in Nova Scotia. Are you here for that interview?"

Bob looked at the appointment ledger sitting on his desk. Uriel must be here for his final job interview. He remembered the Chief's friend made a good impression at their first meeting at his funeral. Bob thought he was done with all the job interviews, but his secretary must have forgotten to write this guy in. Bob smiled and put his hand out.

"Sorry, I didn't hear you come in. Uriel, right? I remember you. And any friend of the chief is a friend of mine. He was a great man. How can I help you?"

"Yes," Uriel answered. "A leader of the Pure of Heart and one of the bravest men I've known in a long time. It's not how you can help me; it's how I can help you, Bob. I see the Stones of Truth on your desk. They're priceless. I know about their power. History and archeology are favorite subjects of mine. One amulet is engraved with the Ibis head of Thoth and the other with the Heart of Osiris. Thoth, an Egyptian god, was a master of divine law and Osiris, another Egyptian god, judged by weighing the heart to find out the truth. The words engraved on each stone are Stones of Truth. They seek the speaker of truth. If a person lies, the stones move away from each other, but they move closer if a person speaks the truth."

Bob watched the Stones of Truth move together. He chuckled, "Well I'll be damned, I think you're right. I've never seen them do that before."

Uriel smiled. "You've hidden them in your desk for months. Today's the day you witness their amazing power. Let's try it out on you, shall we? Do you love a woman?"

"No," Bob quickly answered. "I just like to have fun." The Stones of Truth moved away from each other.

Uriel looked at him intently. "Someone isn't telling the truth," he sang. "The stones look into the heart of a person wherein lies the truth. I'll warn you that their power must be used for good. If their power is abused then they don't work. Imagine the power of a boss who knows when his employees lie to him."

"By the way," he went on, "I met a very interesting man in the waiting room named Randy. He's brilliant. An honest young man. I think he could help you run this company. You should try the stones on him and see what happens." The Stones of Truth moved together.

Bob looked at Uriel and had a good feeling. "I like you, Uriel. How about working for me? I'm offering you a job. We are trying to change the world for the better. What do you say?"

Uriel got up and shook Bob's hand. "I enjoy fighting for good. I'll take the job. I may need to get back with you on when I can start. You'll be hearing from me soon. Thanks, Bob. Oh, and before I forget, the Truth Stones will be very helpful in your interviews as you search for loyal people to work for the company. I'd keep them hidden in your drawer and watch what they do while you question potential employees. It's just a suggestion."

Bob laughed. "You don't take drugs do you, Uriel?"

Uriel smiled. "Drugs? No, not me, never got into them. I do drink every now and then."

Bob nodded as the Stones of Truth moved together. "I guess you don't have to take that drug test after all."

Uriel chuckled and walked to the door. "Randy," he yelled, "he's ready for you."

Bob decided to take Uriel's advice and test the Stones of Truth on all job applicants. He placed the amulets under a shelf below his desk and would observe them while interviewing Randy. He whispered softly to the amulets, "Stones of Truth, seek the speaker of Truth."

CHAPTER 27

Truth Seeker

Randy walked into Bob's office for his interview. He wore jeans and a T-shirt with the words "Big journeys begin with a little step" written on it. He wore glasses and looked like your stereotypical geek.

Bob whispered to the stones, "O, Keeper of the Balance, let no lies be told to me and declare the speaker of Truth. Let their heart be revealed."

Bob stared up at Randy. "Well, Randy, tell me about yourself and why you want to work for this company."

Randy surveyed the room slowly. "Uriel was a pretty cool guy," he answered. "He said you were trying to make the world a better place. I want to be part of that vision. I went to MIT and graduated top of my class. Life's too short to waste. I don't think mankind has much time left."

Bob watched the heart stone of Osiris and the head stone of Ibis move together. "Can I trust you, Randy?"

Randy seemed surprised by the question, almost as if it were an assault on his character. "Yes, of course you can trust me. The question is can I trust you?"

The stones moved together.

Bob looked deep into Randy's eyes. "You can trust me. Actions speak louder than words. All you have to do is look at the company's work and the good it's doing. You wouldn't be here if you didn't want to be part of the war."

Randy nodded in agreement.

After a few more questions, Bob seemed satisfied. "You're hired, Randy. You're going to be my assistant in running this company. I like you, and I can trust you. Your heart is in the right place for our mission."

Randy jumped out of his chair to shake Bob's hands. "I won't let you down, Bob," he assured him.

Bob then showed Randy the Stones of Truth. The young man was initially skeptical but changed his mind after Bob asked him if he thought his secretary was hot. Randy lied and said no, but the stones moved apart. Randy sheepishly looked at Bob. "OK, she is hot," he admitted. The stones moved together.

Bob gave Randy a pat on the back. "You're going to interview all the applicants wanting to work here and find out who is trustworthy for this organization. I'm entrusting you with the stones. Can you imagine how awesome an organization can be when you know the people you hired are honest? I don't want you to ever abuse the stones. No stupid questions and don't invade people's private affairs. Do I have your word?"

Randy nodded, "You've got my word. I won't abuse the stones. My job is to weed out the corporate spies. This job is going to be awesome!"

Bob handed Randy the next interview file. "Let's see how you do."

Randy got started right away. Bob sat back and watched him in action. He wanted to know if the stones worked only for him or if they would work for Randy.

The next applicant lied about whom he worked for and what he did on his last job. Randy even asked if he was loyal to promoting good in the world. The applicant said yes, but the Stones of Truth moved apart on nearly all the questions he answered.

During Randy's next interview, an eager young woman told him about her arrest for shoplifting. She admitted that she'd been young and foolish at the time. She hoped he would understand. She disclosed how it was hard to find jobs because of her record. Randy observed the talismans, and they moved together like magnets of opposite poles drawn to one another. Bob and Randy smiled. They knew who the Speaker of the Truth was. The girl left for her welcome tour.

What Randy and Bob discovered through the many interviews was something they knew all along: most people lie. The talismans' ability to reveal the truth in a world filled with deceit was invaluable, especially in financial markets. No wonder the Nephilim tried to steal them from the Egyptian temple of Isis, the goddess of the Nile. The ideal mother, patroness of nature and magic carried the ankh some called the Keys of Life. In temple wall hieroglyphics, the goddess opened her broad wings to protect the downtrodden. One must have truth.

All candidates at Bob's agency were tested and anyone who failed was shown the door. The Nephilim and Dark Watchers couldn't infiltrate the company. They couldn't figure out how Bob spotted their spies so quickly. Bob chuckled at how frustrated they were getting.

CHAPTER 28

The Fall

It starts with a tiny drop of water falling from the dam's wall. The trickle becomes bigger and bigger until the force of the water breaks through the wall with incredible power and destruction. Ken's management of the Nephilim's resources was terrible. Ellen gave him credit for keeping the massive hemorrhaging of their funds secret from his boss. What he didn't know was that she was the Nephilim's drop of water.

Ken kept the chairman distracted with the playful Mindy. The sexy minx sat in the chairman's lap, passionately kissing him when Ellen walked in on them. She had answered a call by his devious secretary to come up and see him. Ellen did as ordered. The chairman cussed her out for the interruption, not listening to any explanations, as Mindy's proud eyes met Ellen's as she walked out. The siren had hooked her prey and knew Ellen wouldn't be returning to her old position. *What a relief*, thought Ellen. She realized that the chairman's addictions and arrogance clouded his judgment. It seemed Ken was pulling the strings now.

The greatest damage came from one of the Nephilim's chemical companies. A fatal toxin was discovered in their main money making product, meaning they faced major lawsuits. As the poisonous byproducts were banned from use throughout the world, the loss loomed greatly on their balance sheets. Bob's firm aided the victims in court and exposed the chemical's severe damage to the ecosystem and the deaths caused by it. The company's stock fell like a rock into an abyss while Bob's fund profited.

The boardroom hosted an associates' meeting, and Ken handed out reports. He bamboozled all of them with the creative bookkeeping of his accountants. If anyone disagreed with his report, Ken threatened death would follow. The oblivious chairman grinned as he skimmed the papers and saw their false high profits. He told everyone that under his great leadership, the companies would continue to see excellent growth for the next year. This was a lie, of course, because Ken knew the chairman was too busy and infatuated with his new playmate to notice their failures.

Ellen read the financial reports of the Nephilim and learned they were on the brink of bankruptcy. She smiled at how easily the chairman was deceived. Ellen picked up the latest list of targeted individuals for termination, dossiers developed by researchers looking for the Pure of Heart. Her fear was that Bob's name would be on one of them. She breathed a sigh of relief when his name wasn't there.

Bob called her while she was in her surveillance room. "Hey, honey. What's for dinner?"

Ellen loved hearing Bob's low, sexy voice. He turned her on and made her feel alive. Working for the chairman made her feel cold and robotic, and she realized the programming dehumanized her. Her loneliness disappeared whenever she talked with Bob. Like a sturdy rock she could lean on, he held her hand when she suffered through haunting dreams and the painful detox when the poison left her body.

Bob had all the Nephilim's codes, passwords, and files. All her downloads went to his computers. Ellen knew she didn't have much time before someone would get suspicious.

"Bob, listen to this telephone call and tell me what you think. Ken's been acting really weird."

"I hope Ken's kinky telephone sex is on the recording. It will give me a good laugh. Go ahead and play it."

Ellen wanted to explain one more thing before the tape rolled. "One time, I passed Ken in the hall with a coffee in my hand that I'd just bought and he gave me this weird knowing wink. Then he took my coffee and drank it. Next he says, 'Thanks for the coffee. I heard that was your new job and maybe your last.' The whole incident really disturbed me. I felt like Ken was in on a secret."

"Maybe he's worried someone's going to poison him because he's a jerk," Bob answered. "OK, play the tape."

Ellen listened to the weird telephone call on the surveillance tape from Ken's office as she played it back for Bob.

"OK, listen close to what he's saying."

"Hello, Ken," began the recording. "Is everything going according to plan? How's Mindy doing?"

Ken chuckled, "Perfect, and the chairman is quite infatuated with her talents."

"I'm not surprised. Mindy is one of our best. She's spellbindingly beautiful and her kisses would make Judas proud," the mystery voice said.

"The Nephilim are on the verge of financial ruin, and the chairman is clueless. Everything seems to be going according to plan. Keep up the good work, Ken." The phone call ended.

Bob hesitated for a second. "Well, it seems we're not the only ones trying to take down the chairman and the Nephilim."

"Who are Ken and Mindy working for? The caller's voice sounds familiar but I can't remember where I've met him," Ellen said.

Bob furrowed his brows. "I think we need to get you out of there. I want you to keep in contact with me more often. I'll come in there and drag you out if you don't, you understand?"

Ellen knew Bob meant it. "I understand. But first, I'm going to find out what the hell is going on."

Chapter 29

A Serious Problem

The chairman sat in his favorite salon, surrounded by beautiful women. One was doing his fingernails and the other, his toes. His favorite stylist was combing his thick, black mane, when the comb pulled out a mass of hair from the back of his head. All eyes in the room widened, shocked; any giggling and laughter went silent.

The stylist showed him the hair-filled comb. "I believe, sir, you have a very serious problem."

The chairman saw the massive amount of hair falling out. He had already noticed the dark spots on his skin. Anger and fear surged through his body.

"Everybody out of the room," he ordered. "Get out, now!" He threw his drink against the wall. Everyone scrambled and vacated the room.

He gazed into the mirror and what stared back terrified him.

The chairman recognized the signs of radiation poisoning. He remembered awhile back when his old boss, the past chairman, needed to be removed. The late chairman's shocked expression when he realized his loyal friend had poisoned him made him smile at the time. He wasn't smiling now.

Radiation poisoning took a few weeks to kill, with the victim unable to trace the poison back to the killer. A perfect weapon, it killed with excruciating pain and suffering and had no cure. The realization of karma's revenge fell on him like a heavy boulder, suffocating him under its weight. His killer knew he'd assassinated his boss. He could hear their laughter in his ears.

As the chairman's death loomed, he searched for revenge on his killer. Who did it? All his thoughts focused on Ellen. The bitch, taught by him to be a ruthless killer, haunted him. He knew his protégé well. Kidnapping a young Pure of Heart was an excellent plan at first, but now as he gazed into the mirror, he saw the true power of the Pure of Heart. *She's gotten her revenge and now I'll destroy her*, he thought. Rage burned inside him and tears rose up in his eyes. "I'm a dead man walking. I will make her regret the day she was born," he said through gritted teeth.

He'd not been feeling well the past couple of weeks. His joints ached and at first, he thought he was catching a mild cold. A small hope had glimmered in his mind. Denial started to set in. What if he was wrong about being poisoned? He called his doctor.

The chauffeur pulled up and he jumped in the back seat of the limo. The chairman ordered his driver to take him to the medical center. He planned to assemble scientists and doctors to find a cure if he was indeed suffering from radiation poisoning. *No disease could bring down one of the most powerful men on Earth*, he assumed. Then, the chairman felt a presence and a feeling of trepidation filled his soul.

Antar, the father of the Children of the Nephilim, was seated next to him wearing a black suit. He looked disgusted and angry when he gazed at the sickly mortal, whose hands trembled in fear. The chairman looked at Antar with terror in his eyes.

"Have I angered you, Father?" he stammered. "I ask forgiveness and for mercy. I have served you all these years with great dedication.

I've killed hundreds of thousands for you. I beg you. Please save me. I know you have the power to do so. I've been a loyal servant," he pleaded. He leaned over to grab Antar's hand but stopped as he leaned away from him with profound disapproval. Antar could smell death's repugnant stench all around this weakling.

"You've disappointed me for a while now. You're not the one to bring my children into the future. Failure can't be tolerated. I've run out of patience with your lack of success. Another candidate has demonstrated his ingenuity and desire for supreme power. You've grown to be complacent, and now you're going to die for it. Before you're terminated, I want you to clean up the mess you made."

"I can make it right. Just give me another chance," begged the chairman.

"It's too late. Quit sniveling like a baby. I loathe your pathetic, childish behavior and your sloppy work. You've grown soft and lost the drive to accomplish our plan."

The chairman started coughing and spat blood into his handkerchief. His eyes blinked for a second and his vision of Antar disappeared. The chairman's anger swelled. "Someone's going to pay for this. I guarantee it. And everybody who failed me will die. I'm not going down alone. He wants me to clean up the mess, and that's what I'm going to do!"

The chairman dropped his head into his hands in desperation. Any hope he was lost when Antar disappeared. He should've known better to think his coldhearted and vicious boss would show pity on him. His life appeared to be a cruel joke, but he would have the last laugh.

Tests confirmed he'd been poisoned by radioactive polonium 210. He would suffer severe diarrhea and vomiting. The physician predicted death in a few weeks. The chairman knew of the poison and the outcome because he'd killed his predecessor the same way. A horrible death awaited him. He remembered savoring the victim's tremendous suffering. He remembered the glee he felt knowing how efficient a poison polonium was. Polonium didn't come cheap and the chemical had a signature. He was surprised when the doctors told him the polonium came from his own nuclear reactors. The angry chairman left the doctor's office in utter despair.

No antidote available could save him. The only person who knew he had murdered the former chairman was Ellen. Her programming would not allow her to harm him physically, with her own hands, but poison was the perfect weapon because someone else could do the poisoning for her without knowing it. The sickly man figured out her plan. He created Ellen, and she had risen in the ranks to be a vicious killer. The time arrived for revenge against his enemies. A horrific death awaited him but her punishment would be excruciating and merciless. As a long-time pathological killer, he realized his death left no one with remorse. In his lifetime, he'd never experienced true love for anyone. Nobody would miss him and in fact many would be pleased at his disappearance. Madness descended on him and intense hatred filled his heart like a raging fire. If he could kill everyone on Earth, he'd do it out of spite. One more act needed to be accomplished before he left his job. The ailing man pulled out his phone like a gun aimed at his next victim.

Ellen got the call while down in Operations. The chairman wanted to see her in his office later tonight; she was to institute protocol 666. "I will comply," she answered in a robotic tone.

In Ellen's programming, protocol 666 ordered her to ingest cyanide when given the order. The chairman had been her handler since she was a child. His abusive tactics had stripped the little girl of Julia's identity and instead created the cruel, heartless Ellen. But what he didn't know was that his programming had broken down as she matured and especially after she drank from the Wishing Cup that day in Nova Scotia. The deadly snake poison in the honey from the Tree of Knowledge killed Ellen and set Julia free. The truth was revealed and the knowledge of who she really was came back to her. Chief Saunhac held her in his arms and saved her. How many Pure of Heart had he seen hunted and killed by the chairman? Her duty was done and she knew the chief would be proud of her.

She knew the mind control command was still in play, buried deep in her programming. All high level agents of the Children of Nephilim had the fail-safe command within their programming. It ensured total obedience throughout the entire organization. The chairman blamed Ellen for everything and he wanted her dead.

CHAPTER 30

Retribution

Ellen felt like she was walking in a dream but couldn't wake up from it. A robot-like Ellen had no will to stop herself from complying. She saw herself grab the coffee cup and drop the cyanide pill into its murky liquid. Ellen knew her death was inevitable after one sip.

She felt some relief in the fact that once dead, the chairman would have no more control over her. She only regretted losing Bob. Ellen wished that they had taken that vacation, but with Bob's help, the Nephilim would be left tattered and shredded. Ellen typed Bob a farewell, "I love you Bob. Remember me, Julia."

She headed slowly up to the chairman's penthouse office as the sun set and night settled on the City of Lights. She opened the door to the dark and familiar room where she had been abused for years and years. She would comply. Ellen placed the coffee cup on the chairman's desk and pulled up a chair. She'd drink on his order. He enjoyed watching his helpless victim die, as he felt no remorse or pity. Her life would not be in vain; the information given to Bob was priceless and worth her coming back to this wretched place. Bob promised to finish them off and she believed him. She'd leave mankind and the world a better place.

The door swung opened suddenly and Ken rushed into the dark office. He recognized Ellen.

"What are you doing here?" he snarled. "Damn, I'm thirsty! I could use a little caffeine."

Ken spotted his favorite special brand coffee cup on the chairman's desk. He noticed no lipstick marks on the lid and deduced Ellen had not drunk from the cup. He grabbed it and smiled, "Thanks for bringing me my coffee. You've got perfect timing. It's like you read my mind," he said. "Funny how things have changed, Ellen. Before, I brought you coffee. Now you bring it to me." He drank two gulps of the poisoned coffee.

Ellen stood there with her mouth open in shock. Ken looked at her stunned face.

"What's the matter with you?" he asked. "You look surprised. That's a first. It's not like I haven't taken your coffee cup before. Oh, and by the way, it tasted like crap."

Ellen smiled at him and shook her head, "Ken, that will be the last coffee you will ever steal from me."

He started feeling weak and dizzy. His chest felt like it was on fire and he was getting short of breath. He dropped the coffee cup and its contents spilled on the floor. Ken fell to his knees, and looked up to Ellen.

"I knew you weren't very bright Ken, but now it is confirmed," she said as she knelt by him. "Who are you working for? Who is trying to take over the Nephilim? I've known for a long time someone's been infiltrating the organization and trying to take it over." Ken couldn't tell her because he was no longer breathing.

Ellen couldn't believe what he had done. "You are one stupid, damn idiot!" she screamed.

Suddenly, Ellen felt a shadow watching the whole scene. Evil lurked in the dark corner of the room, sitting in a chair. A sinister laugh bubbled up from the black abyss, followed by slow, deliberate clapping.

"Bravo, Ellen," said a man's voice. "I agree, Ken had become quite power hungry of late. I believe Mindy deserves a promotion." The chairman's voice filled the office and she could hear the suppressed anger in it.

"Yes, he's always been a disappointment, but his death was surprisingly amusing. The look on his face was priceless. I surmised your cyanide pill was dissolved in the coffee cup that he drank. Oh well, let's do something more creative, shall we Ellen, for your send off."

The chairman emerged slowly from the shadows, looking like a living corpse. His hair was gone and lesions appeared all over his body. "You know why you're not running from the room, right now?" he asked.

Ellen bowed her head. "I know. Protocol 666 is in progress. I must do as you order. I must comply while you live to command me. You are my master and I am your slave." She held out her hands to be bound. He liked to have women tied up so they couldn't resist. The pleasure registered on his face. His programming worked. It was now time for the final test.

The ropes wrapped tightly around her wrists, bruising her skin. He would beat her and then kill her. He'd have the ultimate control. Ellen couldn't fight back and he'd enjoy every moment of it. The chairman slapped her face hard and her head whipped back from the force of the blow.

"I must say, using Mindy to kill me was a stroke of genius since you couldn't do it."

Ellen looked at him with a smile. "You told me to show Mindy the secret to making the perfect Bloody Mary. The programming has its flaws. At least I know you will soon be dead too. Justice served for killing all the innocent children and Pure of Heart. The protocol doesn't allow me to feel anything. Little Julia isn't scared of you anymore," she said defiantly.

He slapped her again and blood trickled from the corner of her mouth. The chairman pointed his gun at Ellen's head. "I release you from Protocol 666," he said, "and will take great pleasure killing you myself. I want you to feel utter terror before you die."

142

Ellen closed her eyes to prepare for the end as the chairman's finger started to squeeze the trigger.

Right then, the penthouse window shattered into pieces and crashed onto the floor. A well-built man with a black mask over his face fired an AK-47 into the room. There was a rope attached to him as a stealth helicopter flew above in the sky.

"C'mon Ellen, time to turn in your resignation," yelled the masked man. Ellen knew that voice anywhere. She gave a shout of warning, "Watch out, he's got a gun!"

The chairman took his gun and aimed at Bob.

Bang! Bang!

At that moment, Ellen had sprung out of the chair and kicked the chairman in the groin, making him miss his shot. Bob detached his harness and watched a hand-tied Ellen kick the hell out of the chairman.

Bob calmly said, "Honey, step back and let me shoot him."

"I have this all under control, Bob, so let a girl have some fun. He's going to die no matter what. This piece of filth needs to suffer," she retorted as she kicked the chairman in the stomach.

Bob watched as Ellen took her fury out on the sickly looking man. He saw the chairman crawling for his gun on the floor while her blows fell on him. In pain, it was the chairman's desire for revenge that pushed him forward. He would kill her. Ellen's fury possessed her. She didn't notice the madman's intent.

The chairman reached his gun and started to aim at Ellen. His hand shook from all the pain and pent up anger. Bob reacted with the lightning speed of an experienced commando. He pushed Ellen out of the way and pointed his AK-47 at the chairman.

"OK, let's get this over with, you evil-ass bastard. She may not be able to kill you, but I sure as hell can. Adios, sucker." Bob squeezed the trigger, riddling the chairman with bullets.

CHAPTER 31

A Room with a View

Ellen truly died that night as Julia was reborn. Bob freed her hands and hugged her tightly. "I thought I lost you for a second," he whispered. "Don't ever scare me like that again."

Julia loved him more than anything in the universe and he had saved her. She felt lucky that two men, Chief Saunhac and Bob, dedicated their lives to free her from her evil master. She still had some unfinished business with the Children of the Nephilim. The chief's dream was coming true that night.

Bob erased the room of fingerprints and arranged the scene to look like a murder-suicide. He set the bodies to look like Ken shot the chairman and then took a cyanide capsule. Julia admitted the man was a pro and magnificent to watch in action. His years with the Navy SEALs showed as he made sure every detail was taken care of.

"I really did have everything under control, Bob," she scolded.

Bob smiled. "Sure you did, I just wanted to kill him first. You can kill him the second time. Besides, why do you get to have all the fun? What the hell happened to Ken? Looks like he needs to lay off the caffeine. He made a big mistake. Remind me not to buy that brand of coffee."

Julia shook her head. "You wouldn't believe me if I told you. Stupid idiot accidentally drank my cyanide pill."

Bob kicked Ken's dead body and chuckled. "First good thing he's ever done."

"Give me one second to finish off the Children of the Nephilim." Julia bent over the chairman's computer and typed in the destruct code.

"We don't have time to play with computers, honey. The champagne is getting warm so hurry up."

"Don't nag, Bob. Just give me a second."

"I'm not nagging. I'm just pointing out that we're on a tight schedule."

"There, see, you're doing it again."

He shot a steel wire into an open window of a hotel next door. The hook at the end of the line pierced the stone structure. Earlier in the day, Randy had checked into the hotel and left the window open on the balcony. Bob tested the line for strength and motioned to Julia.

"Now hurry up, beautiful, and let's get the hell out of here. I've got a surprise for you." He held out his hands to hold her. She pulled the fire alarm and grabbed her cell phone. "It's all clear," she said.

"Let's go!"

She grabbed Bob's shoulders and he slid the harness on both of them. They glided through the window of the chairman's office all the way to the open window of the hotel next door. He set Julia down and released the line from the walls. The wire dropped down onto the empty street.

They had a room with a view of the Children of the Nephilim headquarters. Bob had ordered champagne on ice and a tray of goodies waited for them in the room, compliments of Randy. The window drapes flapped from the night breeze. The stars gleamed above in the dark sky on a beautiful serene night as the excited couple watched for the climax of their plan to be fulfilled.

The Nephilim had a disaster plan in place in case of a major attack of infiltration. They rigged the building with explosives on orders of Julia's late boss. Julia knew the codes for detonating all the explosives throughout the building. They watched below as everyone exited the building during a fire alarm. The bombs ticked away on all the floors.

"Let's get this show started, shall we?"

Bob popped the bottle of champagne as Julia pushed the buttons on her cell phone, which acted as a proxy detonator. The time sequence whizzed to zero. Five explosions took place simultaneously throughout the building and the chairman's office blew up, ablaze with fire. Fireworks lighted the sky.

Their glasses clinked in a toast. Bob and Julia sat on the bed and enjoyed every moment of watching the building burn. Using the chairman's computer, Julia had confiscated all of the organization's information and released a virus to infiltrate and destroy any remaining files. The Children of the Nephilim's organization was in shambles. Chief Saunhac's dream had come true.

Julia moved closer to Bob. She put her arms around him and passionately kissed him. "I love you. You saved my life."

Bob hugged her and tenderly said in her ear, "Man, it takes a lot to impress you, but I knew I could do it. The chief would be very proud of you right now. I'm proud of you."

"I have to say," Julia whispered seductively, "you know how to show a girl a good time. Once in an elevator and now after burning down a building. What's next?"

Bob turned off the lights and kissed her with all the passion held in his heart. He pulled her on top of him in the luxurious bed.

"Oh, I'm full of surprises."

CHAPTER 32

Dark Watchers Rise

De Villiers sat in his black leather chair and looked out over the London night sky. The Dark Watchers' headquarters in the city commanded huge resources. The leader and the highest-ranking Dark Watcher called for a meeting of all its members. The Children of the Nephilim had been destroyed and lay in ruin. News traveled fast and de Villiers smiled with pleasure. One down, one more to go. He couldn't have been happier. Next, the collapse of the Pure of Heart would all but ensure his power over the entire world.

After the chairman's death, the companies owned by the Children of the Nephilim went bankrupt and their stocks were now worthless. De Villiers' plot to be master of the Nephilim's vast wealth and power had now changed with their destruction. De Villiers' man being killed in the explosion was a surprise twist, but Ken had screwed up his mission and deserved his hideous death.

He also hadn't anticipated the Pure of Heart being such a strong competitor. They were taking Wall Street by storm as their companies thrived. People flocked to join their revolution and their strength grew. Taking down the Nephilim backfired because instead of gaining a strong, powerful ally, de Villiers created a powerful opponent. His plan was askew. The Light Watchers and Pure of Heart were united and stronger than ever.

But de Villiers loved chaos and confusion for it left some great opportunities. Isis, his cat, sat perched on his desk. He gave her a smile. "You naughty cat, what are you doing on my desk?"

She meowed in protest as he picked her up and set her on the floor. The cat jumped on her favorite chair, watching the door. Isis had lived with de Villiers for many years and he felt his rise in power was partly due to his devoted Isis. The spoiled, older cat developed annoying habits and demanded more of his attention. He found his tolerance for the cat getting less and less. The sorcerer didn't need his lucky charm anymore. His pet sensed his love for her disappearing over time. Isis' eyes studied his face, hunting for any affection but finding only impatience.

Mindy knocked on the door, and he called for her to come in. De Villiers beamed with pride at his star pupil. Being gorgeous and lethal were tremendous traits for an undercover spy and this woman possessed them both. Mindy once worked for Interpol and was recruited by the Dark Watchers at the young age of twenty-one for intelligence work on the Nephilim. A femme fatale with a dark past made a great assistant.

Mindy, an incredible actress with a great talent for betrayal found her calling at a young age. The young girl survived by her wits and trusted nobody. She could be your best friend and stab you in the back the next minute. Mindy and Ken delivered all the Nephilim's secret operations and hideouts to the Dark Watchers. De Villiers grasped in his hands her briefs, which contained information about the drug cartels, prostitution rings, and militia of the Nephilim army. The contacts nurtured by de Villiers had come to fruition and many of the Nephilim's handymen clamored to join the Dark Watchers for protection after the collapse.

The Dark Watchers emerged as a secret shadow society with no competitors anymore except the weak Light Watchers and Pure of Heart. De Villiers' gaze devoured Mindy's figure. Her skintight black dress revealed her seductive curves and she complemented her outfit with bright red stiletto heels.

"Well, what do you think of my report?" she asked as she made her way to his desk.

"Excellent work, my dear. And I believe your bank account shows my appreciation."

She smiled and gave him a wink. "I saw your generosity this morning and I thank you for such a prompt delivery. I'm surprised at the destruction of the headquarters, but we got the information out in time. I must be honest when I say I feel no remorse over foolish Ken's death. I thank you for my big promotion. I promise to serve you well. Are all the Dark Watchers coming for the meeting?"

"Yes," he assured her. "Everyone will be there to cast their vote, but I don't see any obstacles to the marriage of the Nephilim remnants to the Dark Watchers. If there are, I'll take care of them. I assure you. The chairman liked to delegate his messy work, but I'm more a hands-on manager. I don't mind getting my hands dirty."

Mindy sat on the corner of his desk, giving him a smile. "You were surprised Ellen survived, but I have to thank her for making my job easier. You used her, didn't you, to kill Saunhac?"

He placed his hand on her thigh, moving slowly up under her skirt and smiled. "I knew what she wanted, just like I know what you want."

Mindy leaned over and kissed him. "Unfortunately, time is running out and preparations must be made for your big day as the Dark Watcher Grandmaster, ruler of one of the most powerful organizations in the world. I better get ready for the meeting and make preparations. Good luck with the vote."

He watched her stroll out and as soon as she closed the door, he felt the chill in the room. The hair on his neck stood up. Isis' hair arched up on her back and she hissed. She felt his presence too.

De Villiers turned his chair and there stood Antar. He'd heard of the Father of the Nephilim but had never met him. He assumed that with the destruction of his army, he had come crawling to him for aid. He smiled at the tall, mesmerizing Antar.

"Have I the pleasure of meeting the Father of the Nephilim?" he asked. Isis stopped hissing as soon as Antar gave her a smile. "Hush ancient one," he cooed, "I won't hurt you."

The Father of the Nephilim lifted his hand and petted the purring Isis.

Antar studied him. "You do, and may I commend you on getting rid of the tiresome and weak chairman. I'm impressed with your plans on the unification of the two dark branches. It's brilliant. My hope is that you will continue the cloning process of the ancient Children of the Nephilim. The plans of a super race have progressed with positive results these past few years. They will make a more efficient and more obedient army than Adam's children."

De Villiers nodded his head. "The program shows great promise and will continue. We are bigger and stronger united than separated. I'm not a passive commander like the feeble-minded chairman. My priority is to continue to hunt down the Pure of Heart and obtain their ancient prizes. Mankind will be my slave."

"Don't fail me or you'll regret it," Antar answered coldly.

De Villiers returned his icy gaze. "I don't scare easily and who knows, you may work for me when this ends."

Antar turned and stared at him with astonishment. "Sorcerer, you want to possess the ring of Solomon? The ring controls the elements and angels. Many have tried and many have failed."

De Villiers arrogantly smiled at him. "I'm not afraid of attempting too much, but rather doing too little. I'm aware of the power of the ancient ring. All of the warnings in legends telling of madness and disaster are utter nonsense. Saunhac, the weak fool, was afraid of its power, but not I."

Antar started to disappear but his words echoed back, "Be careful for what you wish for; it may surprise you."

After Antar left, de Villiers stood up and headed for the meeting, whispering aloud to himself, "Antar, Father of the Children of the Nephilim, will someday kneel and serve *me*."

CHAPTER 33

Poppa Jon Abstains

De Villiers had announced an emergency meeting for all the families of the Dark Watchers. A distinguished elderly Poppa Jon Lafitte strolled into the room. His adversary headed straight for him like a predator chasing his prey. De Villiers kissed both cheeks as ambition shone in his eyes. The message came in loud and clear to the wise old man.

"Welcome, Poppa Jon, my dear friend. Where is your adventurous grandson?"

"He's away on business. He sends his apologies for not attending the meeting. You must listen to an old man instead," he said sternly. "What news are we to hear tonight? Rumors abound about the chairman's death."

"We need a leader, Poppa Jon. Can I count on your support?" The Lafittes abhorred de Villier's leadership and dark guidance. They didn't like the idea of working with the Nephilim, who they found untrustworthy. De Villiers admitted they had a point, but he still needed their vote.

The Lafitte family descended from privateers and over time, they merged their companies into legitimate businesses such as gambling casinos, fishing boats, and weapons sales. They were a respected family that honored a certain code and held the trust of the other Dark Watcher families. Their influence couldn't be underestimated.

"I will listen to your proposals and make my decision," Poppa Jon answered cautiously. He took his seat at the round table with the others and folded his hands, waiting for the meeting to start. De Villiers was ready if the old man betrayed his leadership. In fact, he suspected he would.

De Villiers scanned the table where all the Dark Watchers' representatives sat with their full attention. They had arrived from all over the world. The Dark Watcher families and organizations worked in various businesses, which often dealt with men's vices. The families dated back centuries. Gambling, bootlegging, shipping, and banking were lucrative businesses of the Dark Watchers. They'd infiltrated governments, secret societies, and intelligence agencies. Laws didn't mean anything to them since their tentacles reached deep into all major governments. A powerful underground, controlling many of the countries of the world's leaders, was created ensuring power in the hands of a few elite.

All of the men dressed in dark suits reflecting their shadowed pasts. For generations, their families had worked together in running international businesses. In some countries, corruption ruled the governments so the Dark Watchers deftly handed bribes to officials and blackmailed others. The Nephilim's agenda of hunting down the Pure of Heart didn't interest them. Money and power attracted them more. The Light Watchers played by the rules, but not the Dark Watchers.

"Welcome Dark Watchers," de Villiers announced to the table. "We celebrate a momentous day. I've brought you here for a vote to unite what is left of the Children of the Nephilim and the Dark Watchers. No longer will two entities be fighting one another. The merger will make us the most powerful organization on Earth. As your leader, I bring you this opportunity of riches and great prosperity. However," he paused, "one family sitting here will betray us today." A hush fell over the room.

"Yes, my friends, a Judas sits among us. We all know betrayal is the worst crime."

The men looked at each other with surprise. Poppa Jon stood up proudly from the table and answered de Villier's charges. The only family who could give him a challenge would be the powerful Lafittes. The calm Poppa Jon turned his back on their power hungry leader and faced his shocked fellow Dark Watchers. "We've never trusted the Children of the Nephilim and now he wants us to unite with them. What assurances do we have that they'll obey the rules of the Dark Watchers?" he entreated. "De Villiers may think the Lafitte family betrayed the Dark Watchers, but we find he betrayed the code of the Dark Watchers by asking us to merge with the Children of the Nephilim. We have, over the ages, been separate from them for good reason. The Lafitte family abstains from this vote and finds the merger ill advised."

Isis sat on the table quietly licking her paw when a furious de Villiers pushed her off the table into the wall. The cat screamed in anger and hissed at de Villiers, scurrying out the door. Poppa Jon looked up into the sorrowful eyes of Christ being kissed by Judas in Caravaggio's painting of *The Taking of Christ* that hung on the wall. He folded his hands the same way as the betrayed Christ. He knew what would happen next and he submitted to his fate. No one noticed, for all eyes were on the retreating angry cat. De Villiers pulled out his .44 Magnum and shot the older man. Poppa Jon felt the bullet enter the back of his head. He fell forward onto the table, dead.

With the gun still in his hand, de Villier looked at the shocked members. "I think the time to take the vote has arrived. Be careful how you vote, my friends, lest I know what other traitors lay amongst us. I hope you all take my advice. The times of old men are gone and a new star arises. The Lafitte family will be punished and destroyed for their disloyalty. All for the unity of the Children of the Nephilim and the Dark Watchers, raise your hands." The face of the betrayed Christ looked down on Poppa Jon's dead body where a pool of blood oozed onto the table. Everyone in the room knew the outcome of the vote.

De Villiers now possessed the dark army that he had always wanted. His agenda to seize the Pure of Heart treasures was still in play. Mindy smiled across the room at how easily de Villiers manipulated them. She texted him, "I think we should celebrate your victory tonight with something special. A king needs a queen in this political game." He read his text and knew he was in for a treat.

He texted her back, "I'll have the champagne chilled and ready for you. No one can stop me now."

Everything went according to plan and soon his super race of soldiers would be at his command. Only those who completely obeyed him would survive. The power of life and death gave him such a rush. God and he had a lot in common in that respect. He felt no regret for killing the old man, but he did know his grandson wouldn't be so easy a target. De Villiers would make the destruction of the Lafitte family an example to everyone not to cross him.

CHAPTER 34

One More Time

"Something must be up with Bob," Ash said. "I texted him early this morning and I haven't gotten a response all day. That's not like Bob."

Cordy asked, "What did you text him about?"

"Your wounded friend over there bleeding to death is what. I asked Bob to run a background check on him. I don't like the way he looks, I don't like the way he talks, and in fact, I don't like him at all. He's trouble! The only reason he's with us right now is because he got us out of a big jam back at the hotel and he's an OK shot."

"Get over it, Ash. We decided we needed to trust someone and he's able to get us out of here alive. He risked his life to save us, or did you forget? So will you just give it a rest? But you're right about one thing. It's not like Bob to take so long to call back."

Ash looked at the unconscious Jon. "He better come to soon before we get to the airport. Slap him and see if he wakes up."

"I am not going to slap him," Cordy angrily yelled.

"Hey, no problem. Move over and I'll slap the shit out of him or we can just sit on the side of the road at the airport and wait for everybody to show up."

The limo driver glanced at Ash in the mirror but fixed his eyes back to the road.

Cordy pushed Ash back. "No, I got this." She propped him up against the back seat and started to slap his face. "Come on, Jon, wake up!" she yelled. She repeated it several times and even gave out a Mi'kmaq war whoop but nothing helped. Ash started to move over to help, but Cordy had a feeling the limo driver might shoot him if he hit Jon.

A vision of an elderly man dressed in the robes of a monk sitting in a crossed leg position came to her mind. Many students knelt with heads bowed with swords in their hands and a dragon tattoo on their arms. Her teacher smiled at her. "Remember, Star Child."

She remembered a wise lesson by Master Wong. He said, "Sometimes pain will sting like a bitch, but it works to wake you up."

"Ash, I got this," she said sternly. Ash leaned over and looked over her shoulder, watching Cordy stare at the wound on Lafitte's shoulder. She had one finger pointed at it; with no warning, she jammed her finger into the wound.

Almost instantly, Lafitte came off the back of the seat and let out a blood-curdling scream. "Holy shit, that hurts!"

"Damn, Cordy, that was intense!" Ash said. "Now, don't let him drift off again."

Cordy put her arms around Lafitte. "Jon, focus on my face. We're at the airport."

"I am with the living, yes, chérie?"

"Yes, I thought I lost you but you're back and I need you now," Cordy replied. Jon, still in pain, tilted his thick, dark, curly-haired head and with an ever so small smile, winked at her.

Jon instructed the driver, "Follow the signs to air cargo. My plane will be on the far side next to the jumbo jets. The big planes keep my jet hidden. You can pull the car down next to the plane. My man will recognize the car and let us in. He better," Jon muttered. "I give him a nice bonus every Christmas."

The driver slowed down but didn't stop. The man at the gate just nodded. Ash could see the plane once they got to the other side of the large cargo planes. "Where is the crew? The door is still shut," Ash said.

"Well, there's just one problem. You see, in my line of work, it's best to employ as few as you can," Jon explained. "I never have to worry about them finding out my secrets. As my great-great-grandfather said, 'If you want to keep a secret, don't tell anyone and it will always stay your secret.' No one knows we're here and where we're going except Jacque. He can be trusted. That's the good news. The bad news is, I'm your pilot. So, Ash, I designate you my new copilot. Don't worry, I'll talk you through it."

Ash shook his head vehemently. "No, that's not going to happen! Cordy, let's get out of here and go look for some motorcycles, some Harleys. You know, fat girls. I'm getting good at riding them."

"Ash, the bikes are called fat boys, and no, we're not leaving. Besides, your Mom told me you could fly. She said you flew to St. Catherine's Monastery."

"That was a small, small, small, little plane. This," Ash pointed to the private jet, "this can't be good."

"Come on, Ash, be a man. Go for the adventure in life," Jon challenged. "What the hell. If we stay in Ireland, you die. At least in the air you have a chance. Your destiny awaits you."

Ash had to admit he did make sense. "What did you mean by I would die? What about Cordy and you? Won't you guys die too?"

Jon flashed his brilliant white teeth in a wicked smile that appeared under his dark moustache. "Well, you see Ash, I'm too well-respected and everyone owes me favors. I'm worth my weight in ransom. And for Mademoiselle Cordy, she's way too beautiful and so very rich. I'm sure I could work a deal to keep her with me. So you see, Ash, I'm really only doing this for you." Ash had to admit he was a cocky bastard and Uriel's advice came to him. He needed to keep going and not retreat.

"Welcome to my first jet airplane lesson," Ash said. "Everyone get on board."

Within minutes, Ash strapped himself in the cockpit and Jon walked him through the checklist. He realized why they called it the cockpit - you had to have big balls to fly these jets.

"OK, Ash, just take off the brakes and give it some thrust," Jon guided him with a commanding voice. With that, the plane started to move. Jon got on the radio.

"Tower, this is Lafitte One, ready for takeoff."

Less than a minute later, the tower came back, "Proceed to runway A-6. You are a go, Lafitte One."

Ash looked over at Jon and smiled, "Yeah, I get it, the tower is on your 'Christmas list' too."

Lafitte winked. "OK, Ash," he instructed, "just keep Jennifer in a straight line and remember, small moves. You will be going three to four times faster. The principles of aerodynamics are the same for a small plane as well as a jet."

"Why did you name her Jennifer?"

Jon chuckled. "Named her after Jennifer, an amazing, gorgeous, French film actress. When you pull back on your stick, she'll give you one hell of a ride."

Ash started down the runway. "Can I pull back yet?"

"Hold on, hold on," Jon coached, "not yet and... *now!*"

Ash pulled back and Jennifer threw them into their seats. "I see what you mean," Ash remarked with a sly smile.

Cordy rolled her eyes. "Men."

CHAPTER 35

Stick Rudder Speed

It only took a few minutes for the jet to reach 25,000 feet, and Lafitte talked Ash through setting the autopilot. Lafitte explained that he trained as a pilot in the NATO air force. Interpol recruited him later for special assignments, where his flying skills came in handy. The two men started to bond and become more at ease with each other.

"I'm going to get some rest," Jon whispered weakly. "It should take us only a little over an hour to get to Paris. I'll talk you through the landing, Ash. Glad you're a pilot. I read your dossier. You're very resourceful."

Ash nodded. "I used to be a nobody, and now I've got a dossier. What can I do to prepare?"

"Prepare isn't an option," Jon smiled. "You'll either do or die, my friend, and I of course prefer do!"

He closed his eyes and drifted off to sleep. Ash gazed at Lafitte and noticed that here he was shot in a gun battle, had broken every international flight rule in the book, and still lay there sound asleep with a big smile on his face.

Ash pointed at him. "You sure can pick them, Cordy."

"I didn't pick him," she said exasperatedly. "He picked me. Hey, he saved my life twice now and yours, Ash."

Once the seatbelt sign was turned off and autopilot on, Ash and Cordy grabbed clean shirts. Their eyes filled with tears as they exchanged glances. The weight of Linda's death started to show, but neither Ash nor Cordy were ready to talk about it. The whole time they flew, Linda's name was never mentioned. Their blood stained clothes had said it all.

Lafitte's cell phone alarm clock went off; time to prepare for landing.

Cordy gently nudged the handsome Frenchman. She checked his bandage and the bleeding had stopped. He was still weak but his eyes assured her. "Ash, the most important thing you need to remember is never make fast or large moves. You're used to small engine planes and this jet will be landing at three to four times faster. We may over shoot the runway but don't worry. We will just go around for another try. If you fall short of the runway, that won't be good. Understand?"

Ash repeated the words, "Stick, rudder, and speed!"

"OK, let's get lined up on the runway. It will be the one on the right. Do you see it?" Jon positioned himself behind Ash.

Ash nodded, gripping the steering wheel tightly. "Yes, I got it. Stick, rudder, and speed!"

Jon whispered, "Cordy, you need to get in the back and strap in tight. This guy isn't giving me a lot of confidence."

Cordy sat in her seat and buckled up. Jon calmly instructed Ash in every move and like a team, the men worked together.

Ash took the challenge and landed the jet as smooth as silk. As soon as they pulled up to their gate, Cordy helped Jon get up. He wrapped his arm tenderly around her, feeling his way around her curvaceous back. He knew from experience to take advantage of any situation. The Frenchman wasn't dead but very much alive. Jon started to walk past Ash's backpack and reached down for it.

"I'll get that, Jon. Looks like you have precious cargo with your other hand." Jon winked at Ash and they exited the plane.

Ash went to stand but he couldn't; his legs started to shake uncontrollably. It took a few minutes before he could stand. The enormity of landing the jet had hit him. As he exited the plane, he patted Jennifer on the door and said, "That was quite a ride, lady."

Chapter 36

Linda's Memory

While on the plane, Cordy and Ash freshened up, disposing of their blood-soaked clothes. Jon had texted their measurements and had new clothes waiting for them. Jon demonstrated his eye for detail as everything fit Cordy and Ash perfectly. They then took a limo to George V hotel in Paris, where Jon had booked the Royal suite for the three of them. At their arrival, a valet opened the limo door.

Cordy, her hair in a chignon and sunglasses covering her face, stepped out first. She wore black skin-tight pants, a long-sleeved black silk shirt and a black and silver scarf around her neck. Ash's wardrobe was scaled up with the help of Jon. The handsome archeologist blended in fine with the other wealthy Parisian men in his black jeans, gray blazer and white linen shirt. Jon Lafitte sported Japanese denim jeans, a black T-shirt and a matching black slim-fit blazer that hid his injured arm. The bellhop showed them to their suite.

The elegant room was filled with white roses and gilded sumptuous antiques. The huge luxurious suite was divided into separate rooms for the three of them. The veranda held a wonderful view of the Eifel Tower. Chilled champagne awaited them along with French cheeses, breads, and crackers. A fruit bowl sat on the table with a card, compliments of the house.

Jon assured both of them. He checked the news. The Dark Watchers had done exactly as he said and cleaned up their mess. He held the newspaper and dropped it on the table. The front-page headline stared at them: 'Ambassador's young daughter caught in crossfire of drug deal gone wrong.' Both men involved shot each other in the head. Her funeral was attended by many of the friends she met in the diplomatic corps. Her parents expressed thanks to all those who sent their condolences. Jon had at first hesitated to show Cordy and Ash the paper but thought they needed to know. Sadness filled the room.

Linda's father knew they lived a dangerous life in the State department but had always thought it would be him, not his innocent daughter. Cordy brushed the tears off her cheeks thinking of how Linda's parents' loss was so hard to bear. Memories of the loss of her parents filled her mind and she excused herself to Ash and Jon.

She ran into the exquisite bathroom of marble and gold fixtures and proceeded to sob thinking of holding the dying teenager in her arms. Uriel promised she would be taken care of and she trusted him. Linda was so brave throughout the whole horrible shooting. It took all of her training from Master Wong to resume the inner calm she so cherished. Cordy remembered Linda's last words and she promised to heed her advice. She came out of her room and heard Jon and Ash talking.

Ash was not doing well either. He felt tremendous guilt and sorrow for the girl's parents. Linda wouldn't step down but had to help him. He knew how courageous and good-hearted she was. Ash vowed that he would do everything he could so her life wasn't lost in vain.

Jon decided it was time to bring out his family's secret weapons to fight de Villiers and the Children of the Nephilim. He had some things of importance to show them. Cordy and Ash agreed to go with him just to get their minds off Linda.

Cordy texted Bob and asked him to do something for her parents and for Linda's memory. He texted her back and told her he was on it. Her friend was relieved she was alive and all right. Bob planned to set up a trust for Linda's family and a college scholarship fund under her name for those children in the diplomatic corps. Bob used Ash's and Cordy's names in the condolence card.

Cordy looked at the pale wounded man sitting in the chair. "First things first Jon, we need to fix you up before we go anywhere. Ash help get him to his room. I need to look at that wound."

Both of them aided Jon and placed him on the bed. Ash decided to let Cordy work on him while he gathered more information. The weak Frenchman smiled at the idea of having such a beauty for his doctor even though she was a pet doctor.

He whispered. "Think of me as one of your devoted loving pets, I'm sure you will give me a pet now and then. I'll be glad to give you a kiss in return."

Cordy smiled. "You want to know the surgery I perform most on pets, Jon."

"What is your specialty, my sweetheart?" Jon said in a seductive voice.

"Cutting balls off of males and neutering them. I suggest you better remember that and behave."

Ash chuckled as Jon's eyes opened wide.

CHAPTER 37

Pillow Talk

To say the potential of Ash and Cordy's death became more a possibility with each passing day they possessed the Keys of Life, and the reality of everything all hit home. Danger surrounded them and lurked in the shadows. He checked all the news outlets for anything more on Linda's death. Ash witnessed the power of the Dark Watchers. They could control the news and soon Linda's death became old news. He did find other news on the television.

A reporter announced a breaking news report of a New York skyscraper burning and reports of a missing CEO and president. The corporations represented by the huge hedge fund stocks tumbled. Wall Street reacting at the news saw a crash of the Nephilim's companies and many filed for bankruptcy. Ash knew Cordy's and her grandfather's companies' stock soared on the news. Ash smiled to himself. Bob's strategy worked. He didn't know why the skyscraper was going up in flames but he had a feeling Bob and Julia were behind it. The Nephilim's empire burning to ashes sounded good to him. How many innocents like Linda died at their hands?

Cordy was in Jon's room getting him settled. Ash walked in and looked at a recovering wounded Jon. He saw a handsome, tricky Frenchman milking it for all he could.

Ash asked. "Will he live?"

Cordy's frustration showed. "The bullet went in and out but I still feel some metal. It's got to come out and he won't let us call a doctor."

Jon smiled, "Why should I call a doctor when I have two doctors right here. Let's see, one is a veterinarian and the other is a rock doctor. No offense, Ash, I know you have done more digging but I'm going to go with the vet. My only request is for no cutting of the family jewels. I'm rather attached to them."

Cordy gave Ash a list of things to get at the nearest drug store. He was gone only a short time. When he returned Cordy had fallen asleep sitting in the chair next to Jon. Jon held her hand with his eyes closed.

Ash thought Jon played the sympathy card well. "Let the games begin!" he announced. "I have everything you need." Cordy woke up and didn't hear his sarcasm. "What do you need me to do?"

Jon's eyes met his. "I'm going to need a big shot of scotch before we start." Cordy nodded for Ash to pour him one. She cleaned the wound and grabbed the forceps waiting for the Frenchman to prepare himself. Jon nodded and she pushed the instrument in while Jon tried to keep still and yelled a few curse words.

Cordy did great. She pulled the bullet fragment out in seconds and then grabbed Ash to the side and whispered, "I'm going to let you dress the wound. I know you've the power to help heal him so I'm asking you to do me a favor and help him." Ash looked at Cordy and nodded he wasn't going to refuse her anything nor could he. "Well I am exhausted I'm headed to bed. Ash, will you finish up?"

Ash replied sarcastically. "Ya, I'll finish him off." Cordy gave him a scolding look. "Come on Frenchy, let's get that wound bandaged." Ash placed his hand on Jon's forearm and on the back of the injured shoulder. "I'm just seeing if everything is in alignment." Ash closed his eyes, "I can feel your shoulder is out of place. Let me put some pressure on the front and see if it will go back- in-place."

Jon felt a strange feeling over his body. "Can you really fix it? I'm feeling a bit woozy."

Ash assured him. "I can fix almost anything. It's important that you believe that I can. When I was in Egypt on many dig sights the most common injury was dislocated shoulders. Actually, Jon, yours was not out of place just sore. I guarantee you'll feel like a new man in the morning."

"Thanks, Ash, you're OK. I think we've got a lot in common."

When he came out of Jon's room Cordy sat in her nightgown reading the newspaper about Linda's death. As soon as she said the word "Linda" she fell apart. It tore right through Ash, and they both embraced and started to cry. Ash poured some whiskey in a glass and told Cordy to take a drink. He just drank from the bottle not one but two large pulls. He walked Cordy to her bed, pulled down the sheets, and tucked her in. He bent over and kissed her forehead. "Cordy, get some sleep. You're exhausted."

He pulled up a chair and sat next to the bed. "I'll stay with you until you fall asleep. My mom always said things will look better in the morning. I hope for our sakes it will be true." They spoke not another word but the tears that ran down both their cheeks said it all. Besides, Ash wasn't going to leave Cordy alone with the wounded wolf in the room next to hers. They both held each other's hand tenderly and a silence filled the room.

CHAPTER 38

The Other Woman

Jon passed out after Cordy and Ash took the fragment out and dressed his arm. He fell into a deep sleep and a lovely vision of a woman dressed in white appeared. Her perfect form could be seen when the light shone through her thin silk robe.

"Jon, wake up!"

He didn't want to wake up for he was very weak.

"No, leave me alone, chérie, but before you go tell me who you are?"

The vision's lips laid a trail of light kisses along his neck. Her seductive voice filled his ears. "My name is the Guardian and you must tell Cordy and Ash about the secrets your family has kept all these years. It's time to reveal the Forevers' treasure. Earth and her children are in terrible trouble. You must reveal your family secrets to the Pure of Heart, Ash and Cordy. Wake up, courageous Jon!"

He opened his heavy eyes in the dark bedroom and he spotted a bright light coming from a backpack on the chair. Jon thought, *what the hell is that?* It was quiet throughout the suite. Ash and

Cordy were sleeping soundly in each of their rooms or so he hoped. His curiosity pushed him on. The bright light beckoned him. Jon asked himself if he was hallucinating. If so, calling out for help was out of the question. An image flashed through his mind of Ash and Cordy in bed busy with other pleasures. No sound of bouncing bedsprings came from their rooms. What a shame. Jon wondered for a second if they were lovers and had slept with each other in the past. The magnificent Cordy wouldn't be sleeping if Jon had her in his bed! The light got brighter and filled his room. The fascinated Frenchman stumbled over toward the backpack.

"Don't be afraid, Jon," a familiar gentle voice said as he opened it up. "I promise I won't bite you," the gentle voice teased.

"I'm not afraid, just worried that I'm dreaming or going crazy. All right, I will take a look at you. Your voice tempts me and I must see you. I hope I'm not opening Pandora's Box." He pulled out the bright crystal ball and there before him shone the Guardian's beautiful face smiling at him.

Jon smiled back at her and was mesmerized by her face. She was the mysterious woman in his dream.

"How like a man to think of sex at a time like this. I've found men think of sex almost every five minutes. I need you to focus on the serious task ahead. The whole Lafitte family story needs to be explained to Ash and Cordy. They don't understand. It's your job to reveal the truth."

The sleepy handsome man wondered how she read his mind and figured her powers not to be underestimated.

"What does the Guardian do?" asked Jon.

"She guards and defends Terra, or as you call her, Earth. I was left by the Forevers to keep the balance. Terra's children are in grave danger. You must obtain the Forevers treasures soon for a terrible storm brews. I've seen that you are now the head of your devoted family. It is now your responsibility to keep the powerful gifts of the Forevers safe. If you need me, just call me and I will come. Now sleep, Jon, for tomorrow is a big day. Oh, by the way, Ash and Cordy slept in separate bedrooms tonight." She gave him a knowing wink.

The light dimmed and disappeared. Jon sat in the dark holding the crystal ball.

He whispered into the darkness, "Well, I'll be damned! Wait a minute! Come back! What did you mean I was head of the family?"

Ash and Cordy flipped on the lights in the room and saw Jon talking to the crystal ball.

"Who are you talking to?" asked Cordy.

Jon looked at them with a puzzled look "The Guardian and she told me I must help you."

Ash and Cordy looked at each other and decided right then and there they probably had a partner. The Guardian recruited Jon like it or not.

"C'mon, Jon, try to get some more sleep." Cordy gently wrapped her arm around him and guided him back to his bed.

Jon smiled. "Why don't you keep me company and warm my cold bed?" He lifted the covers for her to jump in.

Cordy chuckled, but Ash gave him a stern look. "I don't think so. If you're cold I'll get you another cover. You need to get some rest."

Jon fell into bed and said in a seductive voice, "The Guardian told me that Ash and you slept in separate bedrooms. What a waste of a romantic night in Paris. I'd keep you entertained all night, Cordy. We could have a menage à trois, if you wish. Think about it." Jon teased Ash and winked.

"Over my dead body," Ash's angry voice shot back.

Jon looked over at him. "I could arrange that very easily."

Cordy held up her hands. "Now, boys, settle down. Ash, cut it out. He's still doped up from the meds I gave him. He's delirious."

Jon lay there on the bed, eyes closed, quietly passed out. She looked back at the sleeping Frenchman and placed the blanket over him. Jon Lafitte had troublemaker written all over him.

CHAPTER 39

Wicked Frenchman

Jon woke up in the morning, surprised that his arm was feeling so much better. He smiled when he thought about Ash's jealousy. A little mischief can't hurt. It makes life exciting. Adventure filled his days and the Frenchman never bored. Women fell all over him but not Cordy. The feisty Jon loved a challenge. He remembered a certain excitement when their lips met. Jon saved her from drowning in the frigid dark waters of the sea. The Guardian knew him well for he already envisioned a passionate Cordy begging him to make love to her. What did the vision tell him? Focusing, he reluctantly left the dreamlike vison and made a list in his mind of what he must do.

The Guardian wanted him to guide them, so a tour of France was in order. His family history was not easily told. Jon's family had many loyal friends here, and he could protect them better in France. It's why they came to Paris. His powerful network here would keep them safe. He moved his wounded arm slowly and pulled the covers off with his good arm.

Jon rose from his bed tentatively and started a hot shower. It felt wonderful as the water dripped on his back and his muscles relaxed. The dried blood washed away, and he examined his wound in the mirror. A shocked face looked back at him. It's healed! He realized at that moment that Cordy had an incredible gift for healing and it wasn't just for animals. Every time the gorgeous woman crossed mind a desire filled him and his chest tightened. He heard her anxious voice calling. He'd left the bathroom door open.

"Jon, where the hell are you?" Cordy's worried voice traveled through the bedroom. She saw the bathroom door open and ran in. Jon stood naked in the shower, singing a lusty French love song in the steamy mist.

Cordy's eyes drank in the muscular physique of the handsome man. The water sparkling over his body enhanced the magnetism of him and his dark eyes. Jon's lusty eyes met hers. He knew when a woman admired his allure. The mischievous man wanted to have a little fun and stir up some trouble. Life wasn't worth living if you didn't have unpredictable adventures. His seduction would start now.

"I can't reach my back to clean the blood off. Will you help me Cordy? My sore arm can't reach back there."

Jon issued her a challenge. Cordy had never run from anyone and she wasn't going to start now, especially from a wicked Frenchman. If she ran away then, she knew he'd take it as fear that she'd succumb to his charms. His intense black eyes stared into Cordy as he held the soap out to her hand. He turned his naked wet back to her and she opened the shower door slowly. The bar of soap she held in her hand glided over the hard muscles of his back. A blushing Cordy rubbed gently and slowly. He had the body of a Greek sculpture and his thick, dark shoulder-length hair gave him a timeless look. Jon kept singing his French love song. His voice was rich and seductive. Cordy thought, *women must fall over themselves with such a sly devil*, as she enjoyed rubbing his back with the fragrant lavender soap.

He turned around in all his naked glory and Cordy's eyes looked at the wall. Jon's voice was soft and sincere whispering into her ear,

"Thank you Cordy for taking such good care of me. I feel like a new man. The Guardian wants me to guide you, and I'll show you Paris through the Lafitte family's eyes." He picked the soap from her hand.

"Paris awaits you."

Ash yelled anxiously, "Cordy, where are you?"

Jon yelled back. "She's in the shower with me. Come join us!"

Ash flew into the steamy room looking at Cordy with a murderous gaze.

"I...I.. was scrubbing his back. He couldn't reach it with his sore arm," stuttered Cordy.

Ash crossed his arms over his chest. "Room service brought up breakfast. Jon looks like he's much better."

Jon heard the word breakfast and he shut the steamy water off.

"Breakfast! Wonderful news! I'm ravenous!" His eyes feasted on the blushing Cordy.

Cordy decided it was best to leave while the steam covered the room. Her eyes never ventured downward. Ash threw him a towel.

"Don't expect us to dry your back. The fun is over."

Jon winked. "Oh, no, Ash. The fun is just starting."

Ash and Cordy looked at each other as they left the Frenchman.

Ash whispered, "Jon appears to be feeling no pain and is all healed up. "

Cordy laughed as she sat at the breakfast table filled with flowers and delicious food. "He looks like he's back in the saddle again and quite feisty."

Jon came over to the table, still drying his curly hair with a towel. He kissed Cordy on the cheek, taking her by surprise. She smelled his Middle East spiced aftershave, and she blushed again when she felt his goatee brush her face. "Thank you so much for caring for me, mon chérie. I am hungry enough to eat even you, sweet Cordy," Jon whispered, loud enough for Ash to hear. Cordy was speechless for a second. Ash threw a croissant straight at Jon's face as he sat down but Lafitte's quick reflexes caught the croissant with his good arm before it hit the target. "Ah, Ash is jealous that I have not thanked him for healing me and saving us. Merci! I love croissants, by the way. How thoughtful you are. You must understand, Ash and Cordy, that we are in Paris. Frenchmen kiss everybody." Jon buttered the croissant and drank some champagne. "Let us toast Paris, and the adventure ahead."

CHAPTER 40

Napoleon's Secret Possessions

Jon opened up the window of their suite and pointed to the Eiffel Tower. The bustling city of Paris could be viewed from their balcony. "At night," Jon told them, "The tower will light up with golden triangles interconnected within its steel structure. The golden triangle symbolizes the Great Architect of the Universe for the Freemasons and Christianity." He watched Cordy's and Ash's faces as he said golden triangles. Both Ash and Cordy glanced at each other and thought, *Does he know?*

"I have other important places for you to see. I knew both of you would appreciate the view. Paris can be a dangerous place if you are not careful so we must be equipped for trouble." He placed before them a steel suitcase with different weapons. Jon smiled.

"Ladies first, I insist."

Cordy picked a Glock-19 and an X26 Taser. "Oh goodie, I'll take these." She placed them in a shoulder holster over her dark blue turtleneck sweater and put on her navy wool jacket, and then her camel-hair coat. The Missouri country girl felt comfortable with guns because her father had taught her how to shoot at an early age. Her aim was precise.

Ash, dressed in gray jeans and a white turtleneck, looked at the Glock 18 and placed it in the hidden pocket inside his black leather jacket. Ever since the archeologist started this journey, guns seemed to be a necessity. Although he was a quick learner and a natural fighter, the archeologist was still better at using his fists than guns.

Jon, dressed all in black, picked up his favorite Beretta 92 FS Brigadier and gently placed it in his shoulder holster. The Frenchman's military training was reflected in his knowledge of each gun. His killing of the agents in the lobby of the hotel in Ireland demonstrated his skill.

"We are now ready to take a tour of Paris, and I'll explain how the Lafitte family plays their part in this ancient war. I assure you both that this Lafitte tour is one of a kind. We must always be on alert. A limo and its driver, one of my trusted men, await us downstairs."

Ash, Cordy and Jon sat in the limo as he began to tell his family story.

"My family has always been full of rebels and privateers. I admit, my ancestors could be ruthless and greedy bastards. The Dark Watchers utilized our talents. Our allegiance is to our family and my grandfather heads the corporation. Poppa Jon has slowly brought our family business back into legitimate trade so our smuggling days will soon be over. My father was assassinated when I was a child. We know being a member of the Dark Watchers doesn't usually guarantee a long life. I attended university and received my degree in astronomy and physics. The government recruited me to be an agent for Interpol. They found my contacts with NASA and the military valuable." He showed Cordy and Ash his Interpol security badge. "My military training kept my family and me alive. Dark Watchers have embedded themselves in almost all governments and secret societies. I'm an example of one of them. We often work with both sides, the Nephilim and the Light

Watchers, but one thing is certain. We never play by their rules, but follow our own.

"Through the centuries, the Watchers, both Light and Dark, infiltrated many companies' boardrooms and their members were placed in high positions all over the world. Our men controlled many news agencies. We have alliances with some of the Light Watchers like your grandfather, Bill. Your little friend Linda died, a sad casualty of this war. We're dealing with very ruthless people here and de Villiers is the worst one. He's positioned himself as leader of the Dark Watchers. My family knows he is a traitor and he set us up to be killed in Nova Scotia. His henchmen planned to kill all of us and take the Pure of Heart treasures. I admit, a good plan to get rid of one of his competitors for leading the Dark Watchers but with your help, he didn't succeed." Ash and Cordy's mouths dropped open at all the information.

"I see you're surprised that I'm a scientist. You thought I was just a pretty-faced thug like the rest of the secret agents." He enjoyed the surprised looks on their faces.

"My family needed me to help run the businesses. We've grown very dissatisfied with the Dark Watchers' agenda and our rising leader named de Villiers. I've never met such a ruthless, power-hungry leader and believe me when I say I've met many greedy bastards. The world news is reporting today that many of the Nephilim's corporations have gone bankrupt and their headquarters destroyed. Your friends Bob and charming Ellen managed to destroy the Nephilim's power base leaving them shattered. De Villiers wants to gather these loose ends and unite them with the Dark Watchers. He's truly a mastermind of deceit and, I believe, a mad man. I don't trust him and my grandfather could be in great danger right now. I've had no calls returned from him for hours."

"I met de Villiers at his art restoration shop in St. Louis looking for the meaning of the symbolism of the hands on Magdalene's statue at the school. He gave me the Wishing Cup and a box with a golden triangle for curing his cat. You're right, he's the puppet master setting up a chain of events. He acted very weird that day. De Villiers knew how dangerous the Wishing Cup was. He never warned me," Cordy said.

Jon grinned at Cordy. The golden triangles were legendary. He discovered them after he searched their bags while they slept, looking for the crystal ball.

"I've seen his cat Isis on his desk. Many sorcerers use cats as their familiars. He named her Isis after the Egyptian goddess of magic. His actions set into motion the Pure of Heart coming into contact with the Guardian. I was hired by the Nephilim's agent Ellen, whom you all know, to assist in the capture of your ship, but I noticed the McDermott pin on Cordy's shirt. Our family owes a debt going far back thanks to one of my notorious relatives, the pirate Jean Lafitte. Your family saved his life, and ever since, we have abided by our vow to assist your family, so that changed everything.

"My family is going to have to vote on de Villiers' proposed merger soon. The vote should be already over. We have had no word from Poppa Jon, my grandfather. I don't think he realized you both possessed golden triangles, which together form the Star of David. These sacred objects possess great powers and only a Pure of Heart can handle them. De Villiers used the Wishing Cup to test Cordy. He's made a big mistake using Ellen to kill you. She recruited me in Nova Scotia to help her and that's when I realized he was after the Pure of Heart treasures. The ruthless bastard wanted me dead, too."

Ash asked, "What's his agenda?"

Lafitte stared at him intensely, "He desires complete power over the world and to build a super race to command. You've heard the legends about giants? He wants to bring them back, but instead of the giants going extinct, mankind will. The Nephilim created a program cloning Neanderthal males for a secret shadow army. They will be programmed to obey only his orders. He also wants possession of all the Pure of Heart treasures. My family is in great danger but so is the world. He's a very clever mad man. Did you drink from the Wishing Cup?"

Ash and Cordy nodded.

"You both lived and so maybe your wishes will come true."

"My great-grandfather Chief Saunhac died to save a Pure of Heart being used by both the Nephilim and de Villiers. Sometimes a pawn in a chess game can turn into a powerful queen. The chief knew how to play the game of war. Ellen possessed the power to destroy the Nephilim," Cordy whispered.

"Some treasures are cursed. The Wishing Cup is one of them. You're both lucky you're alive. Unfortunately, the chief died, but my grandfather said he was a very honorable and wise man."

Cordy's warm voice answered, "Thanks to you for coming to our rescue."

Lafitte's sad face looked at her. "I wish I could have saved Linda too. The little girl died for no reason. The bastard will pay for her death. I promise you."

The limo drove past a large church and Jon pointed to the older church made of white stone. He ordered the driver to stop for a moment so they could see it from the car.

"Saint Sulpice, do you remember the name?"

Ash and Cordy glanced at the church and then Cordy answered.

"In Montreal, we saw the Sulpician Seminary. I remember taking a picture of it next to the Notre Dame Basilica. Ash and I met each other there for the first time." Her warm eyes met Ash's for a second.

A picture of the iron gate with the golden triangles logo flashed through Ash's mind. "I remember you told me about a Bishop Dubourg who trained at Saint Sulpice Seminary in Paris and played a part at the Miraculous Medal Shrine near your family farm. He escaped France by boat to America from the revolutionaries who wanted to kill him. The Sulpician-trained priest taught at Georgetown University and knew George Washington."

Jon pulled out pictures of a carved marbled *Pieta* of Magdalene, Jesus, and Mary, another of an angel wrestling with Jacob, and the last one of a pulpit with a golden triangle with golden light beams spreading outward above on the roof. All of these objects resided in Saint Sulpice.

"Bishop Dubourg played an interesting part in history. He became the Bishop of New Orleans and all Louisiana territories. The painting of the angel battling Jacob by Delacroix is important. It refers to a story in the Bible. Jacob saw a stairway, which angels used to go to heaven and then back down to earth. He lay his head on the stone and saw the vision in his dream. The stone was called the Stone of Scone and is revered by the Scots. They believe the stone must be sat on for the true king to be recognized. The Scots treasure the Stone of Scone and no jewel or crown in the world was as important to them. One more thing, Saint Sulpice has is a gnomon, a piece of a sundial made by the clockmaker Henry Sully. It uses the sun to help calculate time. I want you to remember these because in our travels you'll see their importance. "

Ash thought of Uriel when he saw the Delacroix painting of Jacob wrestling a red-haired angel. He recalled his vision of the red haired angel in a black leather jacket drinking whiskey and warning him of the danger ahead. Abu Simbel's temple builders thought sun position important also, and it was there he found the golden ankhs called the Keys of Life. The Egyptian obelisk of Saint Sulpice reminded him about the connection to Egypt's temples. The *Pieta* reminded Ash of the assassination through time of the Pure of Heart. Jon motioned to the driver to move on.

"Ahh, we're here. Let me show you another man who had the same ambition as de Villiers long ago. His name was Napoleon. We're at Les Invalides, his tomb."

The limo pulled up to a complex of buildings. In the middle was a large building with a dome.

Ash and Cordy followed Lafitte.

"France's military heroes are buried here. Napoleon rose to power after a coup d'etat occurred. Betrayal gained him his position of power. He conceived grand ideas for France to rule the world. Like de Villiers, he searched for powerful ancient treasures. One time, in Aachan's cathedral, he ordered the monks to open the tomb of Charlemagne and give his wife Josephine a sacred necklace found in the tomb. He hunted down and confiscated any sacred treasure he could get his hands on. Like Napoleon, de Villiers believes these objects are so powerful that he can't be defeated if he possesses them.

"A brilliant military strategist, Napoleon invaded Italy. Along the way, he grabbed priceless artifacts and plundered the Vatican. He took Pope Pius VI as prisoner but he died shortly afterward. Napoleon realized the Church would be a better ally than an enemy. After he confiscated Rome's treasures, he decided to use the Church to his advantage by being crowned as Emperor.

"Napoleon came into possession of secret knowledge and certain ancient treasures. I told you to beware of treasures cursed with evil. Napoleon wanted to rule the world, so he possessed some of these. He obtained from the Vatican Judas' 30 silver coins. You remember the Carravagio painting of *The Taking of Christ* that we saw in Dublin? De Villiers owns a copy of it and placed it in the meeting room of the Dark Watchers.

"The Wishing Cup came into his possession later, from his adventures in Egypt. Like Napoleon, he's used war and chaos to acquire sacred relics. His obsession to rule the world corrupted his mind. I told you only a Pure of Heart can handle the immense power; otherwise, men go mad and arrogant with their power. He's an example."

They walked up the stairs and a statue of Napoleon in his uniform with his hand hidden under his coat looked down at them.

Ash said, "He wasn't content with plundering the Vatican, was he?"

Lafitte smiled. "No, his ambition grew and grew."

"He headed for the treasures of Egypt," Ash added. "French scientists and mathematicians joined him and they found the greatest treasure of Egypt. "

Lafitte looked at Ash. "Oui, the Rosetta Stone."

"Colonel Hautpoul and Lieutenant Bouchard discovered the stone's inscriptions on the back and wrote Napoleon about the discovery," Ash explained to Cordy. "The French found it but the English took it as plunder for winning the war in London."

"It took a French man to translate the stone later on and it opened up major discoveries in Egypt. De Villiers sought the hiding place for the Keys of Life but was unable to find them. I believe someone in this room did." Lafitte smiled at the archeologist standing next to him.

"It was the inscriptions at Abu Simbel which helped Champollion decipher the stone," Ash answered. "I found the Keys of Life at Abu Simbel. I wonder if he hid them in the stone I found. Champollion died suddenly by a stroke but was probably assassinated. The secret died with him."

"Who killed him?" whispered Cordy.

Lafitte shrugged his shoulders.

"I doubt we'll ever discover who, but my guess would be the Dark Watchers. They want control of all of the Keys of Life. Ash got very lucky finding the treasure of a lifetime.

"Napoleon went next to Malta and captured the seaport city of the Knights Hospitallers. Malta was home to one Grandmaster Philippe de Villiers de L'Isle-Adam. He obtained Malta in the 1500s for the Hospitallers. Carravagio escaped to Malta and they revealed the Knights of Malta's secrets to him. It gets better — Malta has great megalithic temples. Legend has it that a great giantess and giants built the ancient stone temples located there. The Guardian has existed for a very long time, I think. Our families' history goes back to the Crusades and so does de Villiers'. Our bloodlines are interwoven through time like the hands on Magdalene and Jesus. We've been fighting this war for a very long time."

Ash and Cordy looked surprised. They both shouted, "Grandmaster de Villiers of the Hospitallers!"

Lafitte nodded. "De Villiers and Saunhac ancestors were elected as Knights of Malta in the past. All of our ancestors' paths connect with each other. The Guardian knows all of us."

Ash's face lit up. "The Hal Tarxian altar has the swirls symbolism like Newgrange. I bet the Guardian knows about Hal Tarxian. So it's true, de Villiers knows about the Guardian and the Keys of Life, probably from his parents."

Cordy whispered, "It's an ancient temple like Newgrange. The Guardian said they were throughout the world. De Villiers' family probably knew about the possibility of a technologically advanced civilization existed long ago like Atlantis. Let's face it, the Pure of Heart treasures are high tech. He wants control of the Keys of Life."

Lafitte looked at both of them. "Edgar Cayce, who had the gift of prophecy, believed one day man would find the ancient library of incredible knowledge. They used a laser to encrypt on the unique round crystal colored disk. Scientists just recently discovered that basically unlimited amounts of information can be placed on an indestructible quartz disk. The disk holds technological answers to all the problems plaguing mankind. The Guardian is the key."

Ash and Cordy told Jon about the quartz disk.

Jon replied, "De Villiers wants it all. He'll kill anyone who stands in his way."

Jon then pointed to Napoleon's sarcophagus. "The grave of Napoleon stands before you. This is where my family's adventure comes into play."

Napoleon's red quartzite tomb sat on a green granite base surrounded by angels and crown laurels with inscriptions.

Lafitte continued. "His ambition and arrogance grew after he became emperor. You know that only the Pure of Heart can possess these treasures. Historical records show Napoleon's greatest mistake was his military campaign into the cold Siberian winter. Madness of ambition descended on him. His arrogance and obsession for complete control destroyed him. He thought his army invincible."

Ash and Cordy looked at each other and said at the same time, "It was the Guardian who stopped him. She triggered the Siberian winter. Is it possible? He dragged his army into freezing weather and watched them die of hunger and disease. Does she have the power to control the weather?"

"Napoleon was captured and imprisoned on St. Helena Island. The former emperor became sicker and sicker. He refused to let his secret possessions land in the hands of the English. In New Orleans, some of his retired military men had talked about a rescue of the Emperor from the island. If you remember, Napoleon sold the Louisiana Purchase to Jefferson. The Napoleon House in New Orleans was built for the general by his friends. It still stands today. They decided Bonaparte might be too ill to travel but he'd given them a map showing where his treasures lay. The pirate Lafitte and his family would be entrusted to find and protect these precious riches."

Cordy's astonished look made Lafitte smile. "I thought that was a legend, but it's true."

"Oui, Jean Lafitte the wicked pirate and his loyal men went in the dead of night to St. Helena and obtained the treasure map from Napoleon."

"I thought the legend said the treasure map was all in Napoleon's head," Ash said.

Jon smiled like a Cheshire cat, "Oui, they brought him back with them."

CHAPTER 41

The Mystery of the Templar Preceptor Gerard de Villiers

De Villiers' steely eyes fixed their gaze on the portrait of one of his ancestors dressed in a knight's armor. Isis, his cat, followed his stare and he recited aloud his ancestor's story to his dubious companion. She would not interrupt his train of thought and appeared to listen with interest. How many times did his father drill into him his family's mysterious past? Too many. He listened to his father drone on about the Templar Preceptor who saved the Templars' sacred treasure from king and pope, and so Gerard de Villiers' name became his on birth in his honor. His parents checked his star charts with experts and saw he had incredible possibilities if he used his talents well. A dark shadow fell on one aspect of his horoscope in the House of Capricorn, which showed his fierce ambition could lead to disaster. Imbeciles didn't understand that with greatness comes power. He would become ruler of the world and even of the universe. His namesake was an ancient hero of the Dark Watchers. His story was known throughout their ranks, told to generation after generation. Light Watchers, too, knew the legend of the lost Templar treasure and how it escaped the grasp of the King of France. His father lectured him about how special his family history was and how honorable their task to get revenge on those who opposed their mission of being guardians of the Keys of Life. He petted Isis and began the tale.

"Once upon a time, Isis, there lived a great Templar knight named Gerard de Villiers, who lived during the unfortunate time of October 13, 1307. His noble family belonged both to the Templar and Hospitaller knightly orders. Tensions grew over the years between King Phillip IV and the Templars because of the huge debt he owed them. Instead of paying the large sum owed, the king planned to destroy and kill the Templars and steal their treasure.

"A few days earlier a secret urgent message came to Gerard by a Light Watcher named Joinville, one of the King's trusted advisors. He said the Grandmaster De Molay would be arrested at dawn on October 13. As Preceptor of France, Gerard was charged with protection of the Templar treasury. With incredible haste and stealth, Gerard managed to load all the treasures of the Templar bank and in the night, their ships left dock for the safest places they knew. De Molay had no idea where they escaped. Only Gerard knew.

"Each Templar family promised to guard their treasure. They departed carrying Templar riches brought back from the Holy Land during the Crusades. The Pope and King Phillip sent out emissaries all over Europe instructing monarchs of the countries to arrest and confiscate Templars and their land. If any were discovered, the Church ordered their arrest, and the Inquisition was to discover where their treasure was hidden. The navy of the Templars was lost in the dead of night, never to be seen again. The story became legend passed down from generation to generation.

"Each Templar family who survived vowed to protect certain articles given to them. His family vowed to protect and possess all of them. De Molay and his assistant Geoffrey de Charney were ordered by the Inquisition to burn at the stake for heresy. The legend tells of the curse given by De Molay at the burning stake to Pope Clement V and French King Phillip IV, who each saw their deaths follow his the next year. Centuries later, the Capetians witnessed the monarchy in France destroyed in the French Revolution. Rome's power grew weaker with the emergence of Protestantism. The Templar descendants never forgot the betrayal and his family looked for revenge against all who betrayed them.

"Templar Preceptor de Villiers would have his revenge. Gerard's minions poisoned both the King and the Pope and hid the treasure so no one would ever find it. Alas, some Pure of Heart who didn't trust de Villiers stole some of the Templar sacred treasures and hid them. The angry Templar Preceptor waged a battle to protect and find the lost treasure stolen by the Pure of Heart.

"The Shroud of Turin was long protected by the Templar family Charney, who revealed the mysterious relic to the public. It resides today in a cathedral in Turin, Italy. The Charney family happened to be a relative of Joinville, who played his part in protecting the cherished Templar treasury. Many believe the shroud shows an imprint of the face and body of Jesus Christ. Sacred and very powerful, the shroud was placed on sacred ground, which did not allow anyone to steal it, for the code of the Watchers abided by the law of sanctuary. My family today regrets its loss.

"Unfortunately, the most precious relics could only be held and operated by a Pure of Heart." De Villiers realized how valuable and rare a Pure of Heart could be if they survived. The chairman of the Nephilim saw the value of programming a Pure of Heart to obey his orders, hence Ellen. He initiated a futuristic agenda in which a few Pure of Heart would be controlled and programmed to do their bidding. They would be unaware of their status and hidden with new identities. If de Villiers could get his hands on Cordy and control her, then he could control the world.

The Mi'kmaq Chief Saunhac protected the relics passed down by his Templar ancestors, which now Cordy possessed. Sacred objects were found under the Temple Mount where the original Templars dug in the night. Some called them the Keys of Life left by Noah to help save the world from another disaster.

Only the Pure of Heart possessed the ability to hold them without dying. He spotted Cordy early on and suspected the aunt purposely changed the dates on her birth certificate to protect the little girl. Her astrological chart with her false birth dates revealed an insignificant life but her real birthdate identified her to be one of the greatest Pure of Heart of the Age of Aquarius. "The Nephilim didn't figure out their treachery but I did. I struck a deal with the nun to keep silent. Cordy would obtain the treasures my family desired over the centuries. The treacherous nun broke her promise to me which retribution was made. No one crosses me without punishment.

"We tested Cordy in Saint Louis, didn't we, Isis?" The cat purred softly. "She held the Wishing Cup and lived. Quite impressive, and I believe she drank from the cup which held honey from the Tree of Knowledge in the Garden of Eden. If she did, then her blood carries certain immunities and powers, which will open doors to which I want to gain entrance. Some talk about the legend of the Holy Grail and say the Wishing Cup in the proper hands possesses the same powers. Any other man would have died from the lethal poison. Cordy is our own female Galahad and our Joan of Arc, the purest knight living in our time." The cat purred louder and sat on his lap demanding he pet her.

He stroked the cat and whispered, "She passed our test with flying colors. I have great plans for Cordelia. Just wait and see. I'll make daddy very proud of us. The de Villiers family will once again be respected and feared throughout the world. We will have our revenge."

CHAPTER 42

Notre Dame and Saint Chapelle

Everyone climbed into the limo and Lafitte poured them all a glass of wine as they drove off.

"I think everyone needs a drink."

He handed Cordy and Ash their wine glasses. Both glanced at each other wondering why but decided to humor Jon.

Lafitte's telephone buzzed and he picked it up. His voice lowered to a whisper and he hung up quickly. He gulped down his wine, surprising both Ash and Cordy. Intuition told both of them the news received was very bad. Lafitte's gray eyes glistened with emotion as he slammed the glass down. His voice took a dark and angry tone.

"Poppa Jon is dead, shot in cold blood by de Villiers for abstaining in the vote for unification with the Nephilim." Jon's demeanor turned stiff and cold. His eyes gazed out the window, not ready to meet theirs. Lafitte tried to keep his emotions in check. His heart went cold. He hated de Villiers.

"He'll regret his dishonorable actions in killing a defenseless old man and an innocent young girl, I assure you. My family's gone into hiding for their safety. I'm now the head of the family. Poppa Jon wanted to retire. After all, our businesses were legitimate. He planned for me to take over afterward but now I see de Villiers planned to kill me in Nova Scotia using Ellen to lure me into his trap. His assassins didn't just have orders to kill you but also me. He must have heard about Poppa Jon's plans. My grandfather was very honorable and very popular with the other Dark Watchers. De Villiers plans to wipe my family off the face of the earth. Poppa Jon's retirement was scheduled for the end of the year. He warned me about de Villiers' desire for power. I regret not listening to him. I'll never underestimate the bastard again."

Ash and Cordy felt his sadness. Cordy placed her hand gently on his hand. "Don't blame yourself. No one could have known he would kill your grandfather. I didn't know he'd kill Chief Saunhac. We've got to stop this maniac."

Lafitte's sorrowful eyes stared at them. "We've all lost someone in this war. Let us visit Notre Dame, the cathedral where Joan of Arc was canonized as a saint. Joan's story remains an important one. Her story is all about courage. A Pure of Heart in every way, Joan saved France."

The gigantic cathedral bells rang when they walked in. Cordy could feel the bells resonating through the stone walls of the church. The energy within was like the one she had felt at Newgrange and Knowth in Ireland. The stained glass rose windows illuminated the room with colors of the rainbow. Glass mandalas shined down on the sacred space. The black and white tiled floor spread throughout the building. They were on sacred ground.

The statue of Joan of Arc stood before them. The young woman was dressed in the armor of a knight and carried a flag. Cordy gazed up as Jon reminded them of her history and pointed to the statue.

"Joan's story is of a peasant girl who followed her 'voices' and trusted her belief that France needed to be free. The legend of a Pure of Heart rising up to save mankind couldn't have a better parallel than the rising up of a country girl to be savior of France.

Joan's story is amazing in the fact that she was a peasant girl with no education. Just her faith and courage saved France from English rule. Under impossible odds, she achieved her goal. The statue shows her carrying only a lance, but in her visions, she carried a sword. The protectors knew Joan was a Pure of Heart. At Saint Catherine de Fierbois, Joan found a rusted sword with five crosses. A sword from Heaven, many have called it, as its power was immense. The legends talk about how mysterious events occurred when she found the sword at Saint Catherine's church with the help of her voices. Saint Catherine of Alexandria became one of the voices that Joan heard in her visions."

Ash's ears perked up. Saint Catherine of Alexandria Monastery was a safe haven for his family and a flash of the icon painting of the saint flooded his memory. Brother Michael showed it to him. In the painting, she sat on a throne while at her feet a crystal ball rested atop some books. He thought to himself that it was a painting of the crystal ball of the Pure of Heart and the Guardian.

Jon continued pointing at the statue. "Joan's story ended with being captured by the enemy and tried for heresy. She burned at the stake condemned by men whose affiliations belonged to injustice and evil. The agenda sound familiar. I brought you here because of the Guardian. She wanted to show you what a difference the Pure of Heart can make to change the world. Together, we fight for mankind."

Ash smiled looking up at the statue. "My father found protection at Saint Catherine's Monastery near Mount Sinai. Their libraries protect many ancient texts. I just remembered a painting I saw of Saint Catherine holding a crystal ball that contained a symbol for electromagnetic power of the atom. The Guardian activated the energy within the crystal ball and it looks like she's played a big part throughout history. After thinking about it, I'm not surprised one of Joan's voices was Saint Catherine, who was supposed to be a beautiful woman with vast superior knowledge. Hope is what Joan of Arc symbolizes. I know why the Guardian wanted us to see it."

Notre Dame's altar sat in the center, a stone sculpture *Pieta* of Mary and her son surrounded by a cherub angel and another angel.

Jon walked over to the candles people lit for special prayers. He handed Ash and Cordy a flaming candle. Jon placed the fire on two candles and said a prayer. Cordy and Ash realized Jon had a spiritual side to him.

"One candle is for Poppa Jon and the other candle is for the little girl, Linda. They sacrificed their lives for what they believed in. I pray that I can follow in their footsteps." Jon knelt with his head bowed. Cordy had a picture flash through her mind of a Templar knight resembling her great grandfather Saunhac kneeling at an altar. Kneeling next to him was Lafitte dressed in a knight's armor. Ash knelt next to Jon and lit a candle followed by Cordy.

They knelt together and held a moment of silence for all those who lost their life in the fight against evil. How many over time died to save mankind from self-destruction?

Cordy's hand shook as she lit another candle.

Ash whispered, "Who is that for?"

Cordy glanced at him with tears streaming down her cheeks. "I think Sister Agnes is gone too. In my heart, I know she's with my parents and the chief. All three of us have lost someone in the past few days."

"We're going to make sure their deaths were not in vain. There is always hope."

Ash tried to reassure her but she knew in her heart the reason Bob had not called her was because the little frail nun was gone.

Jon walked around the cathedral telling them the stories of weddings that took place within the cathedral, and even the President of France Francois Mitterrand's funeral mass.

Jon turned to Cordy. "You're from St. Louis, Missouri. The Saunhac family history begins here in France. One of your ancestors became a Grandmaster of the Templars who died in the Crusades with Saint Louis. His bravery in battle was well-known and written about in a Crusader knight's memoirs. Guilliame Saunhac protected the treasures of the Holy Land. The Crusades are an important part of history at our next stop."

They walked just a short way and arrived at the chapel of St. Louis. They avoided security by using the back door to the chapel.

It seemed Jon knew everyone in Paris. The chapel was breathtaking, filled with gold and colors of the rainbow. Saint Louis had been a collector of relics and treasures from the Holy Land. He bought the Crown of Thorns and the Holy Lance relics for a fortune.

"The ceiling is filled with painted stars and fleur de lis. During the Revolution, rebels sacked many churches and emptied them of their treasures. America became a safe haven for these lost relics and treasures rescued by the Pure of Heart. Important contacts made with those who could be entrusted with these treasures resulted in a loyal underground created to hide them. My family was part of that trusted underground. Napoleon knew we could be trusted. We aided the protection and transportation of these treasures. Our smuggling skills proved very useful. Who would ever think a Dark Watcher family could be trusted?"

Cordy held Jon's hand tenderly. "I trust your family with my life and so does the Guardian."

Jon kissed her hand and Cordy blushed.

Ash had to admit Jon was a charmer and a fighter.

The handsome archeologist wrapped his arm around Cordy protectively, looking straight at the conniving Lafitte. "I trust you about as far as I can see you."

Jon chuckled. "Smart man, Ash."

The stained glass windows depicted stories from the Bible and dated back to the 1200s. The windows started at Genesis and ended with the Apocalypse. His mother, Blanche Castile, held a place of honor in Saint Louis' chapel too. Ash picked out the menorah up on the window and the six pointed stars on the roof.

"Lots of Jewish symbolism throughout the church considering Louis wasn't very tolerant of them. But his mother allowed them some freedoms. Blanche of Castile's father educated his daughter in the Greek classics and believed the stars and the zodiac played an important part in our lives."

Jon pulled out from his pocket a photo from the illuminated manuscript titled "The Saint Louis' Bible" and showed Ash and Cordy.

Ash recognized it immediately. "It's the Great Geometrician!"

Cordy looked puzzled. "Who?"

Jon smiled. "He is the Great Architect. The creator of the universe, the architect, uses the compass held in his hand. Mathematics was considered by French monarchy to be divine sacred knowledge, only for the devoted few. They read Plato's and Pythagoras' teachings. St. Louis placed this knowledge in his Bible, as did his mother, Queen Blanche Castile, so that it would be passed onto their children. The psalters show monks looking at the stars and placing data within the books. St. Louis and his mother had great respect for the knowledge of astronomy and mathematics."

Cordy tilted her head. "I never thought of St Louis looking at God like that. I thought all astrology was forbidden by the Church but looking at the zodiac carved in stone and in the stained glass windows, maybe not for the French monarchy."

Ash's face lit up. "Did St. Louis discover sacred treasures on his Crusades or the Templars? Does the Guardian know?"

"Oui, Saint Louis was an architect and builder. He built the chapel to house these treasures. Later on, Freemasonry used the symbol of the all-seeing eye for the Great Architect and so do the Watchers. Saint Louis knew about the Great Geometrician and left a legacy for mankind in his bible and this church. Mathematics is a universal language that transcends time and space. Is it a coincidence in Exodus 3:14 that God says to Moses, "I am that I am?" And the number for Pi is 3:1415 to infinite? You can understand why God holds a compass and his sacred name is written in a golden triangle. Mathematics is the language of the universe." Cordy looked up and gazed at the ceiling filled with hundreds of golden Stars of David. She placed her hand on her silver chain which dangled Saunhac's ring. The symbol carved on the ring hung above her head.

Jon looked at his watch. "Time for us to go back to the hotel and have some lunch. I have to call my family to check on their safety and see if any updates occurred of late."

They headed for the limo and while walking Ash felt eyes were watching them everywhere. He caught in his line of vision two tall men dressed in black walking toward them. Jon stopped for a second to tie his shoe and glanced back to see the two coming up behind them. Cordy looked back at Jon and he gave her a look of warning. Jon started angrily speaking in French, accusing Ash of taking his woman. He caused a commotion by shoving Ash and drew passerbyers' attention. Ash got the message and so when the two men approached closer, he shoved Jon. Lafitte kept arguing loudly at him and Ash clenched his fist turned as if he were going to punch Jon in the face. Instead, Ash clobbered one of the men in the stomach and the other in the face. Jon hit the man behind them, and Cordy kicked the other thug in the stomach, doubling him over. The limo screeched up close to them with Jon's man aiming his gun at the men on the ground. The trio jumped into the limo. The group of thugs recovered only to watch them drive away. They didn't dare open fire in such a public place.

"Good job, Ash. You're not a good marksman but your fists can pack a punch."

"Dark Watchers?"

"Oui."

His trusted driver drove on. Cordy smiled. "They're getting pretty daring out in public like that but they got the message. I think we make a formidable team."

Jon flashed a news report on his cellphone to Ash and Cordy. The latest update coming from Egypt concerned the Great Pyramid of Giza. A humming of a low vibration was reported by archeologists to be emanating from the pyramid, causing the academic world to panic. Scientists said the source of the frequency appeared to be the newly discovered Queen's chamber. "Everyone is abuzz wondering what activated the humming and why it's continuing. The pyramid is supposed to be a tomb, not a generator."

Ash and Jon both glanced at each other and Ash said, "The Guardian awakened the sleeping giant. I wonder what's coming. I've got a bad feeling about it."

Jon grabbed his phone back and scanned incoming information from NASA where he worked from time to time on small projects for the ISS. Information showed a discovery by Spanish astronomers of a possible dwarf planet 10 times the size of Earth, found next to Pluto. Many changes were happening — the temperature on Jupiter and Mars had also been dropping in the past days. "NASA documents show a disturbance in our solar system. Whatever it is, it's affecting Earth, too."

Ash, Cordy, and Jon shook their heads. The archeologist asked,

"What's the Guardian up to? The Great Pyramid is all about mathematics. You think the Guardian activated the Great Pyramid at the same time as we did at Knowth?"

"I think she's trying to save the world and she needs the Keys of Life to come together," Jon said, sounding concerned. "The Forevers left them to save mankind from extinction just like Noah was saved from the Great Flood. One more stop before we get to the hotel. "

The limo stopped near a Carmelite convent next to Montmartre's Sacre Coeur. The all-white church stood on the highest hill of Paris. Its name honored the Sacred Heart.

"Don't you think it's appropriate to use the name Sacred Heart for the symbol of the Pure of Heart?" Jon asked. "Follow me. I want to show you something." Jon opened the car door and motioned them to follow him.

An elderly nun opened the convent door and Lafitte whispered in her ear. She quietly directed Jon to a stairwell and into a crypt below the chapel. Cordy noticed the statue of Our Lady with a rose in a vase. She touched the miraculous medal that hung around her neck and with it, the ring with the Seal of Solomon. She thought of Sister Agnes and started to realize the sisters knew about the Keys of Life and protected them. The nun hurried off to prayers leaving them alone in the crypt.

"St. Louis brought some of the hermits from Mount Saint Carmel during the Crusades here and he established Carmelite houses throughout Europe. This is one of them. The sisters produced a trusted highway to transport sacred treasures through the world. My family worked with them for centuries. Follow me."

Jon carried a knapsack on his shoulder. They headed down into the crypt, which led into a dark tunnel. Ash felt comfortable for the first time in Paris. An archeologist knows tombs and this crypt was an ancient one. He could smell death in the damp dark air below.

They progressed down narrow stone steps and pitch black darkness engulfed them. A tiny flashlight flipped on from Jon's hand and heaviness filled the damp chilly air. A mouse scurried over Cordy's foot. Ash avoided the creature by shifting to the other side of the wall.

As she turned suddenly, a large human skull stared at her. Cordy sucked some air in surprise at the sight. "OK, I'm creeped out down here."

Jon placed his arms around her to calm her, and Ash wished he had thought of it first. Damn, the Frenchman was good. Cordy moved away slowly from the huge skull.

"I'm sorry. What are we doing here?" She wondered. Ash felt right at home and answered her question quickly.

"My father took me to Mount Carmel, and we visited the Stella Maris. He told me the same story as Jon did. Mount Carmel is a sacred place, home to the Essenes from Nazareth called Nazarenes. Elijah, and Pythagoras studied there. A big Neanderthal burial ground lies in a cave there, too. I think our early ancestors play a role in this. We're in a crypt." Ash observed the wall filled with skulls and bones lying in the open on top of one another.

Two tunnels going in opposite directions led from the crypt. A large skull stood watching them on the wall. Jon picked it up.

Lafitte said, "The tunnels lead to Sacre Couer's crypt and Saint Denis. In fact a tunnel system runs through Paris. Only a few know the labyrinth exists under the ground. Ash, take a look at this skull and see if you notice anything."

Ash observed the large skull, recognizing it immediately.

"Neanderthal, I bet. Their craniums were larger than Homo sapiens. What a perfect place to keep a Neanderthal skull in hiding. No one would notice it in a crypt. The latest research finds our extinct ancestor might've been much smarter than we thought. They buried their dead, painted pictures, and some mated with Homo sapiens. Some of us carry their DNA in our blood. Why is de Villiers interested in the Neanderthal? "

Jon bowed his head in respect. "Well done, Ash. Some would call them giants or the Children of the Nephilim. They went extinct. De Villiers wants to resurrect the Neanderthals. Giants return for revenge. He's cloned them with the help of the Nephilim. I've seen their laboratory. Mankind is on the extinction list next if he gets his way. St. Louis found the large skull at Mount Carmel and recognized it was a giant. The Templars transported the skull and placed it in the crypt. He probably thought he could have been a relative and who knows he might have been. Many said Louis IX stood over six foot tall, like his uncle Richard the Lionheart. They would have been considered giants in those days. We're taking the skull and the Book of Enoch with us." He removed a stone from the crypt's wall and inside the crevice pulled out an ancient scroll wrapped in a cloth. Another gem brought back from the Holy Land. He placed them in his knapsack.

Cordy said, "De Villiers gave me the Book of Enoch in St. Louis too, with the Wishing Cup."

A familiar voice echoed from the darkness of the cave. "A gift for a beautiful Pure of Heart. We meet again, Cordelia. Don't move if you want to live."

Out of the darkness strode de Villiers, all in black, as two of his men pointed guns at their heads. Cordy, Ash, and Jon put their hands up. She recognized him as the mysterious store manager who gave her the cursed Wishing Cup. She felt even sorrier for his cat, Isis.

De Villiers smiled. "I'll take the book and the skull, please, Jon. You stand accused of the crime of traitor to the Dark Watchers and the evidence is revealing our secrets to the Pure of Heart. The penalty for that is death."

"I want you to take these two," he ordered the men, pointing to Ash and Cordy, "and put them in the car. I've got a few surprises for them. As far as Jon goes, I'll take care of him personally."

"Did you order the killing of the young girl in Ireland?" Ash asked. "If you did, I'm going to make you regret the day you were born."

De Villiers smiled. "Yes, I did. No one stands in my way, not even little girls. Take them away. And if they give you any trouble, kill them."

The two men pushed Cordy and Ash to the front. One of the men aimed his gun at them while walking behind the pair, while the other grabbed Cordy's wrist, pulling her down the dark abyss. Ash followed with a gun pointed at his head. They disappeared into the darkness with Cordy yelling as he dragged her along. "Don't kill him, please." She hoped someone would hear her call for help.

De Villiers pointed the gun at Jon's head. "Any last words?"

"Did you kill Poppa Jon?"

"Yes, and after you, Sam is next on the list," de Villiers said.

Jon watched carefully as a little mouse that had crossed Ash and Cordy's path in the tunnel swiftly moved onto de Villiers' shiny black shoes and then went up his pants leg.

"Ha ha ha the, joke is on you, de Villiers," Jon chuckled.

A suspicious look fell on De Villiers face, and he wondered why Lafitte laughed at this desperate moment. The little mouse scurried up his leg and bit him in a very sensitive spot.

De Villiers screamed, "Ahhh, what the hell bit me?"

In a moment of vulnerability, Jon rushed him, grabbing his hand. A gunshot rattled through the tunnels. Lafitte's hands grabbed the Dark Master's thick silver hair and yanked hard, ripping out tufts and punching him in the face as they both fell to the ground. Jon watched de Villiers squirm with fear on the dirt floor. Some of de Villiers' hair and blood stained Jon's hands.

"A souvenir to remember you by, de Villiers. I enjoyed watching you scream with pain. Who will be the next Dark Watcher Master after you're dead? You envisioned me taking your place, didn't you? You're wiping out the competition." He started strangling the half conscious de Villiers. "Time to die, de Villiers."

The Dark Watcher Master whispered, "Every second you take will place Cordy and Ash in danger and they'll die. Are we so different, Jon? I want revenge and power just like you. Let's join forces."

De Villiers struggled for breath and saw in the dark corner of the room Antar smiling at the scene before him. The Dark Watcher

Master gasped for air and couldn't breathe. Consciousness slowly left his oxygen-deprived brain. He could hear Antar's words in his head.

Antar whispered in the dark but his voice echoed all around them, "Jon wants sweet revenge. He understands my quest. Do you?"

Jon could think only of revenge for his grandfather, Poppa Jon. A moment of madness descended on him. His thirst to kill needed to be filled. Jon squeezed harder and harder around de Villiers' neck. He heard a whisper in the back of his mind.

"Kill him, and you can be the greatest Dark Watcher Grandmaster in history. You don't give a damn about those Pure of Heart. Power, revenge, money, and everything you desire will be yours. Kill him. Get sweet revenge." Jon tightened more and de Villiers' struggles diminished. A few more seconds and de Villiers would be dead.

A loud bang rang through the tunnel. Jon heard a gunshot, and Cordy wounded flashed through his mind. Ash and she would die if he didn't save them. Lafitte made his decision.

"I'll kill you, de Villiers, when I've got more time. But I will kill you."

He picked up the gun and knapsack and ran in the direction of the gunshot. The Dark Watcher Master rolled on his side gasping for air and bleeding from the punches and mouse bites. The small fighter squeaked and scampered away in the darkness. In the corner, Antar showed his disappointment and disappeared.

Ash had grabbed a loose stone from the tunnel wall in the darkness and slammed it into the face of the Dark Watcher. The gun discharged a bullet into the ground and the Watcher crumbled to the cold earth.

Cordy kicked her captor's leg dropping him to the ground as she punched him in the face. He fell and hit the stone wall landing unconscious at her feet. Jon raced down the tunnel. He stared at Ash and Cordy standing over the unconscious men.

"Ah, you're safe," Jon cried out in relief.

Cordy and Ash couldn't believe their eyes. Jon was alive. She hugged him. Ash patted him on the back. "Glad you made it. Now if you can just tell us which tunnel to take to get out of here."

"Follow me," whispered Jon.

Lafitte led them down the tunnel to the right with his flashlight. Jon talked as they moved through the narrow stone walls. "Some Books of Enochs are different. They were hidden and condemned in some places. We need to compare yours and this one. I'm betting this one has more chapters. It's why de Villiers didn't want us to get it. And if you want to know, I didn't kill de Villiers. He managed to escape me."

"How did you escape?" Ash asked.

Jon smiled. "A little mouse ran up his pants and bit him. I managed to wrestle the gun from him. I left him there with the mouse still biting him as he screamed in pain. I owe that mouse a big block of cheese."

Ash and Cordy remembered the little mouse in the tunnel and they both chuckled. "I wish I could have seen that," laughed Ash.

Cordy looked at Jon and saw blood and strands of gray hair on his hands and asked if he was wounded.

"It's not my blood," Jon said. "I tried to scalp de Villiers." He wiped his hands on his pants.

They climbed the stone stairs and exited into the convent garden where there stood a white stone-carved statue of the Mother cradling her son. A small gate in the garden opened with the key Jon possessed and they ran back to Jon's limo.

CHAPTER 43

The Sword of Heaven

An elderly woman named Marie sat in the pew of Notre Dame Cathedral praying to her favorite saint, Saint Joan of Arc. Every Sunday, Marie came to pray and enjoyed sitting next to the statue of the saint dressed in armor and carrying her banner. A handsome redheaded tour guide sat next to her and she noticed his name tag. His name was Uriel. He must have been a new employee of Heavenly Tours for she had never noticed him before. The young man had a charismatic smile. He whispered in the ear of the old woman.

"Hello, Marie, I see you're praying to Joan of Arc again this Sunday. My name is Uriel, as you can see from my nametag. I wondered if you'd like to know a special story about Joan of Arc that's not often told. I've researched her life and found something you'd be interested in."

Her eyes widened with surprise. "Oh, yes please do tell. I love Saint Joan of Arc stories." Marie remained on the wooden pew and waited for Uriel's fascinating tale.

"It is written in one of the hidden Book of Dreams a chapter in the Book of Enoch, and protected by the Pure of Heart, that the prophet Enoch, the seventh son from Adam, stumbled onto a great stone which fell from heaven. Lightning bolts shot from the stone like Tesla's static electricity formed by cosmic rays. He took this stone and forged a sword which glistened in the sun and whose power could still any storm and destroy any army. Enoch knew of the power of the stars and universe so he hid the sword from the Nephilim. The great prophet knew someday the sword would be wielded by the Pure of Heart to save mankind.

"Noah later came into possession of the sword, deemed worthy, for he was a Pure One and of the bloodline of Enoch. An angel warned him to use the Sword of Heaven wisely for its power was as great as the stars in the sky. The rains fell and the oceans swelled. Noah's ark saved all the animals and his family. The ark sailed through the rain storm for weeks and supplies ran low until the wise man pulled out the Sword of Heaven to stop the Great Deluge. He pointed it up to the heavens and a blast of light flew from the gleaming sword. Noah's hand shook with its great power. The winds stopped and the heavens opened up bringing the sun. Mankind was saved and Earth was repopulated with the cosmic seeds given to Enoch and passed down to Noah.

"Kings lived and died, but the Sword of Heaven remained hidden safely, only brought out in dire times. Poor France was being gobbled up by England during the Hundred Years' War. A young peasant girl named Joan of Arc saw the gleaming Sword of Heaven in a vision. She told her friends where to find the sword — in Saint Catherine's of Fierbois Church, hidden behind the altar. The sword's rust fell away as soon as the Maid of Heaven picked it up. Joan carried the sword into battle against the invading English but never killed anyone with it. The Sword of Heaven helped defeat the invaders, and the girl became famous for saving France. The Nephilim and Dark Watchers worked together to gain possession of the renowned sword and captured Joan of Arc and brought her to trial for heresy. The night before her capture, Joan saw her trial in a dream and Saint Catherine, her guardian, told her to give the sword to her most trusted confident. The girl was taken the next day. Her Inquisitors asked her where the Sword of Heaven was, but she told them the truth, that she didn't know. Only her trusted friend knew where and no one could find him. The innocent Joan was burned alive for being a witch but many years later was declared a saint. Oh, woe to the men who tried her in court. The girl sacrificed her life to save France.

"The Sword of Heaven lay hidden for many years waiting for the day when it was needed to save mankind and Earth from future disasters. Legend said only the blood of a Pure of Heart could wield such a sword. Many tried but died of heart attacks or worse. The Sword of Heaven awaits the wielder whose heart is true and honorable. Many heroes and heroines wielded the sword and those whose hearts were true won the day.

"Many great warriors, such as Napoleon and Hitler, forget the power of Earth's weather storms. Their arrogance made them believe they were invincible. Their armies were both defeated in the Siberian winters. How they wished they had possessed such a weapon. The Sword of Heaven can only be wielded by a Pure of Heart. The time is right for another wielder like Joan. Shakespeare said it, 'What's past is prologue.'"

Marie gazed into the warm eyes of the young tour guide and she nodded her head. "Thank you so much for sharing. I had no idea she wielded the Sword of Heaven, but it makes sense for the Maid of Heaven to carry such a prize." They both admired the statue for a few seconds in silence. Uriel looked at the watch on his wrist.

"I so enjoyed our chat Marie, but must be on my way. My next private tour is scheduled now." He smiled and left the elderly lady pondering if the Sword of Heaven would return.

CHAPTER 44

The Pure of Heart
Gain an Ally

Jon pointed to the Louvre's famous glass pyramid as they drove by. Ash and Cordy leaned over and looked out the window.

"France has its pyramids, too, just like Egypt. The museum holds many art treasures within." He pulled out two copies of paintings from his briefcase, one by da Vinci, *Virgin of the Rocks*, and Poussin's *The Arcadian Shepherds*. The second painting showed shepherds stumbling on a man-made stone engraved with the words Et in Arcadia Ego. "I want you to get a good look at the monument in this painting and remember what it looks like. In time, you will see its importance.

"Nicolas Poussin was named by King Louis XIII as First Painter in Ordinary. One of his patrons was Cardinal Richeliu, who promoted the colonies of Quebec and Arcadia. The New World lands were located in what we now call Canada, though it was first called Arcadia and then Acadia. I believe it's a reference to the land of Acadia across the sea. The monument was left by a technologically advanced ancient civilization discovered by a primitive one. Note the simple shepherds amazed at their discovery."

Cordy nodded, "Acadians lived in Montreal and Nova Scotia and were expelled by the British during the war. The Saunhacs were Acadian. They intermarried with the Native American Mi'kmaq."

Next Jon showed them the *Virgin of the Rocks* at the London Museum and compared it with the Louvre's version of the same painting.

"Da Vinci shows two similar paintings but the London painting has halos whereas the Louvre version doesn't. In the London painting, the angel Uriel is the only one without a halo. Why? Did da Vinci know the angel's veneration was stopped by Pope Zachary's edict in 795? It appears he did. Archangel Uriel plays an interesting part in the Book of Enoch, and that could be the real reason Uriel has no halo. The Pope didn't want to draw attention to this strange forbidden book. The Book of Enoch wasn't considered part of the biblical canon of the Jews but the book is mentioned in the New Testament. It existed in the early days of the Christians, and its scrolls were found in Qumran.

"I think da Vinci saw a copy of one of the hidden Books of Enoch which talked about the Watchers and the Nephilim. The Book of Enoch has five parts, the Book of Watchers, the Book of Dreams, the Book of Parables of Enoch, the Astronomical Book, and the Epistle of Enoch.

"Uriel knew about the ancient war and the plight of the Pure of Heart. He holds a special place as protector of Noah's children and the Holy Family. Da Vinci knew the story and how Uriel warned John the Baptist's family to flee for Egypt where they met his cousin's family. It's the same old tale of how the Children of the Nephilim hunted down and killed the Pure of Heart. The whole story of the Great Flood in the Bible is about mankind experiencing an extinction-level event and the Guardian gathering the Keys of Life to save us. Uriel and she knew where the keys were and mankind needs them again. I think de Villiers wants control of the Keys of Life, and that's why he wants you both. He didn't kill you for a reason," Jon explained.

Ash, Cordy, and Jon headed back to the hotel. All of them relaxed and ordered room service. Lafitte's men surrounded the hotel keeping watch. Night descended on Paris. The Eiffel Tower in the distance, with its lights lit, made an incredible sight. After a few more drinks, the exhausted trio headed for bed.

Later in the evening, Jon tip-toed toward Cordy's bedroom hoping to surprise her with some late night amour. He grabbed the door knob and a light shone from Ash's flashlight onto the Frenchman's surprised face.

"Not on my watch, Jon. Better get back to bed for your beauty sleep."

Jon looked confused. "Oh, so sorry, I must have thought this was my room. It's good to know Cordy's so well guarded. Perhaps I should call you the Guardian. Ah, just what I was searching for." He grabbed another bottle of wine and a glass on the hall table and headed back to his room.

Ash smiled to himself and closed his eyes.

Early in the morning, Cordy woke up and found Jon in a white T-shirt and black pants doing Tai Chi exercises. Cordy watched his graceful, controlled movements. Women all over the world would be drooling at his muscular physique and good looks. Cordy lined up next to him and began following his movements.

"Tai chi aids me in focusing my energy. Who trained you, Cordy?" asked Jon. He watched her move in sync with him.

"Master Wong took me to Hong Kong for training. I learned martial arts and Tai Chi from him. He taught me how to breathe and meditate. The arts opened my mind on how heaven and earth interact together with each other."

Jon and Cordy performed a mesmerizing dance together, moving in total synchronization. Ash walked in and watched the fluid movement. They acted as one but were separate. Jon called out to him.

"Ash, come and join us."

"C'mon, Ash, we'll teach you a few moves. I bet you're a natural," Cordy urged.

Ash stood next to Cordy. He followed her movements.

Jon said softly, "Relax all tension from your body, Ash, and feel the energy flow throughout it. Let go of the tension."

Ash felt the blood flow through his body, and his mind focused on following their movements. He was a natural as he moved as one with them. The door to the hotel room swung open but they stayed in formation.

Bob walked into their hotel room pushing a breakfast tray from room service and found Jon, Cordy, and Ash doing Tai Chi.

"Bob!" beamed Cordy. She still followed the movements of Jon.

"Hello, cupcake, mind if I join the boys and you?"

Ash stayed in synchronization with Cordy. "Where have you been, Bob?"

Bob dropped his backpack and got in the tai chi position with them. "I've been a little busy, Ash, kicking the Children of the Nephilim's butt." Bob's martial arts training kicked in and his body moved along gracefully.

Jon continued with his movements. "Hello, Robert, I see you know tai chi, too. It's helpful with jet lag. Good job taking down the chairman." Sunshine illuminated the room and their movements appeared as a slow, beautiful dance. After ten minutes, Jon finished and bowed. They went over to eat their breakfast before it got cold. Everybody admitted they felt better and more awake.

Ash caught Bob up on what had happened in Ireland. He told him about the Guardian and possessing the Guardian's library of knowledge.

"I sent condolences to Linda's family and set up a scholarship fund in her name for the Diplomatic Brat Corps, as I wrote you," Bob said. "The kids wrote you a thank-you card." He handed it to Cordy. "Her mother and father told me to tell you thanks and that Linda would've loved it. I never want to do anything like that ever again. One of the hardest things I've ever done in my life. Her parents are handling it about as well as can be expected."

He turned his attention on Lafitte.

"Oh, and by the way, Frenchie, good shooting. I saw the video footage from the hotel before the Dark Watchers deleted it." Bob nodded in Jon's direction.

"My pleasure, Robert. You came prepared for trouble, I hope. As you Americans say, the shit has hit the fan. My family's in hiding and my grandfather assassinated. The Lafitte family has been branded traitors by the Dark Watchers. "

Bob leaned back. Sadness filled his eyes as he gazed at Cordy. "I've got bad news, Cordy. Do you want to be alone when I tell you?"

Her eyes filled with tears. "I already know. Sister Agnes is dead isn't she? It's why you came, isn't it, Bob? How did it happen?"

Bob squirmed and looked at her with sympathy. "It's not pretty, Cordy. They discovered her body at the Lough Key in Ireland. She'd been beaten. McDonough and Bill found her body near the McDermott castle. I'm so sorry. Bill's pretty torn up about it. He made all the funeral arrangements with the sisters. I thought you would want me to tell you face to face, not by phone."

Ash put his arm tenderly on Cordy's shoulder. She'd known all along her aunt was dead but knowing she was beaten to death sickened her.

"I should've been there. Maybe I could've saved her," Cordy said.

Ash looked at her with compassion. "The best thing we can do is stop de Villiers. If we do that, Linda and Sister Agnes won't have died in vain."

Jon stared intently at Cordy. "I can promise you this. De Villiers will pay for what he has done to our families."

Bob raised his glass to Jon. "I'll drink to that, Frenchie. Allies, to the death. "

Jon saluted him with his glass. "Allies to the death!"

Bob shook his hand. "Welcome to the Pure of Heart, Jon."

CHAPTER 45

Chartres

After breakfast, Jon drove them to Notre Dame de Chartres in his Porsche. Built in the 1200s, the cathedral still stood, long after the wars had ended and the kings had died. Saint Louis consecrated it. His mother Blanche Castile's heraldry was displayed throughout the original stained-glass windows. Jon showed them a picture of Richard the Lionheart's effigy at Fontevrand Abbey.

"Richard the Lionheart stood six foot four inches tall. A giant among men, King Louis IX's was a relative of Richard. Richard believed he had "infernal blood." He said his bloodline could be traced back to Noah. On his tomb, Solomon's seal, or David's Shield, lies over him.

"Richard took part in the Crusades and wanted to be King of Jerusalem. The two golden triangles, which you possess, put together make this magical symbol. Today, it's more commonly called the Star of David."

Jon parked the car and they walked into the huge cathedral. He pointed to the astrological signs of the zodiac carved in stone and then to the stained glass windows.

"Chartres' stained glass windows go back to the 1200s and up above you is the Noah windows. The window tells the story of Noah and the ark, but it also tells of the Nephilim and the giants."

Cordy answered, "Genesis 6:2, the sons of God saw the beautiful women and took any they wanted as their wives."

Jon nodded. "The giants and the Nephilim are in the stained glass window. The giant with a club in his hand and the one with a spear represent the constellations Orion and Hercules. The female giant could represent Pleiades or Virgo. Sirius is the vertex of the Winter Triangle. We know how important triangles are in this mystery."

Ash looked at the stained glass and saw the symbolism. "Pleiades, and Sirius played very important parts in the temples of Egypt and they're written in the Bible. The Book of Enoch talks about the war. I wonder if the Queen Blanche knew about the mysterious books since they were restricted only to certain officials."

Jon pointed to the giant woman in the stained glass window. "She's a giantess, like the legend at Malta who built the ancient temple. Does a woman dressed in white telling mankind a message sound familiar? Napoleon searched for the ancient objects of power, too." The stained glass window showed a tall woman talking to a smaller human male.

Bob started walking over to the Chartres Labyrinth, a huge black and white maze-like design engraved on the stone floor.

"It's supposed to symbolize the battle between Theseus and the Minotaur," Ash said. "The Egyptians built a huge labyrinth to initiate the members into the ancient mysteries as a sort of a spiritual journey. It's also an ancient Greek story. The House of Daedalus became a master builder, and he designed the maze to keep the Minotaur in prison. The Ariadne's thread helped save Theseus from the Minotaur. That's why it's the symbol for using logic and reason to handle a problem. Artificial intelligence also uses logic to solve puzzles. Have you noticed The Guardian acts like a computer and uses math, the universal language?"

Jon smiled. "Interesting, isn't it? And pilgrims used the maze as the road to Jerusalem. If they couldn't go on a pilgrimage, they would go through the labyrinth and pray. It's a form of meditation. They call it an 11-circuit design."

Bob walked through it and looked up. "The human brain has a right and left hemisphere which looks like the labyrinth. The goal here is the flower in the middle, right? Is that the pineal gland then?"

Cordy looked at him. "Pineal gland, the seat of the soul. The labyrinth consists of eleven rings divided into four sections. I can't believe it. It's like the Keys of Life. The maze is a circle with a cross, a variation of the ankh Ash found in the Temple of Abu Simbel. The quaternity comes from the visions of Enoch and looks like the Celtic cross from Ireland."

"A school existed here, too. There's Pythagoras sitting with his book carved in stone. The Greek master was placed in the sacred church, built using sacred geometry. I have one more thing to show you. It is on a pillar."

Bob, Ash, and Cordy gazed up at the stone pillar to see a carving of a cart carrying a chest being pushed by men. Jon pointed to a pillar with the Ark of the Covenant, which had the words 'The Ark of the Covenant was yielded here.' Jon pointed to the ball on top and the opened chest. "It looks like the crystal ball of the Guardian."

Ash's mouth fell open. "Well, I'll be damned. It does."

Jon looked at his watch. "Time is running out. I will fly us to Toulouse. We are heading for Lourdes." They headed out and walked down the stone steps when Lafitte stopped for a moment.

Jon looked at Ash. "Ash, I noticed you admiring the smooth ride of my Porsche. Would you like to drive it and meet us up the hill? Here's the key. We're going to get some papers, and we will meet you there."

Ash loved Jon's taste in cars and didn't want to pass up a chance to drive the Porsche. "Sure I'll drive it."

Bob, Jon and Cordy climbed the steps up the hill and watched Ash anxiously run to get the car.

A bleep-bleep came from Ash's turning off the alarms and he jumped inside the car.

Ash waved and started the engine.

Jon chuckled. "Well, we know that no bombs were placed on the car while we were inside. Ash has his uses, doesn't he?"

Cordy's mouth opened up when she realized Jon had used Ash to check if the car was safe.

Bob chuckled, too. "Got to say, you're pretty clever, Frenchie."

CHAPTER 46

Saunhac Family Secrets

Cordy had started reading her great-grandfather Chief Saunhac's book of stories about her family's past. The diary had been left to her after he died. It contained the family history she never knew. The chief had wanted to leave Cordy a family legacy to tell her how different families played a part in the ancient war of good versus evil.

She found the chapter on Sister Elizabeth McDermott who was born in Ireland and joined the Ursuline convent at seventeen. Her orders had her taking a voyage to New Orleans, Louisiana, in1809 where she would be a nurse at the hospital there.

At the hospital, Sister Elizabeth became known for her gift for healing. One night, a young boy asked for the sister to come save his poor uncle who was with fever. She was kindhearted and followed him. He took her to a house on Chartres Street where she found the notorious pirate Jean Lafitte. Sister Elizabeth knew that his family members were criminals and very dangerous. The delirious man was shivering with fever. A Christian would not leave the sick man and so Sister Elizabeth pulled out of her case herbs grown in the garden at the convent to help bring his fever down.

He was an incredibly handsome man. Tall, long thick hair, ebony eyes, and a dark moustache befitted the wicked privateer. She had seen his face on Most Wanted posters around the square near the cathedral. Sister Elizabeth held his head up.

"You must drink this, monsieur, please."

His eyes closed. "No, give me some wine. If I die, let me be drinking my French wine."

She shook him and commanded, "Lafitte, drinking wine will just dehydrate you more. You are not ready to die, so drink."

Lafitte's eyes opened and he saw the vision of a woman in white like an angel. He was so tired but he would drink for this angel. Sister Elizabeth sat with him all night and all day. He hovered many times between life and death. She prayed that he would survive.

The next evening, Jean looked up at her as she fed him some beef broth. He asked, "Am I going to die, Sister?"

She smiled. "No, Jean, you are too stubborn to die."

He laughed at her words. "I guess God has some plans for me yet. I owe you my life, Sister. I swear my family will repay you for saving me." He saw the McDermott family crest pinned on her nursing bag.

Sister Elizabeth gave his brother medicines to help Jean get better.

"I will tell no one that I have seen the pirate Jean Lafitte, and I will remember your vow to me."

Saunhac had written a note below the story. *Star Child, remember this secret alliance between the Lafitte family and the McDermott family. Throughout time, the two families have aided one another and entrusted deep secrets to each other. If anyone were to discover their secret bond, the families would be wiped out.*

Cordy had to agree with the chief. The Lafitte family saved Ash and her from drowning in icy waters. She would have to take the plunge and find out what he wanted.

CHAPTER 47

Sword of Earth

Jon's Porsche flew down the highway. Cordy watched the wonderful French countryside whiz by and asked, "Where are you taking us, Jon?"

Jon kept his eyes on the road. "I have to pick something up. I will need all of your help. I read Saunhac's book the other night in Paris. He wrote about Eleanor of Aquitaine and Richard the Lionhearted. I think Saunhac gave you directions, Cordy, using his family book. I know of something priceless that my family and your family guarded for centuries buried at the abbey."

Cordy was surprised. "How the hell did you find my grandfather's book?"

Jon had a wicked smile on his face. "I discovered it in your room."

Bob started to pull his gun out. "Do you want me to shoot him Cordy?"

"I vote to shoot him," Ash chimed in.

Cordy answered, "He's driving Bob, but if you ever catch him in my room again, shoot him!"

Bob placed his gun back in its holster. "Okie dokie, Boss, but I hope we don't regret not shooting the sneaky bastard now."

Jon grinned, "Good thing you all chose to let me live. The Abbey hides the Sword of Earth, Richard the Lionheart's sword. Some say his sword dates back to Solomon. The sword was discovered by the Templars in Jerusalem. One of its powers is causing earthquakes and preventing them. Chief Saunhac knew where the sword slept and that it could come in handy."

Right then, he pulled the car off the road and parked it by a small café. "We'll walk from here to the abbey."

He opened his trunk and pulled out bright light green vests to put over their clothes. He pulled out a tool bag. "We're going there to repair a floor tile. Ash and Cordy bring your backpacks." He handed them workers' passes.

"Follow me."

"Are we going to break the law?" Cordy whispered.

"Looks like it to me," Bob said calmly.

Ash smiled. "Guess somebody else around here is going to be a tomb robber. Welcome to the club."

Bob, Ash, and Cordy put on the vests and followed Jon through a garden to enter a back door. The abbey amazed them as they strolled past where Richard the Lionheart and Eleanor of Aquitaine effigies stood and were once buried. Cordy pointed to the Seal of David on Richard's tomb.

"Saunhac wrote about this in his book. Richard saw the seal as a powerful and protective symbol. He's so tall, over six feet, like you said. He must have seemed like a giant to most men of the time. The ring I possess has the Seal of David engraved on it."

Jon whispered with surprise in his voice, "You possess the Ring of David? Many legends named it Solomon's Ring and Richard the Lionheart believed the symbol had special powers. I do remember a legend about him owning such a ring, but his heart was corrupted by the power. De Villiers wants to possess it badly even though he knows it's cursed to anyone except a Pure of Heart. The ring can cause insanity if you're not a Pure of Heart. Marcus Aurelius said long ago, 'Vanity is the greatest seducer of reason.' The Lionheart was thought to be descended from the Nephilim. He made mention that his bloodline was "infernal". A Christian king carved the very Jewish Seal of David on his tombstone. Remember, David killed Goliath the giant and a little boy shot the arrow which killed Richard the Lionheart."

Ash looked over at Eleanor of Aquitaine. "Eleanor's hands hold a book. She appears to be reading even now. It makes sense for this brilliant woman to be remembered for her search of knowledge. Queen Eleanor of England and France proved education for women, especially royalty, was essential. She became one of the most powerful women of her age."

The abbey's beauty awed them as the sun shone through the windows. The gigantic white stone columns and arches overwhelmed them. Jon directed them to an altar with a triangle on it. He placed the orange cones around the work area and picked up a trowel, hammer, and chisel.

"Bob and Cordy, watch, and stop anyone coming too close."

Bob and Cordy acted like they were examining and cleaning the stone with cloths.

"I'm going to need the archeologist."

Ash smiled.

Jon knelt down and looked at the tiled floor and the altar. "This one." He tapped on the chisel with the hammer and broke the grout. He lifted the stone tile, where underneath laid a metal box buried vertical in the ground.

Jon looked at Ash. "We need the small Key of Life to be inserted into the box. It won't let us retrieve it without it."

Ash pulled out of his bag the smaller key that he found at Abu Simbel. He saw the hole to insert it at the top of the box. A blinking light activated on the metal box.

Ash looked at Jon. "Now what?"

Bob gazed at the blinking light. "I hate to say this but blinking lights are not a good sign."

Jon remained calm. "Turn the key but turn the right way, or it will activate the Sword of Earth. The stone columns will fall and kill us all. It's a test to see if you are worthy, my friend. Don't turn that key just yet."

Bob heard Jon and grabbed Cordy's hand. "Cordy, I think we may just step out for a second here and let the archeologist do his thing."

"I'm not going to leave Ash," Cordy said.

Jon nodded at Bob. "I think you better and run quickly both of you. I will stay with Ash. Now start running!"

Bob pulled Cordy's arm and they headed quickly out the back door to the garden.

They tried to put as much distance as they could between themselves and the abbey. Bob huffed and puffed running toward the car. "I knew I should have shot that damn Frenchie."

Beads of sweat formed on Ash's forehead. "OK, Jon, quit playing around. Which way do I turn the key?"

Jon beamed. "You must choose, my friend. Trust your heart. I believe in you, my friend, Ash. I want to say thank you for healing me. I figured you possess special talents. So choose. "

"Jon, you pick a helluva time to tell me thanks."

Jon knelt beside him. "Better late than never, my friend. I trust you will make the right decision."

Ash thought for a second and took a deep breath. He turned the key to the right and the light stopped blinking. Both men started to breathe. Jon had noticed Ash's penchant for being lucky and his healing touch since Paris. Lafitte deduced the archeologist was much more than he appeared. One thing was clear to Jon — Ash was the real deal. Poppa Jon talked about the gifts and talents of the Pure of Heart, and he had witnessed it for himself.

Jon helped him pull up the metal case. Jon then took a stone tile and replaced it with a small amount of grout. It looked good as new. Ash and Jon walked to the garden and stopped behind a wall. Two security officers passed them as they walked back to their office but didn't notice them. Ash and Jon ran toward the parked car. Both men opened the door to find Bob and Cordy in the car, drinking wine and eating baguettes and cheese.

Ash and Jon were astounded to see them casually eating a snack.

Cordy held out a baguette. "Bob ran into the bakery across the street and bought us some goodies. We're hungry. What took you guys so long?"

Bob handed Ash a cup of wine. "Looks like you chose right Ash. Congratulations!"

Bob drank some wine from the bottle. "I don't need a glass, not after that escapade. I haven't had my heart race like that since being with Julia. And may I say, had a much more enjoyable time, too."

Ash and Jon put the metal box in the trunk. They grabbed a baguette from Cordy and Jon took another bottle of wine. Both men agreed they needed a drink.

Jon drove to the city of Chinon and the Forteresse Royale de Chinon. They sat in the car looking at the fortress.

Jon looked at Cordy. "Saunhacs were Templars. One of your relatives was a Grandmaster. Chinon is where the Templars were arrested and imprisoned by King Phillip. Jacques De Molay was tortured in the jail here. Joan of Arc came to Chinon to convince Charles VII to fight the English. If Joan had never come here, then France wouldn't exist today."

Jon drove to a small airport outside Chinon, where a helicopter was waiting for them.

"I'm going to show you where the Saunhacs lived long ago. Your ancestors' home is one of the most gorgeous places in all of France, Bel Castel. The Cathars, a religious sect who disagreed with Rome, lived here. The Inquisition hunted them down. A great genocide took place here called the Albigensian Crusade in Languedoc. There is a Magdalene statue in Rennes Chateau, a mysterious village, which looks like the Magdalene statue in St. Louis' hands. Cathar legends say they possessed secret treasures. Another reason they were hunted down by you-know-who."

He pointed to a medieval castle, Bel Castel. A charming stone arched bridge went across the river toward the tiny town.

Cordy grabbed her phone and, from the helicopter, took a picture of the stone castle. The view was fantastic. She heard Chief

Saunhac's voice in her mind, *Star Child, you come from a long line of warriors.*

She placed a hand on Jon's shoulder "Thank you so much, Jon."

Jon nodded. "You come from a great family. Saunhac was known for his bravery during the Crusades. He brought back many relics from the Holy Land. The Templars protected and guarded them with their lives."

A flash of light gleamed in the sky. Bob grabbed the binoculars quickly from Ash. "I hate to be a party pooper, but do we have a visitor at 9 o'clock?" He pointed to a small white drone adorned with the symbol of an eye coming at them.

"You've got to be kidding me, this guy never gives up," Ash yelled as he pulled out his gun.

Cordy and Bob took out theirs, too.

"A drone at ten o'clock and moving straight for us."

Bob grabbed his phone and called Julia. Ash aimed his gun at the drone and fired. Julia heard the gunshots on the phone.

"Hello, Bob, I hear gun shots. Having fun, honey? I'm putting you on speakerphone with Randy."

Cordy shot next, hoping to hit the drone as it came closer. Lafitte took evasive actions. The drone stayed right with them.

"We are under attack by a Dark Watcher drone. We need a little help."

Randy yelled across the line, "I'm on it, like a mouse on a cheese pizza." He ran to the computer and pulled up satellite signals. Randy tried to identify the drone signal hoping to jam the connection to its owner. "Tell him I'm trying to jam the drone's signal."

Julia and Randy could hear more gunshots.

Bob shouted, "Ash, would you please do me a favor and try to hit something? Anything would really help. The drone is heading straight for us. You have our GPS coordinates, right?"

Julia watched the radar screen. "Affirmative, we have you and the drone in our sights."

Randy found the radio signal. "The good news, I got it. Bad news, we need five minutes to jam the signal."

Lafitte flew the helicopter downward and weaved to the right. The drone followed. Bob shot at it again.

"Hold on everybody," Jon bellowed.

Lafitte flew down to the river that cut through the mountains and headed for the centuries-old stone bridge. He tried to buy them some time. The helicopter was at top speed headed straight for the arched stone bridge while the drone followed closer and closer. Right before it looked like the helicopter would hit the bridge, he pulled up. The drone flew directly into the stone bridge and broke into bits as it plunged into the river, flames flying.

"Honey, have I told you how much I love you lately? Drone DOA."

Julia slapped Randy's hand. "I love you, too, Bob, but don't call me honey."

"OK, darling, tell Randy thanks. Over and out."

Ash, Cordy, and Jon laughed and simultaneously said, "OK, darling."

Bob answered them back gruffly, "You guys quit teasing old love sick Bob. Just wait 'til the love bug strikes you. I'll have no mercy."

CHAPTER 48

Toulouse Back Room

Jon flew on to Toulouse. Toulouse was connected to one of the first Crusaders, Raymond of Toulouse, who refused the title King of Jerusalem. Jon knew the city well because Europe's aerospace industries were headquartered there.

All of them would stay at a hotel in the city and then drive to Lourdes in the morning. Lourdes would be a two-hour drive for tomorrow. They checked into the Plaza Hotel near River Garonne into connecting luxury suites.

Jon finished with a call from his worried family. "I have to meet a friend tonight. He owns a nightclub here in Toulouse and has some information on de Villiers. You're welcome to come and enjoy the music. It's been an intense week. I think we all deserve some down time."

Ash sat on the couch reading the news about the Great Pyramids and the discovery of a low-frequency vibration detected in the past few days. The media said scientists and archeologists were stumped and couldn't find the source to stop it. As Jon poured some wine for everyone, Ash showed him the article.

"A low frequency resonant vibration coming from the Great Pyramid about the same time the Guardian awakened Knowth and Newgrange. What's she doing, Jon?"

Jon sipped his wine. "I believe temples all over the world are going to activate and possibly power up. Something big has got the Guardian alarmed. The Keys of Life were left to mankind by Noah just for this dangerous time. I'm getting reports out of NASA and satellite data showing disturbing weather patterns, increased earthquakes, and volcano eruptions. Meanwhile, the Dark Watchers keep the population unaware of the changes around them."

Ash grabbed the glass of wine Jon poured. "The Egyptians knew this day would come. That's why they built the pyramids to last millennia. They knew about the Guardian, too."

Jon smiled. "We're not the only ones the lovely lady has charmed."

Cordy and Bob walked out on the veranda together and took in the view. Bob offered to stay at the hotel for the night. "I need to check in with Julia and see how she's holding up. I kind of left her running the business while I'm away and she didn't like being left behind. As you saw today, Julia's an amazing and efficient manager. The Nephilim trained her well. She's enjoying every minute dismantling the whole system. Cordy, your companies are booming and people recognize that eco-friendly companies are winners for everyone. Entrepreneurs are knocking on our doors for funding. We'll give clean water to third world countries and provide a better life for everyone. Julia has a purpose in her life and she's enjoying it. I just need to check in so she knows I'm behaving. Plus a little phone sex can't hurt."

Cordy laughed. "She's got you on a tight leash, huh, Bob?"

Bob grinned. "Oh, I have to admit that woman has me jumping whenever she gives a command. You be careful with those two boys, cupcake. I don't want you to get hurt."

Cordy winked at him. "I know how to handle Frenchie and Ash. Trust me."

Cordy was dressed in a tight black dress featuring a round neck and a mesh cutout bodice with long sleeves. The dress plunged into a deep-V in the back, revealing her alluring skin. A short skirt showed off her legs and her long hair flowed over her shoulders.

Jon smiled at Ash and Cordy. "Let's go have some fun, shall we?"

They took a taxi to La Couleur De La Culotte. The doorman recognized Jon and showed them upstairs to a corner table. The music was playing loudly and the dance floor was full.

They ordered drinks and Jon's black hair fell over his white linen shirt. His gray eyes feasted on Cordy. Ash had to admit, she was a knockout and no man in the room could take his eyes off of her.

Jon whispered to them, "I have to talk to Andre. It's important business. Why don't Ash and you dance or enjoy the music? I'll be right back."

Jon walked into a back room.

Ash and Cordy smiled at each other. "You want to dance Cordy?"

"Oui," Cordy nodded.

The crowded dance floor pushed Ash and Cordy together. A charged atmosphere surrounded them and they felt the beat. He always surprised her. Who would have guessed Ash was a great dancer? He placed his arm on her back protectively. His black shirt emphasized his light hair. Their bodies touched ever so lightly but the electricity in the air was unmistakable.

Jon stared at Andre. "How did it happen that Poppa Jon was killed at the meeting? His bodyguards did nothing?"

Andre's face was full of sorrow. "He's like a father to me, Jon. If I knew that de Villiers was going to shoot him, I swear I would have gone with him. He told me to stay home. Even Sam was ordered to stay home. I think he knew what de Villiers had in mind all along. Lucky for you that you didn't come or you would be dead. De Villiers did some magic or mind control over everyone there. All the families were shocked and scared of him. Some have said he is delving into black magic. No one could resist him. No one!"

Jon hugged Andre. "Thank you for telling me. I want you to tell everyone that I'm happy Poppa Jon is gone and now I am head of the family business. I celebrated tonight with my friends. You know what a heartless bastard I am, right, Andre?"

Andre gave Jon a knowing look. "I'll tell everyone de Villiers did you a favor."

They both opened the door and stepped into the loud and crowded bar.

Jon saw Ash and Cordy dancing on the floor and realized that if he were to have a chance at winning Cordy that he better get down there. Ash and Cordy were enjoying themselves way too much.

He grabbed three gorgeous girls and danced with each one. He exuded sex appeal to every woman in the club. Jon placed his hand firmly on one of the girl's body and let his hands roam all over. Her hands weren't shy, and she put her arms around Jon's shoulders. He came over to Cordy and Ash with his entourage. The girls started to dance with Ash. Jon took the moment of distraction to gently grab Cordy and pull her close to him. Their bodies were rhythmically swaying together. Cordy felt the heat generated by this man and it was definitely a heart racer. The music stopped and Cordy was left breathless by both men.

Jon looked at Ash. "I think it's time for us to get back to the hotel and be sure Bob is all right."

Ash nodded. "OK, let's go."

Bob sat quietly in the living room of the suite talking to Julia on the internet. She told him about the cheerleader outfit she was wearing. A picture registered on Bob's phone. Julia seductively asked, "Do you like my outfit? I'm going to wear it when you get back home."

"You're getting me into the mood, and you're in New York. I can't wait to get back and hold you in my arms."

Suddenly, he heard another woman's voice behind him. "Oh, Bob who are you talking to?"

He started and dropped the phone. He pulled his gun. "OK, c'mon out, baby, let's see what you got."

Julia heard the woman's voice but couldn't see a thing. "Bob, who the hell is that? "

Bob grabbed the phone while holding the gun. "Sorry, honey, got to go! The maid is here with towels."

He looked around and didn't see anybody in the room.

"OK, I'm putting the drink down because I'm beginning to hear things."

"It's me, Bob, the Guardian," whispered the soft woman's voice. "Over here!"

A light shone in the backpack. Bob opened it and pulled out the shining crystal ball with the Guardian standing there, talking to him.

"I needed to talk to you, Bob. Mankind needs to find a clean and safe energy source. A world conference needs to be called to discuss with scientists all over the world about Earth-friendly safe technology. The famous scientist Tesla had some fascinating ideas about free energy. Your corporation is making strides in this area but more is needed. I fear de Villiers will threaten the countries of the world with great devastation. Technology is a double-edged sword."

Bob rubbed his eyes and blinked but she was still there. "Why don't you just give us the technology instead of him?"

The Guardian smiled. "You have to be worthy as a race, and you are not there yet. Someday in the future you will be, if you haven't killed yourselves." The light dimmed and the crystal ball reflected only Bob's face looking at it.

"Hey, where did you go, beautiful? Knock, knock, anybody there?" asked Bob while holding his gun.

He turned to find Cordy with her arms crossed over her chest, Lafitte smiling, and Ash grinning.

"Who the hell are you talking to, Bob? Did you bring a girl up here? Julia will be ticked off," admonished Cordy.

"Robert, you do not woo French girls with knock-knock jokes. You need to try a different technique than that."

"Girls don't like guns pointed at them either, Bob. Have you been drinking too much tequila again?"

Bob mumbled, "I was talking to Julia when the Guardian appeared. I'm in so much trouble."

They all at once said, "The Guardian?"

Bob nodded and poured another shot of tequila. "Oh, by the way, she has a hot voice."

CHAPTER 49

Lourdes

In the morning, they drove to Lourdes, near the foot of the Pyrenees Mountains. Bob asked, "Why do you think the Guardian wants water from Lourdes and Knock?"

"I've wondered that myself," Ash said.

Cordy chimed in. "I know that my family and I are connected to Lourdes. My birthday is on one of the days the vision appeared to Bernadette. My grandfather, Bill, was cured of a skin disease by the waters. I checked the water. It's pure and has some elements in it but nothing special.

"Still, Lourdes is a sacred location visited by the sick. Millions have come to drink and bathe in the spring's supernatural waters. It's about believing in the power of faith and prayer. Saint Bernadette talked about how believing in the power of the water can cure oneself. If you want to get more scientific, studies have found that the mind plays an important role in people's recovery from illness."

Jon smiled. "The Guardian wants the four elements which are the basis of all life. They're fire, water, air, earth and a mysterious secret ingredient. I know the ancient swords of power, and water from sacred sites is an important ingredient for life. I know it all sounds crazy but my family passed down this information for a reason.

"The names are the Sword of Heaven, the Sword of Earth, the Sword of Water and the Sword of Fire. The other secret ingredient brings all these elements together so really you need five ingredients. A pentacle or star is a good symbol for all of them united together. They could be treasures left from a past civilization much more advanced than we are today. The Guardian knows how important the stars influence our lives here. The zodiac signs being carved amid the churches we just saw demonstrates this isn't a new theory but an ancient one.

"We've found water on the moon, Titan, Ceres, and on Mars. Earth isn't the only one. We are entering the Age of Aquarius, the water bearer. It's a time of expanding consciousness, the internet, corporate greed, and Earth changes. NASA is noticing planet changes such as Mars' and Jupiter's climates are warming up. The Guardian must know Earth has awakened. She needs our help.

"Lourdes is on Paris' prime meridian and runs through the Paris Observatory. The spring is special and considered sacred ground, just like Knock's spring. Water has special properties such as polarity, surface tension, and exists in all three states at Earth's temperature. We need water, which is one of the keys of life. Even today we underestimate its power."

Ash nodded. "I remember that Napoleon brought all his scientists to Cairo and Alexandria. He searched for the treasures lost from the Library of Alexandria just like Hitler searched all over the world for objects which tapped into what some people call 'magical powers.' What I'm saying is many people have been on this quest, too."

Lafitte pulled the car up and gave Cordy a stone vase to put the water in. A cross was carved on the front of it. Jon smiled and asked "Does the vase look familiar? My family calls it the Magdalene cup."

Cordy thought for a second and a smile spread across her face. "It looks exactly like the white slender necked vase in Carravagio's *Taking of Christ* painting in Dublin where we met. I remember. It's beautiful." They walked the grounds amid hundreds of tourists.

Ash walked around looking at the different fountains. He wanted to bring his mother a souvenir so he took out a tiny jar that he carried with him in his pocket. He had left one tiny jar filled with water from a sacred well in Egypt in his backpack. He had great respect for the power of faith and believing in water's healing properties. Ash got his water from the fountain labeled Queen of the Apostles. Bob and Jon were off looking at the mountains in the distance.

Cordy went up to one of the fountains and obtained the water from Our Lady of Light fountain. She filled the vase and placed a cork tightly on top. The sacred water from Knock Ireland and Lourdes were now theirs. Cordy knew the connection of Lourdes to the Miraculous Medal was that Saint Bernadette had worn the medal when she saw her vision. The visions occurred all over the world when times were hard and conflict was in the air. The group jumped back in the car and headed out.

Jon noticed in his rearview mirror that a couple of cars were following them.

"Everyone better get ready because we're being followed."

Bob pulled out his gun. "I'm ready, Jon, anytime you are."

Just as Bob said that the cars started accelerating and tried to advance on Jon. Shots were being fired on them. Jon weaved back and forth across the highway at a racecar speed. Bob opened the window and shot one guy in the arm. Ash pulled out his gun and shot the front tire and the window on the car behind them. The car swerved and ran off the cliff bursting into flames as it fell down the deep embankment.

Bob turned in surprise at Ash. "Nice shooting, Ash. You hit something."

Ash shot again shattering the other car's window. "Thanks, Bob, I think I'm getting the hang of it."

One car came alongside Jon, trying to push him over the edge and down the steep cliff. The side driver had Jon in his sight but before he could shoot, Ash hit the front tire of the car making it swerve out of control, holding back the other cars for a few minutes as they tried to avoid hitting the disabled car. It was right then that Jon drove through a tunnel. He turned off his car lights and being farther ahead saw a small country road right outside the tunnel and took it. The other cars sped past them as Jon turned around and headed back taking a different route.

Jon complimented his team, "Well done, and nice shooting, everyone. Ash, I must admit, great idea shooting out their tires."

Cordy and Bob reloaded their guns. Ash whispered to Jon, "Just between you and me Jon, I aimed for the driver."

Jon nodded and realized Ash was a great archeologist but not a marksman.

CHAPTER 50

Rochelle

Jon drove them to one of his family houses at Bayonne, a charming French three-story home overlooking the river. He decided to make them lunch. Quiche and salad, along with assorted breads and cheeses, were set before them. Jon impressed Cordy with his ability to cook. The master of many talents produced a scrumptious dining experience.

Jon began to tell them about the French oral tradition of Mary Magdalene. "A Magdalene cult had developed in France. The legend talks of her coming to Marseille by boat with other saints like Lazarus, Maximin, Sidonius, and Suzanne. She converted many followers in Provence and lived in a cave. Angels fed her and communicated with her. Saint Louis' nephew played a part in finding her grave and later, became a shrine.

"Ancient France had a reputation for miraculous waters, such as the springs at Rennes Les Bains, hot springs for thousands of years. The French wrote many famous legends and troubadours spread them far and wide. One of the tales told of a Lady of the Lake dressed in white with magical powers. She's the one who gives Arthur his famous sword Excalibur. You see the comparison to the Guardian. We are all on a quest and she's guiding us.

"Rennes Chateau and Rennes Les Bains are where images of Magdalene with her hands crossed like the Jerusalem cross can be found. The area was filled with legends of Templars and Cathar treasures hidden in secret caves." Jon showed them the pictures of Magdalene kneeling in prayer at the altar at Rennes les Chateau like the Magdalene Cordy found in Saint Louis.

"You know that Oxford professor who told you the Magdalene at Rennes' name was really de Villiers? The Dark Watcher's headquarters is in London. He's fluent in French and English."

Cordy nodded. "The Saunhac family protected the relics from the Holy Land. He tested me in St Louis. I led him to the Pure of Heart treasure. He knows we have them."

Lafitte looked at her with tenderness. "My family has been trusted protectors and transporters of ancient treasures throughout history. Our families are secret allies fighting against an ancient evil."

Bob asked, "Are you related to Jacques Laffite, the banker from Bayonne who knew Napoleon?"

"He is probably a distant cousin. We're related to the privateers' family from Louisiana. Our family has many branches. Julia's family, the Villiers, is a branch related to de Villiers' ancestors. They're distant cousins. They broke away and wanted to be free. As you can see, it doesn't always work."

Bob took a sip of his coffee. "Why does having bankers and privateers sound like they mix well together?"

Jon chuckled. "Don't forget Napoleon sold the Louisiana Territory to Jefferson at just the right time. No one can say we're not fighters. Some would say America's independence owes our family a huge debt."

Jon brought out small bowls with scoops of blueberry-lavender ice cream for dessert. It was delicious and such a treat.

Jon continued, "Our bodies are made up of ninety percent water. Water is sacred and used in many religions, such as in Christianity for baptism, and in India, many bathe in the sacred river. It's not surprising to me that the Guardian wanted the water from such sacred sites in France. My family has always made their wealth from shipping and the best transportation mode is water. After lunch we will travel to La Rochelle where I have my ships docked."

Bob finished off his ice cream and looked at Cordy. "Julia told me she had a dream about that ring." He pointed to the ring around Cordy's neck. "She said Saunhac told her to find it but it's the diagram on the ring that gives it the power to control the angels. Julia's been researching the Nephilm's library."

"Control the angels..." Cordy fingered the ring hanging around her neck.

"I have to get back to New York. Do you think you're going to be safe here with these two guys?"

"She will be safe with me," Jon shot back. "I guarantee it."

Ash looked at Bob. "I'm going to be sure he keeps his word."

Cordy leaned back. "I'll be fine, Bob. We're going to get the treasures the Guardian wants because I've a feeling the world is going to need them. After watching the weather reports I noticed one massive storm building up in the tropics, and we've been getting some abnormally violent ones lately. My gut is telling me that the world is in danger. It's why the Guardian made contact."

Jon said, "I agree and de Villiers wants these treasures. The Guardian's language is adapting more and more to ours. Have you noticed?"

Bob smiled. "I sure did. I bet Julia heard her sexy voice, too. I've got some major explaining to do when I get back home."

Cordy patted his hand. "We got you covered." She hugged him. Jon's men would drive Bob to the airport.

Jon looked at his watch. "The helicopter is waiting for us at the airport. We better go."

When they arrived at La Rochelle, a seaport on the Bay of Biscay, Jon drove them to Le Thiers Temps restaurant. He knew the owner so getting a table in the popular restaurant was easy. Cordy, Ash, and Jon feasted on smoked duck in mushroom soup, smoked red tuna, and for dessert, crème brulee.

Ash asked, "You seem well known here and almost everywhere in France."

Jon nodded. "Oui, my family owns a home here. After dinner we will go there. It will be safe there. The Lafitte family needs to be near the sea and near a wine garden at all times. And Rochelle is connected to Queen Eleanor of Aquitaine. She let the Templar fleet pay no taxes and the city was given a special charter. The Templars' headquarters here is still standing. Templars developed a role as the bankers of Europe and possessed their own independent navy. They were great landowners and as Ash knows, had quarters at Temple Mount in Jerusalem. Rochelle was where La Salle departed for the New World. He landed in Texas at what was later called Fort St. Louis. It's located at the mouth of the Mississippi. I will take you to the Templar Command on the way to my home."

"I saw something very strange at Temple Mount just a few months ago," Ash said. "A beam of light came down from heaven hitting the Dome of the Rock. My family witnessed it. I have never seen anything like it."

Jon nodded. "I've seen footage of it and what a surprise that you witnessed it. We will have to ask the Guardian if she was responsible. Remember what we talked about, how the Guardian is activating all the sacred places around the world? The Dome of the Rock might have been one of them. We must go. It's getting late."

He drove them by the Templar Command at La Rochelle. "Templar sea maps were very valuable and held by trusted sea captains of the Templar navy. La Rochelle is near the Pyrenees Mountains where Templar members resided. Paris was their headquarters. The city dates back to 1139. A transportation system was developed for pilgrims, supplies, and reinforcements to Jerusalem and Cyprus. After Templars were arrested and jailed, they went into hiding. The Hospitallers inherited the wealth and lands of the Templars. De Villiers' family is related to many high commanders in the Hospitallers. We have always been competitors."

Cordy looked at Jon. "Dark Watchers and Light Watchers battling for dominance. The Children of Nephilim committing genocide over and over again. The Pure of Heart trying to stop them. The war has been going on for a long long time."

"Oui."

Jon drove them to his chateau and his security opened the black rod iron gates. Cordy and Ash surveyed the manicured lawns and the 15th century building. It resembled a fairy castle.

"The chateau contains 21 bedrooms, a pool, stables, orangeries, vineyards and ponds. Poppa Jon bought it after World War II and updated it over the years. We will be safe here.

Lafitte led them on a tour of the house. Each room dated back centuries. A gallery of portraits hung on the walls. Cordy saw it first. Jean Lafitte, the famous pirate and legend, looked down at her with a wicked grin. A handsome devil with long dark curly hair and ebony eyes saved America from the British in the war of 1812. Who would guess that a pirate could make such a difference?

Cordy pointed to him. "Handsome devil, and he knows it."

Ash smiled. "He does resemble, Jon, doesn't he?"

Jon laughed at Ash's comment. "Yes, my naughty ancestor. A businessman, Freemason, soldier, and captain led his men in the Battle of 1815 in New Orleans with Andrew Jackson. Outnumbered and outgunned, Lafitte saved New Orleans and the United States. The tour must come to an end, I'm afraid, for in the morning we set sail for Haiti and then New Orleans. The other swords are located in New Orleans and we need to make a stop in Haiti for provisions.

"Sweet dreams, Cordy, and Ash, my friend." Jon placed Cordy's hand gently in his and kissed it.

Ash rolled his eyes. He hoped Cordy wasn't falling for his nonsense.

As Cordy walked to her room, she reflected on all that the three of them had been through. Their experiences continued to draw them closer, forging a friendship between them. However, the two men confused her and at the same time, attracted her as they competed for her affection. Alas, friendship would have to be enough. There wasn't time for a love affair at this critical moment.

CHAPTER 51

Headed for Home

After a scrumptious breakfast, the three of them were packed and ready. Jon needed to complete the Guardian's request and it meant heading to New Orleans. The morning air was crisp and the sun was shining. Weather reports showed no problems for the next few days. Jon did notice a storm brewing in the tropics, but they'd be ahead of it if they set sail today.

The car drove through the French countryside as they passed quaint farmhouses. Remnants of old castles on mountaintops stared down at them. Cordy felt at peace. After a few hours, they arrived at the port.

Ash and Cordy jumped out of the car as Jon yelled out, "The name of my ship is 'Who's Your Daddy.' It's off the main pier. You'll know it when you see it."

Ash was still upset at Jon for putting his moves on Cordy. He looked at her and said, "Do you want him to be your daddy?"

Without hesitation Cordy pulled back and punched Ash's shoulder. He let out a Mi'kmaq war cry but it sounded more like a whine.

"Be careful what you say, bud, I've been known to snap boards in half."

They arrived at the ship. Cordy and Ash just dropped their bags on the pier. For the first time, Cordy questioned Jon's character and wondered if he could be trusted. The ship resembled the schooner Ash's mom and dad had been kidnapped on.

Jon came up to them from behind and said, "What do you think of her? She is an aft-rigged topsail schooner. She's strong, made of oak and teak, built in the USA."

Cordy didn't say a word but all of the emotions associated with Minah's kidnaping came back in a flood. Cordy had saved Minah from a sex slave trader in St. Louis. She punched Jon's shoulder.

Jon yelled, "Damn, woman, what's wrong with you?"

Cordy didn't say a word. She just picked up her bag and walked up the gangplank, passing the two very alarmed armed guards standing on the deck. She headed to the main cabin in the aft of the ship.

Ash looked over at Jon with a grin and said, "Who's your daddy now?"

Jon threw up his hands. "What did I do now? She's a crazy woman."

Ash and Jon picked up their bags and with the other hand rubbed their shoulders. Jon headed back to the main cabin and saw a pissed-off Cordy standing in the hallway. She was already waving a finger at him. As he approached the doorway, Jon yelled out, "What? What's wrong with you? What did I do?"

"You can move that bed and show me what's in that secret cargo hold of yours. That means right now!"

"That's not a good idea, Cordy. There are things I transport for a premium dollar for people who don't want anyone to know what they are shipping."

Cordy pushed the bed and unlatched the straps that held it in place. "You don't get a say in this, Jon. I'll see what your cargo is."

"Damn, Cordy, I've never done this for anyone but if it means that much to you, I'll show you. I'd trust you with my life but promise me you'll never tell anyone what you're about to see."

Cordy stood there with her arms crossed.

"All you pirates are alike. Open it up! Now!"

Jon answered, "Pirates? Come on, Cordy. We prefer privateer, and besides, I think that I'm exceptional at what I do. The Lafitte family is not like anyone you ever met. And we are great warriors and good shooters. I think you and Ash are glad about that fact. So maybe you should just give me a little slack, chérie."

Jon lifted the door recessed in the floor. Cordy didn't even hesitate jumping into the cargo hold.

"Is there a light down here, Jon?"

"Yes, on the post to your left."

Cordy turned on the light and was surprised at all the boxes and crates jammed into such a small place. Narrow paths between the rows of wooden boxes left room for Cordy to inspect his cargo. Every inch of space was meticulously organized.

Cordy opened a latch on one of the cases, which measured about twenty inches by thirty inches. Inside was a painting. As she pulled back the cover protecting the painting, Cordy could see it was a Monet, the same one she'd seen in the newspapers earlier in the week. The painting was reported stolen from a home burglary in Switzerland. "Damn. I knew it."

Cordy opened the leather briefcase next to the painting. Inside the briefcase were stacked rows of gold and silver bars. "What the hell. He's a smuggler. Why am I not surprised?"

Cordy had seen enough. She stomped up from the cargo hold. Jon reached down to help her up and Cory slapped his hand out of the way. She pulled herself up and turned to Jon and gave him a death glare.

Jon smiled. "Sorry, what were you expecting? Nothing down there is owned by me or the family corporation. Think of this ship as a delivery truck or a mail truck. We just deliver from one point to another. And might I say for a very good price. What were you expecting?"

"I had a friend who was kidnapped and captured by a sex slave trader. Bob told me these ships were used to transport slaves."

"Oui, chérie, they were and are still today, that is true enough. However, this ship was made just for our family. It has never been used for that purpose. My family gave up slave trading centuries ago. The bad karma is a legacy we've suffered for our crimes and why we refuse to ever do it again. The Lafitte family doesn't smuggle drugs, slaves, or weapons. We specialize in unique jobs and this is one of them. I need the money and since we're heading in the same direction, I said why not?"

Jon put out his hand and said, "Truce?"

Cordy reached out her hand very slowly. Jon quickly pulled her in and started to kiss her passionately. At first, Cordy pushed back but then was drawn in. She had never been kissed like this before. It seemed like a lifetime had passed since Cordy had let herself run wild. She found herself pulling this pirate of the high seas in closer and now she was the one doing the kissing. Her whole body was on fire! What Cordy and Jon didn't realize was that Ash stood in the doorway watching their passionate embrace.

Ash cleared his throat and whispered sadly, "Um, why don't you two get a room? Oh, I forgot. I see you two already have a room. Well, I decided to come back and check to see if everything was OK. By the looks of it, Jon, I would say you have everything well in hand." Ash was obviously hurt and disappointed.

With disheveled hair, Cordy looked at Ash and became confused. Why did she feel so ashamed? She threw her hands in the air. "Oh, you two are enough to drive any woman crazy." Cordy picked up her bag and stormed past Ash. She got two feet down the corridor then stopped looking at the doorways on either side. "Which room is mine?" she yelled out.

"Mademoiselle, you would be in the one next to mine, the one on the left."

"Then I guess mine is the one on the right," Ash said.

"No, that is my bodyguard's room. Yours is down the corridor at the end on the right."

Ash turned and headed to his room. "Yep, kinda saw that one coming. Well, I will let you two love birds get back to it. I'm going to stow my gear and get some sleep."

Cordy walked toward her room. "I'm going to get some sleep too." She opened up her door to the stateroom, stepped in, and slammed the door. Ash and Jon could hear a Mi'kmaq war cry come from the room. Ash and Jon gazed at each other with a competitive glare.

"Well, Jon, hope I didn't interrupt anything. Thanks for your hospitality." Ash turned and continued to walk down the corridor.

Jon waved his hand and shook his head, then walked to his door and shut it. As he was pushing back the bed and securing it, he said aloud, "I was so close, and now who knows what will happen. What do they say in the U.S.? Game on, Mr. Archaeologist! Game on!" As Jon lay in bed a smile came over his face. He thought, *you know, Jon, she did pull you in and she did kiss you back, and what passion she has. She is magnifique.*

Ash lay on his bed and realized how much Cordy meant to him. He decided Jon had met his match with Cordy. Time would tell who the best man was but Ash wouldn't give up easily.

CHAPTER 52

Visitors in the Night

At two in the morning, Jon's alarm went off. He'd only had a quick nap because he lay in his bed tossing and turning thinking about Cordy. She's the first woman Jon had lost sleep over. He sprang up and got dressed. He headed down the corridor quietly. Jon started to pass Ash's stateroom, when Ash poked his head out the cabin door.

"What's up, Jon? Something wrong?"

"No, just getting the last of my shipment to take to the US. Can you get dressed and meet me up on deck?"

"Be right there, Jon." Ash took but a minute and when he came out on deck he could see Jon shaking someone's hand. The man headed toward the gangplank. "What's up?"

Jon decided to let him know the situation. "Ash, we've got big problems. It seems that bastard de Villiers has gone and put a price on my head. He wants me dead or alive."

Ash smiled, and Jon noticed how happy he looked. "How much are you worth, Jon?"

Jon gazed at the full moon. "Twenty five million dollars. You know what that means, Ash? It means I'm as good as dead. There's more, Cordy and you have a 50-million-dollar bounty for being captured alive. I'm a bit upset. I should have been worth twice that. Insulted is what I am, so I decided to place a bounty on de Villiers for 60 million dollars. My ancestor, the pirate Jean Lafitte, would be proud. He did the same thing to the Governor of Louisiana when he put a bounty on him. If I could've killed him in the tunnel all of this would be over. The bastard knows I'm coming to get him for what he did to Poppa Jon.

"We're going to have to leave right now. The ship needs a minimum of six for a crew. I've got the two guards who have helped before and I trust them with my life. My bodyguard just got in about an hour ago, he'll help us. That leaves Cordy, you and me. Can I count on both of you even in the worst of conditions on the open sea? Even I have been scared out there. You've got to respect the woman with the deep blue eyes or she'll swallow you up and drag you down to the bottom."

Ash nodded. "We're in. I can speak for Cordy, too. How are you so sure the guards and even your own man won't turn you in for the bounty?"

Jon assured him. "The cargo on this ship is worth ten times that and they never blink an eye when it comes to offers of betrayal. Every bad guy wants to take a shot at getting what is on this ship. They dream about it every time we sail. They've never been able to find us on the open seas. The loyalty of my men is unquestionable."

"Let's get going, Jon. Looks like you're in the same boat as Cordy and me."

Jon smiled. "No, we're on a ship not a boat."

Ash laughed. "It was a joke, Jon. Never mind, let's just get out of here, Frenchie."

"I was hoping you were going to say yes," Jon said. "I'm not sure we'd see another day alive in France if we didn't leave tonight." Jon motioned to the two guards to untie and shove off. "Ash, go look for any big objects that we might hit over by the bow of the ship."

Ash started to walk away and turned his head. "You better respect Cordy, Jon, or I'll see you have a date with the blue-eyed woman and I won't be looking for any money."

Jon saluted Ash. "Message well received, Monsieur Ash. Now, if you please, could you get up front and help?" The ship slowly pulled away from the dock. The full moon illuminated the way and the stars shone above Jon's head while he navigated out to sea. He felt at home on his boat, more than any other place on Earth.

Jon remembered Poppa Jon taking him for a cruise and telling him all about the stars and how to use them to navigate. The moment he gazed up at the jewels in the sky, Jon fell in love. Astrophysics journals filled his insatiable curiosity as he thirsted for the knowledge of the heavenly bodies. He enjoyed working for NASA and his wish was to navigate a ship to Mars or Europa. The deep blue ocean existed below his feet but there was another above his head. A small tear fell on Jon's cheek as he recited a sailor's prayer Poppa Jon had taught him to say while setting on a journey on the sea. The grief hit him full force and in the distance he saw a falling star. Jon smiled, for Poppa Jon had told him it was a good sign. He started to sing, "Farewell my pretty lady, I must sail away." Poppa Jon sang the song often to him as a child. The ship plunged ahead and in the darkness Jon continued to sing.

CHAPTER 53

It's a Great Day at Sea

In the morning, as the sun rose, Jon ordered one of the crew to pilot the ship. Ash and Jon were up on the bow doing their morning tai chi. The sun glowed and warmed the deck of the ship. A clear blue sky, deep blue ocean water and a light breeze surrounded them. As they sailed south the breeze became warmer.

Not too long ago, Ash remembered he had been in the desert sleeping on the hood of his 4Runner. The last cruise he'd been on was with Dirty Dottie and she had him locked up in her cabin. So sailing on Jon's ship was a totally different experience for him, and he liked it. The air felt clean and fresh but the sea breeze had a salty flavor to it. Ash demonstrated great discipline in the art of tai chi. Jon noticed just how proficient Ash had become in such a short time. He made a note to himself not to underestimate him.

Cordy woke up surprised as she felt the ship floating on the sea. She could feel the roll and pitch of the waves and heard the sound of rushing water. Cordy breathed in the warm humid air flowing through her cabin. She was excited to have the opportunity to see such a massive sailing ship in action. She noticed her stateroom was decorated with a woman's touch. She wondered who the woman with the great taste was and about her relationship with Jon.

Cordy went through the drawers and found several string bikinis. As she strolled past Ash's cabin she knocked and saw that he wasn't in. She went in and grabbed a white, cotton, long-sleeved shirt, put it to her face and took a deep breath. She was attracted to his special musk. She put it on and headed for the top-deck. She couldn't believe her eyes. Ash and Jon moved in perfect harmony as they did tai chi. Ash had become a master in just the short time they'd been together. Cordy also couldn't get past the fact from behind they looked like chiseled statues of Greek gods. She walked between the men and took off her long-sleeved shirt. They both turned their heads so fast she thought she heard their necks snap.

Cordy chided them. "Come on, gentlemen, focus." Jon was in awe of the goddess next to him, and Ash couldn't keep from falling over.

"Well, gentlemen, I can see this tai chi class has come to an end." Cordy took two steps forward and turned. In an instant, she stood up straight and put on the white long-sleeved shirt. The two let out a disappointing moan. "A girl has to protect her skin from the sun, you know." Yet the white shirt still showed the red bikini, ever so slightly. Little did she know this would be the true torture all day. Nothing works harder on a man than his imagination.

Cordy spoke a little French, so she looked at Jon and said in her broken French, "Is he still mad from last night?" Jon knew what she was referring to — the kiss.

Jon replied in his perfect sexy French voice, "Surprisingly, no. He's been just fine." Ash glanced at Cordy with surprise; he didn't realize she spoke French. He decided to be silent.

Ash asked, "Jon, where are we headed and what's our ETA?"

"Now that we are at sea I can tell you the first leg of the trip," Jon said. "We're headed to Gonaives, a port city on the island of Haiti. The ship will resupply there and then head out for Galveston, Texas. We will download our cargo and then the ship needs to go to New Orleans, its home port."

"How long will it take us?" Cordy wondered.

"With good wind, we should arrive in Haiti in about eight days and Galveston in about three and a half days after that. The dangerous part will be getting the ship back to New Orleans. If all goes well, it should only take about one day, but that's a big if. I fear everyone and their brother will be looking for me and the ship."

As Jon and Ash put back on their shirts, Cordy could see both of them wince with pain. They had matching huge bruises on their shoulders where Cordy had hit them with her fist the night before, just as she'd done back at Master Wong's DOJO snapping boards with her bare fist. She smiled. Both men needed a reminder to approach her with caution.

CHAPTER 54

Long Days and Longer Nights

Ash had no clue what they signed onto when he volunteered Cordy and himself to become shipmates. Sailors' work was very hard. Paired up with the two experienced guards, Ash and Cordy figured out early on this wasn't a pleasure cruise. Although it was harder than he had expected, Ash enjoyed watching Cordy across the way, learning and pulling more than her weight. Ash felt relief to see her so preoccupied. He could see for the first time that the stress of losing the chief, Linda, and Sister Agnes eased. Fresh ocean air proved healing to both of them.

Cordy was impressed at how Ash could climb the ropes with just his arms. His upper body strength was phenomenal.

At the end of the day, as the sun was setting, Jon rang the dinner bell for his new crew. Jon placed a small but elegant table set for the two Pure of Heart who worked their hearts out at sea. He broke the baguette and handed it to Ash. "Well, you two have come to respect life on the high seas these past days. Here, take this, you earned it."

Ash grabbed the baguette and chomped down. He was so hungry

all he could do was grunt, "Hmm." Cordy didn't make a sound. She knew all about calorie intake but nothing else mattered at that moment except eating the delicious meal.

Jon cat napped throughout the day and knew everyone wondered why he wasn't working as hard as the rest. The captain's job was to navigate, and his job more mental than physical. "Well, you two need to get some rest, tomorrow won't be any different with work load, but you have learned a lot today and should be proud. I'll be taking the night shift and Roger, my buddy here, will make any small adjustments as the blue eyed lady decides to get rowdy throughout the night. I'll need the two of you to report back on deck at no later than 05:00 hours tomorrow. The first thing I need you to do is check to make-sure I'm still awake. There's no time to waste."

"Thanks for dinner," Ash said. "I'm dead and heading for bed." He shook Jon's hand and headed toward his cabin. As he turned he could hear Jon ask Cordy something in French.

Jon leaned over. "Well, my chérie, shall I come join you on my break later tonight? I can rub your sore back among other things to help you relax and loosen you up.

Cordy spoke back in French, "No, monsieur, I'm dead tired and will need every minute of sleep to make it through tomorrow, if you know what I mean."

Jon smiled. "Oui, I understand, chérie." Ash stood still at the top step watching the exchange. As Cordy started to walk away she bent over and kissed Jon on the forehead. Cordy shocked herself when she did that, and wondered if she was being pulled in by the bad boy's charm. She admonished herself, telling herself she should have known better. Cordy knew both of them suffered a great loss. She felt his pain.

Jon asked nonchalantly, "Cordy, if you don't mind, I'd like to visit with the Guardian tonight. She can help keep me awake."

Cordy laughed. "I know better, Jon. You are going to talk stars and constellations with her. Just don't let her fall overboard, Captain."

"Don't worry. I respect wise women. She'll be safe with me. See you in the morning, chérie."

Ash had his cabin door cracked open so he could see if Cordy headed to her room. It was one of the silliest things he'd ever done, because every-time the ship would roll, his door would bang.

As she went by Ash's cabin, Cordy could see and hear his door bang. She knew what he was up to. "Goodnight, Ash." She heard his door close. Cordy smiled and thought, *someone is jealous.*

Jon was well into his late night shift when he finally got "Who's Your Daddy" squared away. She was running smooth and true on autopilot. The Frenchman was accomplished in most everything he attempted but excelled in his ability to sail. He'd inherited his sailing instincts from his notorious ancestor, the privateer of 1812. Lafitte never got sea sick as a child and he was a natural born leader. Jon climbed down to get the backpack left by his shipmate.

When he arrived at his cabin, he reached in and pulled out the two golden triangles and the crystal ball. Cordy and Ash were surprised he was able to hold the triangles as only the Pure of Heart could handle them without harm. But the Frenchman had passed the test earlier in Paris. It was a sign given by the Guardian that Jon deep down was a Pure of Heart. He may not believe it but she knew where his heart lay.

The night sky glimmered with stars and the crisp air blew his dark curly hair. The boat cruised smoothly through the dark waters. Jon climbed back on deck to finish his shift. Everyone had headed to bed and left him alone sailing the ship. He poured a glass of his favorite wine and placed it on a small wooden table. He then set up the triangles in the shape of a Star of David and placed the crystal ball in the indented center. He whistled the children's song "Twinkle, Twinkle, Little Star" as Cordy told him. In seconds, the mysterious Guardian appeared to the handsome Frenchman.

The Guardian had a serene smile as her holographic image stood before him. The statuesque image took his breath away. "Well, hello, Jon, what a lovely night. Not a cloud in the sky." The night air had just a little chill to it but you could feel the warm southern air flow trying to break through.

Jon smiled. "Guardian, you know I am an astrophysicist and

have a few questions for you. The stars fascinate me, and I believe you know about our galaxy and all about Earth."

"The way I see it Mr. Jon, you also hold the titles of smuggler, CEO, and how do they say it now days, Don Juan? or is it Don Jon?"

Jon laughed. "I see myself as a transporter, CEO and lucky. I have a question for you, Guardian. Are you tapping into communications and data systems? Because you are adapting to current times, if your language is any indication."

"I can read and collect all electronic data as well as visual data."

Jon nodded. "I knew you were evolving and learning new information. May I call you Diane for short? Seeing as how it is the last part of your name."

The Guardian smiled. "I've been called many names over the years. You may call me what you will."

"Diane, I like that the name fits. Can you see the stars above us and recognize the constellations?"

The Guardian looked up into the sky. "Yes, a spectacular show of energy is it not? Not much has changed over the years. I see movement but all the main players are intact."

Jon knew the next question would be tricky. "How old are you, Diane, and where do you come from?"

The Guardian smiled. "Asking a lady her age, a French man should know better. My first data collection started long ago. You could say I was born into knowledge but also that I had knowledge."

Jon had to ask the one question that had always intrigued him. "Is there life out there, Diane?" He pointed above his head.

The Guardian gazed up into the ocean of stars. "Why, Mr. Jon, the sea abounds with life, fish, whales and many other creatures. The universe is an ocean of stars but you knew the answer before you asked the question, didn't you?"

Jon pushed to know more and looked straight up to the night sky. "That's not what I was talking about, life out there in the stars."

The Guardian looked up into the sky. "I don't know, Mr. Jon. I have sacred secret knowledge given to me and only the Pure of

Heart can have access to it. Your question opens many doors and some are not ready to be opened. The mathematical probability leaves one to deduce that yes, probably, life exists in the big, vast universe. My job is to protect the progress of life on Terra. What that progress is or when it ends is up to the Pure of Heart. But if we can see life close to the ocean from this ship just a few feet away, then, why couldn't there be life on the other side of the universe in a similar ocean? Water is the key to life. There are many ties to the heavens from the early years, such as the sphinx, the Giza Pyramids, and many other constructed structures. They all point to the constellation of Orion. Even the Pyramids of Giza simulate Orion's Belt, they almost line up exactly. If I were to sail a ship into the sea of stars, I would look to Orion."

"As an astrophysicist, I would say you're dead on, Diane. The Orion Nebula seems to be a haven for possible evolving planets. We are like Jason and the Argonauts looking for the Golden Fleece. Well, old girl, time for me to get back to the task at hand. Don't want us to go in a circle."

The Guardian's voice took a serious tone, "When you first accessed me, I could read a sense of frustration. What was the cause?"

Jon sighed. "Diane, let's just say locked doors don't work for even a lucky man." With that, Jon pulled the two golden triangles out from underneath the crystal ball and Diane disappeared.

Jon stretched his arms over his head and let out a huge yawn. The long days and even longer nights were starting to take their toll on him. He dozed off for a couple of minutes and then was awakened by a bright light. "Diane, is that you? I thought I put you to bed." He instinctively reached to feel the golden triangles and the crystal ball in his pockets then bolted as fast as he could to his feet and turned. A tall stranger in a black leather jacket stood next to him. Jon rubbed his eyes.

"Who are you and how did you get on my ship?" Jon looked around for a weapon but found none nearby. He was screwed.

"Well Jon, do you believe in angels?" Uriel asked.

Jon played along with his curious visitor. "I knew a couple of women who I thought were angels and had fun looking for their wings." He chuckled and repeated his question, "Who the hell are you and how did you get on my ship?"

"My name is Uriel. I'm the angel in the Book of Enoch who warned Noah about the devastating Great Flood and instructed Enoch on the stars above. The one you showed Ash and Cordy in da Vinci's *Virgin on the Rocks* painting? But I'm better dressed and better looking. Leonardo had a sense of humor when he painted me with no halo."

Jon was surprised. "You mean Uriel the archangel, angel?"

"Well I was trying to be modest but yes, some have given me the title of archangel and if you don't mind, I'm not on your ship but about one foot off the deck."

Jon couldn't believe his eyes. "Damn, that's a trick and a half."

The angel leaned forward and Jon stepped back. Uriel spoke in French. "Come on, Monsieur Jon, I just want to give you a pair of sunglasses to take away the pain of looking at me." Jon reached out and took the glasses. As soon as he put them on, he could see the light was coming from a sword partially hidden and tucked behind a long overcoat.

"What can I do for you, monsieur?"

Uriel explained. "It's not what you can do for me. It is more what you can do for yourself. You've set in motion the final showdown between the Pure of Heart and everything that is evil in the world. I didn't want to scare you. I just wanted to get your attention."

"You've got my attention. Just floating above the deck did that."

"Jon, you are already focused on killing de Villiers and losing sight of the task at hand. You must help Cordy and Ash get to their final destination. De Villiers will come to you because he seeks the Pure of Heart and you'll be right with them, side-by-side."

Jon started to get angry. "Don't tell me what my focus should be, ghost!"

Uriel held up his hands in the air. "Whoah, wait just a minute, Monsieur Jon. I'm no ghost. That hurts. You can call me anything but that. If you want to make it through this alive you should take my advice. A large storm is brewing down south and it'll be the worst anybody has ever seen. You'll need something your father kept hidden from everyone, something passed down for many generations. It's the Sword of Orion and it possesses the power to calm the storm and give you time to reach your final destination and goal. The Orion Sword unites all of the swords. You and only you will know where to look; your grandfather would have put it somewhere special."

Jon shook his head. "I don't know what you're talking about. Poppa Jon would have told me about the Sword of Orion and the location."

"As we speak Jon, you are already thinking of where it could be. Remember, Jon Lafitte, you must protect the Pure of Heart above all. You know just how bad of a shot Ash is." They both began to laugh.

"Yes, Monsieur Uriel, you've got that right. I don't think Ash has hit anything he's aimed at yet. He's scary."

Uriel gave Jon a warning. "You must not anchor in Galveston, and you must separate Cordy and Ash to get them to New Orleans. They will fight you on this because they've sworn to stick together no matter what. Everyone in port is searching for two Pure of Heart. One person can make or break this war. If one dies, you could still have a chance. If both die, the world will go into darkness and never recover. All will be lost forever."

"How can you know all this to be true?"

"I was the one who guarded the gates in the Garden of Eden and the Tree of Life. You're a Pure of Heart whether you like it or not. I know you've changed and you'll live if you fight for your people and Earth."

Jon bent over to pick up his vintage wine because he needed a drink. When Jon looked up, Uriel had disappeared. The sunrays peaked above in the horizon and Jon could see Cordy and Ash arriving up on deck.

Cordy smiled. "Well, Jon, how did your date with the Guardian go?"

Jon frowned. "That went great, but it was the talk I just finished with Uriel that was upsetting."

Cordy and Ash glanced at each other. "You saw Uriel?"

"Yes, and by the sound of it, you two must know him well."

Ash gazed at the sun rising in the distance over the sea. "He saved my life. I know he is on our side of the war."

Cordy leaned over the rail, feeling the cool morning breeze. "He can be a great resource, too."

Jon crossed his arms over his chest. "Well, if you've anything else to tell me, get on with it and if not, I am headed to my cabin. It was a very long night. You two get to work. We must make haste to Haiti."

CHAPTER 55

Land Ho

Every day started and ended the same way — long hard nights for Jon, and the same for Cordy and Ash during the day. Dinner was the only time the three of them really spent any time together. But every night at around midnight, Cordy would be woken by the sound of Jon checking to see if her door was locked. She had to give him an A+ for effort.

The seven-day voyage to Haiti was coming to an end and the re-alization that the ship need to resupply was going to be a daunting task with a price on all three of their heads.

Jon said, "Well, you two, we'll be in port in about four hours. The first leg of the trip has been great and we made good time. We will spend one night in the port city of Gonaives, an out-of-the-way city in the northern part of Haiti. The city is rich in history. It was founded in 1422 by Taino people and known as the Independence City. But don't let this little town fool you. It's very dangerous. I have a friend we're staying with and at first light tomorrow we must set sail with no exceptions."

One of the crew let out a shout, "Land ho."

"I'd like to have all three of us do our morning tai chi together," Cordy said. "The exercises promote good team dynamics." The guys agreed and Ash, Jon, and Cordy took their usual places with Cordy in the middle. All three stood moving as one. They'd come together during the trip and their graceful movements in unison painted a balanced picture.

"Both of you've done an outstanding job every day," Jon said. "You've cheated the blue-eyed lady, and we're ahead of schedule."

Ash smiled. "I enjoyed the voyage except one thing annoyed the hell out of me. Jon, did you know you had a rat on board? Every night about midnight a rat starts to gnaw on one of the cabin doors. The lil' bastard has woken me up every night. Did either of you hear anything?"

Jon and Cordy looked at Ash. Simultaneously, they said, "We didn't hear a thing."

"Well, it's no big deal. I don't think the rat got in the cabin, so no harm done." Cordy started to blush and with the warm Caribbean air her face only got redder.

"Well, gentlemen, I think this session is over. I'm getting overheated." Cordy scampered away.

Jon agreed. "Let's look lively. It's time to get "Who's Your Daddy" into port. Ash and Cordy helped drop the sails and the ship coasted to a stop just as Jon dropped the anchor. The docking of the ship looked like poetry in motion as its captain's experience showed.

Jon talked to the other crewmembers and they dropped the dingy. He motioned to Ash and Cordy to come over. "Go below and just get what you need for a short night on the island." They were back in two seconds.

Cordy gazed at the beautiful palm trees and white sand. "I've never been to a Caribbean island before. I can't wait to see and talk to the locals."

Jon put a stop to her tourism idea. "Not going to happen, Cordy. Did you forget when we left France we all had bounties on our heads? My friends on the island want us, to keep a low profile, got it?" Jon passed out handguns to both of them. "Ash, if you have to shoot, don't try to aim — just point and shoot. I think that might work better."

"Very funny." Ash started down to the dingy and once again he could here Jon talking in French to Cordy.

After they arrived at the docks everyone worked unloading the cargo of the ships. They weren't really paying close attention to people because strangers went back and forth all the time. One man spotted them and started to walk down to where they were tying up. As the man got close, Cordy and Ash started to get nervous. Ash started to put his hand on the Glock tucked in his pants.

Jon grabbed his hand. "Hold on, that's my cousin, Ted."

He waved at the man coming toward him. "Ted, long time no see my friend. How has the weather been down here?"

Ted smiled. "Not bad, but they say there is a big mother coming our way from the south, and it's way too early in the season."

"Uh oh, we better not stay too long. You know the drill, Ted, we'll be back in the early morning at sunrise."

Jon looked at Ash and Cordy. "Mademoiselle and Monsieur, that means we will be setting sail with or without you at 6 a.m. sharp. Which means be at the dock, on time." Ash and Cordy nodded and walked toward town.

Cordy asked, "Jon, the town used to be an old pirate hangout, right?"

"In the old days, my great-great-grandpapa Jean would have said a privateer's home port. Today, I just call Gonaives the city of mystery and opportunity. You never know what will happen — it's a mystery — and everyone is looking for the opportunity to make a deal."

Ted pointed. "Jon, Cousin Mike is at the end of the dock in a red truck. He will take you to the guest house."

"OK, Ted, we'll see each other here tomorrow, and call me if you see anything out of the ordinary."

Ash laughed. "Everything looks out of the ordinary. This gives a whole new meaning to the word."

It was midday now and Cousin Mike dropped them off at a small but fortified house just up the street.

"Jon, you have a lot of family down here. Are they originally from Haiti?" Ash asked.

"Let's just say I had some uncles that were not welcome in the U.S. any more so they settled here," Jon explained. "I've got some errands to run and need to collect some information on what is happening stateside. There's a local bar just one block toward the beach. You can hang out there until I get back. I know the owner, Sally. She'll take good care of you. I'll walk you down and be back soon."

CHAPTER 56

Gonaives' Local Flavor

Ash and Cordy walked into Sal's Bar and Grill. The bar made it seem as if time stood still. Like Casablanca, you could imagine Humphrey Bogart and Ingrid Bergman sitting at the bar but the bar still had a Caribbean twist. A DJ was setting up in the corner, getting ready for the night. He pulled out a sign that read, "It's Island Time with Chris Love." A female bartender walked up to Ash and Cordy, a tall woman about six feet five inches with dark hair featuring speckles of gray. "Whatcha tasting today? My name is Sal. Your friend Jon called and said to take care of you. What are your names?"

Ash remembered an old man's advice to never give your real name. "My name is Rick, and this is my girlfriend Lisa." Cordy locked eyes with Ash. She was surprised to find herself his girlfriend but started to smile. Ash returned the smile with interest.

Ash looked over by the DJ. "Are you planning a big night tonight with the music and all the decorations?"

Sal shook her head. "No, just your regular Saturday night. Get down and drunk, same as any other Saturday. You're going to like Chris Love. He's the best DJ on the island."

Chris, a native Haitian, walked with a slight limp. He'd been involved in a boating accident when he was in his early twenties. His leg never healed and caused him many restless nights. Now, at 32, he was one of the best DJs on the island and ran many other lucrative businesses as well. Chris always wore his hair cut short, and his signature dress evolved from the old South Florida look, a white cotton suit coat with no shirt and six-pack abs to drive the women wild. White cotton pants and alligator cowboy boots gave him a unique style. Around his neck hung some type of gold chain accompanied by a one-carat diamond earring.

The music started to play and Cordy was just dying to dance. "Ash, come on and dance with me?"

"I don't want to Cordy." Ash remembered Jon's warning.

"Well, that never stopped me from dancing before." Cordy got up and headed for the dance floor. No one was dancing yet so all eyes trained on Cordy. She'd been cooped up on a boat and was ready to unwind. Ash thought she never got the lecture from the old man about blending in. The good-looking Chris stepped down on the dance floor and started dancing with Cordy. He couldn't miss the chance to dance with such a hot woman. Plus, it'd get the crowd dancing. Every time he would move his head the light would catch the diamond stud in his ear and reflect into the crowd at the bar. Even with a limp, Chris was a great dancer. Everyone at the bar was mesmerized by the delightful dancing couple having so much fun together. Ash knew it wasn't good for them to draw attention to themselves. He jumped down off his bar stool and grabbed Cordy by the arm and headed for the door. All the men at the bar yelled at Ash.

Ash whispered, "What are you trying to do? Get us killed?"

"Don't you ever grab me like that again and tell me what to do!"

Ash knew she was pissed, but he did get them out of the bar without injury. She didn't understand why Ash wouldn't dance with her.

Jon got back to the guesthouse around midnight that evening and peeked in Ash's room. He lay in bed reading and had heard Jon return.

"She's in the next room down the hall, but it won't do you any good. Cordy has the door locked just like on the ship. Oh, and one more thing, she's really pissed at me but Cordy can tell you what happened in the morning in French." Jon shut the door and smiled.

About 3 a.m., everyone woke up to a wild screaming voice in the back yard. Everyone ran to see what the hell was going on. They could see a small fire burning and a man with dreadlocks wearing a skeleton mask holding a cane with a skull on top. Jon, Ash, and Cordy gathered by the window wondering who he was and what he was doing. Jon told them it could be a voodoo ritual. He warned them. "Don't go out there. It's bad juju." The man danced around the fire and had a bright flash of light shine by the side of his head, which must have been reflected by the light of the fire. The scary figure dancing around the flames looked like he cast a spell and started to raise some hell. Ash patted the shocked Jon and Cordy on the back and said, "I've got this one."

Ash walked down the back steps toward the voodoo master. "Yaba yabaphooo on youuu," the figure yelled, rattling bones straight at Ash. Smoke rose from the fire and sparks danced into the air. The closer Ash got, the louder and angrier the voodoo master screamed. He raised his cane with the skeleton head swinging it in the air. Ash got five feet away and the voodoo master started to back away at his boldness. Ash noted he had a limp. The flash of light came from the side of his head once more. The voodoo master reached down and pulled a rooster from his bag. In a split second, he cut the rooster's neck, spraying blood all over himself and Ash.

"Abba dabbba phooo on you," he screamed as loud as he could.

Ash kept moving closer to the voodoo master.

Cordy screamed out, "Stop, don't do it, Ash!"

Jon restrained her from running out. He pulled out his gun.

Ash reached over and grabbed the voodoo master and held onto him as he struggled to get away. Ash bent his head down and closed his eyes. He held onto the voodoo man's arm with all his might. Finally, calm fell over the man and Ash released the man. The voodoo master backed up even further but this time he stood erect and his limp had disappeared. Ash had healed him.

"My juju is stronger than your magic, Chris Love."

Chris smiled. "How did you know?"

"The diamond earring reflected the light, same as in the bar."

Ash put his arm around Chris' shoulders and the two walked into the jungle.

"Take me where we can talk."

Chris couldn't believe his leg felt so good. He'd been crippled for years. Ash introduced himself to Chris and both of them felt a bond immediately. He thought fate played a part in meeting Chris and he wanted to know more about this daytime-DJ-turned-voodoo-master. Chris knew anybody else would have run for the hills when they saw the voodoo master, but not Ash. He was ticked at Ash for breaking up his dance with Cordy. The voodoo master looked for revenge but ended up healed. The spirits worked their magic on him tonight and freed him from his pain. The fearless archaeologist had powerful healing hands and an in with the angels.

Ash told him all about the war against the Children of the Nephilim and the Dark Watchers' Grandmaster de Villiers. Chris knew of de Villiers' reputation. Chris and others were aware of his attraction to powerful objects.

De Villiers had previously approached him in an attempt to acquire his ancestor Marie LaVeau's necklace. "I told him absolutely not. The boating accident happened afterward. De Villiers wanted me dead, but the voodoo queen of New Orleans protected me. You came into my life and cured me. I want to join your quest, Ash. You're going to need me. De Villiers' believes he can rule this world if he summons the spirits of the angelic world. My ancestor Queen Marie could, and he wanted to use me to get to her to help him. She aided the sick and poor when she lived in New Orleans. Queen Marie was respected and feared, but I know she would want nothing to do with his lust for power and viciousness. She will protect us as I will call on her to aid us. A voodoo priestess' powers extend through many worlds of the living and dead."

"What if I told you, Chris, that I found one of the Keys of Life?"

"I would tell you, I hold the Key to Marie. She protects me."

Ash took a drink of whiskey, and then Chris poured them both another and smiled.

"I think you're our man, Chris. Welcome aboard."

"You know Lafitte is a smuggler. You're traveling with a very dangerous man. His family's reputation goes way back. Are you sure he can be trusted?"

Ash shook his head. "Absolutely not, but he's in the same boat as we are, you could say."

Chris smiled and gulped his shot down. "So tell me, what's the story on Cordy and you?"

Ash shook his head and poured Chris another drink. "You got any love potions in that bag of tricks? It's a long story."

"I got all night, Ash."

Ash told Chris about the war between the Children of the Nephilim and the Pure of Heart. He explained his discovery of the Keys of Life at the Temple at Abu Simbel, the miracle seeds found in the golden ankh that could produce food for all the children of Earth.

CHAPTER 57

Never Say No to a Voodoo Queen

Chris fell down on his bed and closed his eyes. It was the first time in a long while that pain didn't wake him. His mind drifted and Chris found himself standing in front of the Saint Louis Cathedral. The church saw lines of people dressed in their Sunday best entering its doors. A smiling black woman in a white lace dress and carrying a parasol grabbed his arm. "Chris, you're here. Let me introduce myself. My name is Marie Laveau."

He stared at his magnificent relative. The woman resembled his dead mother. People said his mother bore an uncanny likeness to pictures of the famous voodoo queen. His mother was even named Marie, after her famous ancestor. The gorgeous lady held her head with a regal bearing and her eyes twinkled with amusement. Marie grabbed his arm and they walked over to a small café named Uriel's. They sat down at a table outside on the veranda, where glasses of wine and a shrimp cocktail awaited them. Marie nibbled on shrimp from the crystal glass and took a sip of wine.

"I want you to meet the owner. Here he is now." A tall redheaded man dressed in white kissed Marie's hand. "Enchanté, Marie." He smiled at Chris.

"Hello, Chris, welcome to Uriel's Restaurant. Notice the wings around the name. The food is heavenly." He pointed to a sign featuring white wings. The café sat on the bustling Chartres Street, right next to the church.

Chris liked Uriel instantly. "Merci. The shrimp is delicious and the wine superb."

Uriel stared up into the clouds. "I believe time is running out, Marie. Better be off soon. One piece of advice, Chris, the best revenge is not to mimic your foe. You're unique and from a royal bloodline. " He kissed Marie's hand, and she beckoned Chris to follow her.

Her laugh tickled the air. "I'm very proud of you, Chris. You've done well, but it's time to come out of hiding. You need to protect Earth's children. You know how to stop de Villiers."

Chris shook his head. "My mother warned me to stay away from the dark sorcerers. He's using one of the most powerful objects to gain power."

Her dark eyes met his. "Your mother knew the danger of going into the darkness, but he needs to be stopped. No one can stop him but the Pure of Heart and you. I will be there with you always. Don't worry about Lafitte. I knew his family well, and they know when to fight against evil. The time is now. Your destiny is with Ash and Cordy. Ash broke the spell de Villiers placed on you. He's been watching you, Chris, and placed a spell on you which made you weak. The Dark Watcher Master saw your potential in his star charts when you were young. The spell affected your leg, causing pain and great suffering. De Villiers' arrogance will be his downfall. The use of dark magic backfires and now it is your right to repay him. I came to mass every Sunday at this church, and it is here where you will defeat his plan to destroy New Orleans."

Chris was shocked. "He's going to destroy New Orleans? Why?"

"He wants to destroy Lafitte and he knows the Pure of Heart treasure lies there. I know, because I aided them. I'll be with you always, Chris. Remember who you are and where you come from. It is your destiny."

"Queen Marie Laveau, how can I refuse you? I'll do it, but how?"

The woman walked along the street with her arm in his. No one noticed them.

"He won't be expecting you so the element of surprise is on your side. A gift will come into your possession. Your heart and will are stronger than his. You will be on your family's turf. If you fail, people will die and so will Earth. You must wear the most powerful gris gris in your possession. The one you wear now around your neck was made by me and handed down. My necklace can be used to summon my help. I will come when you call."

Chris felt the powerful gris-gris around his neck hidden under his shirt.

"I'll not fail you, Queen Marie. He doesn't scare me."

Her intense gaze pierced his heart. "Your suffering has ended, Chris, and your prayers heard by the Lord of Hosts. They sent Ash to you to heal you. The Saint Louis Cathedral holds great power. I know because some of my rituals were performed inside its walls. Fear is his weapon, and courage is your shield. The Eye of Ra and the Watchers lay above your head on the ceiling of the church on the Ark of the Covenant. The Keys of Life were placed in the ark to save the world. The Bread of Angels is one of the Keys of Life. The elimination of hunger is possible. The seeds of life can save the world. De Villiers' wants the Keys of Life to rule. Don't let him achieve his wish or the world's children are doomed. "

They stopped and sat on a bench under a great oak tree in front of the church. Marie held Chris' hand in hers. He felt the strength of his ancestors like a strong vibration.

Chris asked, "What does he look like?"

She was surprised at the question. "You don't see him? Look again my dear and use your heart to guide you. Who is the evilest one here?" Marie's finger pointed to a man dressed in a black suit and hat, carrying a cane, who looked directly at them."

Chris felt his body stiffen and his senses alerted him to danger.

The man slowly headed toward them in a menacing way, and he started swinging his cane. The clouds darkened in the sky and the wind blew harder.

He turned to her with trepidation. "Come, Marie, let's get out of here."

Her voice commanded the evil one. "Leave us, Dark Watcher."

De Villiers sneered at her. "I don't listen to an old has-been fraud like you. I'm here to kill him, and you can't stop me."

The calm woman confidently stood up and stared at the encroaching man. She didn't move.

"Queen Marie does not run from evil. It runs from her."

She called out in a commanding voice, "Zobi, my pet, defend me."

Lightning struck all around Chris and her. The winds blew with hurricane force and yet the threatening man kept coming at them. From under the bench, a red huge boa constrictor slithered straight for de Villiers. Marie's left hand stroked the back of the snake as he passed. The snake wrapped itself around the man, suffocating his squirming prey. Chris watched as the snake proceeded to swallow the man whole, his kicking feet sticking out of the reptile's mouth.

Marie stood up and looked at Chris with great love. "Remember, dear one, evil consumes itself because its hunger is insatiable. Don't be the prey. Be the predator. I will always protect you."

Chris felt hands grabbing him and shaking him. A panic-stricken Ash yelled, "Wake up Chris. We need to catch a boat."

After spending all night drinking, Ash awoke to rays of sunlight peeking through the drapes of the window. Remembering the warning Jon had given about being at the dock at 6 a.m., Chris and Ash tripped over each other, stumbling from their hangovers. They scrambled to the docks as fast as they could run.

CHAPTER 58

Late for His Day Job

At 6 a.m., Jon and Cordy were standing next to the dingy waiting for Ash. Jon broke the news to Cordy and glanced at his watch.

"We must leave, chérie."

"No, Jon. Give him a few more minutes."

"Cordy, it's not possible to wait anymore." She couldn't believe Ash would be late without a good reason. Why did he run off with the crazy witch doctor? Cordy worried all night about him. Jon refused to let her wander in the dark. He trusted Ash and felt he knew what he was doing. She didn't want to leave without him but Jon warned him not to be late. An ache filled her heart as she realized Ash meant a great deal to her. She shouldn't have been so tough on him, especially since Cordy knew she was in the wrong. Jon pushed her over to the waiting dingy. He told her Ash would catch up with them later.

They both jumped in and Jon started to give the signal to leave. Cordy grabbed Jon's hand and smiled. In the distance, two men ran to the dock waving their arms and shouting.

"Wait, wait," yelled Ash.

Ash brought Chris Love with him, and they jumped into the boat together.

"We can't take him with us," yelled Jon.

Ash reassured him, "We need this guy. He's a genuine certified voodoo master so don't tick him off, Jon boy."

Cordy shook Chris' hand. "Welcome to the team, Chris." Jon gave him a warning. "Welcome, but be warned, I'll be watching you. If you give me any trouble, I'll kill you. Understood, voodoo master?"

Chris looked at Ash. "Charming fellow."

Ash nodded, "You have no idea, but my advice is don't piss him off."

"It should be him who should not tick me off. I guarantee he'd regret it." Chris' steely eyes sent Jon a message.

The voodoo master knew instantly he had stumbled upon a life and death adventure. The dingy went around Jon's boat. Chris recognized the name on the infamous schooner. Many thieves on the island attempted to steal her mysterious rich cargo but none of them were seen again or lived to spend their riches. Everyone in the black market called her the death ship. The boat waved an invisible skull and crossbones flag of the pirates to all the island's inhabitants.

Chris was definitely having an "oh shit" moment. Ash and Cordy got to work straight away. Both smiled at each other, relieved to be back together again.

The schooner sailed toward Galveston, Texas, and Bolivar peninsula. Lafitte's family history dated back to the 1800s and they called it Campeche. Ash explained to Cordy and Jon, "Chris Love is Christophe Laveau and great-great-grandson of Marie Laveau. She was the renowned voodoo queen of New Orleans. We're going to need him and his special talents. Just as you're afraid of him, Jon, so are the Dark Watchers."

Jon smiled. "Excellent, he will prove useful against the sorcerer de Villiers. The voodoo master will give the despicable bastard a run for his money."

"De Villiers practices dark magic?" Cordy asked.

Jon nodded. "He trained in the dark arts for many years. That's why he covets the treasures protected by the Pure of Heart. His master plan is to rule not just Earth, but the universe. He needs the ring with the Shield of David, which you carry, to achieve his goal."

Jon gazed out onto the light blue waters and turned toward them suddenly. An idea came to him and he smiled. "I, by chance, possess something important to de Villiers and just what a voodoo master might need. My last meeting with him left me with a souvenir." A basket of dirty clothes sat on the deck. Jon was going to wash them later. He pulled a small sample of de Villiers' silver gray hair from his pants pocket.

Chris smiled at Jon. "Perfect."

Jon pointed to the coastline. "We'll arrive in Galveston by tomorrow and meet up with my most trusted partner in the other half of our American operation."

Cordy wondered for a second, *is Jon a married man? He never said he was in a relationship and if he were, why would the cheat try to sneak in my room every night?* She wondered who this "most trusted partner" was. The way Jon said it, it sounded like he loved this partner. Ash glanced quickly at Cordy and smiled.

Jon threw a blanket at Chris and said, "You sleep up on deck tonight. Don't ever forget that half my crew are highly trained bodyguards, so don't think about stealing anything, understood?"

Chris nodded. He was just glad to still be alive. He wondered why the hell he even came. Lafitte's ruthless reputation and history were well-known among Chris' family. He rubbed the protective amulet engraved with a heart given to him by his grandmother. Chris' family history gave him courage and he refused to be scared for Queen Marie Laveau would protect him. If anybody hurt Chris, they'd regret it.

Later that night, Cordy heard someone try to sneak into her cabin but the door stayed locked. For good measure, she put a chair under the doorknob. She had to give Jon credit, he was a persistent man.

Cordy, Ash and Jon stood on deck doing their morning tai chi exercise when, from the front of the ship, boomed a loud voice, "We're home, boss. Land ho." Ash's head turned forward and he gazed upon the sandy beaches and palm trees of America. Ash's first trip to the United States filled his heart with excitement. And what a trip to arrive here all in one piece!

"Everyone hop aboard the dingy," Jon commanded. "We need to rendezvous with a friend." He handed them life jackets, ironically, since most of the trip they had gone without.

Ash and Cordy's eyes met and both wondered about the extra precautions. Chris grabbed the life jacket with a death grip. He had never learned how to swim. A ladder fell off the schooner and all of them climbed down into the dingy. The small boat floated in the channel all alone with no one in sight as the schooner drifted away.

They sat in the dingy out in the middle of the ocean as a small submarine emerged from of the water.

Cordy, Ash, and Chris gasped.

"You own a submarine?"

Jon smiled. "Doesn't everyone in the smuggling business? Come aboard and I'll show you my prize."

They climbed down into the submarine's control room, which had two men manning the vessel. All of them greeted Jon. What impressed Cordy and Ash was Jon's talent leading his men. A natural- born leader, Jon commanded the deepest respect and loyalty of his men. He showed them to their bunks and the mess hall.

The sub sailed toward Galveston and Bolivar peninsula undetected.

CHAPTER 59

Bolivar Peninsula

Long ago, the Lafitte family businesses settled in Louisiana and Galveston, Texas. Initially the Lafitte headquarters were located on Grand Terre Island and Grand Island near the Bratoria Bay, which guarded the entrance to the Mississippi River. Later on, Lafitte and his family moved near Galveston Island. Privateering and gambling became some of their favorite businesses. Jean Lafitte long ago paved the way for a lucrative and successful international family business. Lafitte's family was filled with bankers, captains, and tavern owners. The family spread across the world and became members of the Dark Watchers. Laws meant little to them.

They'd given up selling slaves long ago and now hundreds of years later their main businesses were shipping, fishing, and casinos. All the family businesses were in jeopardy now that the Dark Watchers branded them traitors. Poppa Jon Lafitte had known all along de Villiers was untrustworthy and capable of vicious retribution if crossed. The time to declare war on de Villiers had arrived. The Lafittes had no intention of losing.

Poppa Jon bought old submarines from Russia and buried them in various locations throughout the Lafitte shipping territories. They served as hideaways and were perfect for cargo stashes. Poppa Jon had bought two other small subs from Russia, which traveled undetected throughout the world. The brilliant plan worked perfectly and was the best way to bypass customs all over. Jon placed a map of Galveston Island and Bolivar Island before them as they sat around the table on the submarine.

"Bolivar is where my ancestor Jean Lafitte left some of his treasures. It's been devastated by hurricanes."

Cordy followed Jon and sat down at the table in the control room.

Jon began, "My ancestor Jean Lafitte was asked by Napoleon's soldiers to try to rescue Napoleon. Legend says he aided Napoleon's effort to escape Elba. Napoleon didn't want the British to obtain some of the treasures of the Pure of Heart. He'd become remorseful for all the damage he'd done. The Emperor confiscated treasures from all the countries he conquered. Napoleon had raided the Vatican treasure trove and found Joan of Arc's ancient sword and buried it with all his other treasures in various safe places. Britain kept him alive because they hoped to obtain all of them. A dead man can't reveal his secrets. One of Napoleon's biggest treasures was given to Thomas Jefferson when he sold the Louisiana Purchase.

"Laffite, Dominque Youx, and General Humbert plotted to free Napoleon and bring him to New Orleans. General Humbert had an affair with Napoleon's sister and she begged him to save her brother. A dying man who looked like Napoleon volunteered to take his place. While on Elba, Napoleon knew he was being poisoned slowly, but he didn't want to die in a prison. A dying Napoleon told them where a sword that fell from heaven was buried and they brought it to New Orleans for safekeeping. Joan of Arc had carried the Sword of Heaven into battle. They buried Napoleon in a place of honor. For centuries, my family kept the sword hidden. But my grandfather told me about the sword's history and how it would someday save mankind. He must have suspected de Villiers' obsession for power. De Villiers wants to possess the Lafitte family treasure and exterminate us.

"Poppa Jon, before he died, had given me a sample of the metal. He wanted me to take it to a friend at NASA and have him run tests on it to find its origins. I got the spectroscopy results and the metal came from a meteorite from Mars that fell on Earth. I think I know where the Sword of Heaven is. Follow me."

Jon walked down the narrow corridor and headed toward the torpedo room. He pulled out the torpedo and opened the cap.

"Should I ask first if the torpedo is armed?" Cordy said. "It would have been nice to know when we pulled out the Sword of Heaven."

"Minor details, Cordy," Ash said.

Jon placed his hand inside the torpedo and grasped the hilt of the sword. He pulled out a gleaming metal sword once held by Saint Joan.

"What does it do?" asked Cordy.

"That is the million-dollar question but the Guardian says we're going to need it. Sword of Heaven, forged from a stone that fell from the heavens. Ancient legends talk about such a sword engraved with five crosses."

Jon placed the shining sword in a wooden case lined with red felt. They walked back to the control room and his man broke the news to him.

"A storm is coming, Jon. The weather forecasters are warning a hurricane is heading for the Gulf Coast in a few days. Some are saying it could be a category five. The stock market is already reacting to the news, and our casinos and shipping are in jeopardy."

Jon watched the storm on the radar screen heading straight for New Orleans. Jon knew in his heart this was the work of de Villiers. Cordy grabbed her phone and called Bob.

"Hello, cupcake, what's the problem?"

Cordy laughed. "Why do you always think there's a problem when I call you?"

"You never call me to chit chat, Cordy."

"Bob, the Lafitte Corporation is taking a hit in the stock market. I think de Villiers is up to something. He may be trying to bankrupt the company."

"I'm on it like a monkey on a banana tree," Bob replied. "I'll get back to you. What are you doing?"

"We just found the Sword of Heaven in the torpedo tube of a Russian sub."

"Oh, I'm glad I missed that one. Were there any blinking lights or ticking clocks seen when he pulled it out? OK, sorry. I'm reliving a scary moment right now. Where are you heading next?"

"I have a feeling its New Orleans, so get ready to meet us there at the airport in a couple of days."

"Do you guys watch the news? A major hurricane is hitting New Orleans in three days. Evacuations have already started."

"Just do it, Bob. This is important. Lafitte says we may be able to stop it."

"I told you I'm on it. OK, cupcake, see you in a couple of days."

Cordy looked at Jon. "Bob is a stock market genius. He can take de Villiers down."

Jon motioned for everyone to follow him. The submarine surfaced next to "Who's Your Daddy." Jon climbed up the ladder near the hatch carrying the Sword of Heaven, followed by his ragtag crew. Cordy wondered what other surprises the Frenchman would throw at them. The schooner sailed away from the submarine, which disappeared into the deep blue sea.

They pulled out of the shipping lane on the Bolivar Peninsula side but they could still see Galveston in the distance. Barges sailed from all over the world and could be seen in the distance bringing goods into port. Large ferries loaded with cars and people passed them. In about five minutes a helicopter headed toward them, and Jon felt a sense of relief. The helicopter's logo was that of his family. The helicopter hovered over the back of the schooner and dropped a wire ladder. A long-haired blond, who could've doubled as a swim suit model climbed down with ease. As she got closer to them, Ash let out, "Wow!"

Jon pointed to the wire ladder and ordered, "Ash, grab the ladder and anchor it for her."

Ash saluted. "I am on it, skipper." Ash had a big smile on his face. This was one order he didn't mind. He took hold of the bottom of the swinging ladder and glanced up. Suddenly, the blonde lost her grip and fell two feet into Ash's strong arms. She let out a gasp. Ash's hand was positioned right on her nicely curved butt cheek.

"Last time we met and you did that, you were cold and wet. Now you're hot and warm. I like the hot and warm better." Ash gazed at her mischievous eyes. He held her in his arms and recognized the woman who had saved his life in Nova Scotia, on the day the chief died.

Jon introduced the gorgeous woman still being held by Ash.

"Everyone, I would like you to meet my sister Samantha, the other half of the family business and my trusted partner. My sister runs our American operations here. She's the best in the business. I love her with all of my heart.

"I've taught her all that I know. She's the best soldier in the Lafitte army. Her courage in battle is like a lion. She is also one of the best sailors in our fleet."

The girl knew how to make an entrance, Ash thought.

Cordy glared at Ash for enjoying the obvious flirtation. She knew Sam didn't accidentally fall into his arms. She knew damn well what she was doing. If Ash didn't watch it, he'd be her willing slave. Cord wanted to smack his head and tell him to snap out of it.

Samantha waved to her big brother and turned to the others. Her voice held a French accent that was both seductive and charming. "You can all call me Sam." She turned, smiling at Ash and giving him her full attention. "I like the shorter name, and all of our associates think Sam is a man. It's good for business. My family found it best in the long run to call me by my nickname, but you, my strong handsome stud, you can call me anything you want." She leaned over and whispered into Ash's ear. "I would still come to your beck and call. Thank you for saving my life. Now, we are even."

Cordy stood tapping her foot on the deck, her hands on her hips. "Ash, you can put her down. She let go of the ladder five minutes ago."

Ash blushed. "I'm sorry, Mademoiselle Sam. I don't know what got into me. It is Mademoiselle Sam? If I'm wrong, my apologies." Ash put her down and she stood face to face with him.

Sam kissed his cheek and whispered again. "Well, my Egyptian hunk, you can grab my ass anytime." Ash started to smile and he could see Cordy getting pissed off. Sam smiled at Cordy and announced the news. "Oui, Mademoiselle. I haven't found any man interesting until now." Chris just stood there with his mouth open. Sam's beauty mesmerized men and the voodoo master stood bewitched by her.

Within seconds, the helicopter took off and two speed boats pulled alongside the schooner. The crew started to move the precious cargo out of Jon's stateroom and onto one of the speedboats. Sam headed down to her cabin. In just a few minutes, the speedboat was loaded and took off. Sam came back on deck wearing a white bikini, like the one Cordy had worn before. Cordy realized for the first time it wasn't a regular bikini when Sam had it on. It looked like a thong and the top just barely covered her "aurora borealis," or northern lights. Cordy had wondered why the ties in the back and sides were so long.

Jon broke the news first. "Well, everyone, the time has come to split up the team for safety reasons. Sam told me before she arrived that everyone is on high alert looking for us. The best way to make sure all of us don't get captured and lose the Keys of Life is to split them up. Sam will take one of you to New Orleans by speed boat and the others will come with me by land. Chris, you're going with Sam."

Chris smiled. "I would be honored to go with Mademoiselle Sam. I'll take good care of her."

Ash chimed in, "I'll go with Sam, too. I'd like to see the mouth of the Mississippi and, besides, someone needs to keep the Keys of Life and swords safe."

Jon nodded. "OK, that settles it. Cordy, you will come with me by land. Everyone keep a lookout for Dark Watchers."

Cordy glanced over at Ash. For the first time since they had met, Ash didn't pay any attention to her. He focused his attention on the river map which showed the route they would be taking. She was sure that Ash's eyes were locked on more than the map. Cordy turned and grabbed Jon's hand as he helped her into the dinghy loaded with half of the treasures of the Pure of Heart.

Cordy glanced back and she could see Ash's troubled face looking at her as if he had just lost his best friend. She could tell he cared deeply for her. Cordy knew Ash would miss her and in her heart, she acknowledged she would miss him. They'd been through so much together. Both of them waved goodbye and hoped it wasn't the last time they'd see each other.

CHAPTER 60

Let the Good Times Roll

Jon and Cordy landed on a dock where they walked across the sand to where a RV was parked. Jon's laughing eyes met hers and smiled.

"Are you ready for a road trip? Let's go in style."

Cordy scanned the large Class A motorhome. It had all the comforts of home — a kitchen, beds, and a shower. She gazed above her head and noticed the machine guns stored on the top shelves.

Cordy pointed at them. "She's packin', I see."

He nodded. "You have no idea how much. Let's hope we don't have to use any of her toys. Time is running out so we should start."

Jon and Cordy headed down Highway 10 in their custom RV. On the other side of the highway they watched the huge lines of people crawl along as they tried to evacuate due to the oncoming hurricane. The evacuation meant the roads were. Massive amounts of cars were driving bumper to bumper and the line was agonizing long. People were stranded on the side of the road as cars broke down, and others tried to jump the line by riding the emergency lane. Traffic was gridlocked. Fortunately, Jon knew the back roads to bypass the highway.

"They aren't going to get everyone out in time, are they, Jon?"

"No, Cordy and that's why I hope the Guardian can help us stop this monster storm. As well as lives being lost, my family's business will be destroyed, which is what de Villiers wants most all."

Jon found a small alcove off the highway. He pulled in and found a storage shed filled with gas cans stacked on top of each other.

"Gas becomes a priceless commodity when a hurricane hits. I've learned to be prepared. Jean Lafitte lost his whole fleet in a huge hurricane that hit Galveston. We have a history of losing money and lives via hurricanes. Poppa Jon told me to never forget that the Lafitte family are survivors of many misfortunes. I'm pretty tired, Cordy, and was wondering if I could take a small nap."

Cordy nodded. "Sure, Jon, go ahead. I think I need one, too."

In the quiet of the RV, Jon took off his shirt and lay down on the bed. His eyes were closed. Cordy decided that the wicked Frenchman looked like an angel with his dark hair and five o'clock shadow.

Jon whispered, "Come, chérie, just take a rest for a few minutes. I hate to sleep alone."

Cordy could feel the electricity in the room and her heart was racing. She slowly lowered herself onto the bed and lay next to him. Jon rolled over and put his arm gently over her. He felt a surge of adrenaline and decided to snuggle close to this amazing woman.

"You know why the McDermott family and the Lafitte family formed an alliance?"

Cordy whispered back, "No, my grandfather Bill never told me why."

"My ancestor Lafitte fell in love with a beautiful Ursuline nun named Sister Mary McDermott. She saved his life and that of his brother. He asked her to marry him but she refused to break her oath to God. She never left the convent but our family vowed that the McDermotts would never be harmed. Do you believe in reincarnation, Cordy?"

"I don't know but sometimes I think it's possible," she whispered.

Jon lightly brushed a kiss on her neck. "I wonder sometimes if I'm like my ancestor Jean who fell in love with a McDermott. I think you resemble her and me, him. Their love was never consummated but ours could be."

An uncomfortable silence filled the RV.

Cordy felt a tingle all over her and she jumped from the bed.

"You get some sleep, Jon. I'll take over driving."

Jon rolled back over and smiled. Cordy was definitely a challenge, but he liked challenges.

CHAPTER 61

Antar and de Villiers

De Villiers sat in his office gazing out the window over the city as Isis lay sleeping on his lap. The Dark Watcher pondered his next move against the treacherous Lafitte. He stopped petting his precious pet when Mindy walked in with the latest reports.

"Have they killed him yet? I hope so or I'll be very disappointed."

"I'm afraid not. Now he's back in America. Lafitte placed a higher bounty on your head after he got wind of the bounty you placed on his," Mindy whispered, anticipating his reaction.

De Villiers' rage filled the room. He roughly pushed an unsuspecting Isis off his lap. The cat screeched in pain and ran from the room.

"What do I have to do to get someone to kill Lafitte? I would think 25 million dollars would have done it. I want a dead Frenchman, and I want it now! Everyday Lafitte is not buried, he is a day closer to killing me! Get out of here and stay out until he is dead!"

Mindy backed away from him and closed the door. She had never seen him so furious. She'd noticed de Villiers was becoming more and more obsessed with maintaining complete power. She wondered how long it would be before he turned on her. Mindy pulled at the tightening neck of her sweater and felt anxious. Her master wanted Lafitte. She would give him his nemesis.

With the lights off and curtains drawn, de Villiers lit two candles on an altar filled with magical books and talismans. He put on a long dark robe.

De Villiers pulled out an old canvas bag that held ancient Roman coins. He placed a coin over a piece of paper with Jon Lafitte's name written on it. "I want him dead, and call for the dark ones to rid me of him."

He picked up one of the coins and called Antar's name. "Antar."

In a dark corner of the room, Antar came out of the shadows. "You rang?"

De Villiers set the coin down.

"They work. One of the most evil talismans, Judas' silver coin can be used to call the ancient Forevers. I want to know how to destroy Lafitte. Can you help me?"

Antar smiled. "I think we can do business. Information is power and I have some valuable information. Earth is being affected by a multitude of forces. A great storm is coming to the Gulf and that is where Lafitte's empire rests. His family possesses the Swords of Power, which are priceless. He's going to need all of them to fight the wind and ocean. You can take the swords from him and let New Orleans sink back into the sea. If you can't kill him, then destroy his empire and steal his treasure."

De Villiers pulled up a report on the monster hurricane bearing down on New Orleans. He was delighted at the information. Lafitte's casinos and shipping would be destroyed by the devastating winds and flooding. The Lafitte dynasty would be gone forever.

"You can go now, Antar," commanded de Villiers.

Antar stood for a moment and didn't move. The silence in the room was incredible. A person could hear a pin drop. Antar seethed with anger at being dismissed so nonchalantly.

"Judas' bag of coins suits you well, de Villiers. Betrayal is what you are all about. You betrayed the Nephilim and the Dark Watchers. Your loyalty is only to yourself. It will be my pleasure to leave you."

He then disappeared into the shadows.

De Villiers whispered, "Someday, Antar will kneel before me and I'll be his master."

He called Mindy and told her to tell all the Dark Watchers to sell their stock shares in Lafitte's corporation. Anyone who disobeyed would be killed. All Dark Watchers were ordered to kill Lafitte. "I want my top men to hunt him down. I want them to bring me the Pure of Heart alive and their treasures."

De Villiers played with one of the Judas coins in his hand and pondered, *How will he pay the bounty he put on me if the Lafitte corporation is wiped out? I'll bankrupt his empire and who knows, he may commit suicide and save me money. I'll make him so desperate that he'll regret the day he was born.*

CHAPTER 62

Sword of Water

As soon as the dinghy was out of sight, Sam asked Ash if he wanted to go swimming. She kicked off her sandals and jumped in the warm Gulf waters. "Come on, Ash. What's holding you up?" Ash still had the bad habit of not wearing any underwear. He jumped in with his jeans on.

Chris laughed. "I wish I wasn't the only islander who can't swim right now."

Sam swam over to Ash. Every time a wave would come in, Sam's spectacular breasts would lift out of the water. Ash wanted to look away but somehow they held his gaze.

"Help me with my top?" Sam asked mischievously. "It came loose when I jumped in." As soon as Ash got the ties loose to readjust them, Sam pulled away and Ash ended up with her top in his hands. Sam's seductive voice called out.

"Well, you bad boy, swim over here and give it back to me." Ash's face flushed beet red. It took Sam only two seconds to grab onto Ash. She pulled him tight against her. She could feel that Ash was equally excited.

Ash had been away from Cordy for just ten minutes and he had already found himself compromised by a voluptuous seductress. *Could a bad situation get worse?*, he thought. In one second, it did. Sam took a deep breath and in one great jerking motion went under the water and unbuttoned Ash's jeans. She was staring at one of the largest one-eyed sea snakes she had ever seen. When she came to the top of the water, she pulled Ash close again. They both let out a gasp as their warm bodies touched one another, and Sam rubbed up against Ash again. Ash pulled back reluctantly and said, "I can't."

Sam's surprise showed in her eyes. "What do you mean? You could lift me out of the water with that thing."

"No, I mean I don't know how," Ash confessed. "I'm a virgin."

The French siren couldn't believe her ears. "Oh my, at your age? What's a woman to do? Looks like it's your lucky day. I know all about how to make love and would love to teach you. Don't be shy."

Ash shook his head. "No, I am saving myself for my wife."

Sam chuckled. "OK, I am a certified captain. Just say you do, and I will do you."

Ash tried to put some distance between him and the French woman but she moved closer. "Not going to happen because I don't know you."

"I can't think of a better way to get started."

Ash began to swim away and as Sam started to follow him, another speed boat pulled up. Her sailor yelled out, "Captain Sam, they are coming fast, and it doesn't look good. We spotted them on radar."

Sam turned back to look at Ash and watched him climb up the rope ladder butt naked. The captain yelled out, "What an ass, Ash! Magnifique!"

Ash ran downstairs to get his clothes and came back with all the important artifacts. Sam grabbed a T-shirt laying on the deck and fired up the speedboat's engines. Chris stood, mesmerized at Sam. They left the other boat in the distance. Sam winked at Ash and smiled. "Don't worry, Ash, you will be safe with me. I saved your life once and I know how to get around in the bayou. They will never find us."

Ash grinned back at his captain. "It's not them I'm afraid of."

"Don't worry," Sam assured him. "I will be gentle with you."

"OK, tell me where we are headed?"

"My old great-great-pappy Jean Lafitte designed a secret transportation system in the bayous all the way to New Orleans. The canals stretch more than 40 miles and go through some of the most breathtaking swamps, but make no mistake, some of the most deadly, too. What most people don't know is that Napoleon's Imperial Guard came to the New World and settled on Campeche where great-great-pappy Jean built a two-story brick house called Maison Rouge.

"A magnificent home and built like a fort. Canons could be seen from the upper story. My great-great pappy Jean rescued Napoleon and brought him back home to Campeche and then to New Orleans. We're headed to Baratoria Bay, the long-ago home base of the Lafitte family privateers. My family knows these waterways well. All of us were raised to sail the sea. We have a stop to make at his grave site."

Ash turned his head and did a double take. "Are you telling me you're taking us to Napoleon Bonaparte's grave site?"

Sam nodded. "Well hell yeah, and also John Paul Jones as well. We have to pick up something very valuable — lost treasure my family guarded for centuries. What good is adventure without a pirate's buried treasure? My brother Jon told me where to look. He knows all the family secrets, and someday I will too. We are headed to the village of the Lafitte family ancestors. Baratarians cherish my great great pappy Jean. He is said to be buried in an unmarked grave right next to the bayou. The three good old boys are said to be side by side."

"They say my grandmother still walks the grave yard at night and visits the good old boys, just like your old Pappy," Chris said. "My family says Queen Laveau met Jean Lafitte, the pirate, when she was a young girl. He fought in the Battle of New Orleans and saved the country from Britain. Queen Laveau aided the sick and dying during the infamous yellow fever outbreak. Our families passed on their respect for their ancestors."

She smiled at Chris. "Lafitte said he saved America from the grip of a dark society. The Children of the Nephilim made a grab for control of the United States. Our family is notorious for playing both sides and having no allegiance to any country. So many people think naively when they listen to history. No one knows there's more to the story than gets told."

Sam expertly wove the boat through the bayous. Spanish moss hung on the water oaks as egrets flew over their heads. Ash thought the wild bayou's beauty was magnificent. Every once in a while, an alligator could be seen peeking up out of the water.

He thought of the crocodiles swimming in the Nile and how the Mississippi River had its alligators. He could hear Isis' name echoed in the Mississippi name. He wouldn't have wanted to miss the boat ride through the bayou and was glad he followed Sam. He could only trust Cordy's strength of will in handling Jon.

Six hours later and the boat came to rest alongside a graveyard.

"You stay here," Sam ordered Chris. "Ash and I will only be two minutes. If someone tries to steal the boat, shoot them with this rifle." She handed Chris a rifle.

"Come on, Ash, shake a leg, or even your third one," Sam said.

Ash and Sam jumped on land.

"Let's get this show going."

The sunset filled the sky with red, offering one last burst before dark. Chris watched them disappear into the cemetery. He hoped they treaded with care. Nobody wants to wake the dead. They get grumpy. They walked down two rows of white-washed headstones before finding three unmarked graves.

Sam laughed and pointed. "OK, big man. Those are the ones."

Ash put his hands on his hips. "Sam, can you stop with the jokes, please? They make me uncomfortable."

Sam couldn't help ribbing him one more time. "OK, long fellow, just kidding. We want the grave to the left. Jon said the treasure would be with John Paul Jones, another great captain with the reputation of a pirate. The other graves are said to belong to Napoleon and Jean Lafitte."

"What about the body?" Ash asked.

"The heat down here pretty much takes care of that in less than three years. Come on. Let's get the top off before someone comes along. Did you bring the Keys of Life? We need to insert the Keys in the hole right there." Sam pointed to a small hole on the side of the stone grave. Ash pulled the key out of his pocket and inserted the smaller golden ankh he found at the Abu Simbal temple in Egypt. They heard a mechanism unlock the grave's stone top.

They pushed the grave open and inside of the tomb was a narrow leather pack. Ash grabbed it and pulled out a shimmering sword.

Ash looked at the markings of Aquarius, the Egyptian hieroglyphs for water, engraved upon the sword and realized he held the lost Sword of Water. In his pocket, he pulled out a tiny stone alabaster jar filled with holy water his father had given him. He put a tiny drop on the shimmering blade and pointed to the bayou's dark waters. Chris watched as the waters parted and left a walking path for Sam and Ash.

Chris laughed. "You can part the waters like Moses. Wonder what other tricks it does." On cue, the Sword of Water dropped raindrops on Chris' head. He stood on the boat soaked head to toe. "OK, you made your point so stop already."

Sam and Ash ran back to the boat and after they climbed in, Ash tipped the sword downward. The dry path they had walked was now filled with water. Chris dried his hair with a towel. They took off for New Orleans as fast as they could. Sam navigated the bayou with a masterful touch. Chris tried his charms on the captain, and Ash stayed away from Sam as much as possible. All of them watched in awe as the dark clouds from Hurricane Justyce slowly headed toward New Orleans.

They pulled into New Orleans just after dark and parked in a secret boathouse just off the Mississippi River downstream from

Jackson Square. Sam took Ash and Chris to Jon's New Orleans house. The rich furnishings throughout the house created an elegant atmosphere. Chris had to admit the Lafitte family knew how to live in luxury. He missed Haiti and his friends but knew New Orleans needed to be saved from the great storm headed for her. Queen Marie Laveau's hometown held a special place in his heart. Chris wanted to give the city a fighting chance to survive and somehow, he felt the Pure of Heart could save New Orleans.

All of them were exhausted from their trip and decided to get some shut eye. No news came from Jon and Cordy as they weren't able to contact them. The storm blocked communications. Ash decided to lock his bedroom door at night, just in case, for his protection against a wily vixen. His door knob jingled but the mysterious night caller found it locked. He smiled and knew the caller wasn't Chris, but a seductive Lafitte lady on the prowl. He grabbed the Book of Dreams and the Book of Enoch, studying the diagrams and words on the books' pages. In the late hours, Ash discovered important information on the pages of the ancient texts. The coded knowledge handed down to Noah provided him with a ritual which could save New Orleans.

On one of the scrolls Jon had taken from de Villiers, Ash read about a story of the heavens causing severe changes on Earth. Enoch left the treasures of the Pure of Heart to Noah to help them survive cataclysms through time. Immense storms, earthquakes, famine, volcanoes and drought would appear as signs to the Pure of Heart. He drifted off to sleep and dreamt about Cordy. He prayed she was safe but knew as long as Jon was around, it wasn't possible.

CHAPTER 63

Downturn

B ob, Julia, and Randy sat in awe of the catastrophic hurricane headed right for New Orleans. The monster roared and destroyed everything in its path. The Bahamas were decimated by the massive winds of up to 200mph. Florida took a huge hit and though weather forecasters predicted slower wind speeds, Hurricane Justyce didn't weaken. New Orleans looked like it'd be worse off than after devastating Katrina.

Reports flooded in detailing huge casualty numbers, and the winds increased. Lafitte's businesses' stocks tumbled and de Villiers sold all his stock as soon as he could at extremely low prices. All the Dark Watchers' families sold their holdings. Many decided to place their margins on Lafitte's companies falling further. Bob heard through his Wall Street friends that they were only getting orders to sell. The panic was spreading.

Bob looked at Randy. "Anybody got any ideas on how to save Frenchie? I don't care if he goes bankrupt but Cordy wants to save his ass, so anybody got any ideas?"

Julia scanned the terrible charts. "De Villiers is vicious. He knows Lafitte needs to be crushed. He's the only other contender for the Dark Watcher Grandmaster position. All the other contenders are terrified and after this, nobody will oppose him. Sorry, I'm at a loss, even though I want to pay him back for setting me up. We know the storm is going to devastate Lafitte's casinos and fishing businesses. Insurance will only cover so much. Let's face it. He's going to file bankruptcy."

Randy watched the stock sell off. "You know, if we knew the storm wouldn't hit New Orleans and would miss Lafitte's businesses then we could clean up. Dark Watchers are betting on New Orleans being destroyed but if the city survives, the Dark Watcher losses would be in the billions. Didn't you say Lafitte could stop it?"

Bob knew about the Swords of Earth and Heaven. Lafitte told him that New Orleans could be saved with their help. A revelation hit Bob. He had a crazy plan.

"Randy, I want you to listen to the rumors around the world on Lafitte's Corporation. What if we buy all of the Lafitte stock at the lowest price with the idea of becoming a major stockholder in Lafitte Corporation and affiliates? Timing is so important here because we need to buy, buy, buy on the cheap, buy all the shares owned by the Dark Watchers before they know the storm is gone. If we don't get the signal then we just have to let Lafitte's businesses collapse. But they have to stop that hurricane."

"Are you crazy? How do you know the hurricane isn't going to hit?" Julia and Randy pointed to the television. All the weather experts talked up the coming disaster.

"Lafitte says the Pure of Heart treasures can save New Orleans. I believe him. Randy, get on all the exchanges around the world and when I call you, buy all the cheap shares you can buy. New Orleans will be saved and so will Cordy. Lafitte's Corporation will have a new majority holder. Timing will be so important here. If we jump too soon, we'll waste Cordy's entire fortune and if we move too late. Lafitte goes bankrupt."

Randy grabbed his computer and coat. "I love this. My adrenaline is on major overload. You know this could be the greatest stock deal of the decade. I know just what you want, Bob, but you have to be there to let me know if the hurricane is going to hit. I'm taking the stones with me for insurance. Oh, and Bob, try not to get killed down there. I like working for you. But I'll need a raise after this."

Bob gave Randy a thumbs up. "I'll be at ground zero and call it in. You keep me updated on the stock price. Good luck Randy."

Randy rushed out the door.

Julia didn't like Bob going in the path of one of the worst hurricanes of the century. She grabbed him by his dress shirt and gave him her pep talk. "Honey, I think your plan better work because if it doesn't, you're going to need a life jacket. I want hourly reports. If I don't hear from you then I'm coming in to get you. Understood?" She hugged him.

Bob held her and kissed her lips gently. "I know you're worried but I trust Cordy. Anyway, we've got to save New Orleans. People can't be evacuated fast enough. Millions of people will die if we don't try to save them. Look at the mass chaos down there. " He pointed to the television set. Thousands of terrified people were rushing to escape with their love ones. No one could leave fast enough.

Julia held him close and whispered, "I love you Bob but please promise me you'll be careful. I don't want to lose you."

Bob caressed her hair and gazed into her worried eyes. "I promise. I'll be good and try not to kill too many Dark Watchers. I'm coming back."

Bob called Cordy and told her his plan.

"Let's do it," Cordy said.

CHAPTER 64

Lafitte's Shortcut

Cordy noticed while she drove that four suspicious black SUVs had pulled behind them on the abandoned highway. They'd been waiting for them.

"Jon, wake up," Cordy yelled. "We've got trouble following us."

He jumped up and put on his shirt. "Let me take over driving, Cordy. I know a shortcut. We're going into Cajun country, Saint Martinsville." He turned the RV down a side road and pushed a button that put steel side panels over the wheels of the RV and steel plates over the windows. The RV had turned into a tank.

The four black cars started shooting, but the steel protected them. Jon pushed a button that lifted the rear bumper as two machine guns fired back at them.

"Wow, I love this RV."

"I engineered the improvements myself. I see only three cars back there now."

Cordy looked at the monitor. "You hit one. Only three more to go."

Jon pushed another button, exposing a small rocket launcher. He watched the monitor zero in on one of the cars and fired. The rocket launcher blew the car up, making it flip into the air.

"Let's see if they want to follow us now."

As predicted, the other car halted its pursuit and watched its comrade burn.

Cordy saw the sign for Saint Martinsville. She knew they were in the heart of Acadian country or what common folk called Cajun land. Long ago in the land of Arcadia, settlers came here to escape oppression from Nova Scotia. Cordy's family lived in Nova Scotia and along the Mississippi near Saint Louis.

They flew past the church where Longfellow's statue of Evangeline sat. "Evangeline" was the name of the poem he wrote about the Acadians expulsion from Nova Scotia to Louisiana. It told of a young woman who searched for her fiancé only to find death wherever she looked.

A statue of the Atakapa Chief holding a peace pipe stood in front of the church reminding Cordy of Chief Saunhac. Many Acadians intermarried with the local tribes living there.

"We're in Watcher territory."

Lafitte noticed her eyes focused on the church. "The chief, statue of Saint Martin the soldier, and look, the angels' symbols used by the Acadians. Legends brought back with them from their home over in France. Inside the church, Saint Bernadette and a grotto, which resembles Lourdes, lie near the altar." All signs were pointing the way. Lafitte glanced in the rearview mirror. The cars were nowhere in sight.

Rain started to fall. They reached a one lane small drawbridge used to allow boats to ride up and down the bayou. The bayou was flooded and in a few more hours, water would be spilling over the bridge. Tricky business, but Jon had driven over the bridge many times.

"Cordy, we need to blow the bridge so they can't follow us. After I drive over the bridge, I want you to take this grenade and pull the pin. Aim for the bridge. They can't follow us if the bridge is out."

Jon slowly drove over the old bridge. The RV barely fit. "I'll be parked by that shed over there and wait for you."

Cordy grabbed the grenade and opened the door. "Got it."

She pulled the pin and threw it at the drawbridge. The grenade landed on the center of the wooden bridge, and an explosion put a hole in the middle of the bridge. Nobody would follow them now.

Cordy walked back through the mud to where the RV was parked by a decrepit woodshed. As she turned the corner Jon stood there with his hands up.

"What's wrong, Jon?"

A man dressed in black stepped out of the shadows and pointed a gun at both of them.

"I've been waiting for my nice big bounties to show up. I knew Jon would be tempted to come this way. The wait was worth it. I want both of you to walk slowly down to where my car is parked behind those trees by the river. Don't try any funny business or somebody is going to get hurt."

Jon headed down to the car. "Henri, I can offer you more money than de Villiers."

Henri laughed. "You're a traitor to the Dark Watchers and a dead man. Have you seen the stock market, Jon? The casinos will be closed and bankrupt after this monster destroys the whole Louisiana coast. I don't deal with traitors, especially poor ones."

A soggy field made their walking slower and menacing rain clouds loomed over head. Cordy started to recite the words taught to her by Chief Saunhac. "Ah ae ta ho. Ae ta ho ta he."

Her voice vibrated and the air felt charged. Henri kept his eyes on Jon and Cordy but hundreds of copperheads, water moccasins, and alligators from the river slithered in the high-grass field. They heard her call. Henri was unaware of his assassins crawling up behind him. The hissing sound made him look behind him. He felt the first bite on his leg. Henri screamed in pain, and he shot at them. Terror filled Henri as he saw the field covered with slithering snakes. One snake after another bit him and he didn't have enough ammunition to kill them all. He was losing consciousness as their poisonous venom entered his blood stream. Finally, he collapsed on the ground. The snakes covered his body, biting him repeatedly and his screams of terror and pain filled the air. Two large alligators finished him off.

Jon turned around and couldn't believe his eyes. The field was filled with snakes and alligators. Cordy and Jon had backed up to the riverbank and their path was blocked by the venomous snakes and hungry alligators.

"What do we do now?" Jon anxiously asked. "I can't reach his gun."

Cordy remained calm and remembered the Atakapa Chief statue they passed a few minutes ago. "Follow me close. They won't attack us. Chief Saunhac taught me how to call to the spirit world. We must be slow, and no jerky movements. Snakes are only aggressive when they are provoked."

She kept chanting her grandfather's song. The Mi'kmaq song called on nature's allies to aid her. Jon grabbed ahold of her ribs. He thought if he was going to die, let him have one last feel of Cordy's body next to his. All the French men would smile on him for his ingenuity.

Cordy stopped and could not believe where his hands were placed.

"Really! Jon, get your damn hands off my boobs and put them on my waist. Make sure to follow my footsteps unless you want to be alligator bait."

"Pardon, it was just a Frenchman's instinct at work. If I'm going to die let me have a bit of heaven before I go. They're very nice, chérie,

by the way."

The snakes and alligators were still preoccupied with Henri's dead body.

The pair moved as one, walking together slowly through the hissing and slithering snakes. A path opened up to where the parked RV stood. Cordy chanted over and over again. A large rattlesnake slithered closer. There was something sinister about the snake. He rattled his tail, and he coiled up ready to attack. The snake blocked their path but persisted in its aggressive manner. Deep in her mind, a vision flashed of a devious de Villiers chanting and holding a coin in his hand.

Jon whispered, "De Villiers' sorcery and tricks, the snake is a minion of his."

"You're right, but I've got someone who can help us. We're standing on Native American sacred ground. I feel it."

Cordy closed her eyes and envisioned her great-grandfather Saunhac and chanted the words louder and louder. The air carried her words on the wind. Her mind envisioned him standing in front of her. Two hawks flew on the chief's arms. "Star Child, gaze up into heaven and see your brothers."

Cordy glanced up into the sky and saw two hawks flying toward them. They swooped down and killed the rattlesnake. Their path clear, Cordy and Jon walked slowly past the remaining animals as the hawks feasted on the rattlesnake. She thanked her great grandfather for hearing her cries for help. The chief told her long ago that she wouldn't be alone.

They climbed into the RV and headed to New Orleans on the back roads. Jon had witnessed Cordy's amazing ability to communicate with animals. The reptiles had heard her call for help and rescued them. The hawks saved them from de Villiers' dark magic. Jon thought, *Cordy bested the Dark Master.* He was realizing more and more what an amazing woman she was.

CHAPTER 65

New Orleans

Mass hysteria and chaos seemed contagious. Store shelves were empty and the streets abandoned. Everyone with a car had evacuated inland and the highways were lined with traffic. Hurricane Justyce was heading straight for the Gulf.

Jon ordered his casinos closed down to protect his employees. The RV had a gas generator that would aid them if the electricity went out. Jon stored gallons of fuel near his home for such emergencies. He pulled into his large driveway on North Rampart Street. The two-story hundred-year-old house was decorated with wrought iron balconies and had a courtyard with a fountain. Jon ordered the window shutters closed and the house readied for the hurricane.

Cordy and Jon rushed into the exquisitely decorated house and found Sam lying on a sofa and Chris sitting in a recliner, watching the television.

Cordy realized Ash wasn't there. Sam jumped from the sofa and hugged her big brother and Chris hugged Cordy. A panic set in.

"Where's Ash?" Cordy asked Sam. "He's alright?"

Sam smiled. "Oh yes, the bookworm is in the cellar, though I don't know why when he could have a scrumptious French meal upstairs."

She winked at Cordy, making it very clear she was the French meal Ash missed.

Cordy didn't like Sam's attitude one bit, and she really didn't like Ash being called a bookworm. Jon and Cordy sat down by the television to watch the frightening news. Disaster warnings flew across the screen.

Massive evacuations were being conducted but some roads were closed because of car accidents. Many people were trapped in the midst of the killer storm. The military helped with evacuations of the elderly and hospitals. The huge storm's winds increased. Scientists were baffled at its strength and how early in the season the hurricane had arrived. The emergency shelters were full to capacity. In Saint Louis Cathedral, everyone prayed for a miracle.

Jon looked at the business news. His corporation's shares were plummeting on the news that his casinos, fishing and shipping businesses would be destroyed by the category five hurricane. His family's legacy was on the verge of utter destruction while he was at the helm. He felt despair and yet he held out hope for he believed in the Guardian.

Cordy and Jon jumped to attention when they heard a bang at the door.

Bob knocked on the door holding a rum-filled hurricane alcohol glass. He carried a bag of beignets for Cordy.

"I've heard the best way to ride out storms is through alcohol. Right, Frenchie?"

Jon shook hands with Bob. "Welcome, Robert."

Cordy ran into Bob's arms. "Hello, cupcake. Grandpa Bill told me to say he loves you. I brought you a treat. Where's Ash?"

Ash heard the commotion upstairs. He ran up hoping to see Cordy and emerged around the corner with a book. Ash was obviously relieved when he saw Cordy and their eyes met and locked together. The archeologist knew in his heart that nothing had happened between Jon and Cordy. He turned and smiled at Bob.

"Bob's back! Where's my drink?"

"You're on the job, I see," Bob said. "What did your dad say he found in the Book of Dreams?"

Ash grabbed Bob's hurricane glass and took a swig. "I think I know what the Guardian's idea is. It's written in the Book of Dreams but we have three different versions of the Book of Enoch. Each Book of Dreams reveals something special. Cordy possessed one, my dad another, and de Villiers, the third. My dad's scrolls show a diagram in which a certain ritual on sacred ground could prevent a great deluge and disaster. The map is set on a crescent river and a square. The other Book of Dreams refers to Solomon's Temple. The ancient diagram of the First Temple is a square courtyard leading into the main temple. The Temple Mount in Jerusalem or what some refer to as Mount Zion is where some believe the original one was located. King Solomon protected all the sacred relics there dating back to Noah and Moses. An old Crusader legend talks about finding Solomon's treasure. The Saint Louis Cathedral is very similar to these diagrams, and New Orleans is named the Crescent City. The square is Jackson Square.

"The four Swords should join with the Sword of Orion. We need to find the Sword of Fire and the Sword of Orion. Orion symbolizes Osiris, the god of Resurrection in Egypt. In Egypt, we have the great Nile, but here we have the great Mississippi whose name echoes that of the goddess Isis. A coincidence? I don't think so. I think both of the swords are here, and we need to find them. The other books give instructions on how to get them all to work together. The Book of Dreams predicted the changes in Earth would occur again."

Ash gathered them all around him.

He placed the diagram in front of them on the mahogany dining table. Jackson Square, surrounded by a wrought-iron fence, matched the diagram in the Book of Dreams. Four statues of pagan gods and goddesses placed in four of the corners mimicked the four swords. The Sword of Orion rose in the middle at the highest point. Andrew Jackson's statue stood in the center of the square.

Chris observed the diagram over Bob's shoulder. The voodoo master had been working on de Villiers' voodoo doll. He smelled of incense and his painted face gave Bob a shock.

"Who the hell is this guy? What are you smoking buddy? Got any extra?"

Chris smiled and introduced himself. "I'm the voodoo priest. Just call me Chris. I knew you'd be a cool dude, Bob." Chris rattled his bone necklace at Bob's face to square away any bad spirits.

"We need a voodoo guy? You've got to be kidding me. What's next?"

Chris rattled his bone necklace around Bob again.

"Get the hell away from me."

"You must be cleansed of all negative energy," Chris said. He grabbed the hurricane glass and took a gulp. "Thanks, Bob."

"Chris is here to distract de Villiers," Jon explained. "He's made a voodoo doll of him and we're going to make his life miserable. Is it finished?"

"Oui, I took the hair you pulled out of de Villiers' head and placed it on the doll. I must say he's a masterpiece."

Everyone watched Chris pull out a doll dressed in red with de Villiers' peppered gray and black hair on top of its head.

"Queen Laveau would be proud. You never cause harm unless harm is aimed at you. De Villiers chose his fate by attacking us and trying to kill us. Karma plays a part in this equation. Shall we try it out?"

Jon pointed to a lit candle on the table. "Let's give him a fever, shall we?"

Chris said a few words and dangled the doll over the candle.

In his office, de Villiers pulled at his Armani shirt and noticed his armpits were sweating. What the hell was going on? He pulled his shirt off and turned down the air conditioner to 60 degrees. Isis sat on his desk watching his discomfort. He grabbed a cold water bottle from his fridge as beads of sweat dropped from his forehead.

Chris pulled it away. "We need to do it randomly so he won't catch on, but I guarantee it works. Jon got lucky grabbing his hair and pulling it out."

Bob grabbed his glass back and took another gulp. "Voodoo dolls. What's next, a snake charmer?"

Jon smiled at Cordy. Her eyes met his.

A gorgeous woman with a knockout figure grabbed Bob's glass and took a sip. "I'm Sam, Jon's sister."

His eyes drank in the gorgeous woman drinking from his glass. Good thing Julia wasn't here or he would be a dead man right now. He couldn't help admire her figure and face, but he could see her eyes homed in on Ash. *What a triangle we've got here*, Bob thought. Sam had trouble written all over her. Julia thought Sam was a man, and Bob knew she'd be on the first plane down here if she got wind of seductive Samantha. What a kickass team they had.

The television reported the devastating news about the hurricane breaking records and the catastrophe awaiting New Orleans. A deluge of water and high winds were headed straight for them. Scientists said they had never seen anything like it.

They watched the business news and announcers reported the catastrophe of the Gulf would destroy Jon's casinos. De Villiers' minions used the media to build hysteria in the stock market.

"Bad news travels fast, Jon."

"Oui."

"Julia, Randy, Grandpa Bill, and I have thought of a way of saving Jon's ass and kicking de Villiers. You have to promise me that these swords can protect New Orleans."

Jon looked at Bob with hope in his eyes "The Guardian said we have a chance, and I believe her. The Forever ones left these powerful artifacts for a reason. It's to save mankind and Earth's children. I think I know part of the answer as to what is going on. It's a disturbance in the gravitational forces in our galaxy. An astrologer discovered a huge planet four times as big as Earth coming into our solar system. Our planet enters the galactic center too at this time. NASA satellites spotted huge storms on Saturn and Jupiter. Earth seems to be affected, too. Storms and wind speeds will increase until the rogue planet returns to its long elliptical path. Earth experienced the same phenomenon and the Forevers knew this day would come. The Keys of Life are tools left for mankind to survive."

Cordy grabbed Bob's hurricane glass and took a gulp. "What do we need to do?"

Bob gave up ever seeing his hurricane glass again. "I don't know about Earth but the stock market could save Jon's corporations and bring de Villiers down a notch. The one ace we have is the swords, but can they stop the hurricane? We need to ask the Guardian."

Bob laid out a strategy map. Julia and Randy planned to buy Jon's plummeting stock shares from the Dark Watchers using Cordy's money.

"Cordy, take another swig from that hurricane glass because if this plan doesn't work its back to fighting little chihuahuas at the vet office for you," Bob said. "If it works, this plan could kick de Villiers where it counts, and I'm talking his money and power. All we need is very precise timing and to snuff out a hurricane. No biggie."

Jon poured all of them a glass of whiskey. They all gulped down their glasses, slamming them back on the table.

Cordy hoped they could do it because if they didn't, Jon's family would be devastated and she would lose all of the money given to her by Grandpa Bill. The worst part was that de Villiers would be more powerful than ever. He couldn't win. If he possessed any of the Keys of Life, mankind would be his slave and Earth would never be the same.

Jon nodded. "Let's do it." Cordy shook Jon's hand. "Partners."

Bob made the call to Julia and Randy. "It's a go, baby."

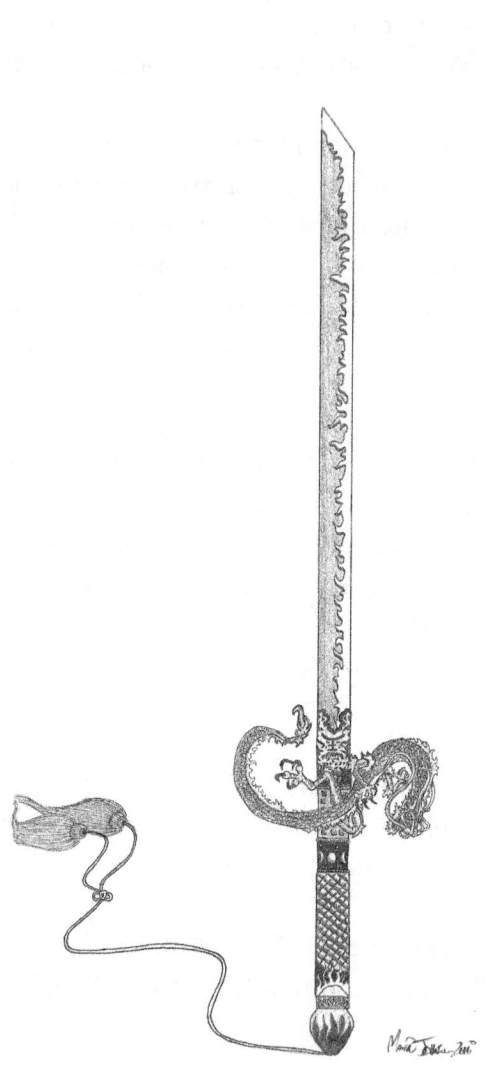

CHAPTER 66

Lafitte Family

Jon strolled into the family library and closed the door. He pulled a dusty book from the bookshelf, The Lafitte Family History. He remembered Poppa Jon reading it to him. The Lafitte family crest blazed on the cover. He opened the book and began to remember.

The Lafitte family history went back to the Crusades. In 1234, Gombaud de Lafitte owned an estate in the village near Bordeaux, France. Guillame de Lafitte, brother of Gombaud, served under the Preceptor of Aquitaine, who at the time was Guilliame Saunhac. Lafitte watched the rise of his master to Templar Grandmaster and rode into battle in the Seventh Crusade. The young Lafitte served him well and carried many of the sacred relics and treasure for Saunhac. The Templar knight's devotion to Saunhac brought him promotions of rank. Over the centuries, Gombaud 's chateau and land grew some of the finest wines in the world. The Lafit tes had a magic touch in producing wine and loved the sea. The Lafitte family served with loyalty and guarded many Templar treasures. Over time, they found the Dark Watchers suited their expertise and became a leading family in the organization.

The most notorious Lafittes were the brothers Jean and Pierre who created one of the largest pirate syndicates of its time. Their birthplaces were not known but Jean told his friends he was from Boudreaux though others say Haiti. The brothers landed in New Orleans to begin their pirate careers. They set up a base in Barataria Bay. The brothers had legitimate businesses in New Orleans which helped them to funnel smuggled goods to happy citizens of the city. They used the intricate web of bayous to smuggle goods without detection. One of the major goods passed through and auctioned at a place called "The Temple" were slaves found on Spanish and British ships. Piracy was their business and they attacked many Spanish ships loaded with immense treasure. The handsome Jean with his dark curly hair and beard drove the Southern ladies aflutter when he walked past them on the street of New Orleans. Pierre ran some of the legitimate business and both brothers' loyalty to one another was unquestioned.

In 1812, America and Britain went to war and the pirates continued their raids. Governor Clairborne decided to place a reward on Jean Lafitte's head for $500. In turn, Lafitte offered a higher reward for Clairborne. The governor didn't find it amusing. On one rainy night in 1814, Pierre Lafitte was caught by Clairborne's men and placed in jail. Later in the week the British approached Jean Lafitte with a deal for his aid in the capture of New Orleans. His brother Pierre would be freed and the Lafittes rich. If he agreed to aid the British, Jean Lafitte would be well-compensated. Jean had grown fond of the young and struggling United States and sent news of the impending British invasion to the head of New Orleans' defense. The next day, Pierre escaped from prison. The brothers were united again but knew what they had to do.

General Andrew Jackson rode into a desperate New Orleans discovering the city had no defenses. Jackson saw the scouting reports and knew he was out gunned and out manned. He had heard of Lafitte's warning. He needed men who knew how to fight the British. A messenger sent to the notorious brothers brought a plea for help. Jean met with Jackson secretly in the upstairs of Lafitte's Blacksmith Shop and asked for all his men to be granted pardons if they fought for America. Jackson agreed to his terms. Pardons were issued to all of his men and his family by the U.S. government. Fear filled the streets of New Orleans and the women and children fled to the church at the Ursuline Convent for safety. Bishop Dubourg said mass in the chapel. Sister McDermott prepared the hospital for casualties. Lafitte sent her a message. The letter told her he and his men had decided to fight the British and he would be in her debt for as long as he lived. The pirate revealed his deep love for the gentle nun and hoped she loved him, too. She had nursed him back to life. His family and her safety meant everything to him. The dark haired Lafitte marched proudly into New Orleans with Jackson. Desperate times deserved desperate measures and this was one of them. Sister McDermott prayed to Our Lady of Prompt Succor that Lafitte survived.

The Battle of New Orleans started on December 23, 1814. The British reached the Mississippi, stopping all boats from getting in. Their ships began firing on New Orleans but artillery experts who were friends of Lafitte, Renato Beluche and Dominique Youx, fired back hitting their targets with pinpoint accuracy. British reports had failed to reveal the Lafitte cannons and gunpowder and the Brits were surprised to realize that New Orleans' defenses were stronger than thought. The easy target turned into a devastating slaughter of British soldiers. Lafitte's men were expert riflemen and the British uniforms made easy targets. Outnumbered by the thousands, Laffite and his men won the day. Jean's men demonstrated incredible bravery and Andrew Jackson heaped many compliments upon them. Jackson knew America owed the Lafitte family great gratitude. One had to wonder if America would have survived if Britain had taken New Orleans.

Soon afterward, the Lafittes grew tired of the quiet life and decided to side with the Spanish. They settled in Galveston, creating a colony and base of operations. They called their colony Campeche.

A letter came to Jean from Napoleon, who was captured on Saint Helena. The Lafitte family had been on friendly terms with the former emperor. Both men admired each other for their military strategy. Napoleon wanted Jean to collect and protect precious relics of great power that he had gathered from Egypt, France, and the Vatican.

The British could not possess these powerful treasures. Lafitte and his men decided to aid the remorseful Napoleon. In the dead of night, the two men met at Elba. Napoleon told Jean that over the years, he hunted down these treasures of the Pure of Heart. He had come to realize he couldn't die knowing that his jailers would possess them. Jean gave him his word that his family would protect them. A map given to him by the ailing ruler showed the location of the buried treasure. Jean sailed off into a stormy night with the dying Napoleon. A dying volunteer who looked exactly like Napoleon gave his life to the cause by ingesting the emperor's poison-laced food. Over time, the British had been poisoning the man. Napoleon was not to escape again if they could help it. Napoleon smiled at Jean as they saw the land in the distance which he had sold to Thomas Jefferson in the Louisiana Purchase.

"My only regret is that I will not die in my home country, Jean. I wonder if my prisoners will identify my brave substitute to the world."

Jean looked at the beautiful sunset. "They won't tell anybody for fear their superiors would kill them for negligence of duty. Plus the humiliation that the great Napoleon escaped *from them not once but twice is too much. They will discover a dusky bluish corpse and think it was their poison that changed you. No, Bonaparte will die a free man and the treasures of the Pure of Heart safe. I give you my word."*

Jean was true to his word, and only he knew where Napoleon was buried. Legends talked about the great escape of Napoleon but no evidence could be found. History is written by the victorious.

The Lafitte family became the caretakers of some of the long-lost treasure of the great Bonaparte.

Jean continued his smuggling, but his operations were hit with a devastating hurricane which destroyed his colony and ships. Lafitte's empire came crashing down. Jean wondered if karma played a hand in his collapse. The guilt of selling human flesh on the open markets filled his heart. His family decided when the USS Enterprise showed up the time to go underground was now. They packed and left in the dark never to be seen again.

The Lafitte family later pledged to go into more legitimate businesses and refused to have any more dealings in slavery. They remained Dark Watchers, but Lafitte never forgot the debts they owed to others. The family had a code and loyalty. Many clients liked and respected them. Karma followed the family through time and Poppa Jon told his children that soon the family would be known for their legitimate businesses. The Lafitte empire spanned all over the world, with headquarters in New Orleans. Had the family paid enough for their dark past? No one knew. Only time would tell if the weights of justice fell in their favor.

Jon thought, *My family devoted their lives to protect these treasures.* His grandfather died trying to oppose the poisonous de Villiers and now another McDermott's life was in the crosshairs of darkness. The heavy burden of his family's obligations weighed on his shoulders. He would need all of his military skills as a former Interpol agent to keep them safe. He closed the book placed it back on the shelf and thought, *one more time a Lafitte will try to save New Orleans.*

A handsome devilish grin spread across his face and his heart filled with love for Cordy. She had placed her fortune in danger without hesitation to save his family's empire from bankruptcy. No one had ever done anything for the Lafittes like her. What a magnificent woman! His family knew this day would come. A McDermott had saved them again and they owed her everything. He admired her courage and her fighting attitude. Someday, her bedroom door would be open and he would enjoy kissing those luscious lips. Maybe this Lafitte would find happiness.

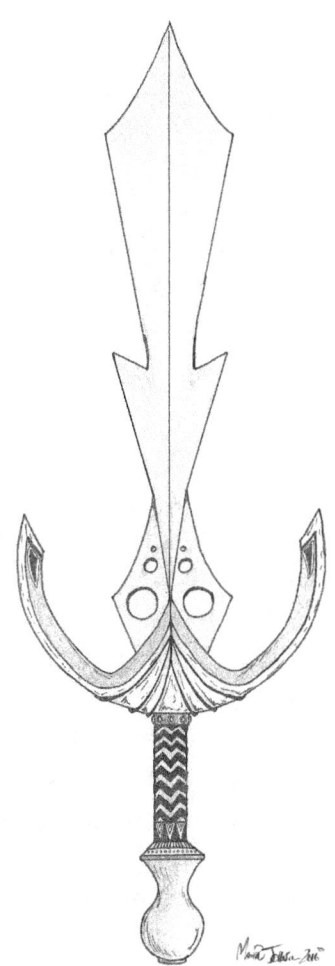

Chapter 67

Sword of Fire

The front doorbell rang and Jon turned on his surveillance cameras posted above the door. He could see a small older Chinese man standing next to a tall younger man dressed all in black. Jon didn't recognize them and took his gun out of his holster.

"We've got visitors, everybody."

Bob grabbed his gun and got next to the door.

He nodded to Jon. Cordy grabbed her gun and hid behind the couch. Jon pointed to Ash to answer the door. Jon aimed the gun at the door. Ash opened the door slowly. The elderly man smiled at him.

"You can all put your guns away, and please tell Cordy that Master Wong is looking for her."

"Don't shoot anybody, he's a friend," Cordy yelled.

Cordy jumped out from behind the couch and ran to the door.

"Master Wong, I'm so glad to see you. Is Peter with you, too? Come in, and everybody put your guns down and come meet my friends. Master Wong and Peter, let me introduce Bob, Jon, Chris, Ash and Sam."

Master Wong bowed. "I'm glad to meet you all. We're here to assist you in finding the Sword of Fire."

Bob looked at Jon and whispered. "How did he know?"

Cordy hugged Peter Woo. Her friend at the karate school in Saint Louis saw all the guns pointed in their direction.

Peter smiled. "I can see things are a bit tense around here."

Cordy nodded. "You have no idea, Peter. A hurricane is heading for us, and a bunch of dark ops guys are hunting us down. Times are a bit tense right now. Everybody, put your guns down! They are friends. What's the Sword of Fire?"

Master Wong sat down on the couch. "I am one of the leaders of the Pure of Heart and, like Chief Saunhac and Sister Agnes, have been asked to defend them and protect their treasures. Let me tell you a story. Once upon a time, a great Chinese warrior created a sword made with the fire of a volcano. The volcano smoked with the fire of a great red dragon from heaven. Lava deep from Earth and metals possessing incredible powers were used to forge the blade. On one side of the sword, the blade was carved with the symbols of the moon, sun, and stars. The sword goes by many names but my people call it the Sword of Fire. You need the Sword of Fire and I know that Lafitte knows where the sword is located. We're here to help you. I've been a trusted friend of Cordy's aunt Sister Agnes and her great grandfather Chief Saunhac. I promised that I'd protect Cordy. Peter came with me to help. We must all be of one mind, so let us begin the tai chi to unite us. All of us must be of one heart. We fight a war against a monster and must prepare ourselves. Take your positions."

Master Wong led them through the intricate motions. Peter, Sam, Jon, Ash, Bob and Cordy moved all in one fluid dance with the old master. A complete calm settled among them, and they flowed like a river as one. They ended with a bow.

Cordy smiled at the elderly man. "I'm so glad to see you both, but these are dangerous times. You're both very welcome, and we are honored for both of you to join our army. We can save New Orleans and rescue millions of people and animals at the same time. Well Jon, where is this Sword of Fire?"

Everybody looked at Jon. "Poppa Jon talked about a sword hidden at the Ursuline convent where a nun named McDermott placed it in a wall upstairs or buried it in the garden. Ash possesses the Keys of Life, and I think we're going to need them. I don't think any of the swords would activate without the Key of Life."

Master Wong spoke, "We need to find the sword before de Villiers does. He's using the chaos and hurricane to seize it. An ancestor of mine died in the hospital of yellow fever when he brought it for safekeeping from China in the 1800s. The sister promised to keep it safe. The Pure of Heart for centuries have kept it hidden. They must have known this day would come."

"We can all go tonight," Jon said. "The alarms are off because of the electricity being shut down. It's now or never. Master Wong may have saved the day with this information."

"Everybody gear up and be ready to move out in ten minutes. We're splitting up into two groups. Cordy, Sam, Master Wong, Chris, and Peter will head for the convent. Bob, Ash, and I will head to the Lafitte Black Smith Shop and pick up a key my family hid there centuries ago."

Both groups snuck out and headed in opposite directions, checking to see if they were followed.

Security guards and police were swamped with emergencies. Nobody would be guarding the grounds. De Villiers knew the sword could be his.

His minions were already searching the Ursuline convent for the sword. The convent, built in the 1700s, was one of the oldest buildings in southern America. Downstairs was used for the school and upstairs the hospital, storerooms, and library. A third building was where the Bishop often resided. A garden with trimmed hedges formed a square, and a path through the courtyard led to the statue of Prompt Succor surrounded by statues of kneeling saints.

Master Wong and Peter snuck up on de Villiers' men, knocking them out. Sam and Cordy stumbled on two more in the garden. Cordy admired Sam's fighting abilities as both women knocked the surprised Dark Watchers to the ground in a few seconds. Peter,

Master Wong, Cordy, and Sam headed upstairs. Before they arrived at the convent, Chris had told them legends said secret treasures or vampires lay upstairs in the convent. Cordy looked around in search for Chris.

After a few minutes upstairs, they found Chris, who had knocked out another Dark Watcher with a hammer left by construction workers.

Chris smiled. "No vampires here, but there is a guy who's going to have one helluva a headache when he wakes up. Look over there."

The Dark Watchers had dug a hole in the brick wall. Peter took his flashlight and saw the bronze case.

"We got here just in time."

Chris helped him pull it out. Master Wong examined the case marked with ancient Chinese writing. The old man gave a sigh of relief. "We've found the Sword of Fire but we need the keys to open it. Let us hurry and find the others." They ran down the stairs and headed for the garden in back.

Cordy recognized one of the sisters' statues from Saint Louis named Saint Rose Philippine Duchesne. She remembered walking with her aunt in a small town named Florissant, meaning valley of flowers. The nun had a school located there. The church's stained glass windows contained the all-seeing eye. Cordy remembered the symbol as a child and now knew the eye might mean Watchers territory was near. Cordy realized the nuns created an underground network that helped hide the sacred relics. Sister Agnes had revealed to the innocent Cordy the secret kept by them for millennia.

The Ursuline convent's history played a huge part in the war of 1812. The sisters prayed in the chapel for the safety of New Orleans. The city now trembled in fear again and needed another miracle.

Master Wong, Chris, and Peter waited and watched over the unconscious Dark Watchers while Sam and Cordy planned to take care of any stragglers.

Sam and Cordy walked through the chapel in search of any remaining Watchers. Cordy saw the carving of da Vinci's *Last Supper* on the altar. Another sign. She remembered the same artwork on the altar in Montreal at the Notre Dame Basilica. The Acadians seemed to use da Vinci's art works as a sign. The symbols of the Pure of Heart were becoming more obvious to Cordy. The Watchers still remained unconscious and no one was detected around the perimeter.

Sam gave the signal. "All clear."

Master Wong, Peter, and Chris proceeded to the manicured garden where Cordy and Sam waited for them.

A white concrete wall bordered the back of the grounds and they climbed over it. Everyone had abandoned their homes so they walked out the backyard gate of the convent's neighbor's home without notice.

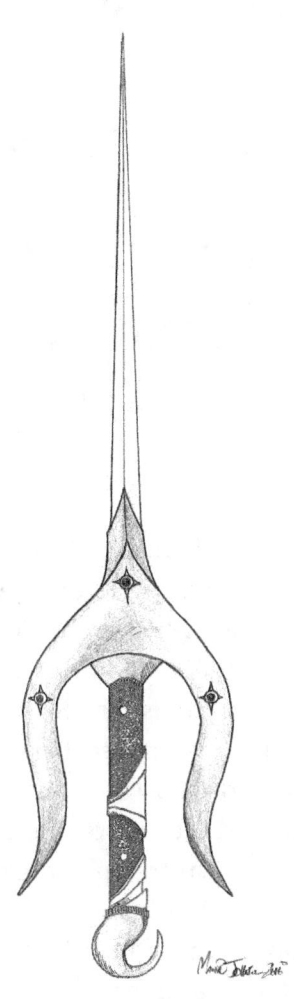

CHAPTER 68

Lafitte's Blacksmith Shop

Jon, Bob, and Ash ran to Lafitte's Blacksmith Shop to grab a key left by Lafitte's ancestors, Pierre and Jean Lafitte. The Lafitte brothers started a blacksmith shop in New Orleans in the 1800's and used it as a front for their operations. Jon believed that without the key nobody was going to use the Sword of Fire.

The old blacksmith-shop-turned-bar was closed and shuttered for the storm. Ash, told to keep watch, stood behind a wooden shed in the yard. Lafitte picked the lock on the back door, which led to a storeroom. Bob watched Lafitte open the door with ease.

"I admire your talents, Jon."

Jon winked at Bob. "I learned to pick locks when I was a baby."

The door creaked open and the room was pitch black. Visibility remained poor for both men. A chair crashed on top of Jon's head and he fell to the floor. The door slammed behind Bob and his gun was grabbed from his hand. A square-faced man held Jon with a gun aimed at his head. Bob heard the click of a gun in his ear and slowly stood up. The Dark Watcher recognized Lafitte and smiled.

"Welcome, Jon. We've been expecting you."

"I see you are now de Villiers' minion," Lafitte answered. "We can defeat him if you let us go. I can pay you more than he can. Don't be a fool."

The Dark Watcher laughed with greedy eyes. "I'm going to be very rich because of you, my friend. You're bankrupt, Jon, didn't you know? The Dark Watcher families got our money out just in time. We want Bob to call off his stock market friends and let bankruptcy destroy you. The weather stations are calling it a one-in-a-million hurricane. De Villiers desires the collapse of the Lafitte Empire and he always gets what he wants."

Lafitte scanned the room for more Dark Watchers but only two stood before him. One with a gun aimed at his head and another aimed at Bob. *Most of the Dark Watchers must be at the convent, searching for the Sword of Fire*, he thought.

The man holding Bob gave him a phone. "Call them off. Now, and no funny business or you're both dead men."

Bob called Randy and Julia on a three-way conversation over a speakerphone. "Randy, change in plans. Don't buy Lafitte shares. Let them crash. I repeat let them crash."

Randy and Julia looked at the Stones of Truth. They pulled apart. Bob was lying. Bob never lied. He was in danger.

"Alright, we will stop buying the shares," Julia said. "Bob, I'm worried. The weather reports are horrible and very scary. I love you always, remember that."

"I love you, too. Bye." The Stones of Truth moved together. Julia knew Bob loved her and she knew what she had to do. Randy gazed into Julia's angry eyes.

"If they hurt that man, Randy, I swear I'll kill them all, including de Villiers."

The Stones of Truth moved together in Randy's hand. Randy grabbed his coat and went to meet with his international team of traders. Wall Street was in for a shock. As soon as news came in, he knew what to do and so did Julia.

A battle rage-filled Ash proceeded to rush the flimsy wooden door. The wood door split, hitting the Dark Watcher and knocking both Bob and him to the floor. Ash grabbed the gun from his hand and pointed it a struggling Lafitte and the surprised Dark Watcher leader whose gun remained pointed at Lafitte's head.

"Aim at his feet, Ash," Lafitte yelled. "Aim at his feet. You can do it. Save New Orleans and my family."

Bob hit his assailant over and over again in the face wrestling him on the floor.

The leader yelled at Ash and Bob. "I'll kill him. Put the gun down."

Time slowed down in that second. Ash heard a whisper in his ear.

Antar stood in the shadows. "This is your opportunity to kill Jon and have Cordy all to yourself. Be like Adam's son Cain, Ash. Eliminate the competition. Kill him. You know she probably went to bed with him. Get revenge. Kill him."

"Shoot him, Ash," Jon commanded. "I trust you. I've always trusted you from the beginning."

Ash gazed in Jon's eyes and knew what he had to do.

Bang, Bang! The Dark Watcher seemed surprised. A trickle of blood came down his hand where his trigger finger had been severed by the bullet and the gun fell to the floor. Jon turned around and knocked him out on the floor. He gazed at the stunned Ash.

"I knew you could do it, Ash. Great shot, my friend."

Ash was shocked. "I didn't."

Bob finished off his Watcher by strangling him to death.

Ash remained stunned for a second. "I was aiming for his feet."

Lafitte patted him on the back. "I know, and I'm very grateful to you for saving my life."

Jon felt along the brick wall behind the bar and pulled out a loose brick. A rusty old key rested within and Jon placed it in his pocket.

"Let's go back to the house and see if the others have found the sword. Time is running out. I feel it." The winds were picking up and the clouds overhead darkened. The men ran down the street and prayed that the others had been successful and safe.

CHAPTER 69

Soniat House

Cordy, Master Wong, Peter, Sam and Chris flew down Chartres Street. The streets were deserted and occasional debris tumbled down the road that shared a name with a cathedral Cordy visited in France. The stained glass windows in Chartres Cathedral talked about the giants and the deluge.

Cordy ran past a hotel built in the 1800s called the Soniat House. She stopped in her tracks for there, standing at the door, was a vision of Chief Saunhac wearing the Mi'kmaq flag as a tunic. The white tunic with a red cross had on one shoulder a symbol of a crescent moon and the other, a pentacle. It gave the chief the look of a Crusader knight. He waved to her to follow him.

Master Wong noticed the mesmerized Cordy walking to the house with wrought iron balconies. He stopped and looked up at the name placed on a wooden board above it. He recognized it immediately.

"Where is she going?" Peter asked.

"She sees an old friend," the old master replied. "We must follow her and keep her safe."

Peter yelled for Sam and Chris to hold up.

Cordy opened the door to the Soniat antique store and behind the counter sat a petite, gray-haired lady wearing glasses.

"Can I help you my dear?"

Cordy scanned the room and the chief pointed to a picture on the wall. It was a photo from the 1900s of a man in his fifties sitting in a chair.

"Yes, who is he, may I ask?"

The old woman chuckled. "My dear, he is Soniat, the builder of this house. He comes from an ancient French noble family named the Saunhacs. The family goes way back to the middle ages and Crusades. One of them, Guilliame Saunhac was elected a great courageous Templar Grandmaster. Soniat brought to Louisiana some of the relics from his family in France. Their family plays an important part in Louisiana history. Would you like to buy the picture? It's on sale. The storm will destroy everything in the next 24 hours, so say the price and he's yours."

Cordy turned the painting over. Part of the back cover was torn, and a piece of paper wedged in the back.

"Do you take gift cards?" Cordy pulled out two cards worth $20,000 given to her by Bob to give to whoever she wanted.

"Of course."

"Keep the rest of the money for yourself for being so helpful."

The old woman smiled. "I never got a tip like this before. You must take a look inside the Cathedral. There is a stained glass picture of a knight kneeling. He's missing an eye. Grandmaster Saunhac lost an eye in a battle. You'll recognize him. Do you want me to wrap it for you, my dear?"

"No, I'm in a hurry. Thank you."

Chris shook his head. "Antique sales, my mother never could miss any. I guess she's not the only one. A super hurricane is coming, and we're antique shopping."

Sam admonished him. "Shut up, Chris. Can't you see Cordy found something?"

"What did you find?"

Cordy pulled back the cover on the picture and pulled out a yellowed paper with a map of the Saint Louis Cathedral and diagram on it with a sword and three stars.

"A message from an old friend sent just for you, perhaps?" Master Wong asked.

"I think the chief sent me here to find the Sword of Orion."

Cordy showed them the paper, and that's when Ash spotted them.

Ash ran up to her. "We got the key. Did you find the Sword of Fire?"

"We did, but Cordy discovered Orion's Sword is near the cathedral," Master Wong answered. "In China, we call it the 'Punishment.' Three stars make a pattern of the sword above us: Theta, Iona, and Orionis. The diagram points to where it's buried. I never thought we would find it here."

Jon grabbed the paper. "I know where this is. Let's go while we have time."

They charged to the Saint Louis Cathedral, which stood deserted. Everyone had already been evacuated.

Jon picked the lock of the Cathedral and they entered a magnificent church, which had already survived many catastrophes. Cordy looked up at the stained glasses depicting Saint Louis' life. She found the knight Saunhac kneeling down with his one wounded eye covered with a cloth. Templar Grandmaster Saunhac knelt before Saint Louis and an Arab Magi in green robes holding a key on a pillow. Jon looked at the rusted silver key with a square handle. It seemed to be the same one.

Cordy saw a stained glass window where Blanche of Castile taught her children. She followed Blanche's raised hand, which looked like a serpent's head, pointing to a riverside cave where a spooky ghostlike figure peeked out. She got chills when, in the corner, a red lamp appeared to look like a sinister eye surrounded by ghostly faces. She took her phone out and took pictures of each stained glass window.

Sam yelled to the others. "Hey, take a look at this one!"

A group of Crusader knights carried a box with a red cross on it from the Holy Land. The window showed the knights reverently bringing back the relics from the Holy Land. As they carried the box, they looked like the Jews who carried the Ark of the Covenant.

Bob yelled up at the front of the church. "Take a look at this, everybody. I found another key. Look at Saint Peter, and Saint Paul is holding a sword."

"The same statues were at the Ursuline Convent chapel where we found the Sword of Fire," Master Wong said.

Jon read the paper, which was written in French. "It's a replica but the real one is buried in Saint Anthony's garden. Saint Anthony is known for finding lost items. Follow me." A door led to a garden in the back of the church.

Jon pulled out his cellphone. "I took pictures of the back of the church a few years ago. I had strange things show up. Look, here is the picture."

Ash saw the streak of light in the picture and strange orbs. "I've seen this phenomenon in the temples of Egypt. The power source seems to be over here." No one was around, and the storm clouds flashed lightning above them. The trees started shaking from the winds.

In the garden, a statue of the Sacred Heart stood facing an obelisk commemorating French sailors lost at sea. The statue's history was well known to residents of New Orleans.

"The obelisk resembles one in France at Saint Sulpice. The alley over there is called Pirates Alley, after Laffite. Everything makes sense. The paper says to dig here. Look in that shed over there and see if you find any shovels."

Ash kicked the door and it opened up. A gardener had left a couple of shovels in the corner. They dug near the cornerstone of the church. Peter and Ash dug deep and saw a bundle wrapped in cloth. Ash smiled. "We found it."

He pulled open the bundle and the long rusted metal box. "Let's get back to the house," Jon ordered.

CHAPTER 70

Jon's House

A consultation with the Guardian was imperative. Cordy placed her golden triangle on the table and Ash set his on top, forming a Star of David. The crystal ball sat on top of the triangles. With the lights in the room turned off, everyone waited for the Guardian to appear. Bob smiled as he watched Master Wong and Peter in awe of the bright light that revealed the woman in white. The surprise and pleasure were apparent on both men's faces.

The Guardian stood before them. "Pure of Heart, you summoned me?"

"Guardian, do you monitor a great storm heading for our location?" Ash asked.

The Guardian nodded. "Affirmative. You're in great danger. I'm monitoring all transmissions, and wind speeds may exceed over 200 miles per hour."

"Guardian, we need to know if the Swords of Water, Air, Fire, and Earth can stop the storm," Ash asked. "We've found Orion's sword too."

"Yes, they can assist you if used correctly. The Book of Dreams will instruct you on how to position the swords, and Orion's sword will connect all of them. I would review the Book of Enoch for further instructions. If done correctly, you can save New Orleans. If you fail, the winds will decimate the land like an atomic blast. I will assist you any way I can."

She disappeared.

"I'm on it," Ash said. "I checked out the Book of Dreams, and my dad sent me a ritual for the winds. The Books of Enochs are different. Cordy's book and de Villiers' version have the Book of Dreams but they're different. I examined them both and found a secret code. My dad's helped piece them together. I discovered the ritual of the swords and pieced them together using my experience with the Egyptian ceremonies."

Cordy placed her hand on Ash's shoulder. "Let's open the Sword of Fire and Orion's Sword."

Ash grabbed the Key of Life and Jon held the key from the blacksmith shop. Jon inserted his key into the box and turned. Everyone held their breaths as he opened the lid. Another wooden box sat inside with a hole and cross on the top, where Ash inserted the small Key of Life and turned the lever. The lid opened and Ash pulled out the Sword of Fire. The Sword started heating up while in Ash's hand.

Master Wong placed his hand over Ash's. "The Sword of Fire calls for one of the family of the dragons. Peter and I have ancestors from these ancient houses." The old master grabbed the hilt of the sword and raised it in the air. The Sword of Fire illuminated with bright red fiery light and pulsated with energy.

"Quiet, old one," Master Wong whispered. "The time is not yet right."

The sword's heat disappeared and the metal cooled. Master Wong showed Peter the sword of his family. Peter Woo bowed in reverence to the ancient weapon of his forefathers. The Chinese inscriptions engraved on the sword told of the great power of fire from the dragon.

Bob grabbed one of Jon's whiskey bottles and took a gulp. "I can't wait to see what the hell Orion's Sword does and who's going to hold it. Uh oh, here she goes again." The bright light appeared and illuminated the room, and the Sword of Fire brightened in Peter Woo's hand.

The Guardian reappeared, surprising everyone. "Hello, Bob. The Sword of Orion produces many different functions. I suggest using its laser beams. If you point the rod into the storm, the laser will hit the center and disintegrate the pressure within the storm. The winds will immediately stop. The laser power gets its energy from the other swords, which must be placed in the four corners of the square. Each sword represents the keys to producing life. The Orion Sword must be higher and pointed to the sky. You must choose the wielders of the other swords well. If you choose wrong, the wielder could die or the circuit could be disrupted."

Jon, Ash, Cordy, Sam and Chris looked at Bob. "She knows your name Bob. Go ahead and ask her suggestions for who the wielders should be?"

Bob took another swig of whiskey. "Guardian, honey, who would you suggest for the wielders?"

"I love being called honey by you, Bob," the Guardian answered seductively. "The four statues in the square will help decide. Bloodlines, age, gender, and the heart of the wielders should be considered, but the swords will choose their wielders. You're running out of time. The storm is coming so don't be late, honey."

Chris laughed at Bob. "Looks like Bob Mr. Honey is the Guardian's honey."

"She's assimilating our language to hers to make communication easier," Jon said. "The Guardian knows we have emotions, so she's trying to mimic us. She's a fast learner."

Ash grabbed the Orion Sword off the table. "Let's see what this baby does, shall we?" He pulled out the Key of Life and inserted it into the hole on the rusted metal box. As soon as they heard the click of the Key of Life, the box started shaking and the door opened on its own. Everyone's mouths dropped in surprise as Orion Sword rose out of the box levitating in the air above them.

Jon whispered. "Nobody move. The Orion Sword is choosing a wielder. Don't make any sudden moves." The Orion Sword shone with an intense golden light similar to the sun. The sword stood in front of Chris and a scanner ran across his face.

"What the hell!"

It moved next to Jon scanning his face and then to Sam scanning her face. Peter, Master Wong, and Cordy received the same treatment but when the Sword scanned Ash, it flashed a rainbow of lights. Ash reached for the Orion Sword and the lights dimmed leaving only an ancient sword with three stars.

Jon patted Ash on the back. "It looks like we have a wielder."

Cordy picked the Sword of Water case and opened it with the Key of Life. Sister Agnes told her about her connection with Knock and Lourdes so it made sense she might be its wielder. The sword was engraved with the words the Answerer and Retaliator in the ancient Gaelic. On Jon's dresser, two stone vases filled with the sacred water from Lourdes and Knock shook while she pulled the sword out of its case. Cordy instinctively grabbed the two vases with the other hand and the Sword of Water stopped shaking as well as the vases. The corks of the vases popped open and three water drops from each vase elevated in the air and fell on the blade. The sword emanated a pulsating electric vibe, releasing static electricity.

"Whoah, I think we have a wielder," Chris said. "Water, fire, earth, and air are the fundamental material for life but the spark of consciousness is the secret ingredient to unite them together."

Jon opened the Sword of Heaven's case with the Key of Life. His family had kept the sacred sword for millennia. Joan of Arc's sword was carried by her in her quest to save France from Britain. Who better to wield the Sword of Heaven but an astrophysicist? He gripped the sword and the metal started to sparkle and twinkle. A strong wind blew through his house, moving chairs and knocking down paintings.

"The Sword of Heaven commands the winds," Peter said. A small lightning bolt flew out and hit a chair. Smoke and fire engulfed the chair, and Sam rushed over with a fire extinguisher from the kitchen to blow it out.

Jon whispered the command, "Hush." The Sword of Heaven reverted back to its former state.

Sam smiled at her brother. "That question is settled. Jon wields the Sword of Heaven. Anybody object?"

Silence filled the room.

Peter, Sam, Bob, and Chris were left for the Sword of Earth to choose. Bob took another swig of whiskey.

"I'm not wielder material. Never liked swords, preferred machine guns. What about you, Chris?"

Chris stepped back. "I'm a lover not a fighter, what can I say?"

Peter held the case holding the Sword of Earth for Sam and bowed. "Ladies first. Sam is a mighty warrior and a beautiful sword needs a beautiful lady."

She smiled at Peter with great respect and pulled out the sword Richard the Lionheart found in Jerusalem. The metal sparkled and a resonating vibrational frequency emanated from it. Dishes and tables shook.

"Quiet, oh most beautiful one," Sam commanded. The room stopped trembling instantly.

Ash worked on the formula and nodded his head. "Perfect balance, two men and two women for the corners of the square and the Sword of Orion in the middle and above them so they all connect. They form four triangles, and the Mississippi River, like the Nile, will accentuate their powers. The Egyptians placed many temples along the Nile River believing running water increased magical powers. We've got a shot at saving New Orleans."

Jon handed everyone a Mardi Gras mask. "We need to hide our identities just in case."

There was a sparkly blue one for Cordy, a glittery green one for Sam, a shiny red one for Master Wong, and a silver and gold one for Jon and Ash. He handed Chris, Bob, and Peter black masks.

Bob smiled. "I love black. Some of my greatest comic characters wear black masks. I just never thought I would. Where's my cape?"

Peter and Chris laughed as they put on their masks.

The television's volume increased as a weather warning flashed on the screen and the news blasted away. The monster was headed straight for them. They didn't have much time left.

CHAPTER 71

New Orleans Jackson Square

All of them watched the television news update. Weather Channel analysts announced that Hurricane Justyce was heading straight for New Orleans. Analysts believed the city would take a direct hit. The state of Louisiana was in a state of emergency. By this time, evacuation was impossible. Residents were told to take emergency measures and hunker down.

"It begins, just like the Guardian said it would," Ash whispered. "The storm will hit like a bomb."

"OK, let's do it," Bob slapped Jon on the back.

"Everyone is leaving the city," Jon said. "No one will be there. I can pick the lock to the iron gate. De Villiers' men will be searching for us so everyone stay sharp."

Bob pulled up a map of Jackson Square from his computer. "Ash and I scoped out the area, and it has to be Jackson Square. The position in the city is a focal point. Jon opens the gate and we all go to the corners. Now here is the tricky part. The Guardian didn't tell us which corners for each relic but I do know the center of the square is General Jackson on his horse. Who's going to climb up and point Orion's Sword into the air? It's going to be very dangerous because lightning is a real possibility, so I'm glad Orion's Sword picked Ash for that job. What do you say, Ash?"

"I'll do it," Ash volunteered. "I've always wanted to be the center of attention. I've got Egyptian bloodlines and Orion's Sword looks very Egyptian."

Bob grinned. "I think you're climbing up on Ole Hickory."

Cordy smiled. "I'll take the Sword of Water and the sacred water in the alabaster jars. My family is connected to Our Lady of Lourdes and Knock."

Jon nodded. "I'll take the Sword of Heaven. My family protected it for many years. Sam should wield the Sword of Earth."

Master Wong stood up holding the Sword of Fire. "I'll command the Sword of Fire. My family helped create it. We've all become one with our swords."

"Peter, Chris, and I will protect you from de Villiers' men," Bob said. "I know they're going to find us." He passed out guns and ammo to them.

A familiar voice filled the room around them and a light shone from the crystal ball. The Guardian spoke. "Bob, you should bring me along in case you need me."

Bob shrugged his shoulders. "OK, I guess I'm holding the Guardian. Thanks, honey."

Ash placed the Keys of Life in a backpack with the books and other treasures. "Peter will take these and guard them with his life."

Peter nodded.

Chris ran to the freezer and pulled out the de Villiers' voodoo doll, which had frost on it. "I'll keep de Villiers busy. He must be freezing to death by now."

Jon chuckled. "I would love to see it. Chris will keep him distracted."

Little did they know that de Villiers had turned the heat up in his house and grabbed all of his blankets. He could swear his fingers were experiencing frost bite. The Dark Master shivered. He knew Lafitte was responsible for this. De Villiers took the warning but vowed he'd get revenge by watching their empire go bankrupt.

Bob looked at the map of Jackson Square again. "Peter, there's a natural ledge here that looks directly down on the square. You can give them cover and provide us with an escape route. The river will be to your back. When it's all done, run for the river where the boats are docked. Everybody put on bullet proof vests. I'll call Randy as soon as I see we've stopped the storm. He'll buy all the Dark Watchers' shares for pennies and watch Jon's stock skyrocket when the storm is gone. Let's move on out, while it's still dark. The storm clouds have blocked out the morning sun."

The Dark Watchers were in a bind as they were short staffed because of the evacuation. No money could make some men stay in New Orleans. A few stayed, hoping for an easy big reward. On the other hand, the good news was that police were at a minimum so they wouldn't get any interference from them. They knew Jon's home was a fortress so they would have to bide their time.

Bob opened the back door. "It's time to go, everyone. I'll cover you. Everybody wear their masks."

They all followed Jon into the backyard, where he opened a gate he shared with his neighbor. Everybody ran through the neighbor's yard and found a gate to a back alley. They rushed through the alley and found the street Chartres. They headed for St Louis Cathedral and Jackson Square in the dark as lightning streaked the sky.

The streets were empty. The wind started to pick up and sirens could be heard in the distance. Debris blew through the streets and trash cans flew and fell. They dodged the flying objects and kept on course.

Jon opened the black wrought-iron gate to Jackson Square. No lock could keep a Lafitte out. The gate creaked open and everybody ran to his or her appointed spot. God and goddess statues stood marking the corners. Jon looked at Dionysius, otherwise known as Bacchus, standing next to a holly tree. Bacchus stood next to a vine holding a book. "The Sword of Heaven shall be here. I love wine, how appropriate."

Cordy saw the goddess holding a sickle. "I'll go to moon goddess with the Egyptian water jars and in the other hand, hold the Sword of Water. The moon governs the tides and oceans. Everything fits."

Master Wong, wearing his traditional robes over his clothes, headed for the older god with the beard who looked like Zeus. "The Sword of Fire controls lightning bolts like Zeus."

Sam went to the last statue of the Earth goddess holding a cornucopia of flowers. "The Sword of Earth belongs here."

Cordy watched as Ash climbed up on the statue horse of Andrew Jackson with the Sword of Orion. The wind started picking up and he almost slipped off. He climbed on the back of Jackson's horse and raised Orion's Sword but nothing happened. The Book of Dreams talked about opening the gates to Heavenly Jerusalem where the archangels resided. The plan outlined was similar to that of the construction of the Saint Louis Cathedral and the grounds surrounding it.

Everyone stood at the four corners of the squares holding their swords as Ash rode Jackson's horse holding the Sword of Orion. Energies swirled about each sword, and an angel stood next to each one. Uriel stood behind Lafitte but yelled to Michael when he saw the swords' energies weren't at their optimum levels. Gabriel stood behind Cordy and Raphael stood behind Sam.

"Mike, switch with me," Uriel shouted. "The Sword of Heaven is more your style while the flaming Sword of Fire is mine." The two archangels switched and all the angels took on different colors. Blue robes for Gabriel, red robes for Michael, gold yellow for Uriel and green for Raphael, together representing the colors of the rainbow. The Metatron known as Enoch, all in white, stood by Ash at the top of Ole Hickory.

Everyone noticed a surge in energy but still something was amiss.

Chris grabbed de Villiers' voodoo doll and pinched his foot. De Villiers, in his home office, yelled in pain. The dark sorcerer had placed a Judas coin in a large vial of water marked New Orleans, swirling it violently to simulate a whirlpool of water. Repeated pinches of pain randomly came every few minutes on the mad Dark Watcher master. He couldn't focus due to the pain. He thought, *damn that Lafitte*. He knew the Frenchman was the cause.

Chris kept up the pinches and sometimes a pin prick on the voodoo doll.

Everyone wondered why the swords still didn't work. Cordy had a revelation.

She yelled out, "One of us must be in the wrong spot. What do we fill all flower vases with? Water! Water makes plants grow. Sam, let's switch."

They switched to different female goddesses.

"Yes, you're right. The goddess is Hecate and she rules Earth," Sam said. "She's known as the earth shaker. I see it now."

The crystal ball lit up brightly in Bob's hand. He stood below watching Ash. The swords started sparkling, the gold ring engraved with the Solomon Seal on Cordy's neck trembled, and the Sword of Fire crackled with static electricity, reaching closer and closer to the Sword of Heaven. A stubborn Antar stood above Ash, holding a shield which blocked the energies of the swords.

Lafitte yelled out to Cordy. "Use the ring, it's our only chance."

The wind was getting stronger, and the ground was shaking vehemently. All the energies were converging on the Sword of Earth. Sam held on tight as the earth began to shake.

Cordy placed the ring that her grandfather had given her on her finger.

She gazed up at Antar. "I order you to release the Swords. You must obey."

Antar scanned them, still blocking the energies from uniting with the Sword of Orion.

"If I release the shield then Ash may die. Are you ready to be responsible for his death?"

Ash's eyes met Cordy's with a deep tenderness. "Do it, Cordy. We must save New Orleans."

Cordy's eyes teared up. "Do it, Antar! Now!"

Uriel's eyes met Antar's. "You must obey the ring." Antar removed the shield as Cordy ordered. Enoch's sorrowful eyes met Antar's.

"You haven't won, and I vow I'll return." Antar disappeared.

Bob held the brilliantly lit crystal ball. Cordy held the necks of the water jars, whose corks popped to release droplets of water. They rose in the air, dropping on the shiny Sword of Water. The energies of all the swords now converged on Orion's Sword.

Bob and Peter kept an eye out for de Villiers' men. No one could have missed seeing the bright lights filling the square. A camera crew rushed to the square and started filming the bizarre group of crazy mardi gras-like drunken revelers. A weather watch crew stood stunned as they watched Ash sitting on top of the horse with a magnificent sparkling sword.

"Are you filming this?" the announcer asked his cameraman. "Tell me you're getting this."

"Oh yeah, we're rolling."

"Ladies and gentlemen, people have gone crazy in New Orleans and have climbed up on Andrew Jackson's horse. Mass hysteria has hit New Orleans. Lightning may kill this obviously drunk young man."

The Orion Sword lit up like a laser beam and a vortex of energy developed around it. Hurricane Justyce pelted them with rain and wind. Hail began to shower down. Bob, Chris, and Peter kept alert hoping for a few more seconds before de Villiers' men would find them. The lights from the swords connected with the Orion Sword and a red beam of light shot up into the sky like a high powered massive laser beam aimed at the clouds.

"I command you to stop the Hurricane Justyce" Ash yelled. Ash held on for dear life with his arm around Jackson. The energy headed straight into the eye of Hurricane Justyce and the heat beams instantly dissipated the hurricane. The winds stopped at that moment and the energy beams quit once the storm disseminated. The sun peaked out on the horizon and the clouds lifted.

Bob made the call to Randy in New York. "Buy, buy, buy, Randy! We did it! Tell Julia, we did it!" Randy grabbed his computer and started buying Jon's company stock. The shares he bought were the first to open the stock market. The bell had rung in New York's stock exchange and as the Dark Watchers sold their shares Randy bought them up at bargain prices. His friends thought he was mad. The Stones of Truth knew Bob spoke true and Randy knew the storm stopped. The news channels had not yet reported that Hurricane Justyce was no more and a miracle had happen. The meteorologists sat in their office stunned. Where did Hurricane Justyce go?

Randy heard the Dark Watcher brokers laugh. They called him a lunatic, and television announcers got ready to interview losers of the day. Randy smiled. They would be in for a surprise.

The force of the static energy blew off Ash's clothes and his hair stood on end, slightly smoking. Cordy ran over, grabbed an empty plastic margarita glass left on a park bench and dumped water from the square fountain on his head.

Ash, now naked and wet, stood there shocked. "Thanks, Cordy."

"Sorry, your hair was on fire." Her hair stood up, as did Jon's, Sam's and Master Wong's, owing to the static electricity produced by the swords.

"Why do I keep losing my clothes?"

Sam smiled. "I don't mind and I bet Cordy doesn't either."

Cordy blushed, making Ash smile. The old master took off his outer robe and handed it to Ash. He put it on and tied the robe together.

"Thanks, Master Wong. It's a wee bit short but it will do."

Master Wong smiled. "You're very welcome. We did it, Pure of Heart. New Orleans is saved."

The camera crew clapped and the announcer reported, "The winds are gone, and it appears New Orleans has seen another miracle. Andrew Jackson saved it in 1815, and it looks like he saved the city again. What an incredible light show!"

Bullets whizzed by their heads, ricocheting off an oak tree. Shots rang out coming down the street from de Villiers' men. Bob sprayed them with his machine gun. Everyone ducked behind the Jackson statue.

"Head for the docks, everyone. I'll cover you. Here they come! Run for your lives."

Everyone pulled out their guns, firing at 10 of de Villiers' commandos.

Shots flew around, and Cordy and Ash crouched low behind a large Spanish oak tree. They both were shooting their guns. Ash used all of his ammo and had to reload. He didn't know what had gotten into him but he knew he'd only get this one chance to ask. She shot one of de Villiers' men in the leg.

"Cordy, I have to tell you something. It wasn't until we were separated that I knew how much I love you." He fired his gun at a couple snipers.

She turned her head, surprised at his declaration. Bullets whizzed by her head.

"I was afraid to tell you because of all the responsibility that you carry on your shoulders." Ash looked deeply into her eyes. "Cordy, will you marry me?" He fired shots over at the trees.

Cordy's face lit up, but she didn't know what to say. Shots hit the tree splintering the wood. "We'll talk later. You picked a heck of a time, Ash."

All Cordy and Ash could do was try and make a run for it toward the boat. They headed for the docks. Peter covered them from his position. The camera crew's camera fell to the ground and the crew ran for their lives. Police sirens could be heard in the distance.

They ran for the docks but were trapped. The river blocked their way out. Everyone fired back. Master Wong saw four of them huddled by a tree. He commanded the Sword of Fire to hit the tree with fire. The flames flew to the tree making them flee.

Peter smiled. "Awesome shot, Master."

Jon looked at Bob. "We're running out of ammunition."

Bob nodded back. A rumble of an engine of a speedboat could be heard heading for them coming down the river.

"Uh oh, we're going to be attacked from the river. Jon, Peter, keep them off of us in the front. Sam and I will fire on the river rats."

Sam positioned herself and aimed at the speeding yacht coming up the river.

She yelled to Bob. "It's a woman driving the yacht."

Bob smiled. "That's not just any woman, that's Julia! Don't fire, Sam! She's coming to our rescue."

Julia pulled the boat to the dock and grabbed a gun, shooting at de Villiers' men. Bob smiled and ran toward her. "That's my girl."

"It's time to go everybody," Julia yelled.

Bob, Master Wong, Peter, Sam, and Chris jumped aboard. Julia dropped her gun and headed for the steering wheel while Bob covered for the rest of them.

"How the hell did you find us?" Bob asked.

"I've got a GPS tracking device on your phone. Who's the hot chick with the sexy voice you call 'honey'? I'm the only one you call 'honey,' got it, Bob?"

"Not now, Julia. I'm a little busy." Bob fired at two commandos running toward them.

Ash climbed aboard wearing Master Wong's robes. Cordy fired and jumped aboard, followed by Jon.

"Hit it!" Cordy yelled.

Everyone fired away as the boat flew down the Mississippi River, leaving de Villiers' men at the dock shooting back at them. Ash and Peter fired their guns from the back of the boat making de Villiers' men duck for cover.

Cordy hugged Julia. "I'm so glad to see you."

Julia held the wheel tightly. "I'm not going to miss all the fun. Hey go downstairs and get more ammo. I have a feeling we're going to need it."

Cordy tried to avoid Ash and ran down the stairs only to run into Jon, covered with the blood of a Dark Watcher he had killed. He grabbed her tight around her waist. "You're alive, Cordy. I thought I lost you. I never want to feel that desolate lost feeling again. You saved my family and risked everything for me. Will you marry me? I love you. What do you say?"

Julia yelled, "Cordy, we need more ammo."

"Got to go, Jon. We'll talk later." She privately thanked Julia for breaking up an unbelievable proposal by Jon. Cordy handed several cartridges to Peter.

"Peter, here's more ammo."

Randy rang Bob's cellphone.

"The news broke five minutes ago that the hurricane disappeared. No one can explain it. Jon's company stock is skyrocketing. I think you guys made the Internet. Everyone wants to know who the mad streaker is, the one who climbed on Jackson's horse. The media wants to know who those masked men and women were at the square. The camera crew said you're all drunk but I know better. Cordy bought out all the Dark Watchers' shares for pennies. They now have to do with their margin calls too. I'm drinking champagne in celebration. Did Julia find you?"

Bob kissed her. "Yes, she did, gotta go."

She yelled at Bob, "Don't you ever leave me at the office again. Where's Chris' voodoo doll? I brought something special for de Villiers from home. I owe him big for trying to kill me."

She pulled out a plastic bag with leaves of poison ivy in it.

Chris smiled as he dropped the voodoo doll of de Villiers in it and zipped it up. Chris and Julia shook hands.

"I love how this woman thinks."

"Get lost, Chris. She's taken."

Julia kissed Bob with all the tenderness and love in her heart.

A spectacular rainbow gleamed in the distance as the storm broke up and the sun pierced the sky.

CHAPTER 72

Afterglow

A do-not-disturb sign hung on the doorknob of the suite at the luxurious Vegas hotel. Dottie and her beau had decided to have some fun and enjoy a weekend of sin.

It was one of the best vacations that she had ever planned. Her new beau was dressed in his Navy best and captain's hat, and she wore a shimmering gold satin dress. She loved strolling with her charming paramour down the Vegas Strip at night. The lights shone all around them.

Her captain popped a little blue pill and was ready to go. They headed for a night of all-out sexual bliss. Dottie admitted that her lover's stamina impressed her. Finally, he lay snoring away with a happy smile on his face. She laid in the king-size bed and flipped on the television. The satisfied woman held a water-vapor cigarette and took a few puffs as she watched the breaking news report flashing on the screen. New Orleans had everybody talking. The hurricane had produced record-breaking winds that terrified the whole world, and her captain was worried about some of his friends' boats docked on the coast.

The camera crew on the ground announced New Orleans had been saved. Hurricane Justyce had disappeared, and the experts were at a loss as to why. Millions celebrated the saving of their city. People ran around the bars on Bourbon Street, spraying champagne and cheering. The station showed a surreal video of a crazy drunk climbing on top of President Jackson's monument with what look like a lightning sword of some sort. Sparks of light flashed from the sword. The weathermen had never seen anything like it. Dottie had never seen such a spectacular light show. The handsome masked drunk reminded her of someone, but she couldn't quite place him.

Dottie laughed. "He had a few too many hurricanes. I'm surprised he climbed up there in the high winds and lightning. What a hunk! Look at those muscles."

Dottie's memory kicked in and a thought flashed through her mind. No, it couldn't be. Something reminded Dottie of a man in her past but that man wouldn't be climbing up Ole Hickory. He was a proper young professor of archeology, not a wild man holding a lightning rod in a hurricane. The guy she's thinking of must be from one of her wild parties or a strip-club dancer she knew.

The newlywed took another puff from her cigarette and leaned forward. Dottie racked her mind to try to remember where she might have seen this guy before. He looked so familiar. An excitement filled her body when she saw the masked man's firm ass. *No, it couldn't be him. I'll be damned, the same hair and body type.* The camera zoomed in for a close up. A laser beam blasted from his hand and four lights connected with it, zooming straight up into the air.

"Holy shit, what the hell was that? He's been hit by lightning! Oh the poor guy is fried."

The light faded and the camera zoomed in on the wild-haired hunk of a man whose naked ass filled the television screen.

Dottie fumbled through her covers and grabbed her glasses.

"Ash man, is that you?"

The bride inched closer to the set and watched the television replay of the drunken streaker sitting on Jackson's horse and practically falling down. He stood there in his glory while a woman dumped water on his smoking head. Another camera close-up of his bum made Dottie press her face up to the television set. Dottie wore a big grin as it dawned on her that she knew him well. She vowed that she would never forget him or his behind.

Dirty Dottie smiled and chuckled. "Well, I'll be damned. It is you, my Ash man. It is you."

CHAPTER 73

De Villiers' Office

Isis sat on the carpet near the window watching de Villiers scratch his arm and then his neck. After being smacked by her master, the cat stayed some distance away from him. She had lost all trust in him. His temper flare-ups made her wary. Isis avoided the Judas coins that he placed near him. The cat sensed the evil force emanating from the ancient coins. She watched as the Dark Watcher Master scratched more and more his reddened skin.

Mindy took a deep breath before she opened the door. The news she brought would infuriate him. The files were tucked under her arm. She knocked on the door and then walked in.

Her files fell to the floor.

"What the hell happened to you?"

De Villiers' face was swollen and he looked at her with blood shot eyes.

"Call the doctor and tell him it's an emergency. It seems I've come into contact with poison ivy. The rash is all over my body. I'm going mad with the itching."

"How did you get poison ivy in New York City?" Mindy asked incredulously.

"I don't know but I've a big hunch this is someone's idea of a bad joke. Jon Lafitte is behind it. I can tell you that. You're going to tell me that he's still alive. I saw on the television the saviors of New Orleans."

Mindy took a gulp. "They escaped by boat up the Mississippi, but my men are in hot pursuit. They'll find them and grab the Keys of Life and the ring soon. The good news is they have the treasures we need."

De Villiers scratched his neck. "Don't fail me again, Mindy. This will be your last chance."

Mindy sighed. "The Dark Watchers are calling in, furious about losing their money in the stock market. Lafitte's corporation gained after the hurricane news broke. The Dark Watchers have lost millions, and our stake in Lafitte's family business is gone. I can't believe they stopped a category five hurricane. I can't believe it!"

"Get out, and call the doctor! I want them and the Keys of Life as soon as possible. You're personally seeing to this mission, got it Mindy?"

"We'll get them soon. I promise." Mindy rushed out the room.

Antar sat in the dark corner enjoying de Villiers' pain. He placed his hand on Isis, giving her a pat on the head. The cat purred at him. "You failed. I'm not surprised. You've underestimated them every time. Why didn't you kill them?"

Furious, de Villiers seethed at Antar. "Someday, you'll be taking orders from me and I'll have you kneel before me."

Antar glared at him. "Never!"

De Villiers placed his hands together. "I need your help to corrupt them. A corrupted Pure of Heart is easier to kill."

Antar gazed into Isis' mysterious eyes. "I tried to feed their anger and lust for revenge but they resist me. We both failed this time, but there is always next time."

De Villiers scratched his neck again and looked again at the chair. Antar had disappeared.

"I'll get my revenge, Lafitte. I'll get my revenge, and Antar will kneel at my feet."

CHAPTER 74

Bob and Julia's Honeymoon

Julia drove the boat to Baton Rouge where Randy, driving an RV, waited for them. They had lost de Villiers' men on the Mississippi and now Julia had a big surprise for them.

"You're all invited to mine and Bob's wedding. I got our marriage license and all we need is a preacher."

Master Wong stood up. "I'm a certified minister. I would be proud to marry you both."

Bob smiled. "Sounds good to me. Let's do it."

Randy looked at his watch. "Everybody hop in. Just call me the wedding planner. I've got everything arranged but we're on a tight schedule. Hopefully, we won't get attacked during the ceremony. Last time I scanned the area, they had lost your trail."

Cordy's heart was in turmoil. Lucky Bob and Julia. They wanted to get married and had no doubts about it. She was torn and just didn't know what to say to these two crazy men. Her life had been a series of murders and escapes from death. How in the hell could these men want to marry her? Both of them were wonderful guys.

What was she going to do?

Randy pulled into the driveway at Lake Hope where a white plantation-style house stood. Everyone was shocked at how ornately decorated it was. White wedding bows adorned every window of the two-story house, which was surrounded by manicured gardens. The house was expecting them. Julia had surprised the hell out of Bob. Julia and Bob grinned at each other. The front door opened and Randy ran into the furnished elegant home.

He beamed with pride as he stood by the door. "I did it, Julia! Come on in, everybody."

"Everyone go up to the rooms marked with your names," Julia ordered. "Your wardrobe is waiting for you."

Everyone stood there stunned.

"Get going! You all meet down here at 1800. Chop, chop."

"You heard the woman, get moving." Bob kissed Julia and they sprinted upstairs.

Chris smiled as he looked at the sound system and music selection. "I've got the music. Oh, we are going to have one hell of a party."

The rest ran upstairs because they knew Julia would shoot them if they were late.

Julia opened the door to the bridal suite, which had rooms connected to one another. A giggling Julia shoved Bob through the door where a black tuxedo laid on the bed. She pulled out her white wedding dress hanging up in the closet. Julia wanted to marry Bob more than anything in the world. She realized it when she thought she might never see him again. Time was ticking. Julia put her dress on and fixed her hair.

Cordy read the instruction booklet that she found on her wrought-iron bed. She was the maid of honor. Her dark purple bridesmaid dress and high-heeled shoes fit perfectly. How the hell did she know her size? Julia was amazing. She walked into Julia's room and was breathless at how stunning Julia looked in her wedding dress. The sleeveless white satin dress with lace overlays perfectly fit her figure.

"You don't look like you need any help getting ready. Julia, you look so beautiful. We have an old custom in my family of pinning money on the bride's dress." Cordy picked up the bottom of her hem and pinned the money underneath the back of her dress for luck. As Cordy knelt down, Julia spotted the ring with Solomon's seal engraved on it.

Julia gasped. "You've got Solomon's ring. The Chief told me to find it in one of my dreams. Cordy, do you know how powerful that ring is? It makes the angels obey the one who possesses it. Many men have gone mad carrying the ring, but you seem to be handling it fine. I think the Chief wanted me to tell you of its power and to warn you. De Villiers will do anything to possess it. For the first time in my life, I'm free and I owe it to all of you. I'm ready to start my new life. The ring is very powerful and very dangerous. You must be careful."

Cordy kissed her and realized at that moment that she couldn't commit to anyone while she carried the ring. The only way she could be free was to stop de Villiers.

Ash walked in and found his gray best man's suit and lavender shirt with suspenders. Everything fit perfectly, even his shoes. Sam and Jon would be bridesmaid and groomsman. Peter would assist Master Wong with the ceremony. The time came and all of them assembled downstairs in the garden. Spanish moss hung from the trees and white chairs sat in front, decorated with white lotus blossoms and an arbor of purple flowers.

Chris started the music and played the classic Pachelbel's "Canon in D" while Cordy hooked arms with Ash and walked down the lane. They both noticed that a statue of an angel watched them go by.

Ash smiled at her. "This could be us. Get used to it, Cordy."

Cordy grinned at him. "I'll get back to you on that question you popped in the middle of gunfire."

Handsome Jon walked down with the exquisite Sam. Jon gazed at Cordy and gave her a wink. Sam gave Ash a wink. Cordy noticed and thought about how the French loved amour. Master Wong stood at the altar with Bob, who anxiously awaited his beautiful bride. Cordy thought Bob cleaned up well and looked damn good in his tuxedo.

Chris played the wedding march song and ran up to escort the beaming Julia. They marched down and Bob took her hand. They gazed into each other's eyes. Peter handed the candle to Master Wong. The old master instructed them both to light it for they were now one and after a small speech, he told them to say their vows. Bob vowed to be obedient, but who was he kidding? He'd obey anything that woman said. At the end, Master Wong pronounced them man and wife. They kissed and everybody clapped and cheered.

Randy took pictures with his cellphone and they celebrated with a wonderful feast. They partied all night and the wedding couple snuck off.

Bob jumped into bed and watched Julia waltz in wearing her white negligee. She turned out the light and fell into Bob's arms. Both of them needed each other desperately. Bob placed kisses all over her body, whispering how much he loved her. Julia looked up in his eyes. "I love you, Bob. Let's make the most of this night so we will never forget it."

"I love you, Julia. I've always loved you. Plus, I promised to be obedient."

A familiar voice rang out in the bedroom. "Congratulations, Bob and Julia."

Both of them yelled out.

"Oh, shit!"

Julia looked around, "Who the hell is that? Her voice sounds familiar."

Bob scrambled in the dark and grabbed the shining crystal ball he had placed on the table in the room.

"Cordy gave her to me for safekeeping during the fire fight," Bob explained. "Julia, meet the Guardian, and Guardian, meet my wife, Julia." He placed a pillow over the crystal ball and rushed into bed with his bride.

"Goodnight, Guardian."
"Goodnight, Bob."

EPILOGUE

After the celebration ended that night, Cordy realized that even at a time of war, hearts and souls could still come together. She was tired and exhausted from avoiding conversations with Ash and Jon, and she pondered her course of action alone in her room.

The plantation house was overwhelming in its grandeur — 12-foot-tall ceilings, detailed crown molding, every detail was hand-crafted. The only way to describe it was art at its finest. Cordy's room was the largest bedroom in the house, and she was sure Bob had his hand in the arrangements. The room was perfect. The only thing spoiling the room's beauty was the two locked doors. The room was connected to Ash's on one side, and Jon's on the other. Bob always had a sinister sense of humor.

Cordy hadn't been in the room for but a minute when she heard a quiet knocking from the door to her right. "Cordy, are you there?" Ash whispered. "Can we talk? I need to talk with you. When we first met, we talked nonstop, but since we've been on the run, we've had little time to talk. I miss that."

Cordy said nothing. She remembered how great it felt to have someone interested in conversation rather than her chest. Ash turned out to be clueless when it came to romance, but his goodness and sincerity were overwhelming and he made her feel safe.

Ash hadn't even stopped talking when the doorknob to her left clicked, making the same noise she had heard every night on the ship. Jon was trying to get in to the hen house. She smiled and shook her head. He was defiantly persistent.

Bob had no clue that both men had proposed marriage to her.

The rattling of the doorknob became louder and more vigorous, followed by sweet whispers that would make any woman swoon. Cordy was no exception. This man could really unlock any women's treasure chest. She moved closer to Jon's door, and with each step, her heart beat faster. She was like a moth moving toward a burning flame, and her imagination was starting to take over her body.

Suddenly, from across the room, Cordy heard the doorknob start to turn on Ash's side and she could make out a loud voice speaking in French.

Ash had decided to fight fire with fire. "Je t'aime. I love you madly."

Now that just made her mad. Ash's French was perfect, and she realized that he must have understood everything the whole time that she and Jon were talking on the ship. And now he thought he could speak a little French and she would come running. She was angry. Ash had a lot of nerve trying to open her door after he had hidden his knowledge of French. She felt like an idiot. She also felt ashamed at how she treated him. It made her mad at herself.

Cordy stormed across the room but as she got close to Ash's door she realized Ash was trying to be like Jon because he thought that was what she wanted. He loved her and part of her ached for him. Cordy put her hand on the doorknob to Ash's room and started to turn the key. She was going to give him a peace of her mind. Then it dawned on her that Ash could never be like Jon and Jon could never be like Ash.

Cordy fell to the floor and for the second time in her life, she felt lost. The first time was when her parents were taken from her. Tears ran down her cheeks as she began to sob, her chin quivering. The flow of sorrow ran over her as she remembered the loss of the chief and the stealing of young Linda's life. Linda should have been alive.

A light came from the other side of the room, by the bed, and a voice said, "Cordelia McDermott, are you the Mi'kmaq warrior princess descended from a line of Pure of Heart or are you a marshmallow?"

Cordy was not surprised or scared. She knew the voice and light belonged to Uriel.

"Cordy, get up and come over and sit down." Uriel turned on the lamp next to the bed. Cordy got up wiped off the tears on her face. She walked over and sat on the corner of the bed. Uriel was propped up against the headboard with pillows behind his back. A bright light shone from under his long dark coat. She felt a great calm come over her body.

"OK, Uriel, where is the light coming from?"

"Some call it the Flaming Sword, some call it the Sword of Righteousness. What I can tell you, Cordy, is that it protects the Pure of Heart. Where there is light, darkness cannot exist. Now, Cordy, let's get back to you and why you're crying. What is your problem?"

"I have two great men who have asked me to marry them, and I am in the middle of a war. I just don't know which way I should go. Should I pick door number one or door number two?"

He looked at her with tenderness and softly whispered, "Oh Cordy, yes, you do."

"Uriel, you don't understand. I can't see the way," she desperately answered.

"Cordy, you have always known the way." Uriel reached to his left, opening the nightstand and pulling out a worn Bible. He tossed it down to her. "Everything you need to win the war is in there. What are some of your questions?"

Her voice shook with trepidation. "What if I don't have the will to see this through?"

"Open the Bible."

Cordy opened the Bible randomly, and the page opened to Matthew 22:14.

"Go ahead and read what it says, Cordy."

"For many are called but few are chosen."

"Cordy, never lose sight of who you are and where you come from. If you stop, all will be lost. Sometimes you just have to go on faith and trust your heart to guide you. You must reach out to everyone that can help you, trust in yourself, make your decisions, and move because time is running out."

Cordy looked up, her face bright with determination. "I have made my decision. I know the path I need to take."

"If you need help, all you need to do is ask," Uriel said.

"If you were going to move valuable artifacts and treasure during the 1500s, it would've been by water. The rivers were the highways, and the oceans, the super highways. We have to stay on the trail of the artifacts. And remember, a wise man once said, 'the common eye sees only the outside of things, and judges by that, but the seeing eye pierces through and reads the heart and soul, finding the capacities which the outside didn't indicate or promise, and which the other kind couldn't detect.'"

Uriel smiled. "Well Cordy, you're quoting Mark Twain. I knew him well. He was one great riverboat captain."

"Looks like we're headed up the mighty Mississippi. She'll give us some of the answers. Now if you don't mind, Uriel, I need to get some sleep and with the two doorknob rattlers, that might be impossible. They're just going to have to wait." Cordy got up to change for bed and when she turned, Uriel was gone.

Little did Cordy know that Jon and Ash were pacing back and forth like caged animals in their rooms. They were each mad as hell thinking that the other was lying in Cordy's warm bed. They could hear the muffled sounds of a male voice in the next room. In their attempt to see more, each one had snuck on her balcony and could only get a glimpse of men's boots lying at the bottom of the bed. The male guest was hidden by the drapes over the window. Each man returned back to his room with worry, not realizing Uriel's visit was taking place.

Ash grabbed a towel and wrapped it around his waist. He decided to take a shower to clear his mind, and Jon grabbed a bottle of Scotch to drown his sorrows.

At the same time, Jon and Ash decided to take one more look at Cordy's locked balcony door. When Jon poked his head out of his room, he saw Ash do the same. The two men gave each other a glare and made for Cordy's balcony door just as she was turning off her light.

"What were you doing in my fiancé's room earlier?" Jon whispered.

"I was going to ask you the same thing, Frenchie," Ash shot back.

"When did you ask her?" Jon shot back.

"Back at Jackson Square, just before we jumped into the boat."

"Well, you beat me. I asked her when she got on the boat. I never made it into her room tonight. Her door remained locked after all my declarations of love."

Ash was shocked. "Neither did I. So who was lying on her bed talking to her?"

They looked at each other with disgust. The spurned lovers turned to go back inside realizing their balcony doors had locked behind them. Jon was in his boxers, and Ash had only a towel wrapped around him. They climbed together over to Cordy's balcony.

"You'll need to climb down the trellis and go around back and unlock the doors," Jon ordered Ash. "The master key is in the kitchen."

"I am not one of your employees," Ash said, shaking his head. "Jon, you can't order me around. Plus, I'm wrapped in a towel."

They could hear a voice in the garden below the balcony but couldn't see who it was. They decided to climb down the trellis together because neither one could trust that the other would unlock their door. The problem was already getting worse. They were in Louisiana, and the mosquitos were out in full force. Both men were bitten everywhere by the bloodsucking vampires. Halfway down, the wooden trellis started to give way and they began to fall. The cracking noise attracted Sam and an inebriated Randy, who had stepped out onto the veranda for some fresh air. The unsuspecting couple looked up at the commotion above their heads. Ash's towel got hung up on the trellis and he fell, naked, atop a surprised Sam, knocking her down on the ground. Jon fell on Randy's back, all four of them sprawled out. The group seemed to groan in harmony.

Sam was enjoying every moment. "Oh, my!"

Ash's face was nestled in Sam's chest, and she couldn't resist holding his butt. She took great pleasure in sampling the goods.

Randy, lying on his stomach, started yelling, "Hey, get off my back! Get off!"

Cordy heard the noise and came out on the balcony. "What's going on down there?"

She looked down and couldn't believe what she was seeing. "Well, it didn't take you two long to move on to other options."

"It's not what it looks like," Jon yelled. "I am not that kind of guy."

Cordy stood in her nightgown with her hands crossed over her chest. "Mr. Menage a trois, I don't know what kind of guy you really are. What about you, Asho?"

Ash was still attempting to pull himself off of Sam and told himself to just tell the truth. "I don't know what happened. One minute I was climbing down, and the next thing I knew, I was on top of Sam."

Cordy's heart filled with jealousy. "Yes, naked I can see."

Sam got off the ground while staring at Ash's body. She yelled up to Cordy, "Sometimes when something long and firm and hard falls from the sky, a girl just has to hang on and hope for the best, if you know what I mean." She winked at Cordy.

Cordy let out a frustrated cry and slammed her door as she went back to bed. As she drifted off to sleep, she had to smile and think, *he was a spectacular naked man.*

About the Authors

Carolyn Schield and Tom Vorbeck are a unique brother and sister team who decided to write a thrilling, adventurous and mysterious trilogy. The Keys of Life, the first book of the trilogy, brought them together after they had drifted apart over the years.

Carolyn writes articles for alternative media and international magazines. She lives in Texas with her husband and children.

Tom is an award winning artist. His work can be seen at the Holocaust Museum in Washington, D.C.

Carolyn and Tom hope to share with their readers their passion and excitement for life.

Their first book is Keys of Life: Uriel's Justice. The book has been a #1 Top 100 Amazon best seller for historical fiction, historical thriller, and historical fantasy.

For more information are readers can visit our website:
www.urielsjustice.com
www.facebook.com/urielsjustice
www.amazon.com/Keys-Life-Justice-Carolyn-Schield-ebook/dp/B00JHV5TEK

www.ingramcontent.com/pod-product-compliance
Lightning Source LLC
Chambersburg PA
CBHW071155020726
47502CB00002B/416